Da's Legacy

The Shillelagh and the City

Timothy M. Shannon

ISBN-13: 978-1500338640
ISBN-10: 1500338648

ALSO BY TIMOTHY M. SHANNON

Da's Shillelagh - A Tale of the Irish on the Niagara Frontier
Chat Room – The Adirondack Campaign
Attica – Journey Down the Rabbit Hole
1965 – Journey to a Rich Land
Beyond the Lazarus Gate
Tales from the Chicken Coop

PREFACE

In this sequel to Da's Shillelagh, the storm-tossed Reddy family faces the turmoil of a nation hurtling toward Civil War. Having survived a harsh life on the Niagara Frontier, culminating in the Great Seiche of 1844, which sent a twenty-eight foot wave crashing into Buffalo, the family is left to pick up the pieces and struggle onward.

Chapters

1

1845
THE WAY FORWARD

As Sean's leg mended and Mary's belly swelled, the tenacious city of Buffalo had reinvented itself. As the stunned residents continued to search through the debris for the missing a mere week after the seiche had battered the city, late season canallers were again arriving in the city to offload their cargoes and partake of the infected district's delights. The day after the ruinous waters receded, the flooded saloons had opened their doors to the thirsty boatmen and the painted ladies had put on fresh powder and damp dresses to relieve the newly arrived men of their wages and virtue.

The canal and tow path were free of debris and sewage for the first time in years. The wave that had swept through the burgeoning city, taking scores of boats and lives with it, was past, and commerce would not wait for mourning. The Guard had collected the bodies and organized gangs to clear the wreckage to make way for the shipments from the West. The hubbub of a thriving port that had been so abruptly halted came back threefold leaving no time for self-pity. Life surged onward as the wave ebbed and the city prepared for the onslaught of winter. By the following Spring, the port of Buffalo was back at full capacity.

Katie hummed quietly as she rocked her fussing, curly-haired grandson to sleep. He was gaining weight now, but during the hunger of the winter following the flood she thought she would lose both him and Mary. The family had all sacrificed to give Mary more of their scant food, but still the young mother had had trouble producing enough milk for a growing boy and the two of them eked by with barely enough to sustain life. As the city recovered, food became cheaper and more plentiful. Mary and the baby had slowly regained their strength, and Katie finally had a nice chubby cheeked lad to fuss over.

The winter had been hard on Katie as well. The scant food and long dark nights had cast a shadow on her soul. She mourned the loss of her parents, of Jimmy, of her home and of her Seneca mother, Wings Spread Wide. In the dark days of January, she had stopped going to early Mass at St. Patrick's, instead, she turned to drink for the elusive solace she was seeking. Neither Father Smith's prayers to the Holy Spirit nor the baser spirits of the bottle had helped. She just sank further into despair. It wasn't until Sean had come home during a spring tempest and found her lying senseless in the mud that things turned around.

Mickey O'Rourke cooked a mash that people claimed would put hair on a toad. No one, not even Mickey himself, was quite sure of what the mash was comprised. He tested it on himself, consuming most of what he produced and would have gladly told you what went into it if he could remember. The liquor's chief merits were the low cost and the mind numbing, muscle freezing impact of the "Divil's own brew."

After staying awake all night with the baby while Mary tried to regain her strength, Katie labored tirelessly, washing the piles of her clients' linens and clothes. Hands raw and cold from the frigid water, back aching from bending over the tub and weary from the struggle to get by, she decided to spend a couple pennies on Mickey's brew to ease her miseries so she could finish her work.

Mickey had set up in the remains of a ruined canal boat left high and dry along the creek by the great storm. Half the boat had been torn off and he had covered the gaping hole in the overturned hull with canvass from a shredded sail. Broken boards and branches had been tied, nailed and jammed together to form the wall to the lee with another bit of canvas providing a porch where Mickey spent his days tending his foul brewing mash.

Katie found him slumped forward by the fire. She couldn't distinguish which of the dizzying odors hanging in the still air was him and which was the mash. The combination was enough to turn a vulture's stomach. She was considerate enough not to pinch her nose, but she couldn't hide the fact that the stench was strong enough to make her eyes water.

"I'll take a jar of brew, Mickey," she announced.

He looked up, eyes unable to focus.

"A jar, Mickey."

"You, K-Katie?" he asked surprised to see the fine lady before him.

"If you please."

He waved his hand at the open barrel and turned away to vomit on the sand.

"Ah, 'tis a elegant drink I b-brewed, K-Katie darling. Will kill the pain and put the hair on your ch-chest."

"I'll not be needing any hair, thank ye," she replied handing him two pennies and dipping her jar in the barrel.

"You're a fine lass, you are, K-Katie Reddy. Fairest o' them all."

He fell off his stool and lay staring into the sky.

"K-Katie of the woods, the q-queen of the faeries. The v-vision of every m-man's dream. Queen Mab must be - your mother, true."

"Get on with it, Mickey. You best be putting down the brew and let your dreams have their way. You will kill yourself with your bitter potion sure, no matter how sweet your tongue be."

He belched and rolled on his side to leer at her.

"Right you are, lass, but I'll be a-dreaming o' you."

She laughed and walked back toward the farm. Weary beyond bearing, she rested on a pile of bricks from a chimney tumbled by the storm and took a sip of the whiskey. It tasted of burnt tar and burned unbearably going down. She almost spit it out, but the warmth in her chest spread, numbing her, promising to deal with the pain. She pinched her nose closed her eyes and took a long swallow of the foul brew.

Mary was up, tending to the baby when she returned to the house.

"Can you take the wee one for a moment. He's nursed the life out of me, and I have to lie down afore I fall down."

"And I'm not as washed out as those filthy linen? Who was up with the lad through the night while you lolled about in the bed?"

"I didn't mean."

"No child. Sorry, I don't know what is wrong with me these days. I am just so tired. Tired of a cruel god who burdens us with more than we can bear, while the wicked prosper in their evil ways. I dread what next he will send our way. Give me the lad. Go rest. I know ye must build your strength."

Katie set down the jar, smiled and took the baby.

"Be off with you, Mary! And you, you come tell Katie about your day, me boyo."

Mary smiled nervously and lay down on the straw tick in the corner. She watched warily as Katie rocked her baby, Terence, and drank from the jar. A heavy rain started drumming on the roof, and lulled by the sound, she drifted off to sleep.

Mary woke in the darkness to Terence's cries. The wind had increased and rain was still lashing the sturdy cabin.

"Katie?" she asked the darkness.

Getting no reply, Mary crawled from the bed and felt her way to baby Terence, who lay wailing on the dirt floor in front of the rocker. Katie was no where to be found. Mary took the baby back to the warm bed and propping herself against the log wall gave the distressed boy her breast. He fussed a moment or two and then sucked contentedly as Mary again fell into an exhausted slumber.

Sean and James trudged through the driving rain after a back breaking day of scooping grain from the holds of ships to fill the canal boats waiting alongside. With his bad leg, Sean stayed dry in the hold scooping the grain into the wheelbarrows while James and the other men rushed through the downpour across the wet, slippery planks, futilely trying to shield their loads from the cascading rain. Joe Sullivan was fired when he slipped on the plank and fell into the harbor between boats, losing his load. Work halted momentarily as the men watched him barely escape being crushed between the rocking boats before making his way to shore.

The foreman cursed the men back into motion and screamed to the crowd of idle men by the slip, "A full day's pay to the man that fishes out the barrow and joins the gang on the plank!"

Five men jumped into the harbor, swam to the floating wheelbarrow and dragged it to shore where a row broke out amongst them. Billy Cunningham was the last man standing, and he proudly rolled the wheelbarrow onto the plank, joining the endless procession of bone-tired men emptying the hold of the schooner.

James was too tired on the way home to ask his father what he thought of the Sullivan incident. It didn't matter, though. Sean was too tired to think of anything but the agony raging through his back. They trudged on through the mud, oblivious to anything but the ground in front of their feet.

"I hope Katie has come up with more than carrots and squash for the stew," muttered James.

"Aye," agreed Sean pausing to straighten his back. "No meat for a week. How is a man to survive on carrots?"

The two men stood in the merciless downpour and tried to peer into the darkness.

"Strange, there is no light from the cabin," observed Sean. "We should have seen it afore now."

"Mary," said James.

The two men hurried on rushing into the cold dark cabin.

"Mary! Katie!" they called.

"Here, James," said Mary.

Sean lit the candle on the table and gazed at Mary and the baby shivering in the corner.

"And where is the woman of the house?" demanded Sean.

"I don't know. I woke to Terence crying. She was nowhere to be found. I must have fallen asleep. I think she was drinking some of Mickey's brew."

Frowning and tilting his head to the side, he stared at the door quizzically and then pulled the lantern down from the shelf. He turned to James.

"Get a fire going, James, and throw whatever you can find into the pot. I am going out to find Katie. Lord knows what has become of her."

He brushed back the wet hair dangling over his eyes, lit the lantern and stepped back into the tempest with thoughts of last October's storm preying on him. The icy wind blew stinging, horizontal torrents of rain against his face. He pressed on, shielding his face and eyes from the blast, trying to spot Katie in the dim light cast by the lantern.

"Katie!" he screamed into the roaring wind. "Katie, darling! Where are you?"

His words swept away by the gale, he staggered toward the outhouse. He swung open the door and raised the lantern to peer inside. Then a terrific gust of wind rushed through the opening and tore the flimsy structure loose, sending it tumbling into the darkness.

"St. Patrick, St. Bridgid, for God's sake, help me find her," he pleaded.

"Katie! Where are you, Lass?"

He turned a complete circle, not knowing which way to go. He started to walk toward Mickey's when he thought he heard a faint cry from out of the darkness back toward the house. He stood still, straining to hear above the wail of the wind. Then he heard it, plaintive and soft.

"Oh, Sean."

He rushed toward the sound and stumbled over Katie's prostrate body, dropping the lantern.

"Katie," yelled Sean crawling through the mud to find her shivering in the dark. "Are you all right. Lass? What happened to you?"

"I'm cold," she moaned. "It's so dark. I can't see."

"I'll get the lantern."

He reached over and drew the lantern close and held her in his arms, looking her over carefully.

"I don't see anything wrong. What happened?"

"I don't remember. 'Tis so dark. Get the lantern. How can you see?"

"Why the lantern, Katie. I see you plain."

"I can't see the lantern," she gasped. "What's wrong with me eyes?"

She turned to her side and vomited in the mud. Sean picked her up from the quagmire and stumbled with her back to the cabin.

"Make room on the bed," commanded Sean laying her gently down.

Mary pulled herself out of the bed, carrying baby Terence with her.

"Put him down and help me get her wet dress off." he directed. "James throw more wood on the fire."

Katie's lips were blue and she lay shivering in the dim light while the two removed her clothes and tamped her dry with dry sheets from her laundry pile.

"What happened, Katie?" asked Mary.

Katie stared uncomprehendingly, unable to answer.

"Take off your clothes and warm her, Da," said Mary.

He shed his wet clothes, dried himself and climbed into the bed drawing her icy body close.

"She's blind," he groaned.

"Blind?"

"Blind."

As Katie's shivering subsided and her breathing calmed, Sean fell asleep cradling her in his arms. Mary picked up Terence and fed him while she and James ate the vegetable stew from the steaming pot and watched over the two sleepers.

Morning arrived with a bright sun drying the muddy ground and bringing the chirping of early spring birds. The door burst open, casting the blinding sunlight into the dark cabin, followed by the laughter of the young ones.

"Ma? Da?" called Danny. "We're hungry! We stayed with the Clancy's during the storm."

Sean squinted into the light.

"Quiet now," warned Mary. "Ma's feeling poorly. There's food in the pot, Where are the girls?"

"Prolly stayed at work 'til the storm stopped," offered Michael. "I woulda."

Sean looked at Katie sleeping soundly and stood. He pulled his trousers on and took a few spoonfuls from the pot.

"You two stay and help Mary with the baby. Ma is sick and needs her rest."

"What's wrong with her?" asked Michael.

"Just look after her. James and I must be off to the docks. Don't let me hear you left or I'll whip the Divil out of you. Got that, you hooligans?"

"Yes sir," they replied in unison.

Katie stirred and opened her eyes.

"Come back to bed, Sean. I'm cold and you don't have to get to the docks before the sun does."

He stared fearfully at her blind eyes and raised a hand in warning when Danny made to speak.

"Go back to sleep, darling. I'll be back before you know it."

He turned to the boys.

"Let her sleep and keep the house quiet. Say some prayers, and she'll be better tonight when I get home."

On his lunch break, he heard that they'd found Mickey O'Rourke dead from his latest batch of whiskey. He went to the foreman and told him he had to go take care of his wife, because he feared she had been drinking from the same batch as Mickey.

The foreman growled, "If you leave, don't come back. It's up to you. Plenty o' men waiting ashore for your job."

Sean leaned on his shovel stared at him in disbelief.

"A woman drinks o' dat Divil's brew ain't worth da time o day," added the foreman.

Rage flashed in Sean's eyes, and he smashed the sneering foreman in the face with the wooden grain shovel. The mighty blow laid the man out cold on the slip and cracked the shaft of the wooden scooper. He spat on the miserable blackguard for good measure and went home to take care of the woman who had stood by him through a lifetime of struggle.

Katie was sitting on the side of the bed with her head cradled in her hands when he returned home. She groaned when he threw open the door spilling the brilliant sunlight into the dark cabin.

"Oh, my eyes," she moaned. "Close the door. I can't take the light."

He pulled the door shut behind him.

"You can see then, Katie?" he asked.

"The light hurts my eyes and sets my head to throbbing, but I can see nothing but the light. I'm so sick and my head hurts me so."

"But if you see the light, your eyesight must be coming back."

He took the kettle off the fire and brewed a pot of tea while Katie lay moaning on the bed. Mary sat rocking the baby and stared at her father-in-law sadly.

"Are you up to taking the wee one for a walk outside?" he asked Mary.

"I'm so tired, da."

"I know, darling, but Katie and me need a little time."

Mary handed him the baby and wrapped her shawl around her shoulders. He handed the baby back and she cradled him under the woolen shawl which James had salvaged while picking through the debris left by the flood. They had replaced their wardrobes and furnished the house from the piles of flotsam left by the retreating waters.

"I'll stop in at Murphy's and see if any new cloth has come in. The baby will be outgrowing this soon enough."

"Thank you, Mary."

He nodded toward Katie.

"You know this can't go on any longer."

"Aye, we need her with us."

Mary left and Sean sat next to Katie propping her against him in the bed. She groaned clutching her head in her hands. Sean held the cup to her lips, and she took a tentative sip.

"Now, Lass, you can do better than that. We have to get that poison out of you."

He held the cup to her lips and she took a long draught. Her eyes widened and she leaned away from him and vomited on the floor.

"What did you give me?"

"Here drink another."

She glared at him angrily and then drank a little more. This time it stayed down.

"I wish I could just die," whined Katie laying back. "I can't stand the pain, and why should I? There ain't nothing but pain and suffering in this world for the likes of us."

"Enough of that talk, Katie Dailey. You've moped and whined around here long enough. You almost killed yourself last night. Now drink some more."

She did as she was told and sighed as the warm liquid settled her tempestuous stomach.

"I didn't mean but to ease my mind a mite. It's been hard, Sean. What have I done to deserve these trials?"

"That's not the way of things and you know it, Katie Dailey."

"It's Reddy now. Katie Reddy."

"Not if you go on like this."

"I'm sorry."

"Sure enough Mickey O'Rourke did kill himself with that witch's brew of his. They found him this morning."

"My God."

"God knows I've tried to be patient with you, Katie. But you would have tried the patience of Job. I'll have no more of it. Mary and Terence need you. The children don't know what to think. We've been working around you, wondering where the Katie of old has got to. You're dragging us down with you. The children need you. I need you. We all need you, woman. The baby will die if you don't put aside your troubles and shoulder your crosses."

"But I…"

"No more "but I's." You cost me my job today."

"You lost your job?"

"No, you lost it!"

"I."

""We need to work together if we are to get by in this land. We are a family, and if we all do our part, we'll get by."

"I've been so lost and alone."

"You've been through hell in this short life, but you are not alone. I'm with you in this Katie, and God knows there will probably be more hell to come. We need each other to face whatever comes our way. Are you with us, Katie? We need you."

She buried her face against his chest sobbing, "I'm so sorry, I'm so sorry."

He stroked her hair purring, "I know Katie darling. I know."

It took a few more days for the poisonous brew to completely work it's way out of her system. She gradually regained her strength and sight, but from that moment on, she regained the mantle of the strong, supportive woman she had always been. As spring brought new life to the land, Mary and the baby prospered from Katie's renewed spirit, and Katie and Sean thrived along with them.

2
CANAL STREET
1847

Within two years of the great flood, streams of Irish fleeing the potato blight now flooded the resilient city. Canal boats piled high with immigrants and manufactured goods poured into the harbor night and day. After discharging their cargoes they were loaded with the bounty of the interior to carry back east to the growing nation. Buffalo's population swelled with men and women desperate for work and a new life in a new world.

Captain Brennan guided "The Western Star" toward the commercial slip while his passengers marveled at the activity along the canal. Scores of people hurried along pulling carts, stacking barrels, guiding mules, hawking goods, butchering livestock and dumping waste into the canal. The immigrants pinched their noses against the stench and gaped open-mouthed at the dozens of canal boats arrayed in front of them while they waited to be guided to a berth alongside the crowded towpath.

"We'll be berthing by the 'Mary Beth' I'm guessing," said Captain Brennan. "Just get your belongings together, and you can cross over her and the next few boats to the shore."

"Won't they mind us crossing over?" asked Liam O'Connor.

"I'll be waiting most the day afore my turn to unload. You cross over and if any give you trouble, tell them to see Captain Brennan. That'll settle 'em, sure."

"Thankee, Captain."

The boat bumped into the 'Mary Beth,' and Captain Brennan tied up alongside.

"Mind the Sleveens. They will take you for all your worth. Just follow the towpath to the harbor to your ship and don't trust anyone. Mind the wee ones don't get snatched along the way."

Cara's eyes widened and she drew Seamus and Honora close. Patting the bulge in his coat pocket, Liam smiled reassuringly at her.

"We've come all this way and have only a night to pass in Buffalo. We'll make it all right."

"You're in for the worst of it here. I'll not be the only one noticing the jingle of coins in the basket. Best get to the ship and spend the night aboard. There is nothing but divilment ashore for you in this Satan's den. Best be on your way before the sun sets."

"We're for Ohio, Cara!" whooped Liam as he hefted his duffle bag over his shoulder and stepped across onto the roof of the Mary Beth. He reached back and swung Honora and Seamus across as Cara stepped tentatively aboard clasping the heavy basket tightly in both hands. As they stepped to the next boat, a weathered woman with a child at her breast emerged from the cabin squinting in the bright sunshine.

"G'day to ye," he said. "Where did ye ship from?"

"From County Clare, out of Galway. Three months past," answered Liam.

"Would you be knowing a Danny O'Reilly from Innis?"

"That I would not."

Her shoulders slouched a little more as a further wave of weariness settled on them.

"He was to follow when he saved the fare. I have been waiting these past two years."

She ducked back into the gloom of the cabin. Liam exchanged an empathetic look with Cara who squeezed his arm thankfully as they passed onto the next boat.

They stepped onto the roof of the fifth boat where Liam helped Cara onto the wharf. As he passed the children up to her, a large red-faced man emerged from the cabin snatching Liam's duffle bag.

"And what do you think you're at?" roared the man.

"Going ashore to find our ship," Liam warily replied reaching for his bag.

"Not without my port fee, you won't," growled the Captain pulling the bag out of reach. "That will be a dollar a head, or I keep your poke."

"There is no port fee," said Liam.

"You step aboard me boat; you pay the fee."

"Captain Brennan said to see him if any had an issue."

The man grabbed Liam's duffle and stepped back.

"That blackguard? I'll settle him in me own time," he said reaching out his open hand. "Now, the four dollars or your poke goes into the canal."

Liam bent and charged, butting his head into the man's midsection and driving him over backwards. He grabbed the duffel and stepped nimbly ashore leaving the cursing man struggling to catch his breath.

"Hurry now!" exclaimed Liam. "We need to get clear of the slip."

The family soon vanished into the swirling mass of humanity that crawled about the district like a swarm of ants on a discarded bit of meat. A string of curses followed them as the red-faced captain climbed ashore to collect his ransom. Watchman Micah Curly appeared and intercepted him as he climbed ashore to pursue the family.

"Would you be forgetting to unload and open a place for the others, Captain Clark?" he asked pleasantly.

"Did you not see that villain assault me? I want him arrested!"

"For keeping your hand out of his pocket? Get on with you now, or you'll be the one seeing the magistrate."

Clark scowled and hopped back aboard.

"You're plaguing the wrong man, you uppity Mick," he called from the cabin.

"Mick Head o' the Watch, boyo, and don't let that slip your mind. I'll be keeping an eye on you."

"That eye best be in the back of your head," murmured Clark.

Micah leaped on board, dragged Clark out of the cabin and drove the shillelagh into his midsection. Clark bent forward and Micah slammed the club down on the back of his head sending him senseless onto the deck. He rolled Clark over and slapped him repeatedly to bring him back to consciousness. He grabbed Clark by the hair and pulled his head up to scream into his face.

"I have eyes in the back o' my head, and sharp ears as well. If you trouble me again, I'll finish the work I started today."

Micah rapped his shillelagh on the deck for emphasis and let Clark's head fall back to the deck. He stepped casually ashore to continue on his rounds with Watchman O'Malley.

"Ah, O'Malley, 'tis a fine thing to get your blood flowing early in the afternoon," he said stretching his arms back loosening his shoulders. "I owe the good captain my thanks. Looks to be a fine day ahead."

"I'd be wary of him," cautioned O'Malley. "His heart is as black as the peat."

Liam parted the crowds with Cara close on his heel tightly clutching the hands of children. A gaunt-faced woman crashed into him and thrust her hand into his pocket. He grabbed her wrist, twisted it and turning her aside, pushed onward.

"That how you treats a lady?" screamed the foul smelling hag. "May your little Irish dick rot off and feed the fishes."

"Lady?" laughed Liam. "I couldn't swear that you was even human."

"Filthy Irish pig."

Liam waved dismissively and Cara hustled the children down the crowded street away from the wretched woman.

Loafers stood in doorways and alleyways eyeing the passing throng, watching for any sign of vulnerability. Two evil looking thugs laughed and called out when Liam thrust the woman aside.

"You passing on horse faced Annie? We have a just ripened one for ye. Turned twelve just last month."

Cara gasped and Liam pushed through the throng to get by the purveyors of vice.

"Take a hold of my belt and keep the wee ones close," he ordered Cara.

"How far?" she asked. "The stench takes my breath away."

"Can't be far. I can see the masts just ahead. Hang tight."

They passed from the dens of iniquity lining the towpath to the busy harbor. Here the crowd was engaged in legitimate commerce, not the marketing of flesh and spirits. Men hoisted heavy pallets onto ships lying at anchor or onto waiting canal boats, as wagons rattled to and fro with teamsters cursing and horses neighing. Merchants and shippers compared tallies and kept close watch on the stevedores swarming the ships and docks, cursing any moving too slowly or mishandling the cargo. Steam engines hissed and whistles blew, announcing the arrival and departure of ships. A heavy pall of black smoke pouring from the myriad smokestacks hung low, drifting inland over the chaotic scene to stain buildings and people alike a sickly brown. The young family was repeatedly jostled by the crowd and the little ones began to cry. Cara hushed them promising a taste of honey for brave children.

Liam stepped over a pile of rags and a hand grabbed at his trousers. He looked down at a pair of wild eyes staring from the filthy face of a wretched drunk lying in the street.

The man moaned, "A penny for me poor wee ones, sir. They be no bigger than your'n. Just one penny to give them something to fill their bellies. Davey McGillicutty will be in your debt evermore."

Liam kicked free of the man.

"Liam!" exclaimed Cara. "Think of his children."

"The only children he has are in the bottle lying aside him."

The man started to weep.

"Oh 'tis true, 'tis true. They perished in the flood. 'Twas God's judgment on Davey McGillicutty. If only he would let me forget."

Liam wavered, his hard eyes softening as he dropped a penny in the quivering mess that was all that was left of Davey McGillicutty. He led the family away toward the docks ignoring the blessings called down upon him by the pitiful man.

The schooner "Sandusky" was being loaded when they approached the wharf. The first officer screamed orders from the deck as a gang of laborers scurried back and forth to shore grumbling against the man, the labor and the luck that brought them to Buffalo.

"Ahoy, the Sandusky!" cried Liam.

The officer glanced disdainfully at the shabby Irishman, and called back, "What business have ye with the Sandusky?"

"We've booked passage to the Ohio, sir. May we come aboard."

"We sail tomorrow at nine bells. You can come aboard at seven bells."

"Might we spend the night on board and save the cost of a room?"

"Am I to be an alms house, now? Seven bells not one minute before. Now be off. I have work to do."

The officer turned away to scream at a man resting his load on the gunwale, and feeling invisible once again, Liam led the family away from the docks.

"Now what?" asked Cara.

"We find a place to lay over. We can't stand out here with all of our belongings. I'm afraid we look a mite easy to the thugs and hooligans laying about. We should get away from the water and find lodging for the night."

"We have only so much silver, Liam."

"What can one night cost us? A few pennies?"

"If you think it best."

A scrawny barefoot boy with a confusion of unwashed red hair sauntered up to them. He skittered to a stop a few feet away and putting both hands in his pocket, leaned forward, cocked his head to the side and asked, "You looking for a clean bed for the night?"

"Not now, boyo" said Liam turning away.

"A penny a head for the big people and two for a penny for the wee ones."

Liam turned around.

"You'll not beat that price if you look a hunnert year."

"A room of our own?"

"A penny more for the big ones."

"No bugs?"

"It ain't no palace, but it'll do for the likes o' you."

Liam looked at Cara.

"Well?"

"It's only four pence and we need a safe place to lay over."

"Very well," said Liam. "Lead on lad!"

"Carrot's the name," said the boy. "Follow me."

"Do you think they named him Carrot because of the hair?" whispered Cara, "or was it the dirt still clinging to him since they pulled him out of the garden?"

Liam laughed and said, "Four pennies is four pennies."

The family followed along, back the way they came, passing the same loafers and whores who sized them up once again. Liam kept the family close together and hoisting his bags over his shoulder, he kept his free hand on the handle of the pistol in his coat pocket. A horrible stench assaulted their noses as they cut away from the canal down Erie Street. Cara wrinkled her nose and gaped at a two-story high pile of manure quivering and glistening in the sun like some monstrous living thing. On closer inspection she saw tens of thousands of flies crawling over the surface of the fetid heap of manure next to a livery stable.

"Here we are," said Carrot proudly pointing to the stable. "Mother Shannon's Horse and Irisher's Hotel!"

Cara gasped, "A stable? Are we the Holy Family, now?"

"Don't be an arse. The horses are up front. The Irishers in the building out back. 'Tis a fine hotel. Mother Shannon stays there herself!"

"Liam!" whined Cara.

"Long as we are here. We'll give it a look see."

"That's a man to be respected," said Carrot. "Keeps his mind open and his woman in her place, he does. Right this way."

They walked around the building past the corral to a ramshackle two story building. The roof sagged in the middle, with dozens of missing cedar shingles. There were traces of faded white-wash on the curling boards and the windows were covered in thick brown soot.

Stepping into the gloomy interior, they were greeted by a loud cackle, "Why Carrot, ye've found me a nice young family. How pretty de wee ones be."

A toothless old crone stepped from the shadows to tousle the children's hair with gnarled hands covered with an oily grime. A faded Mother Hubbard dress hung limply from her stooped shoulders. The tattered edge ended mid-calf to reveal hairy bare legs and twisted feet.

Her unique aroma added to the stench of the manure pile, and Cara felt her stomach turn.

"They wants a room all private," said Carrot.

"Oh, I see," smiled Mrs. Shannon. "De President suite it is. Dat will be five pennies each and five for de room."

"Carrot told us four pennies for the lot."

"Oh he did? He must not have heard of de Marquis' expected visit. Four pennies is for special families what is kin and such."

"Good day, Mrs. Shannon."

He turned and bumped Cara causing the basket of coins in her hand to jingle quietly. Mrs. Shannon's eyes widened and she cocked her head to the side.

"Rein in your horse, a mite. The Marquis hasn't arrived as yet, so maybe I could give you de room for one night. Five pennies for de lot of you. How's dat den?"

"Good day."

"Oh you're a hard one to take advantage of me motherly ways. If Carrot said four pennies, den four pennies it is. Do you want me to keep dat basket o' coins safe for you, dearie?"

Cara clutched the basket tightly and took a step backward. Liam reached into the basket and pulled out a few nails.

"It's just a bag of nails we brought with us from the old sod to make our new home with some of the old. Good Irish iron to keep the fairies away."

"Well that's an idée I never heard afore. T'inking on the fairies never caused nobody no harm, though. It's dem what ignore de wee folk suffer at dere hands."

"I don't think we should stay here," said Cara.

"Why you won't find a safer place in Buffalo. Up on de second floor. No window. Only one way in and one way out."

"Let's be off, Liam."

"You are such a lovely family. I can't bear ta see you wandering de streets with all de hooligans about. Two pennies and de room is yourn."

"We'll take it," said Liam handing over the two pennies.

"De necessary is out back. Carrot show de nice family the room, and den I have another errand for ye."

3

IN THE DARK HOURS

Cara and the children waited in the dark room, lit only from narrow shafts of sunlight shining through the cracks in the rough hewn boards. The children fidgeted and tried to peer through the cracks in the wall.

"I don't like it here," said Seamus. "It smells worse'n the privy in New York."

"We must wait for the morning to board our ship," said Cara gently. "Then we'll have all the fresh air of the West to breathe."

"Where's Da?" whined Honora. " I'm hungry."

"He'll be back soon with our dinner and water."

The door banged open and a shoeless man with scraggly hair and whiskers stood peering into the room. Cara leaped to her feet and hid the children behind her.

"Well, what have we here?" the man muttered lecherously. "Something to suit my fancy I'm guessing."

"You have the wrong room, sir!" she replied indignantly.

"Pity, that, but I'm willing to make the best of it if you are, lass."

"Get out!"

"Not so fast. I'm willing to pay, after a fashion."

Cara shrank back from the evil smelling man as he stepped into the room and started undoing his trousers.

"I'll just come in and be about my business with you. Won't take long and I'll leave you and the wee ones be if you are nice to me."

"My husband."

"He don't have to know, darling."

"Have pity. Leave us be."

He grabbed her by the hair and pulled her against him.

" 'Tis going to happen. Don't make it hard on yourself, Lass."

"What's this, now?" yelled Liam from the hallway.

"Nothing, mate. Just stepped into the wrong room in the dark."

"Oh, Liam. He was going to take me by force!"

Liam grabbed the man by his oily hair and bashed his head into the door frame and booted him down the corridor. The man ran for the exit.

'We have to get out of here," insisted Cara.

"But I've already paid."

"We can spare the pennies, but not our lives."

"Do you think it will be any better out there? We're better off with a door we can bar."

"It isn't safe here."

"I won't leave again, and I can stand watch 'til dawn."

"Keep your pistol cocked and ready."

"Aye, that I will."

"Can we eat, now?" asked Seamus.

Liam rubbed the boys head and said, "Sure and we need to keep up our strength for tomorra's voyage. Shall we feed 'em then, Cara?"

"We should wait a while and offer our hunger to the Blessed Mother," teased Cara.

"Ma!" exclaimed Seamus.

The parents laughed and doled out the meager dinner to the children. Cara and the children fell to sleep after eating and Liam drowsed in the dark stuffy room as the sun went down and the last of the light and the street hubbub of carts, peddlers and children faded into the stillness of an early spring night. The croaking of frogs in vernal pools lulled Liam to sleep and he didn't hear the click of the latch as a silent hand tried the door.

"Liam!" hissed Cara. "Did you hear that?"

"Huh?" he muttered slowly awakening.

"Cock your pistol," she said raising her voice. "Someone's trying to get in."

The jiggling of the latch stopped when she spoke and footsteps could be heard going away from the door.

"What was it, Cara?' asked Liam, now fully awake.

"Someone was at the door, and you had fallen asleep. He went away when I told you to cock the pistol. This is a den of evil we've come to, sure."

Gunshots, curses and shouts of laughter now filled the street, a chorus of revelry replacing the sounds of the bustling daytime business district. The denizens of the dark had emerged from their daytime hovels to haunt the night.

He tried to wedge the door shut, but the decrepit hinges gave way, leaving them more exposed to danger. He piled their belongings on the floor just inside the doorway and put the basket of coins behind him under the straw mattress.

"It would be foolish to venture out now, Cara. I will be vigilant the rest of the night."

"And me wide awake beside you!" she declared.

The two huddled together staring in the darkness toward the door while the soft breathing of the sleeping children was repeatedly overpowered by the chaos on the street below.

The street noise subsided in the wee hours of the morning and Liam struggled to stay awake. Brought to full awareness by the creaking of the door, Liam heard a soft whisper on the other side of the door.

"You sure this is the room?" whispered the disembodied voice.

"Aye," answered another. "Carrot said dis be de one, true. A basket full o' coin, he said."

"Think the woman was bluffing about the pistol?"

"Sounded scared to me, she did."

Liam cocked back the pistol which clicked loudly and distinctly in the still room. The men at the door dashed away without another word. Liam grinned and uncocked the pistol.

"We can relax now," said Liam. "That will be the last of our night visitors. They've no taste for a bellyful of lead."

They settled back resting against the wall. Cara nestled into Liam's shoulder and drifted off to sleep. Liam held her close taking in the scent of her hair and the warmth of her soft body. He fought sleep, knowing he would soon be on the "Sandusky" where he could sleep at his ease. Eventually, despite all his effort, he dozed.

He awoke to whispers in the hall.

"In there?" a voice asked drunkenly.

The door tore free of it's hinges and crashed into the room. Liam leaped to his feet and fired at the man in the doorway.

"He's kilt me!" exclaimed the man collapsing to the floor.

Liam saw that he had just shot Davey McGillicutty, the drunk to whom he had given the penny. Before Liam could quite comprehend what he had just done, four men rushed in behind the fallen drunk. The first into the room tumbled over the pile of their belongings Liam had stacked in their way and Liam laid him low with the butt of his pistol. Trying to defend his family, he rose and set himself to meet the next attacker, but he was struck across the face with a spiked club and driven to his knees. The other men gathered round pummeling him with lead saps until he fell senseless to the floor and beat him to a bloody pulp. Cara screamed and the children began to cry as one of the men tore at her clothes

"There's no time for any o' that. Silence the lot of them," growled the leader as he held a lantern aloft to take in the room.

"You want me to do for dem?" asked the man struggling with Cara.

"No, ye gobswipe. Bash the bitch and stuff the wee one's mouths wit rags. We can sell the lot o' dem to de German. He'll find a use for 'em, sure."

While the others bound Cara and the children, the leader rummaged through the pile of meager belongings looking for the basket of coins that Mother Shannon and Carrot had seen.

Frustrated searching in the dim light, he slapped Seamus in the face and screamed, "Where is it?"

Seamus nodded toward the straw tick and the man tossed it aside. He grabbed the basket and plopped down on the overturned mattress to count the coins.

"I'll stay with our property whilst you three dump the bodies."

The men grabbed McGillicutty by the arms and legs and carried his limp body from the room.

"Thank ye for your aid, Davey," cackled the coin counter to the corpse. "Give my regards to the missus and the wee ones."

The murderers guffawed and carried on taunting the dead man as they dragged him down the stairs past Mother Shannon.

"See you clean up after yourselves," she admonished the men. "I'll not be always picking up after you."

"When you take a bath, we'll clean the whole blamed place," mocked one of the men.

Turning to the brigand counting coins she demanded, "Give me my cut, ye blackguard, and I'll be off to me bed."

The coin counter handed her a few coins saying, "Off with you now. We've more work to do."

"I'll be expecting a piece of what the German pinches from his purse when you hand them over."

"You're an evil old crone," mumbled the man.

"An' you're the divil himself," she laughed.

A splash from the canal caught their attention and Cara groaned.

"Well I'm off to me bed."

When the men returned and picked up Liam's lifeless body, tears filled Cara's eyes, and she moaned pitifully as she watched them carry her love from the room. Dreading what would happen upon their return, she struggled futilely against her bonds. The children stared wild-eyed at her struggles, their muffled cries barely audible through the rags stuffed in their mouths. Another splash from the canal extinguished their last hope.

4

THE WATCH

Mary rose before dawn, fanned the coals back to life and swung the pot over the fire to boil. She shivered in the cool pre-dawn air and warmed her frigid hands over the flickering flames. The room would not warm until long after she departed for the mayor's mansion, but she and Micah would need a good hot breakfast to see them through the day. She trimmed a couple of beets, and threw them into the pot along with some millet collected from the fields, and a slab of smoked sausage. She set the teapot to boil and went to the privy knowing Micah would soon rise to the heady aroma of breakfast stewing. He was a good man, fallen on hard times like the rest of the city. He worked hard and knew that he would soon rise back to prominence in the thriving port. The loss of his parents and their property weighed heavily on him, but he was a strong man, who would not let anything hold him down for long. Her whole family was like that. True, her mother had taken the latest trial badly, but she was on the mend and pulling her and many others' weight once again.

Years of strife had taken their toll, but as her Da, Sean Reddy, had drilled into each of her brothers and sisters, "The Reddy's do not give up readily!"

How many times had she heard that, growing up with family and boarders filling their home? Slamming the privy door behind her she saw O'Malley headed her way.

"Morning Missus."

"You're a mite early this morning, Hugh O'Malley."

"Couldn't sleep. I was a mite queasy and had troubling dreams."

"Did ye stop off at one of the dives on your way home last night?"

"Aye, Mary. That I did. To my everlasting shame and regret."

"You will never learn. Will ye?"

" 'Spect not," he admitted. "Is the chief up?"

"Come in have a cuppa, and we shall see. I have to hurry if I'm not to be sacked by the housekeeper."

"Hot tea? I'll always be your slave, Mary."

"Then fetch me a bucket of water, darkee."

"What's that I hear from your lips Mary Curly?"

"I was just joshing with Hugh."

"Way things have gotten lately, we don't josh about that. What about Malachi? Is he just a darkee to you?"

"Micah, I was just having a little fun. You know how I feel about Malachi."

"Aye. I just hear those words and worse every day on the rounds. They are good people, and I don't want to hear them called animals. Look at what the British are doing to our families back in Ireland. Are we any better if we do the same to the Negro?"

"All right, Micah," said Hugh as he brought a bucket into the room. "You know she didn't mean anything. It was me started the whole slave thing anyhow."

"There is going to be trouble," answered Micah. "You mark my word. All these new Irish coming in and taking the jobs. Nothing good can come of it."

"Don't our lads have the right to work?"

"That they do, but the wages go lower and lower with every boatload coming ashore. There will be trouble between the two, even though it is the bosses profiting from their struggles. We should work together."

"Never happen."

Mary poured out the tea, and the three sat quietly sipping the warm vitalizing brew. Micah leaned back in his chair and smiled at Mary.

"Just a mite tired, I guess. You're a good lass. Sorry I jumped at you."

"You're right though," she replied. "It's all that we hear around the dinner table. The men blaming the Negroes for the low wages."

"Well let it go. We all need to be getting on with the day. I'm for a steaming bowl of the gruel."

Mary scooped him his portion and gave him a quick peck on the lips as she set the steaming bowl on the rickety table.

"That should sweeten it for ye," she laughed.

Micah pulled her into his lap and gave her a long passionate kiss in return as she struggled to pull free. She stood up, straightening her dress and primping her hair.

"Micah Curly! Have you no decency? In front of Mr. O'Malley for heaven's sake!"

"It weren't for Mr. O'Malley's or heaven's sake. It were all about me."

"You will be bringing the vengeance of the Lord down on the lot of us if you go on in your ways."

"The Lord's the one made you so pretty, Mary. It weren't me."

Mary blushed.

"Oh go on with ye. I'm off to me work."

She picked up her newspaper wrapped lunch and stepped out into the darkness.

"Save a bit of that vigor for when you come home," called Micah with a bit of a smirk lighting his face.

"Lord forgive us," she prayed to the early morning sky.

Turning to O'Malley he asked, "Did you get the cart wheel fixed?"

"Good as new. Waiting for us on the towpath."

"Best be getting on with it. Don't want any of the swells coming across the night's refuse."

"It will wait a bit. I'd like another cuppa, and I had something to ask you private."

"Sounds serious."

"'Tis."

Micah poured them another cup of tea and sat across from O'Malley.

"Last night some of the boys over to Mooney's were talking."

He paused and took a sip.

"They are of the mind that something should be done about the troubles back home. They are getting up a group."

"To send money? The British will just confiscate it."

"No, guns."

Micah set down his cup and leaned forward.

"And what did you say?"

"Nothing. I'm just telling you what went on. But..."

"But what?"

"My family is still over there."

"As is some of mine."

"What do you think?"

" 'Twill just be more bloodshed. The British are too strong. They have every weapon of modern warfare at their disposal."

"But if we send guns..."

"No use for it. Just give the British cover for killing more of us. Who were these people at Mooney's?"

"Called themselves 'Young Irelanders' or 'Fenians'. Don't know which."

"Sounds like they think they are Finn Mac Cool and his Fianna reborn."

" 'Tis bad over there."

"I know. I know, but we got our own worries here. Put it out of your mind. Sky is brightening. Time to be on our rounds."

The two men adjusted their coats, checked that their clubs were handy and secured their pistols. Stepping into the cool morning air, Micah shivered and turned his collar up.

"Jaysus!" exclaimed Micah. "Won't the lake ever give up the gales of winter?"

"It'll warm soon enough."

"I canna wait 'til the end o' August, mate. I need a little heat this day."

The two laughed and hurried along to generate a little heat. When they reached the towpath, O'Malley grabbed the handles of the push cart and followed Micah, who strolled along the canal peering into the dark waters looking for the night's refuse.

"Over here, constable," called a woman from one of the canal boats. "Whew! I'm thinking this one been a-floating for a bit o' time."

Micah crossed over the boat and saw a bloated body bumping against the boat. The putrid, naked body was scarred with fish bites and swarming with blowflies. Micah wrinkled his nose and called to O'Malley.

"Bring me the hook and I'll drag him to the bank."

O'Malley passed the shepherd's crook to the woman who handed it to Micah. Before he could get the hook around the man's torso, he had to push it away from the bat. He poked the bloated corpse puncturing the decomposing flesh. A foul rush of air spewed forth causing Micah and the woman to turn aside losing the contents of their stomachs.

"Lord a mercy," groaned the woman. "Get that thing away from here."

Holding his breath, Micah looped the hook around the man and floated him to the bank. He and O'Malley pulled the man out of the filthy water and threw him onto the cart.

"Whew, he's a ripe one, sure," gasped O'Malley.

"Someone didn't want us finding him to soon," said Micah. "See the rope around his leg? Must have tied on a stone to keep him down. He look familiar to you?"

"He don't look human to me, poor soul."

The two continued their search, stopping to check a few drunken sots lying in doorways, under carts and huddled in the open.

A couple of hundred feet further on Micah spotted two more in the water. One, fully clothed, was floating free and the other was hung up naked on a broken piling.

"Will you look at that? These ones look fresh at least."

Stepping closer and reaching out with the hook, he said, "Yep, the blackguards were busy last night."

He pulled the floater in and they threw him on top of the first body.

"It's Davey McGillicutty," said O'Malley.

"Now who would want to do that poor soul?" wondered Micah. "There was no harm nor profit in him. Shot him, too. Don't make no sense."

The second body was jammed in the pilings and try what they would, they couldn't pull him free of the close set poles.

"There's nothing else to it. Down you go O'Malley."

O'Malley climbed down the piling and standing on a cross beam wriggled the body loose.

"Throw down a rope."

Micah lowered the rope and O'Malley tied it around the body. Micah grunted and looping the rope around the post, pulled the body up as O'Malley pushed it clear. O'Malley scrambled back up and the two of them hoisted the lifeless man into the cart. They continued along the canal finding nothing more.

"Let's rid ourselves of this foul smelling lot," said O'Malley.

"Right."

As they turned to push the cart away from the canal and up the steep slope toward their headquarters on the Terrace, Micah spotted a woman clinging to a young sailor as the two of them stumbled to and fro along the street. She struggled against the sailor's storm tossed body, leading him toward the open doorway of a wretched shack.

"Just a minute, isn't that Laura Jensen? And with her head uncovered?"

"Shall we give her a ride then?"

"Let's. She's been nothing but trouble since she came."

He called out, "Stand to, Laura Jensen!"

She pulled on the sailor, trying to get him into her room, but he pulled back saying, "I'm not for no trouble."

Micah took her by her arm and said, "Laura, you should know you can't be taking your hat off on the street. You will have to come along with us to see the judge."

"Get off me, ye fecking arse. Always coming down on poor Laura you are. Think ye can roust me ever day, ye do."

Micah pulled her arms behind her back and fastened the manacles on her. Then he and O'Malley hoisted her onto the cart atop the pile of corpses. The added weight released another blast of foul decomposing gasses.

"Ohh!" she exclaimed. "Get me off, damn ye. I can't stand the smell."

"Just some more cold fish to keep you company," laughed O'Malley.

"Ye filthy Irish bastards, " she hissed .

"You bring it on yourself, Laura," said Micah. "Now quiet down, see the judge and pay your fine."

She glared at him and wriggled herself to the side of the cart pinching her nose and taking short breaths through her pursed lips. The cart rumbled over the cobblestones and the second body bounced to the side. O'Malley grabbed the dangling arm and rolled him back to the center of the cart.

"Hey," said Laura.

"Laura," warned Micah.

"Dat one groaned and moved."

"What?"

"True."

Micah helped her off the cart and saw movement. He pulled the body over and the man groaned distinctly.

"Cara," moaned the man.

"O'Malley, is that the immigrant we saved from Captain Clark?"

"Hard to tell with all the bruising, but I think so."

"If it is, what happened to his nice young family? Best dump the dead ones and get him to the hospital. Laura, this is your lucky day. Be off with you and don't let me catch you tempting the sailors with your bare head."

"Don't need no bare head to get no man. I got me ways."

"That you do," laughed O'Malley. "Long as they be blind drunk."

"Feck you, ye pig."

"I'd as soon do a pig as you, Laura."

She whirled away and stomped huffily back to her hunting grounds to look for her escaped prey. The two men dumped the bodies on the side of the street and picking up the handles jogged toward the hospital with Liam O'Connor slowly regaining consciousness and moaning with every jolt of the wooden wheels rattling across the cobblestones.

5

CARA

Cara cried out when she opened her swollen eyes. She couldn't tell if she was blind or if their was nothing to see in the darkness. Her bruised, naked body shivered from the cold, sending spasms of pain through her battered head. She had been used. That she could tell, but bashed senseless after seeing Liam killed, she had no idea by how many and for how long. The memories of the night's terror came rushing back in an overwhelming torrent, and she raised up sending another shaft of excruciating pain through her brain.

"Honora?" she gasped through clenched teeth. "Seamus? Are you here then?"

She raised herself on all fours and started feeling around in the darkness. Finding herself alone in the tiny space, she collapsed and began to weep uncontrollably.

A sudden loud crash against the door was followed by a disembodied voice cursing, "Damn your noise! Shut your keening ye bitch, or I'll give you more of the same!"

"My children?" she whimpered.

"They are long gone. The German will decide for them."

"You can't."

"I did, and you'll be earning me some coin or joining your man in the drink."

"They're so small. What will become of them."

"They don't stay young long oncet the German gets aholdt o' them."

"NO! Help! Somebody! Let me out! My poor wee ones!"

The door crashed open and in the dim light of a candle from the next room, the disembodied voice took flesh and beat the defenseless woman mercilessly, raining down blows with a lead sap until his anger and energy gave out.

The savage man stood erect and kicked the moaning woman in the ribs for good measure and snarled, "You'll learn to do as you be told soon enough, dearie."

Reeling from yet another thrashing, Cara retreated into a dreamless stupor waking in the dark a few hours later. Though she wanted to scream in pain upon waking, she gritted her teeth and stifled her cries for fear of another beating. As she lay panting on the muddy floor she could hear movement in the outer room.

"How's the new girl coming along?"

"Had to learn her who be boss."

"Ye didn't ruin her?"

"Nay, just thumped her a bit about the body and put her to sleep with a gentle tap on her pretty little crown."

"The German wants to talk. Think she'll hold?"

"She's out, and even if she comes to, she won't be able to move for a day or so."

"Check on her and let's go over to the German's"

Cara closed her eyes at the sound of the approaching footsteps. The door swung open casting light on her abused body.

"Jaysus! Did you kill her?"

"Just did her enough to set her straight."

"Well lay off. We can make a lot of coin off one as pretty as her. Don't want you scarring the likes of her."

The door closed and Cara listened as the footsteps retreated. She lay still for another fifteen minutes listening intently for any sound. Hearing nothing, she made her way to the low doorway. She felt about for a latch and finding none, she pushed gently outward. The door gave slightly. It was latched on the outside. She pushed harder and the door seemed to give a little more.

"It'll give," she muttered.

She stepped back from the door and rushed it, slamming her shoulder against the decaying wood. The door responded with a loud crack, bouncing her to the floor. She lay crying on the muddy floor waiting for the pain to subside. She rose and charged the door again. It burst open slamming into the wall and caroming back at her. Panting to control her agony she pushed the door open and stepped into a slightly larger room. A small wooden table with a couple of rough hewn benches stood in the middle.

A pack of cards sat on the table alongside a couple of glasses and a half eaten loaf of bread. Empty bottles lay scattered about the muddy floor and a short ladder in the corner led up to a trap door in the low ceiling. Hungry as she was, she ignored the loaf and limped to the ladder. She cried out when she lifted her arm to take hold of a rung and grimacing in pain used her left arm instead. She pulled herself up a rung and leaned against the ladder as she reached for the next rung with the same hand. She climbed the few rungs and tried to swing open the trap door. It wouldn't budge. She climbed up another rung pressing her back against the door and tried to force it open relying on the strength of her legs. The rung she was standing on cracked and she tumbled into the mud.

Wearily she used the bench to pull herself up and then stumbled back to the ladder. She climbed the ladder again and started pounding on the door.

"Help! Somebody, let me out! For the love of God, somebody please help!"

She wept and cried out, all the time pounding futilely on the door. Exhausted she leaned against the ladder panting and sobbing pitifully. "Oh please," she moaned. "Ye canna all be divils in this cursed city."

The door creaked and swung upward. She raised her head to the blinding light.

"Well, what have we here?" asked a gruff voice from above.

6

DUG'S DIVE

"What you doing in ma cellar?" asked the gruff voice.

"Please, help me."

The short, heavy set black man bent down and pulled her up by both hands. She cried out in pain.

"Sorry, Missy. You hurt real bad?"

"What you got there, William?" Asked Malachi.

"She hurt, Malachi. Never shoulda let those two in here. They had the look."

"Give her somat to cover haself wit. And pour her a drink whilst you at it. I'm goin' for de Watch."

"My wee ones," sobbed Cara. "They've kilt Liam. We have to find my wee ones."

"Settle yoself, Missy," said William pouring her a glass of Blackjack. "Malachi be back with de Watch soon 'nough. Dey gonna hep you, sure."

Cara looked around the room shivering against the dampness and wrinkling her nose against the reek of sewage permeating the small space. The dim light revealed a low ceiling no more than five feet high with beams hanging even lower. Rats scurried across the floor and she jumped back when one brazen rodent ran across the bar in front of her.

"Don't fret none," said William. "Dat jus' Ol Scratch making hisself to home and checking you out."

Four or five surprised black faces stared from the dark corners of the room at the muddy, naked body that had just arisen from the depths and was now leaning against the bar. Mud matted her damp hair against her bloodied, swollen face and streaks of the gray ooze hid some of the blue and yellow contusions left by the lead sap on her torso and legs.

"Here now, what you looking at?" chided William as he covered her nakedness with a blanket. Don't the lady deserve a little respect?"

"Nekked don't get no respect round here," commented one of the men.

"Timothy, you get yo sorry self outa my 'stablishment. No call fo dat kinda talk round heah!"

"William, I jus sayin'."

"I knows what yo sayin', boy. Dis lady ain't like dat. Not yet anyway. Now git 'afore I bus yo head open."

Timothy shook his head, rose from his bench and ducking his head in a half crouch to clear the low beams, made his way to the stairs leading up to the towpath.

"Yo a hard man, William."

Cara smiled through cracked lips and took a sip from the dark liquid William had poured for her. She coughed and steadying herself against the makeshift bar, took another sip feeling the drink warm her insides and dulling the pain.

"Where am I?" she asked.

"In ma place, Dug's Dive. William Douglas at yo service."

"Where?"

"On the tow path, by the ditch."

"We walked by yesterday and I didn't see a Dug's Dive."

"Ya gotta know where to look. Most white folks don't care to look."

"I have to go. They took my little ones. I've got to find them before…"

"Micah be here in a minute. He a good man. He hep you fine 'em."

She sighed and drained the rest of her glass.

"A mite more?" she asked.

He poured her another glass.

"Go easy now," he warned. "I makes it ma own self. Has a real bite to it."

She leaned forward resting her head in her arm on the bar. In a moment she was sleeping fitfully. Stuffing a whole pickled pig's foot in his mouth from a jar on the shelf behind the bar, William looked intently at Cara sleeping peacefully on the bar. He pulled the foot out of his mouth and gnawed on the gristly meat thoughtfully. He set the foot down on the bar, brushed her hair away from her face and gently pet her head.

"Yo res' easy, lil Miss. Ol' William be lookin' out fo you."

A rat leapt out of the shadows and scurried off with the pig's foot.

"Damn yo hide, Scratch," cursed William tossing an empty bottle at the fleeing rodent.

The sound of heavy boots thudding down the stairs from the towpath caught the attention of the denizens of Dug's Dives. Fearful of recognition, three or four crouched lower turning their faces to the wall to avoid a trip to see the judge.

"All right, Malachi, I'm hurrying," said Micah stepping hunched down into the dark interior. "Just let me get used to the dark."

A couple of the men slipped out behind Micah brushing past O'Malley and up the stairs.

"Scurry away you rats," laughed O'Malley. "Might not get you today, but we'll be meeting up soon enough."

The men hurried away without a backward glance.

"What you got there, William?" asked Micah.

"Knew I shouldna let no Irish in my 'stablishment. They was keepin' dis li'l lady prisona down da hole."

Micah stepped up to the bar and pulled the lantern close to Cara's face.

"She the immigrant's wife?" asked O'Malley.

"Sure as I am Micah Curley."

"Thank the Lord," said O'Malley.

"What about the wee ones?" Micah asked William.

"She been going on about dem. I tole her yo hep her fine 'em."

"You did good this time, William. I'll remember."

"Thank ya, suh."

"Who did you rent the room to?"

"Don't rightly know but his fus' name. It was Dooley an' he had a friend come by ever day name a Fas' Eddy."

"You ever hear of them, O'Malley?"

"Can't say that I have."

Cara opened her eyes and stared vacantly at Micah. Her eyes widened and she latched violently onto his arm.

"Constable! You've got to help me. They kilt Liam and stole me wee ones!"

"Liam isn't dead. We found him and took him to the hospital."

"Oh Jaysus, Jaysus. The Lord be praised!"

"You look sorely beat yourself. We best get you to a doctor."

"No! We have to find my wee ones! I am fine."

He pulled her to her feet and led her to the stairs.

"No you're not. You come with us and tell us what you know on the way. Me and O'Malley will take up the search. William gave us the names of the two who held you here."

They climbed the few slippery steps up to the brilliant sunshine of the towpath. The three of them shielded their eyes from the bright light and gratefully breathed in the fresh air blowing in from the lake.

"What can you tell us?" he asked while they stood waiting for their pupils to narrow.

"I don't remember much. First they kilt Liam and then they did for me. They bashed me again and again. Oh, I can't remember."

"Think hard, now. Did you hear them say anything?"

Putting her hand to her groin, she said, "I know they used me, but I don't remember…"

"They never talked?"

"I was put out of me head! If I made a noise, they beat me down. I don't know. Let me think. Let me think."

Micah led her up the stairs to the street above the path. Hooligans and street walkers watched from alleys and doorways as he led the weeping woman away from the district.

"Poor thing," said one older woman watching bare-chested from her window.

"Get used to it honey!" laughed another leaning against the side of a dance hall. "I've had worse! It's part of the life."

Micah glared at the trollop and led Cara toward the hospital. She stopped suddenly and pulled away heading back toward the district.

"Hold up! The hospital is this way."

"Wait, wait. I remember! The one said, 'They are long gone. The German will decide for 'em'."

"Probably Engel," said O'Malley.

"Angel?" asked Cara.

"Aye, Engel," said Micah. "Though a fallen angel, sure. O'Malley, get her to the hospital and meet at the Smith Block. If we hurry, we may get there before he has a chance to move them."

7

SOMETIMES FORTUNE SMILES

Mary carried her bucket and the canvas dust covers into the library with the housekeeper carping at her from behind.

"Girl, make and get those tiles a gleaming before Mr. Johnson comes down, and then get busy in parlor. You're a lazy one, you are. Why they ever hired a Irish I'll never know. No other respectable house will have the likes of you around. Well, I've got my eye on you. Don't think I don't count the silver every night before I go to me rest. Hurry up, now."

"Yes M'am."

Mary spread the canvas cover in front of the fire place, sprinkled water onto the coal ash and shoveled it carefully into her bucket. She leaned into the fireplace and scrubbed vigorously with a wooden hand brush, scouring the soot from the scorched bricks. Twenty minutes into her arduous task, the door to the library opened, and Mr. Johnson stormed in followed by a harried looking clerk. Mr. Johnson sat behind the massive mahogany desk and glared at the man standing before him.

"I just thought you should know," stammered the trembling man.

"Oh you thought, did you?" Johnson exploded.

"Excuse me, sir," said Mary rising to leave. "I'll finish up later."

"You'll do no such thing. Get back to work!"

"Yes sir," she answered meekly bowing her head and kneeling to pick up her brush.

The housekeeper hurried into the room.

"Is something amiss?"

"Yes dammit!"

"Mary, pick up your things and leave!" growled the housekeeper. "You are dismissed and don't be expecting references."

"Not her. Let her finish. Be off with you! It's this blamed idiot that has got my goat."

The housekeeper flushed and glared at Mary as she left the room closing the door behind her.

"Now what of Furhman?

"Where's he been the last few days?"

"Dead sir."

"Dead?"

"Done for by an Irish whore. Buried a hatchet in his head, she did. They pulled him out of the water yesterday. The Watch found her drunk trying to sell his watch."

"The company watch?"

"The same, sir."

"Now what do I do? Where am I going to find a clerk who can keep the books and deal with that Irish scum along the docks?"

"It will take time to find the right man."

"I don't have time. I've a business to run."

"Beg pardon, sir, but my Da." cut in Mary.

"What? Get about your work, girl."

"My Da. He clerked on the docks for the Rathburns."

"What's your name girl?"

"Mary Curly."

"I don't know any Curly who worked for the Rathburns. Those sons-of –bitches cost me a pretty penny. Now leave off and mind your work. Or do you want me to call Mrs. Zimmerman?"

"My Da's name is Reddy, Sean Reddy, and he clerked the docks for Mr. Lyman Rathburn before the trouble. Now he's a scooper."

"Sean Reddy, your father? He was the only honest one in that house of rapscallions, and an Irishman at that. A scooper? Hmph!

What a waste. Have him come by my office tomorrow morning, nine o'clock sharp."

"Oh thank you sir!" beamed Mary.

"I like the tiles to sparkle."

"Yes sir!"

Mary labored happily for the rest of the day and hurried home to meet Micah as the sun went down over the placid lake. The light wind coming off the lake was just enough to blow the brown haze coming from the city's chimneys and smokestacks inland, freshening the sulfurous air. Through the clear air over the lake she clearly saw small craft sailing back and forth to Canada and the southern shore. In the distance, just beyond the horizon, a trail of smoke rising from a Great Lakes steamer stood out in stark contrast to the clear blue sky. She wondered if it was the Western, where her brother James was to get a berth, coming in for a late arrival or some other steamer heading for Cleveland. So much depended on the ships. The great fortunes of men like her boss, Ebenezer Johnson, depended on the trade flowing back and forth through the port and on to the canal her parents had worked so hard to build. Ma had built a business running the boarding house and Da, even though he was Irish, had made a place for himself amongst the Buffalo business barons before the Great Flood had washed it all away. With James getting another berth on a ship, and Da going to work for Mr. Johnson, the family fortunes seemed to be turning bright again.

She went home finding their place empty, though Micah should have been home hours before. Pushing aside the strangeness of his absence, she rushed off to tell her parents of their good fortune.

8

THE SMITH BLOCK

Micah hurried as quickly as he could through Daugherty's Alley while trying to avoid the piles of garbage, horse droppings and human waste scattered about. He came upon a woman cutting a slab of meat from the carcass of a mule that lay still hitched to the overloaded cart that had broken its heart. The scrawny, undernourished mule had dropped in its tracks, and its cruel master had gone off to get drunk knowing the alley's denizens would soon pick the carcass clean. The weary woman swatted at the swarm of flies sharing in her good fortune and jumped back when a two foot rat darted from a gaping hole in the mule's abdominal cavity. The rat, carrying a putrid morsel in its mouth, dashed over Micah's foot and disappeared beneath the boards of a dismal shed. He heard the cry of a small child from within and peered into the tiny space. Seven children in various states of undress huddled together in the back of the shed on boards salvaged from a downed fence that had been laid haphazardly over the muddy ground. Noses red with dripping phlegm and eyes blurred from illness and smoke defined the poor wretches miserable existence.

"Please sir, a penny?" asked the tallest rising barefooted in the mud.

The rest of the children joined her begging, "Jus a penny, sir, please."

"What do ye want wit me babies?" asked the woman sawing on the mule.

"These all yours?"

"I should think so. Who else would be having 'em?"

"Seen the German?"

"I sees lotsa dem."

"You know who I mean."

"I don't nevah see things 'round here."

"I'm looking for two small children."

"Take your pick 'o the litter. They ain't no use ta me."

"Bah, how are we ever to make things any better if your kind won't lift a hand?"

She lifted her skirt and presented her bony haunches.

"Ye sure it's a hand your after?" cackled the woman. "Have a go, luv. It'll take your mind off your troubles and only cost twenty pennies."

He threw a handful of pennies on the muddy floor in front of the forlorn children and left not caring to watch the poor lost souls scrambling in the mud for the pennies while their sainted mother laughed derisively at his kindness.

He made his way to the crumbling brick edifice standing on Seneca and Carroll known as the Smith Block. Over three hundred of the destitute dwelt within the dark, derelict warehouse that enclosed a courtyard filled with foul open latrines. The sickening stench seeping from the pits permeated the clothes, hair and lungs of the inhabitants. Families had actually set up housekeeping within the tiny structures that had served as outhouses during the building's better days. You didn't have to look or ask a tenant of the block to know whence he came, your tortured nose spoke volumes before you laid eyes on the unfortunate. Cholera regularly bred here spreading throughout the tenement and the city at large, clearing room for the unending waves of immigrants and replenishing the ranks of the hopeless dwelling in the hovels of the city. Many of the new arrivals, out of money, out of strength and out of luck, found their way to the block and other bleak houses of the ward where they waited for an act of Providence to save them or kill them. The lucky few found work and moved out, but just as often, the indigent found death and were carried out.

Micah spotted Adolph Wittman, the landlord's agent clearing the two and three penny lodgers from the basement of the building. Micah stepped down the creaking stairs to look over the emerging mob. The lowest of the low, these men and women filled the basement room on the coldest nights. A single kerosene lantern hanging from a pipe cast a feeble glow into the damp space, barely revealing two tiers of bunks made from sheets of canvas stretched between wooden rails comprising the luxury three cent accommodations. Two-cents bought the soft side of planks that the frugal landlord had salvaged from a fallen structure across the way and laid on the mud beneath the premium bunks. Micah watched as over thirty of the miserable were driven back onto the street.

"Adolph, a word."

The agent glared back sulkily.

"What now, Mr. Curly? I cannot be held to account for every murdering thief that comes my way."

"Does the German still keep lodgings here?"

"Engel? He pays his due. Never no questions about that."

"Still recruiting his pickpockets from your tenants?"

"I don't know nothing about that. I told you, I can't be held to account for the doings here. These animals are just that, animals."

"Is he in?"

"Can't say."

"Which is his room?"

"It's in the back."

"Show me."

"I've no time for that."

"Now, or I'll run you in for harboring a known criminal."

"You can't do that. I told you, I don't pry into my renters' business. I run a respectable lodging house."

"Try me, Johnson can always find another manager while you're waiting to see the judge."

Wittman stared defiantly and then pursed his lips and, resigned to his weak position, shook his head in defeat.

"Follow me then."

"Micah!" hailed O'Malley. "Wait up!"

"Cover the other door. I'm going in."

O'Malley jogged around to the other side of the building and Micah followed Wittman into the "respectable" lodging house through the empty door jamb. On the left side of the entry way a door, hanging from one hinge, opened on a ten by twelve room. Three women, sitting on boxes, huddled around a stove spewing smoke from the battered stove pipe into the room, glanced up and turned back to warming themselves when they recognized the agent at the door. Alongside the women eight small children stood staring anxiously at the pot of cabage bubbling on the stovetop.

"Up here," said Wittman starting up the stairs on the right of the entryway.

A pile of rags under the stairs moved and Micah noticed a worn woman drowsily nursing her infant. At least one of them had something to eat for the time being, thought Micah. He put a coin in the woman's hand and followed Wittman up the rickety stairs to the second floor corridor. The corridor, dimly lit by muted light seeping from the open doors was lined with people propped against the wall. Piles of rags and debris filled the spaces between the islands of light, and the stench was overpowering. Struggling to see in the dim light, the two men stepped around the obstructions, careful to avoid the numerous holes in the sagging floor. Children cried, men cursed and from one forsaken room came the keening of a mother whose child had just surrendered to the croup.

After they had traversed about a third of the dark corridor, a man shouted from behind, "It's the Watch come for ye!"

A half dozen men darted from the corridor and rooms ahead.

Micah turned to Wittman and said, "Which room?"

"Second door down," he answered pointing at a room one of the men had just fled. Micah ran to the doorway and spied a young girl chained to an iron ring bolted to the filthy floor.

"Stay with her, Adolph!" he shouted as he chased after the fleeing man. Micah tripped and fell over a pile of rags that groaned from the impact. A pair of panicked eyes stared up from the rags as Micah regained his feet.

"Heaven save me!" cried the pile.

Ignoring the startled man, Micah ran after the fugitive. He bounded down the stairs at the end of the hall taking them three at a time. He was just a few steps behind and leapt to catch the man at the landing.

There was an earsplitting crash as the rotted floorboards gave way and Micah found himself snared in the jagged gap in the landing. He pulled himself out of the hole and lay gasping on the wobbly floor. His quarry, guffawed at his predicament and scurried outside past O'Malley who had been bowled over by the other fleeing men.

"Shite," groaned Micah.

He got up on all fours and then stood shakily against the wall. An eight inch splinter protruded from under his armpit and he cried out when he tried to jerk it free.

"Damn," he sighed as he slid down the wall to sit wearily in the corner.

"O'Malley!" he shouted. "I need you."

O'Malley climbed the stairs and stepped warily around the hole in the landing.

"Did you get him?" asked Micah.

"Which? I caught the first, but the rest just slammed into me and they all got away. Are you all right?"

"For now. Get the girl from up there and tell Adolph I want to speak to him about the boy. We all should get to the hospital."

O'Malley noticed the splinter dripping blood down Micah's side.

"Jaysus!"

"Get the girl. Careful of the fecking stairs in this death trap. Hurry up."

O'Malley found Adolph staring at the frightened four year old girl who was yanking desperately at the chain.

"She's bound up tight," said Adolph.

The girl's soot covered face was streaked with tears. She panted fearfully from the exertion and blood oozed from the chafing of the leg iron.

"Mama!" she sobbed over and over. "The bad men got me."

"There, there," soothed O'Malley. "I am with the Watch. I've come to take you to your Mama."

She stopped pulling on the chain and looked at him suspiciously.

"See," he said showing her his badge.

"Mama?"

"She's fine, lass. I will take you to her."

Her eyes filled with tears once more.

"Mama," she sighed.

O'Malley knelt beside her examining the chain. The leg iron had been cruelly attached above her knee. Blood seeped from the scraped skin and her lower leg was pale from the pinched veins. They would need a smith to free the iron. He examined the iron ring attached to the floor with no visible screws. Moving Honora behind him he braced himself and pulled the chain with all his might. The floor board groaned, but the ring held fast.

"Grab hold here," he directed Wittman.

They two men pulled in vain.

"You too, lass, on the count of three. One, two, THREE!"

All three strained against the chain and the ring tore loose with a loud snap.

"That will do for now," panted O'Malley. Now to get you and Micah over to the hospital. You're to come along, Adolph. We have some more questions for you."

O'Malley picked up the trembling girl who clung desperately to his neck.

"What's your name, lass?"

"Honora."

"That's a mighty fine name. Do you know where your brother be?"

Fear animated her tear brightened eyes, and she shook her head slowly.

"Don't be afeared, Honora. Micah and I shall find the lad. We found you didn't we?"

She nodded, hugged him tightly around the neck and laid her head on his shoulder.

"Now, to take you to your Ma."

9

CITY LIFE

Seamus had stopped crying. The others only mocked him. Though not much older than he, the other boys' eyes were flinty and uncaring. The Golden Rule had no place at Hauptman's Tannery. Here the adage had degenerated into "Do Unto Others Before They Do Unto You." Hardened from seeing nothing but disdain and cruelty in their short lives, the tannery boys did as they had been done unto. They took his scraps of food and beat him when he protested. They took his flimsy blanket and beat him when he cried. They took his innocence and mocked him when he prayed for deliverance.

There was one lad whom everyone else left alone. Tobias was one of the German's darlings. These chosen ones slept on the floor above in real beds with straw tick mattresses. They were fed separately and lorded it over the tannery boys confined to the basement. Seamus' tormentors all aspired to move up with the boys who slept late and roamed the infected district's streets into the early morning hours. They dutifully performed their tedious work hoping to be rewarded and brought up the stairs.

Three days after Seamus was confined to the dark cellar, one of the specials failed to return. The boy, his throat slit ear to ear, was fished out of the canal that morning. There were murmurs about a drunken sailor and stolen purse, but no one knew for certain or much cared. The tannery boys pissing into the vat to soften the raw hides were abuzz with speculation and boasts that they would be the next chosen to move upstairs.

Seamus ignored the excited talk and concentrated on his work, hoping to scrape enough hides without any nicks and avoid another beating. He fished a hide out of the foul vat and rinsed it lightly in the trough that channeled fresh water from the nearby creek and poured the tainted residue back into the creek where it would find its way to the lake. Preparing to scrape the remaining fat and hairs from the hide, he wrung out the excess piss and chemicals and clamped the hide to the rack. He had almost grown accustomed to the stench of rotting flesh when he slept, but working with the toxic mixtures and decaying skins still made his eyes water and turned his stomach. He had never realized that the straps and bridles and pouches and even the boots he wore had such a hellish origin. With his nose plugged with bits of cloth to fend off the putrid odors, Seamus panted through his open mouth like a dog on a blistering summer day and knelt before the noxious hide. Holding the sharpened tool with both hands, he carefully scraped the taut skin clean more cautiously than any barber ever shaved the fanciest nabob's face.

A whack on the back of the head caused him to slip and slice the hide.

"Oh no," he whined. "That'll do me."

"Leave that be and come with me," said a youthful voice from behind.

Seamus turned and saw the dreaded Tobias staring vacantly from his good eye at him. He was a few years older than, Seamus, about ten or eleven. It was hard to tell. He stood akimbo, his crooked body turned sideways, presenting the right half of his face to Seamus. Curly red hair hung lazily over his forehead just touching his chubby rose colored cheek; the picture of the perfect, cherubic child. Seamus stared fearfully at the beautiful child.

"I have no time for any o'dat," said Tobias grabbing Seamus by the ear.

He pulled the frightened boy to his feet and turned to look him directly in the face. Seamus whimpered.

" 'Tis a pretty sight, ain't it?" growled Tobias.

Seamus stared at the ruined face before him. A few wisps of hair sprouted from the left side of his scalp amidst patches of bright red blotches and white scars. A black hole was all that remained of his ear, and his eyelid was sealed forever by the scars covering the dark side of his face.

"The German wants you. Do what he says or this could be your fate as it was mine."

"Yes, sir," muttered Seamus trying not to look at the devastated visage.

Tobias laughed.

"That's the first time anyone has called me sir."

The two boys walked past the gawking tannery boys standing idly by the vat.

"Get busy afore he sees you," barked Tobias.

The boys scattered instantly, gathering their tools and slaving away industriously with no need for further urging. They stole a glance or two at Tobias and the skinny new boy ascending the stairs and many a resigned head hung in dejected silence.

"Here boy," said Engel when the two stepped into the ornate office.

Seamus sat on the horsehair couch alongside Tobias. The German, his right arm tucked into his vest atop his prodigious belly, sat behind a flimsy pine desk barren of all but a kerosene lamp, a bottle and a smoking cigar in an iron ashtray. The man picked up the cigar with his left hand and leaned back in his chair, puffing hard to keep the cheap weed lit, as he looked the boy over carefully.

He hunched forward over the desk and slurred, "Some sonuva seaside doxy done for Griffin. Best cut purse I had."

He sat back, cocked his eye and stared hard at Seamus.

Laying aside the cigar, he picked up the rum with his left hand, used his teeth to pull the cork and took a long swallow from the bottle. He popped the cigar back into his mouth and leaned forward on his elbow, propping his chin on his fist.

"He'll do, Tobias."

"Yes, sir," answered the ruined boy.

"Tobias here will be your Guardian Angel. You listen to him and do what you're told. If you do well, you get a good bed and plenty o' good eats. You don't and, well, Tobias, you explain that to him. Do you understand, boy?"

"Yes," Seamus answered softly.

"Yes, what!?" shouted Engel leaping to his feet.

"Yes! I will do as I'm told," cried Seamus.

Engel crossed the room and slapped the boy across the face.

"Yes, sir! They are the only two words I ever want to hear from your lips! Understand?"

"Yes, sir," sniffed Seamus.

"And none of that sniveling."

"Yes, sir."

"Both of you to the cart. It's time to earn your keep. Mind, I'll be watching."

The two boys walked down the stairs and through a door leading to the small interior courtyard. A grizzled old man, in a slouch hat pulled low over his eyes stood by a cart with a swaybacked mule attached, while two of the tannery boys loaded cleaned hides in the back. Two of the chosen boys were in the cart covering themselves with the hides and Tobias climbed up pulling Seamus along behind him. The ragged old man told them to lie still and covered the lot of them with hides. He made sure that they could not see out of the cart and then climbed up to the driver's seat.

"Keep still now," he cautioned as he drove the cart out into the street.

The cart rumbled along rutted dirt tracks and cobble stones jostling the boys in the back.

"Where we going?" asked Seamus.

"You'll know soon enough," replied Tobias. "Just do as I tell you, and you will eat your fill tonight."

"Yes, sir."

"Today, you just watch Runner and O'Neil. They have the knack. Don't forget, I'll be watching yuhz, and the German has others about keeping an eye on ye and me as well. He sees everything."

"Are we going to pick up more hides to clean?"

"We de specials. We picks de immigrants clean not de hides," burst out Runner.

The three chosen boys started laughing uncontrollably.

"Shut your gobs!" cursed the driver. "There's swells about.

The boys quieted and the cart rumbled on toward the waterfront. Seamus lay still in the darkness under the hides.

"I don't want to be no robber," whispered Seamus. "Ma and Pa would be 'shamed of me. I'll go back and scrape hides. I'll be careful and work faster than anyone ever."

"Ye dumb Irish monkey," said Tobias angrily. "Don't ye understand? You do what the German says, or he does for you. How do you think I got this way?"

"Did you fall in a vat?"

"The German done it. I was too a feared to grab a purse and run. When I couldn't deliver, he thought I could make more begging. He broke me back to make me crooked, and when that wasn't enough to bring a tear to the eye of the swells, he poured coal oil on me face and lit me up. He'll do the same or worse for you. Now shut your gob."

"Oh Da, how could you let them take me?" sobbed Seamus,

"I said shut your gob," Tobias hissed jabbing him in the side.

The cart rumbled to a halt and the driver pulled back the hides.

"Okay, out with you now. Be back at the normal time or they'll come looking for you."

The boys climbed down from the cart that had backed into the gap between two brick walls. Seamus followed them to the street and hurried to keep up with the older boys off to earn their keep.

10

CONFEDERACY OF THE RESOLUTE

Afraid to walk the streets of Buffalo, Cara and Honora waited with Katie for Sean to return from the Commercial District. His new position generally kept him late, but the family's prospects were good once more. Honora sat in the corner playing with baby Terence while Katie, Mary and Cara prepared the evening meal. There would be meat tonight and everyone moved with a lightness of heart that had eluded them during the deprivation of the long winter.

Margaret and James came in with a jug of liquor to a chorus of "Fáilte! Welcome!" and answered cheerfully with "Bless this home and all in it!" Hugs and kisses were shared all around and Margaret fussed over how bright Terence was, exclaimed how pretty Honora was and how bright things were now that things were on the mend, while Katie and Mary put out the dishes and put on the kettle. James and Micah uncorked the jug and the party was underway.

After reuniting the aggrieved family, Micah had brought Cara and Honora to stay at the farm with his in-laws while Liam recovered. Micah's wound was still bandaged, and though he grimaced whenever he stretched his arm, he was back at work, rooting out scoundrels and searching for the lost boy in the countless hovels of the District. With little hope for the boy, the women spoke sadly, yet hopefully, of the future.

"Four days on the job and already Mr. Johnson is thanking me for sending Da to him," proclaimed Mary.

"With Sean clerking for Mr. Johnson and James on the new berth, the tide has turned," said Katie. "Anything is possible again. Sean was approached about the farm just this week."

"Will you sell?" asked Micah.

"With the factory smoke fouling the air and the water going bad, the crops are suffering. We can't hold out much longer. Nothing much grows any more on the land, but the city needs room to grow and they plan on putting in new streets for homes and businesses on the land. Dirty air and water ruins the farmer but doesn't slow progress."

"The ward is growing too crowded for a farm," added Mary. "Ma and me was thinking we could build a new house here for all of us."

"Sean said, we stick together as a family and nothing can stop us," declared Katie. "Though 'tis sad to think of so many others trodding the land that Ma and Da cleared before the war."

"Time moves on, and so must we," said Micah.

Katie nodded in agreement and stirred the bubbling pot.

"So tonight's the night," beamed Mary taking the baby from Honora.

"At last," sighed Cara. "It will be good to fill the hole he's left in the bed and get on with our life."

"Is he fit, then?" asked Micah. "I never thought he would make it through the night."

"He is a tough old piece of blackthorn, he is. There are still problems, but I can take care of him now. Anything new?"

"No, the two murdering brigands have vanished and Engels denies anything. He even offered money to help your family. He is a sly one, but I'll bring him down one of these days."

"Poor Seamus."

"Don't give up hope. We may still find the lad. Lads such as him are worth something alive. No one benefits from a dead boy."

"But what must he be facing?" sniffed Cara. "The poor wee lad."

"I'll bring him back to you sure as we found Liam."

Bernadette, Erin and the twins entered the crowded room laughing boisterously and disrupting their elders' conversation.

"Out of here, clean yourselves for supper and our guests," ordered Katie. "Your father will be home soon."

"Aw, Ma," said Michael waving dismissively. "That can wait. We're tired and hungry."

"Gnaw on this," said Mary tossing him a raw carrot.

"You think this'll hold a working man?"

"Working man are you now?" teased Mary. "And you just off the teat."

Michael thrust out his lower lip, clenched his fists and stomped out of the room followed by Mary's laughter.

Sean came into the crowded cabin, spun Katie around, and taking her into his arms, kissed her passionately. She beat her fists against his chest and pushed him away.

"Enough of that!" she exclaimed. "Your children are standing by."

"And just how did the wee darlings get here, Katie dear?"

She pushed him away again, and he moved to capture her once more. She held out a boiling pot menacingly, and he backed away laughing, spying the familiar jug on the table.

"Pour me a gilly, Micah. We have cause to celebrate!"

"Micah poured a cup which Sean tossed down and gasped, " 'Tis an elegant brew you have there, son."

Micah poured himself a cup and followed suit.

"Right you are, Sean. 'Tis good that Liam is leaving the hospital, but you seem a mite too happy to be cramming another into this little cabin."

"Sold. Lock, stock and barrel."

"Sold?" repeated Katie.

"Sold, except for one corner lot above the high water mark. That is where we shall build our new home with the money from the sale and what we all can put in," he said quietly. "No notes, no liens, no greedy banker or acts of God to take it away this time."

Katie set the pot down on the table, sat in his lap and kissed him.

"What of the children?" asked Sean.

Katie cocked her head and asked, "And how do you think the wee darlings got here, boyo?"

"Oh, Ma" moaned Erin her face flushing bright. "We are going to see the sisters at the hospital."

"And don't you think they know how you came to be here, Erin?" teased Katie kissing Sean once again for good measure. "You will have a beau someday, and then you will be dancing to a different jig, I'm thinking."

"This is more than my eyes can bear," groaned a freshly scrubbed Michael covering his eyes as he crunched on a carrot.

The laughing family trooped outside of the cramped cabin. The twins picked up the handles of the cart Micah had brought along and ran ahead of the cheerful group to the hospital to bring Liam back to a good home cooked dinner and his anxious family.

11

THE WARD

Seamus had gone to a warm bed with a full belly for the first time since he had watched his father murdered. Sleep, however, evaded him and he tossed fitfully listening to Tobias' breathing settle into the quiet rhythm of sleep. He didn't know what to do. Terrified of Tobias and what the German had done to the disfigured boy, he knew he must obey or be killed, or worse. Yet, hadn't his mother warned him of the dangers to his eternal soul? Would he spend eternity in the sulfurous pit of Hell because he was too afraid of his captors? His mother had told him of Hell, but he had seen the face of Evil itself in the dead eyes of Tobias and the German. Was there an Angel of God that looked over him like his mother said? He had only his mother's word on that. The Devil was real enough. He had given him hot food, a warm bed and a promise of dreadful harm if he dared disobey.

Accustomed to rising with the sun, Seamus woke with the first rays. No one stirred in the room he shared with the chosen boys, but he could hear the cursing and grumbling of the tannery boys below in the damp cellar. He pulled his blanket up to his chin and stared at the shadowy rafters above. A huge rat skittered across a beam and leapt to the table below. It sat upright on its haunches sniffing the air and glancing furtively about, hungry but wary. Sensing no immediate threat, it nibbled on the scraps remaining from the evening meal.

O'Neil coughed and the rat darted from the table into a hole in the wall. A moment later, Seamus saw the rat peek out of the dark hole and emerge cautiously into the room, pausing at the edge of a shaft of sunlight. It sniffed for any scent of danger and crossed into the full sunlight. A blur of orange fur flashed in the patch of sunlight and the rat wheeled about. Too late, it let loose a pathetic high-pitched squeal cut short by the pouncing cat. The cat chomped down on the rat's rear leg and then backed away from the doomed rodent freeing it to crawl away using only its forepaws. The cat jumped in front of the struggling creature and batted it with a paw. The rat reversed course and the cat bounded atop the panicked rodent, again taking it in its sharp teeth and flinging the wounded animal against the wall. The rat tried to flee once more and the cat bit into its neck and carried the dead rat outside.

"That's how the German works," said Tobias from the bed next to him. "Doesn't just out and kill his prey. He likes to toy with you first. He likes to watch you suffer and struggle. He only lets you die when it suits his purpose."

Seamus stared at Tobias' scarred face and started to cry.

"Go back to sleep. We don't have to go to work for a while yet. For ill or good, you ain't a tannery boy no more. Today, you work the street."

Sleep was the last thing on the small boy's mind.

Malachi effortlessly worked the great billows hanging from the rafters. His heavily muscled bicep pumped rhythmically, like the steam pistons driving the grain elevators and locomotives along the waterfront. With his leather gloved left hand he turned the iron rod that lay buried deep in the glowing coals. Blazing sparks shot forth, bounding off his leather apron to die upon the dirt floor.

He had a good life now. Trained as a smith on the Boswell plantation, he was much sought after in his new home in Buffalo. As a young man, he had made his way north meaning to cross over to Canada, but found that the people of Buffalo were willing to let a skilled tradesman stay unmolested. He was never considered an equal, but as a Negro man in a free state he could make his own way without a master telling him what to do and when to do it. At least that was how it had been until the starving Irish had swarmed the city. Now the newly arrived Irish and the vastly outnumbered free Negroes fought over the lowest of jobs. Wages fell and hours increased with the struggle. Vying for survival, his fellow Negroes and the Irish immigrants had found a new form of slavery in the prosperous port. Mutual desperation kept tensions high and a Negro, even a skilled man like himself, had to tread carefully in the rapidly growing city.

He pulled the rod from the coals and carefully eyed the glowing tip. Satisfied it was ready, he took the hammer in his right hand and pounded the rod around the curved end of the anvil forming an oval loop. He flipped the loop onto the flat of the anvil and taking a chisel, cut the glowing loop free of the rod. He fit the cut piece through a length of chain and pounded it closed adding a new link to an anchor chain.

A noisy disturbance drew his attention to the throngs passing by the small shop. He saw a nondescript young white boy dashing through the crowd pursued by a man shouting in a language he had never heard. The boy vanished into the milling crowd leaving his pursuer to stand shaking his fist futilely after him.

"Another picked clean by dat gang o' babies," Malachi mumbled to himself as he thrust the rod back into the coals.

He saw the beggar boy with the terrible burns leaning against the bridge forlornly eyeing the passersby with outstretched hand. He seemed to be talking to someone out of sight.

"Po' baby," sighed Malachi. "Won't be long 'fo no one give him pennies. Getting too old."

The boy pointed and Malachi saw a new boy, even younger, step into the sunlight. The young boy shook his head, and the beggar boy slapped him violently. The young boy hung his head in resignation, ventured forth again and tugged on the coattails of a well-dressed man escorting a woman toward the wharf.

"Off with you!" shouted the man swatting the small boy to the cobblestones and checking for his wallet.

The woman ignored the fallen boy and waited for her escort to take her arm again.

"Damn urchins," cursed the man leading her away.

Seamus stood up and rubbed his backside. He looked over to Tobias and shook his head. Tobias pointed to another man leaning against a porch post further down the street closer to Malachi's shop. Seamus nodded and started toward the man.

"Lordy," muttered Malachi laying down his hammer, "Dat mus be de boy Micah was lookin' fo."

Seamus stepped up to the man by the post and looked around furtively.

"Please, mister," he whispered. "You gotta help me. Bad men kilt my Pa and took me from my Ma."

"Is that so, lad," growled the man who grabbed him by the collar. "Would you betray the German, now?"

Staring into the face of the man who he had seen kill his father, Seamus screamed and struggled to escape his clutches, drawing the attention of a few in the crowd.

"There you are, ye whelp!" shouted the killer. "Your Ma has been worried sick with yer running off agin."

Seamus kicked the man in the shins.

"Damn your hide, lad," cursed the man slapping the boy. "Come home with me to yer poor weeping mother."

The watchers in the crowd continued about their business, and the murderer openly dragged the struggling boy down the street past Malachi's shop.

"Hold up," said Malachi. "Dat's de boy was stolen."

"Yer daft, Nigger! Mind yer own damn business."

Malachi grabbed the man with an iron grip.

"Leave off de boy."

"He's me sister's lad."

"Let de Watch sort it out."

" 'Tain't none 'o dere business neither!" yelled the man.

Malachi pulled the boy free.

"Help!" cried the man taking a wild swing at him. "Dis crazy nigger is stealing me boy."

Malachi pushed the man aside.

"What's dis?' called a man from down the street.

"A nigger is stealing de boy," answered a whore staring angrily toward Malachi.

"No nigger is taking no white boy from his Da," shouted the man. "C'mon lads."

A gang of men charged Malachi.

"He ain't de boy's daddy!" yelled Malachi.

"Help me, lads," yelled the murderer. "Dese niggers is getting outa hand."

The men charged and Malachi retreated into his shop pulling the boy in with him. One of the men paused long enough to pry a cobblestone loose and let it fly. The stone glanced off the side of Malachi's head drawing blood and staggering the huge man. The men rushed him, and he grabbed his hammer swinging wildly at the enraged mob. He connected with the first man through the door. The man crumpled before him and the others stopped the assault. More men gathered outside and calls for weapons drowned out Malachi's protestations.

"Get the watch!" screamed the whore.

A man ran off to find the Watch and the murderer screamed after him, "Hold off on dat. We can settle dis nigger ourselves."

The crowd roared its approval and more cobblestones hurtled toward the smithy. Men tore loose boards to use as clubs and quite a few knives made an appearance. Finally a man with a pistol stepped forward and fired. Malachi stumbled back and fell to the floor. The murderer grabbed the boy's hand and dragged the boy out while the mob rushed in to beat Malachi to death.

Seamus screamed, "Don't let him take me! He's not me Da! Leave the darkee alone and help me."

No one seemed to hear or care, and Seamus was dragged away to his doom screaming for salvation.

Micah and O'Malley were watching the stream of wheelbarrows unloading the freighter into a canal boat, while over at the Dart elevator a steam engine scooped grain from the hold of another. The waterfront swarmed with men transferring the bounty of the nation from one section to the other.

"That's the future we're looking at," said Micah. "Machines will free us all for a life of ease."

"Too expensive," said O'Malley. "A lot cheaper to use an Irishman 'til he drops 'stead 'o paying for a machine and all the coal to keep it running. A little bread, a little whiskey is all it takes to keep us going."

Micah laughed, "True, but the machine is going to replace those lads soon enough."

"Mr. Curly, sir," called the man who had run for the Watch. "Trouble at Malachi's."

"What now?" asked Micah.

"It's about Malachi and a boy. They will kill him sure."

"Not Malachi," said Micah.

The three men dashed toward the smithy and spotted Seamus struggling against the murderer's hold.

"That's the man what run from the Smith Block," said O'Malley.

"Get him!" shouted Micah.

The man saw them coming, released the boy and ran off. The two started to run after him, but the man who had come for them called after, "Leave him go. The mob will kill Malachi."

Micah turned and ran toward the smithy.

"Bring the boy," he directed the man as he and O'Malley sprinted to rescue Malachi.

The two men started to push and pull their way through the crowd yelling for them to leave off.

"We have the boy!" screamed Micah. "Malachi was protecting him from that killer."

The bloodthirsty mob fought them, trying to keep them back while the others pummeled Malachi. None cared for the truth. They just wanted an excuse to attack a black man who was better off than themselves. Micah laid one blocker low with his shillelagh. He and O'Malley beat their way into the shop and pulled the enraged men off Malachi.

"Leave him to us!" shouted one of the hate-filled men.

"He's innocent!" shouted Micah. "The boy is the one we've been looking for. Make way and let the boy tell you himself."

The crowd parted and the frightened boy stepped forward tentatively. The crowd quieted as he spoke.

"The dark man tried to help me," he explained looking up at the angry faces. "The other man kilt me Da and was going to kill me, sure."

He looked at the bloodied man lying in the dirt and hugged him around the neck.

"It be all right, boy," said Malachi through bloody lips. "Mr. Curley will take care that you get to your Ma and Pa, and I be hoping Mr. O'Malley will take care that I get to Dug's Dive."

"What do ye t'ink 'o dat?" asked the whore who had called for the mob. "A nigger wid a white man's heart."

She stepped into the room, dipped a rag into the cooling trough and proceeded to clean Malachi's wounds.

Enjoying the task of cleaning the smith's muscled form she cooed, "Mr. O'Malley and I will see to you Malachi, don't you fret none."

12

THE GERMAN

Engel was furious. Not only had he lost a promising young ward, his two best henchmen were now on the run, and if he hadn't taken care to keep the young boy unsure of the tannery location, he'd be in jail already. As it was, he had sent Tobias, Runner and O'Neil to Cleveland until things cooled down and planned on following the lads as soon as he settled accounts with his partner. He knew that he had little time before the Watch came calling.

Why God had let the Irish find their way to America, or for that matter, had ever created the besotted race, was a mystery beyond his knowing. They were a curse upon the planet and upon the good men who trod the same ground as the subhuman wretches. He never would have spent his days in a foul tannery, scrimping to make a living if it hadn't been for the drunken curs. A master mason, he had been lured to America to build the cursed canal with promises of high wages and social stature. But God and his damned Irish terriers had ended that dream in Lockport.

He and his fellow masons took pride in their work. The "flight of five," two sets of five locks climbing the escarpment, was their pride. Each stone precisely cut and fitted without mortar, while the Irish tarries with their iron drills and child "powder monkeys" took no pride in their mindless labor. A forty foot wide cut had to be made through the mound of dolomite above the locks for the canal. It was an amazing feat, but the Gilly boy with his sixteen rounds of whiskey was all the brutes thought about as they held the iron drill for their partner to hammer, drilling holes in the solid rock for the powder monkeys to fill with black powder and blast the rock away.

The young boys would climb into the crevices of the cut to ram powder into the hole, light a hand rolled fuse and make a dash for safety. Many times the fuse burned too quickly and the young boys didn't get clear. The end of the day was the worst. Everyone was bone-tired and the Irish were drunk from the whiskey they drank to ease the pain of their tortured muscles.

On that most wretched of days he had been guiding a block into place as it was lowered by winch from above. A chip of stone kicked loose by one of the men above rolled under the block. He signaled the men to raise the block and reached in, extending his arm full length to push the stone aside with his chisel. At that moment a powder monkey set off his charge. A shudder went through the earth and Engel pulled back his arm.

A man above cried, "Scheiza!" and the block fell, crushing his hand between the two massive stones.

Later he learned that the unfortunate boy had packed too much powder into the hole. When the fuse was lit it burned too quickly and the boy was blown apart before he could run three paces. An errant chunk of the shattered rock had struck one of the men hoisting the rock in the back of the head and he fell dead on the spot. The others could not hold the weight of the massive stone. The rope flashed through the block and tackle, dooming Engel.

Ignoring their fallen comrade, the men climbed down to Engel, who lay trapped and screaming beneath the block. The foreman grabbed a stone saw and sawed through the shattered bones below the elbow. Three men carried him screaming mindlessly to the smithy, who cauterized the bleeding stump in the blazing furnace, stopping the bleeding and screaming as the excruciating pain knocked him senseless. In a matter of seconds, he had gone from a master stone mason to a useless cripple.

He was cared for in the infirmary for a few days until he regained his senses. They put what was left of his arm in a sling, paid him his back wages and the Irish pig of a boss sent him on his way. Wracked with pain and seething with hate, he vowed to exact his revenge on every Irishman or boy he came across.

"This is what I could raise," said Liborious pouring out a stack of coins on the table in front of him.

"That isn't near enough, and you know it."

"It's all I can muster. Most of the money is tied up in hides."

"I'll take it, Liborious, but I'll be back for the rest."

"It's all you'll be getting. You brought the law down on us, and I'm the one who will have to explain. That has to be worth the rest."

Engel glared furiously at him. Liborious shrank back and put his hand on the pistol in his belt. When he saw the butt of the pistol, Engel softened, leaned back and smiled. Scooping up the coins he ambled toward the door and paused before exiting.

"You're a hard man of business, Liborious. You have me over a barrel, but I can't say I wouldn't do the same to you. I'll be off. Mind though, I'll be back to settle accounts."

13

JUSTICE SERVED

Engel and his murdering gang were nowhere to be found. Micah and O'Malley had followed every possible lead to no avail. They visited all of the tanneries in the area hoping to find someone who would talk. Most had boys working alongside the men, but no sign was found of the felonious boys Engel had dispatched to fleece the unsuspecting. The two men sat down with Malachi and William at Dug's dive and, based on their conversation, concluded that the man who had tried to spirit Seamus away was Dooley O'Hara. Both he and Fast Eddy had vanished, probably fleeing down the lake or back east.

Liam O'Connor had recovered and started working on the docks. The long days of Summer brought ships and canallers by the thousands. The port boomed and Micah and O'Malley had more robbery, murder and chicanery than they could handle. Engel and his men became a dim memory not to be thought of again until one morning when Micah sat reading the Buffalo Daily Courier to O'Malley over a cup of tea.

"Our Colonel Scott seems to have the Mexican War well in hand," said Micah.

"I heard he was a force to be reckoned with back in '13," put in O'Malley.

"Katie's Da was captured with him at Queenston."

"If her Da was anything like Katie, I'd a like to know him, sure."

"He stood his ground when the regulars ran and died trying to stop the British burning Buffalo."

O'Malley leaned forward and asked, "What's it say about the war in Mexico?"

Micah cleared his throat and read.

"Captain Kirby Smith, of Scott's 3rd Infantry, reports:

"The Mexican Army can do nothing and their continued defeats should convince them of it. They have lost six great battles; we have captured six hundred and eight cannon, nearly one hundred thousand stands of arms, made twenty thousand prisoners, have the greatest portion of their country and are fast advancing on their capital which must be ours,—yet they refuse to treat!"

O'Malley nodded knowingly and said, "Can't be long now. Strange, we hunt down those who kill one man and name them murderer. You kill a thousand and are proclaimed a hero."

Micah sat up straight and rattled the paper in front of him.

"Listen to this," he said.

"An Irish gentleman (if any such creature exists)."

"It doesn't say that..."

"It does," he replied pointing to the offending line. "Don't interrupt or I'll lose my place."

"An Irish gentleman (if any such creature exists) has established a thriving, though somewhat unusual, business on the brink of the great falls. Like the Pied Piper of Hamlin, Dooley O'Hara has discovered a novel method of dealing with the Falls village rat population. He pays the youth of the village a penny for each noxious rodent they capture and triples his investment by selling the hapless creatures to the customers of his drinking establishment for three cents. The intoxicated patrons gladly pay to load the vermin onto miniature birch bark boats, set them ablaze and send them squealing over the raging cataract. Who says the Irish have no usefulness? We wish good luck to Mr. O'Hara and good riddance to the filthy rodents!"

He set the paper down and beamed meaningfully at O'Malley.

"Could he be our O'Hara?" asked O'Malley.

"Only one way to find out. I'm going up there to visit the upstanding Irish gentleman, to see for myself if any such creature exists."

Sitting outside the next morning, Micah and Mary contentedly sipped their tea while they soaked up the first warm rays of the rising sun. Wisps of light mist, backlit by shafts of golden sunlight filtering through the willows, rose from the dancing waters of the creek. The empty street was stirring with the muffled sounds of men performing their morning rituals before setting off for the harbor.

"I don't want you anywhere near that iron beast," said Mary.

"You're being silly, woman."

She bit her lower lip and laid her hand on his shoulder.

"And how many times have the blessed things blown apart?"

"They took care of that long ago, Lass. Nowadays, they put a car full of cotton bales behind the engine. If the engine bursts the cotton keeps the passengers safe."

"It goes too fast. All the way to Niagara Falls in three hours. Ten miles in one hour! No man was meant to travel that fast."

"Men do it everyday now. It is safe. It is the future. Soon there will be trains going to Albany in two or three days time."

"Don't go, Micah. What does one highwayman more or less matter?"

"It matters. Give a kiss, Lass and be off to Mr. Johnson's. I'll be home before you."

She pouted, curling her lips to the side. Micah pulled her toward him and kissed her, gently straightening her pouting lips.

He leaned back and smiled, "That's better, luv. I'll be by to walk you home tonight."

He walked to the train station and had second thoughts himself when he saw the chugging beast spewing smoke and steam into the clear morning air. Mary was right about the damned things exploding. It happened more than he cared to think, and a pile of cotton wouldn't stop the cars from running off the tracks. The train ran on half inch iron straps nailed to wooden railroad ties resting loosely on the rail bed. The twelve foot straps were cut at angles at the joints and spiked to a square piece of the wooden ties every six feet. The nails used to secure them often worked loose from the shifting weight of the locomotives and cars. Plus the hot summer sun expanded and distorted the rails enough to shift the bands of iron rails out of place and send them slashing through the bottom of the passenger cars. Stir that in with the mix of makeshift wooden trestles and you had a recipe that would try the courage of even the most intrepid adventurer.

A portly man sporting a stovepipe hat stepped up, and bumping him with his carpet bag, urged him aboard.

"On or off, mate. The beast is not about to eat you. 'Tis a miracle of science, it is."

Micah smiled, nodded his head and climbed uneasily aboard. He settled into the cane seat beside a young man as the portly man and his bag took up the seat in front.

"Good morning," he said.

The young man nodded and turned to look out the window.

The shrill whistle blew three times and Micah grabbed onto the seat in front of him when the car lurched forward. Clutching the seat nervously as the train slowly picked up speed, he gazed out the window at the passing cityscape. So much had changed in the last few years. New streets and buildings seemed to sprout from the earth while he slept. He had to crane his neck to get a glimpse of the sky over the tall brick edifices that now defined the growing port. On the outskirts of the city the train picked up speed. He found he had to look toward the horizon, because the trees and brush close by flew past in a blur, upsetting his normally cast-iron stomach. After a few moments, he released his grip on the seat in front of him and started to enjoy the sensation of controlled speed. It was truly a marvelous age they lived in. Steam had transformed shipping and industry with whistle blasts and the rhythmic chugging of engines. Magnificent steamers plied the Great Lakes. Steam engines loaded and unloaded the grain, and factories no longer needed running water to turn their machines. Just as steam had conquered the water, the steam locomotive now conquered the land.

Outside of Black Rock the train stopped, and he and the other passengers had to get off to clear a herd of cows from the tracks. Consequently, the train arrived in Niagara Falls a half hour behind schedule. Even so, he had a two hour wait for the train to be resupplied for the return trip, plenty of time to complete his mission and get a quick look at the legendary falls.

An omnibus, a horse drawn multi-person carriage, was waiting to carry sightseers to the hotel, but his business was elsewhere, so he bypassed the line and walked down the dirt track toward the rapids. He intended to walk along the rapids, but was soon diverted from the river by a high fence that blocked the view of the rapids and the falls ahead. Spaced at even intervals along the way were shuttered windows and doorways attended by hostile men who charged for a view of the wonder. Annoyed he hurried on to a doorway with a sign stating "The Flaming Raft of Death 3 Cents."

"Is Mr. O'Hara about?" he asked the pug guarding the door.

"Three cents and you'll know soon enough," growled the man.

Micah sighed and gave the man the three pennies.

"Right this way, gent," said the man graciously opening the door.

A cold damp blast of air rushed through the open door blowing his long hair back from his face. The roar of the massive cataract filled his ears, drowning out the excited cries of a small group of men and women pressed against the safety line, keeping them a few feet back from the rapids. All were staring expectantly upstream at a man pushing a blazing birch boat into the current with four panicked rats skittering around the flames. The death boat tossing about in the rapids was swept toward the precipice to the delight of those gathered at the edge. The rats abandoned the burning craft and swam for the shore, but the current was too swift. The small crowd ooed and ahhed as the unfortunate rodents were swept over the brink along with the flaming boat to plummet to their deaths.

Micah joined the crowd and peered down at the rocks a hundred feet below. He could see other sightseers standing on an island with a narrower falls and through the mist beyond, the much larger Horseshoe Falls. The chill mist, the thunderous roar and cascading water overwhelmed him. He had always known of the falls, but had never imagined the raw power of the wonder. The sight momentarily made him forget his mission until the laughing crowd greeted the proprietor with applause.

"Drink up," said Dooley. "Have to make room for the next group."

One of the men drained his cup and holding it forth said, "I'll have another, Mr. O'Hara. A fine spectacle. Makes one appreciate the beauty of it all to see the nasty little creatures meeting their doom."

"Hear, hear," agreed the others

"Why thankee," he said refilling the man's cup and pocketing the proffered coin. "I does me best to make your visit worth the trip, I does."

The man drained his cup and the group started for the door in the fence. When the group broke up, Dooley spotted Micah. He pushed past his appreciative clients and through the door with Micah a few steps behind. The ticket collector at the door grabbed Micah by the arm as he came through and jerked him backward. Reacting instinctively, Micah rammed his shillelagh into the man's midsection. The man grunted, doubled over and let loose his grip. Micah saw Dooley turn a corner into an alley by a dry goods store and sprinted after him. By the time Micah reached the alley, Dooley was nowhere to be seen and Micah was winded. He leaned against the side wall of the store catching his breath and trying to figure out where the cold blooded killer had gone. He heard the scrape of a boot in the gravel behind him and spun around just in time to ward off a knife thrust to his back. Sweeping the blade before him menacingly, Dooley moved in driving Micah against the wall. Micah pushed Dooley back in desperation. Sunlight glinted off the blade as Dooley rebounded from the wall and circled slashing the blade at Micah's face.

"I'm a sending you home piece by piece," he hissed.

Micah waited for the charge Da's Shillelagh ready at his side.

"Think that Irish stick is going to stop me?" taunted Dooley.

He slashed at Micah's throat. Micah ducked to the side and swung the shillelagh down on Dooley's thrusting wrist. Dooley screamed and the knife slipped from his hand falling to the ground. Dooley stooped to pick it up and Micah swung the club at his head. Dooley blocked the blow and darted away along the fence hiding the river from view. He pushed his way past one of the men hawking views of the rapids and disappeared behind the fence.

Micah chased after and saw Dooley making his way through the shallow rapids toward Goat Island. He ran to the edge of the water just in time to see the man slip and get swept up by the rushing water. Dooley struggled against the torrent carrying him helplessly toward the brink of the falls.

"Sweet Jesus, save me!" he screamed.

The shocked bystanders on shore watched in fascination as the man hurtled toward his doom. Micah ran along the shore following the man's futile struggle against death. Dooley slammed into a rock a few feet from the precipice and clung to the slippery moss covered outcrop begging for salvation. Micah pushed past the gawkers leaning against the safety line and cut the rope. He ran to the river's edge tying a bowline into the end along the way. He tossed the rope toward

Dooley. It fell short downstream from him. Micah hauled it back in and threw again. This time the rope landed upstream and the current carried it within a few inches of the panicked man who proved to be too frightened to reach for it.

"Ye have to try!" shouted Micah above the roar as he prepared to try again. Dooley, his eyes closed tightly against his peril, clung desperately to his slimy haven unable to answer.

"Open your eyes, damn you! Here it comes!"

Dooley looked fearfully into Micah's eyes and nodded his assent. Micah cast the rope underhanded in a high arc over the turbid water and onto the man's back. Dooley grabbed the rope, and in the process of looping the rope under his arms, slipped into the rapids and was swept over the edge. His arm looped around the other end of the rope, Micah was dragged down the river bank after him. Micah clung to the rope and scrambled to his feet. He rushed to a sapling on the shore and ran around the small tree securing the rope. Some of the onlookers took hold of the rope and the men pulled the half drowned man back up the face of the falls and onto the river bank. Micah rolled the gasping man onto his back and attached the manacles to his wrists.

He smiled and jerking him to his feet in front of the befuddled crowd drawled, "I won't be letting you cheat the hangman, would I?"

By the time the two boarded the train for the trip to Buffalo, Dooley had recovered sufficiently to bargain with Micah.

"I've put aside a bit," he said while Micah locked one of the manacles to the frame of the seat. "You can have it all. I'll head out West. Ye'll never see me agin."

Micah stared silently out the window.

"I know how I can get more. There's the German. I know where he keeps a pot o' coins in Buffalo."

"The only thing you're going to get is another rope. This time it'll be around your neck. Shut your gob before I shut it for you."

The day had turned unbearably hot and with the windows closed against the thick black smoke belching from the engine's smoke stack the temperature inside the car soared. Micah moved to a seat across from Dooley and the clattering, rocking motion of the car soon lulled him and the rest of the passengers to sleep.

Dooley watched and waited. When he was sure that Micah had fallen asleep, he braced himself and pulled on the chair leg with all of his might. The floor board creaked, and he sat back up checking to see that no one had heard. He hunched down and pulled again. The leg pulled free of the cracked wood of the floor with a sharp snap. Micah stirred, but did not wake. Dooley slipped the manacle from the chair leg and stepped softly to the door. The train lurched casting him into a sleeping woman's lap.

"Lord help me!" she cried out waking Micah.

Dooley untangled himself from the hysterical woman and ran for the door. Micah dove at the fleeing man and the two of them tumbled through the door onto the stair platform between the cars. Dooley rolled on top and pinned Micah with the manacles pressed against the constable's throat. Micah thrashed back and forth trying to break free, but unable to breathe, his struggles subsided into a vain attempt to pry the manacles from his throat. The train jolted abruptly as it crossed onto a trestle. Dooley eased the pressure on the manacles and slid Micah to the edge of the swaying platform.

"Nothing can save you," whispered Dooley. "Relax an I will get it over with quickly."

Micah renewed his struggle, but Dooley pressed down on his throat and Micah soon passed into unconsciousness. As he faded into blackness, he heard the shriek of metal and Dooley's scream.

Micah awoke with his head dangling over empty space, a heavy weight pinning him down. Twisting his head, he saw Dooley slumped against him, his body impaled on a ten foot strap of iron that had broken loose from the wooden rails to tear through the floor of the platform and imbed itself in the wall of the car after piercing Dooley's heart. The motionless train rested precariously on the rickety wooden bridge that creaked ominously underneath. The woman upon whom Dooley had fallen during his escape attempt, trembled ashen-faced in the doorway gnawing the fist that she had crammed into her mouth.

14

1848
THE OTHER RAILROAD

It was early at The Gothic Hall. The real action wouldn't start until the sun had sunk into Lake Erie, and the wharf rats had scurried from their back breaking labor to make their way to the saloon. A more genteel crowd graced the establishment at this hour, and Micah was meeting Sean and James to discuss the finances of the new family home to be built on the site of the farm. The sale of the land had financed the cost of a house, but the men had agreed to pool their resources to build large enough to house them all, take in boarders and open a shop.

Before he had time to settle into his chair, Christopher, the establishments refined Negro waiter, was at his side pouring a glass of water.

"Will you be having your usual, Mr. Curly?" asked the white-gloved man.

"Not tonight, Christopher. Bring a bottle of the good stuff. James and Sean will be joining me."

"Very good, sir. How are you feeling? I haven't seen you since you caught Dooley on the train."

"The rail is what caught Dooley. He had me, true."

Christopher laughed.

"Now, there you go again, Mr. Curley. Malachi told me how you ran Dooley down at the falls. He said the devil helped Dooley get the better of you for sure. That man was evil through and through and sold his soul long ago. But Jesus be watching over brave men of the law, and He is the one threw the rail into that man's black heart."

"Malachi is the hero of this tale. He saved that poor boy from Dooley and Engel, and what did he get for his troubles? My Irish lads almost killed him."

"True, but that Irish Doxie been making it up to him ever since."

It was Micah's turn to laugh.

"She's a wild one. He was safer with the lads."

"Malachi never had much sense when it comes to women," agreed Christopher.

"Mind if we sit with you Judge?" asked James cheerfully. "Christopher, I think we will be drinking something with a bit more bite than water."

"I was just going for a bottle, Mr. Reddy," offered Christopher.

"Right you are, Christopher. None of that rot gut the Judge poisons himself with."

"None of that, James," said Micah. "The council is only considering me for magistrate."

"And they will find no one better on this side of the Atlantic," said Sean as he took the seat across from Micah.

"Thanks Da, but there are those who would not agree."

"Since when do the drunken sots you've locked up get a say in who is to judge them?" asked James.

"Not all the sots are in jail, by a long shot," said Sean.

"There's no shortage of them on the council," whispered Christopher with a wink as he set the bottle on the table.

The three burst out laughing and James yelled for Christopher to have a drink with them. A number of hostile looks were directed their way from the other patrons. Christopher stiffened and backed away from the table.

"Thank you kindly, gentlemen," he said loud enough for the onlookers to hear. "It is not my place to drink with fine folks like you. I am here to serve you and the rest of the fine people of Buffalo."

"And a fine job you're doing, Christopher," said Sean. "You are the main reason we come here."

The other diners went back to their dinners. Christopher bowed and backed away from the table disappearing into the kitchen.

"Now that was a stupid thing to do," hissed Micah. "You could have cost him his job."

"I know. I wasn't thinking. Christopher is such a fine man, I forget he ain't white."

"What's done is done," said Sean. "Have you decided to throw in with us, Micah?"

"I just wonder if we risk going too far," said Micah. "There is enough money from the sale of the farm to build a nice house. Why get a mortgage and risk our future."

"To risk going too far is the only way to find out just how far you can go," Sean answered looking Micah calmly in the eyes. "That's how we dug the ditch and that's how this city came to be."

Micah looked pensively at the glass in his hand, resting his elbows on the table.

He raised the glass, shrugged and said "I'm in!"

As one voice they shouted "Sláinte," drained their glasses and slammed them down on the table. Sean refilled their glasses anticipating many a toast to come.

Two men sitting in the corner of the room eyed the celebrating men, making no effort to conceal their contempt.

"Drunken Irish pigs," drawled one of the men to those around him. "First they try to serve a nigger and now they disturb the rest of us with their drunken Irish revelry. Is there no fit place in this wretched city for fine Southern gentlemen like ourselves?"

His colleague shot him a warning glance.

"Curb your tongue, Phillip," he said quietly "We don't want to draw any unnecessary attention to ourselves. We shall soon be done with our business be done with this place and be done with the likes of them. It will be back to Kentucky to collect the bounty."

Phillip nodded grimly toward the waiter Christopher and poured himself another drink.

"As you say, Seth. As you say."

"Bring on the special, Christopher," called James. "You have three hungry men with a night of drinking ahead."

"Yes," agreed Seth. "I think he'll do just fine."

Phillip and Seth watched from the shadows as James stumbled against Micah and Sean when the three men left the Gothic Saloon at ten that evening. Though the three had fully intended to drink every drop of whiskey in the well stocked cellar, the thought of the long hours of labor before them in the morning and the few hours left to sleep won out and they were lured home to their beds.

Katie, Mary and Margaret had been discussing the living arrangements for the new home when they heard the intoxicated men singing the latest hit song to sweep through the dance halls.

As I was walking down the street
Down the street, down the street,
A pretty lil gal I chanced to meet
Under the silvery moon.

Buffalo gals, won't you come out tonight?
Come out tonight, Come out tonight?
Buffalo gals, won't you come out tonight,
And dance by the light of the moon.

The singing paused and “Katie, Darling, Won’t you come out tonight?” echoed down the street.

The three men guffawed.

Hearing Sean’s inebriated voice, Katie groaned, “Oh, Lord. I might a knowed they’d get into their cups.”

The singing rose in volume and what little harmony it had once possessed, fell proportionately.

I asked her if she'd stop and talk,
Stop and talk, STOP and talk,
Her feet covered up the whole sidewalk,
And she was fair to view.

Buffalo gals, won't you come out tonight?
Come out tonight, Come out tonight?
Buffalo gals, won't you come out tonight,
And dance by the light of the moon.

The men burst through the door, and taking the women into their arms, danced back out to the street.

I asked her if she'd be my wife,
Be my wife, be my wife
Then I'd be happy all my life,
If she'd marry me.

Buffalo gals, won't you come out tonight?
Come out tonight, Come out tonight?
Buffalo gals, won't you come out tonight,
And daaaannnnce by the light of the moo-ooon.

Sean fell over backwards pulling Katie down on top of him.

" 'Tis those big feet of yours," teased Sean. "Might as well try dancing with an elephant."

"Elephant is it?" squealed Katie, pushing away from him "I'm the best dancer you will ever meet. I could make my fortune in one of the halls. Now get up and off to bed with you."

James brayed like a donkey, "An don't let the fairies be getting you, laddie!"

"That goes for you too! James Reddy and you, Micah Curly," she ordered. "The whole besotted lot of ye."

The men retreated sheepishly to their beds while the three women stood with hands on hips glowering after them.

"Lord forgive me, but I love those damned men," sighed Katie.

The women laughed and followed after their mates to bed.

"Goodnight Christopher," said the manager locking the door behind him.

"Goodnight, sir."

Christopher shivered and drew his thin coat close when he stepped off the porch into the fine mist blowing in from the lake. The light rain fell cold but soft on his skin and quickly soaked him through.

"Bed will feel good tonight," he muttered to himself.

The gloomy street was quiet, his shoes sloshing through the muddy puddles the only sound. He wasn't overly superstitious, but the stillness combined with the dense fog raised the hackles on his neck. He sensed something was wrong, but he dismissed it as only the primeval dread that lurks in the darkness. He whispered a quiet prayer and hurried toward his home, unaware of the two men watching from the shadows.

"Take him now, Seth?" asked Phillip.

"No need. We know his habits. We do it nice and legal tomorrow. There's plenty o' business in the trade to be had hereabouts. Don't want no trouble with the law 'bout it."

The day had dawned clear and crisp. The late September leaves blew from the trees in a blizzard of brilliant red, orange and yellow confetti. Katie left Erin and the twins still deep in the revitalizing sleep of youth while Mary and baby Terence played by the hearth. She enjoyed the solitude of the early morning streets as she made her rounds to drop off and pick up the week's laundry from her commercial clients. The few coins she collected had added up over the years and soon the family would be in their new home, and she could give up the lowly life of a washerwoman. Her hands were scaly red claws from the harsh lye needed to properly launder the bundles of soiled linen and clothes. She slid a rough hand over her face feeling the rasp of the ill-treated skin against her smooth cheek. Life was hard for the Irish. Despised and relegated to the lowest of trades, the price of life for most in Buffalo was hard labor and suffering, with whiskey and an early death the only solace to be found.

But Katie had learned the hard way that giving in to despair was the surest path to misery and defeat. That was not to be the lot of her family. Together they would make a place for themselves. They had done it before and they could do it again. If hard work and discipline could see them through the canal days, that course of action would serve them well again.

She saw Christopher sweeping the street in front of the Gothic Hall. He smiled, set the broom aside and waved.

"Morning Miz Reddy. It's a fine day to be alive."

"Good morning to you, Christopher."

She handed him the bundle of clean linens.

"I love the fall, plenty too eat, not too hot, not too cold."

"Yes'm. It does a body good. Let me put this away and fetch the washing."

Katie leaned against the porch rail idly watching the early morning stillness overcome by the rising bustle of the waking street. A line of freight wagons moved slowly toward the market forcing pedestrians to work their way around. Up and down the street, merchants were opening shop. They swept puddles away from the entrances, lowered awnings and put sample merchandise out front. Malachi, the blacksmith, was pumping the bellows, sending clouds of coal smoke out the chimney to compete with the clouds of smoke drifting up form the steamers plying the harbor. Micah and O'Malley were slowly making their way up from the harbor stopping to talk with sleepy-eyed merchants along the busy street.

"Here you go, Missus," said Christopher emerging from the saloon with a soiled bundle of table linens.

A man stepped up and took hold of Christopher's arm, causing him to drop the bundle. Katie tried to catch the falling linens but froze halfway down when the man spoke.

"Christopher Webb, I am here to return you to your owner," said the man displaying a badge.

"I don't have no owner," said Christopher stiffening and pulling back.

"Don't make this any harder on yourself," warned the man pulling back his coat to display a six-shooter.

"I'ze a free man."

"Is this the nigger, Phillip?"

"He da one what run off from John Clements."

"I'm arresting you for stealing yourself from your rightful owner," said Seth grabbing him by the arm.

Christopher shoved him and turned to run. Phillip pulled a lead sap and smashed him behind the ear. Christopher grunted, grabbed his head and fell to one knee. Katie pushed the slave catcher away when he went to strike him again.

"Micah!" she screamed.

A few passersby stopped and lined up behind Katie.

Seth pulled his gun, and pointing it at Katie, declared, "I will kill the next person who interferes."

Katie stared back defiantly, but with the barrel of the gun aiming menacingly in her face she backed away. Phillip laughed and pulled Christopher to his feet.

"That ain't right!" yelled a negro man getting down from the back of a wagon.

"Back off," warned Seth aiming at the man who stopped short.

"I ain't afraid to use this. This man is a runaway slave and I am just doing my duty."

"Your duty to collect the bounty," said another negro in the growing crowd.

Seth looked around nervously at the crowd of mostly black faces glaring at him.

"I'm taking him. Don't try to interfere. Bring him, Phillip."

Phillip pulled the dazed man away from the hostile crowd.

"Do something!" insisted Katie.

"Arggh," cried Seth dropping his gun in the dust.

Malachi held Seth in a bear hug. The man was squirming to get away, but he could not break the hold of Malachi's massive arms.

"Run, Christopher," called Malachi.

Katie and two negro men pulled Christopher free enabling him to run off.

"What's going on here?" demanded Micah as he and O'Malley ran to the scene.

Seth and Phillip broke away from the angry mob and dashed back to their hotel.

After listening to Katie, Malachi and others on the scene, Micah led the seething throng of all colors in pursuit of the fleeing slave catchers who had attempted the abduction. Cornered in their room, the men gladly surrendered to Micah to avoid the vengeance of the incensed mob screaming for their blood. He sent O'Malley for reinforcements and met the crowd in the doorway of the hotel where he faced down the angry shouts.

"Give them to us!"

"We'll show them they ain't on the plantation!"

"No Slavers in a Free State!"

"Out of the way, Micah!"

Micah raised his hands passively and stepped into the crowd.

"Now, now. We got them fair and square. Let the law handle this."

"They're the law! He had a badge."

"That piece o' tin ain't no good in Buffalo," Micah replied. "Let me handle this."

"Step aside, or you will get hurt," growled a large, thickly muscled Negro.

Micah recognized him from the docks. The man grabbed Micah's arm and effortlessly pushed him aside.

"Scrapper, you know better than that," Micah shouted into the man's glaring face. "You do something like that and you'll be the one to hang."

"Don't care 'bout no rope," he growled. "Dey got's my woman and chillun. Ain't no slaver going to come up here and take one o' us."

Malachi pulled the man back and said, "Ease off, Scrapper. You know Micah. He a good man."

The crowd calmed, the shouts giving way to sulky murmuring. Seeing O'Malley and two other watchmen force their way through the crowd, Micah waved his arm dismissively.

"It's over. I have them in custody and am taking them to jail."

He pulled Phillip out to the street with Seth following close behind. The watchmen surrounded the frightened men and cleared a path through the crowd. A fist shot over O'Malley's shoulder striking Phillip in the side of the head. He crumpled to his knees. O'Malley and another watchman bent low and hoisted the fallen man back to his feet. The raucous crowd cheered the knockout punch that had laid the slaver low, and flowed into the Western to celebrate while the watchmen led the frightened men to safety.

The unfortunate slavers had blundered into Buffalo totally unaware that it had become a center of anti-slavery sentiment. Up until then, Negroes had been able to live openly as a small but vital part of the community. When Frederick Douglas came to Buffalo to speak a few years earlier, he found audiences eager for his message. He spoke day after day in ever larger venues. The members of the Baptist church voted to open their doors to him, but even this venue proved too small. Finally, the open park provided the only locale spacious enough to handle the thousands of anti-slavery supporters. The spirit of commonality born during the frontier days, when a man was assessed by his abilities and not his color, still held sway in the growing community and the acceptance of Douglas' message was genuine.

Still shaken by the Kentuckians brazen act, the negro community met that night and formed a vigilance committee to monitor the movement of other "bloodhounds" set on capturing negro men, women and children to collect a bounty in the South. Money was raised within the Negro and White communities, and a lawsuit was filed against the two slave catchers who were fined and sent home.

Bolstered by the rout of the "bloodhounds" and the court victory, the anti-slavery movement in Buffalo spread, and Sean was chosen to join the delegation to the State Democratic convention in the spring, advocating for the Wilmot Proviso that would guarantee freedom to all Negroes who lived in the newly acquired Mexican territories of Arizona, California, Colorado, New Mexico, Nevada, and Utah. Manifest Destiny had expanded the country and the evil of slavery with it. To abolitionists, slavery was a threat to the soul of the country, but to the swelling Irish immigrant population crowding into the First Ward, it was a threat to their livelihood.

15

SAINTS AND HOOLIGANS

Tannery boys, newsies, collectors, rag pickers, stable boys, pickpockets, beggars and sundry other cast offs ruled the streets. They saw all, heard all, felt and tasted all, and learned the harsh lessons of a city's underbelly. Childhood ended once your Ma could put you out of doors with an older brother or sister serving as the only buffer against the marauding gangs of street urchins. If your Ma gave you a piece of bread, you soon learned not to take a bite in view of others who would make it theirs. You didn't take off your coat when you overheated playing ball, or you would go without when the weather turned colder. You didn't catch the eye of an older boy, who would bloody your nose just to see you cry, and you didn't cry if he did bloody your nose. Innocence and weakness attracted predators, and it was best to go unnoticed until you were big enough to fend for yourself.

This was the world of the youngest living in the "infected district." Children of the better off lived elsewhere and had servants or a parent at home who would watch over them. They went to school or were taught at home, preparing to assume their rightful place in society. The children of the district were on their own, unless one or both of their parents had the time and foresight to guide them to better themselves. Choices were few, but choices there were. Catholic children, who were at last allowed to attend public schools, had to endure the proselytizing of the Protestant school masters and the scorn of their classmates. Katie and others took in children teaching them their numbers and letters and with the arrival of the new bishop, Catholic education would soon offer another way.

Michael and Danny had thrived under the close watch of Katie, learning to read, write and cipher as well as any under her tutelage and earned a place in the new school. Sean spent some evenings showing the pair how it all came together in his accounting books. Michael was easily distracted by any and all possible distractions, but Danny had a fine hand and knack for the books and soon was helping his father with work he brought home to finish.

"As alike as two peas in a pod, and different as day and night," sighed Sean after a particularly vexing session with Michael.

"Danny takes after you and Ma," agreed Katie. "And Michael? Michael is all Da, ready to take on the world without a thought or a care. They are both good boys. Michael will blaze a path though the forest and Danny will straighten it out after."

"If we don't wring their wee necks first," sighed Sean.

"Wee? Not so much anymore. They will soon be as tall as you."

"They will do us proud, Katie. That they will."

The Reddy family had as close a bond as any that have trod the old sod or the new. The parents adored and watched over the children and the children idolized them in return. Daily lives were shared over the evening meal, and what little free time they had was spent together. But, boys are boys, and Katie and Sean had never suspected even half of the harrowing exploits the boys engaged in while growing up in a city filled with vice and crime. If they had, they would have locked them away for the rest of childhood.

The journey to and from their schooling was a straightforward walk along Seneca Street passing the fronts of bustling shops and small industries which made for a direct and safe passage to and fro. Naturally, the boys soon tired of the walk. The back alleys of the same street however, were dirty, smelly warrens of mystery and peril waiting to be explored.

Michael was still rubbing his bottom after the school master released him with one last reminder from the hickory switch.

"Are you all right?" asked Danny noting Michael's grimace and the tear leaking from his eye.

"Ah he hits like a wee lassie," he answered.

"I don't know why you rile him so. It earns you a licking every time."

"He don't know nothing. Always telling us we will burn in Hell unless we lose our Papist ways. We ain't Papists. We're Irish, and don't we have a Irish Bishop now?"

"I don't listen to him when he goes on like that."

"It ain't right and I don't care how many times he beats me!"

"I don't think you shoulda called him a bloody British pig."

"Did you see his face? He turned bloody red, he did. Thought he was 'bout to explode!"

"He did! He did! I got sprayed sitting two seats behind you when he started sputtering away."

Michael rubbed his butt again.

"Have to admit that first whack was a good 'un. Oh look!"

He pranced over to the bakery window and stared at the pies spread out in a row.

"Wouldn't you love to live here smelling them pies all day and night?" he asked.

"I would," agreed Danny.

"Here, now," called the baker standing in the doorway. "Get away from me window. You're dirtying the glass you are."

"Ah who wants your dirty old pies anyway? Probably gots worms in 'em," said Michael.

"Get on wid you," said the man making to back hand him.

The two boys scurried across the street dodging between slow moving hand carts and tired horses pulling overloaded wagons. A knot of men stood outside the Democratic party headquarters shouting angrily at each other and gesticulating wildly.

"What's that all about?" asked Danny.

"Just politics. Men is always shouting politics at each other."

"What's politics."

"Something men is always shouting about."

"Oh."

"C'mon," said Michael running back into the street and hopping on the back of an empty farmer's wagon trundling their way. They sat watching the smoke and steam from the harbor district rise slowly to dissipate in the hazy sky. The commotion gave way to the steady clip-clop of the weary horses' hooves and the boys leaned against the empty baskets happy to be carried home to supper. A chorus of shouts disturbed their repose, and they hopped off to investigate the hubbub echoing down an intersecting alley.

Several distraught men were hurriedly emptying an overloaded two wheel cart that had collapsed on a scrap collector. The collector lay gasping beneath the wheel that had pinned him to the ground when the axle broke.

"Jaysus, boys, get her off me!" he cried.

"That should do it," said one. "Now get down here and help me lift the cart."

Danny walked over to get a better look at the injured man. The man's leg was twisted at a bizarre angle.

"You all right, mister?" he asked.

"Get away from the cart," shouted one of the rescuers. "We don't need someone else to be fretting over."

Danny backed away and the men lifted the cart. The injured man cried out and fainted when he was pulled from underneath.

"Be off with you," said one of the men.

"C'mon," said Michael.

Instead of going back to Seneca Street, he made for the alley running behind the buildings. The alley was piled high with rubbish, ash piles, broken glass, pipes, bricks and sundry other manner of debris. A dank odor of decay overhung the back ways and as they passed along, the unmistakable stench of rotting flesh overpowered the rest. The boys picked up sticks and poked through the piles of trash looking for hidden treasures. Danny picked up a shiny brass ball from a broken carriage lamp and put it in his pocket. Jealous, Michael climbed atop a pile and started sifting through the debris.

"Get down offen that," said Danny. "Ma will kill you if you come home stinking of garbage."

"There's lots 'o treasures here for the finding."

"We can look for a while, but we better get home soon."

They walked along the alley for a ways and came upon a row of stockade fencing blocking off private yards from the alley. The piercing squall from a cat startled them, causing Danny to drop his books in the mud. A scrawny tomcat tore past them pursued by a pack of yelping dogs. The cat slipped under a gate with the dogs in hot pursuit. The dogs couldn't quite squeeze under. They pranced about barking at the gate until one started digging frantically underneath. The dog clambered through followed by the rest of the pack. The cat leaped to the top of the fence and dashed nimbly along the uneven boards to safety. The barking dogs quieted and a low menacing growl emanated from the enclosed yard.

A faint whimpering could be heard and then a small frightened voice, "Mama."

Michael climbed to the top of the fence and saw the pack of dogs growling at a toddler backed into the corner. A small terrier had a hold of the white dress the toddler was wearing and pulled the unstable youngster to the ground. Seeing the toddler's peril, Michael yelled and jumped into the midst of the pack of dogs. He kicked the terrier and danced around kicking wildly at the rest. A large dappled mutt with matted down fur chomped onto the back of Michael's leg. He collapsed to the dirt as the rest pounced.

The gate flew open and Danny darted in brandishing a broken two-by-four. He bashed the dappled mutt sending it yelping out the gate and kicked and batted the rest through after the whimpering pooch. He stood gasping for breath and closed the gate behind the fleeing mongrels. He turned to Michael lying in the dirt.

"Are ye hurt bad?"

"Me leg is bleeding something fierce," sobbed Michael. "Help me up."

When he tried to get to his feet, his leg collapsed and the two boys fell to the earth.

"I'll get help," said Danny.

"No, Ma will kill me sure."

"Mama?" cried the toddler.

"Is the wee lad hurt?" asked Michael.

"I don't think so. Just scared."

Two men came out of the door in the rear of the building.

"What's all this ruckus?" asked the first through the door.

He picked up the toddler and glared down at the boys lying in the dirt.

"What have you done to Nelson?"

"Please, Mr. Baker. You got to help Michael. The dogs was going after Nelson, and they chewed Michael up something fierce."

The other man bent down to look at Michael's leg.

"Looks bad. Hope the dog wasn't mad."

"They was plenty mad cause we stopped them from getting Nelson," said Michael.

"What did the dog look like? Did it have foam coming out of its mouth?"

"I don't think so," said Danny. "He was just mean."

"Best get you to a doctor," said the man.

"We can't afford no doctor," said Michael. "My Ma will kill me sure if I cost her a doctor."

"I know your ma, boy. Don't you worry about paying the doctor. You took care of my boy, and I'll take care of the doctor."

Not a word was mentioned when the boys reached home. Michael waited outside while Danny checked to see if the way was clear. Ma was busy in the kitchen when he motioned Michael in to sit at the table. Michael hobbled to his seat and laid his books out on the table to do his homework. Katie noticed him working industriously at the table.

"And why would you be doing your schooling with out me harping on ye?" she asked sarcastically.

"We learned a lot today and I don't want to forget any of it," beamed Michael. "He ain't so bad a school master, I guess."

"ISN'T!" said Katie. "Isn't."

"Isn't," agreed Michael. "Isn't it am."

Katie rolled her eyes and went back to the fire to stir the pot of stew.

The boys had managed to keep the day's adventure from their mother. A feeling of satisfaction accompanied by the smallest iota of guilt set their minds at ease. They wanted to tell their parents of their heroic deed, but they knew Ma's retribution for their disobedience would be swift, so they congratulated themselves on their cleverness and waited at the table for dinner.

Sean came home a few minutes later and gave them a curious look when he saw them at the table.

"What have ye done this time?" he asked.

"Nothing, Da," replied Michael innocently.

"Just waiting on Ma's stew," put in Danny.

"Nice day like this, you would think I'd find you outside."

"You know Ma's stew," said Danny.

"Good old Ma's stew," agreed Michael.

Sean looked at them suspiciously and then called to Katie, "Set another plate Katie. Micah will be by to plan the move."

"I can't believe it is time," answered Katie.

"Cut hay while the sun is shining."

"Don't get me wrong. I am ready to leave this shanty, sure."

The door creaked open and Micah stepped in carrying a rifle that he leaned against the wall.

"Why the gun?" asked Sean. "I didn't expect you so soon. Is it trouble?"

Micah glanced at Michael and Danny sitting at the table noting the tear in Michael's trousers.

"Nothing to worry about. We been hunting a pack of wild dogs that went after the Baker boy."

"Dear Lord, is the wee lad all right?" asked Katie.

"Thanks to two brave lads he is."

He looked directly at Michael and Danny who were cringing at the table.

"What happened?" asked Sean.

"Mr. Baker was watching Nelson while the missus was at the ladies' tea. He put Nelson out back to play and the pack of dogs dug their way under the gate. Mr. Baker was busy with a customer and didn't notice anything was amiss until he heard a real hubbub from the back. Dogs were yelping. Boys were shouting, and then one of the lads let out a piercing scream. When Mr. Baker came out he found Nelson crying by the door and two lads lying in the dirt. One of them was bleeding bad from a bite."

"Was it a mad dog?"

"Don't think so, but I thought I better check on the lad."

He turned to the boys sitting uncomfortably at the table.

"So which of you got bit?"

Katie and Sean turned on the two boys, eyes wide and nostrils flaring.

"What in the name of all the Saints have you two been up to?" demanded Katie.

Danny hung his head and Michael shrugged his shoulders smiling impishly.

"It weren't our doing!" exclaimed Michael. "Honest."
"It WASN'T your doing," corrected Katie.
"Wasn't it am."

16

CONCEIVED IN IRELAND BORN IN AMERICA

To be Catholic in Buffalo was a burden and to be Irish Catholic was a damnable blight. The majority of the Irish lived along the docks in the midst of Buffalo's expanding industrial section, cut off from the finer areas of the city above the Terrace. Their small homes built in the constricted space between the Buffalo Creek, the tracks and the lake, were set amongst grain elevators, railroad yards, smelters, breweries, tanneries, factories, schools and churches. Ubiquitous taverns, saloons and boarding houses full of single laborers imparted an ominous and immoral atmosphere where swarms of children ran freely amongst the dregs of humanity.

The immediate environs of the canal were known as "the infected district," and calls for reform were issued almost daily in the press. Good-hearted souls made attempts, establishing the Orphan Asylum and public schools where the Irish were at first banned, and later subjected to the anti-Catholic teachings of the school masters. Countless families strived to train their children in the midst of the ward's poverty and debauchery. Rejected by the German Catholics of St. Louis Church, the Irish gathered in homes and a rented hall on

Main to hear the Mass. In 1841 St. Patrick Church was built on the corner of Ellicott and Batavia Road to serve as the first English speaking church in Buffalo, but Irish Catholics were still held back by the prejudices of the city. In 1847 that began to change. Buffalo was to have a new Bishop, an Irish Bishop.

The Diocese of Buffalo was established and The Prefect Apostolic of The Republic of Texas was named Bishop. With a special affinity for the Irish, Bishop John Timon set about elevating their station. The six thousand Irish had found their voice at last.

Katie scrubbed Michael's face as the boy squirmed against her ministrations.

"Ow, you'll rub me face off!"

"My face, not me face. I'll not have you talking like the hooligans along the ditch."

"It's MY face you're rubbing off, not yours!"

Katie laughed and held him at arms length inspecting her efforts. She spit on her thumb and removed a smudge from behind his ear.

"That will do. How you manage to get dirt in every nook and cranny is beyond my understanding. You want to look good for the new Bishop, don't you?"

"Do we have to go? The lads are meeting to build a boat for the race."

"Michael Patrick Reddy! He's Irish like us, and we should all be proud to see one of our own in so high a position. Besides, the whole family will be there to pray for Da's safe journey to the convention."

"I guess."

"Born in Pennsylvania, conceived in Ireland, is how he paints himself," said Sean as he spun Michael around for a quick inspection. "Imagine an Irishman who was the head of the Church in the Republic of Texas is our Bishop. Makes a man proud to be from the old sod for a change. How's me hair lass?"

"MY HAIR!" sputtered Katie.

"Your hair always looks good, Katie dear."

"Ah, what's a woman to do with the likes of you two? Hurry now, I'll not be late!"

As the new Bishop processed from the small church the congregation lost all pretense of solemnity and burst into cheers for the

Irish lad made good. They milled about long after he had departed unwilling to let the momentous occasion end. A new day was dawning for the Irish.

"Praise be!" exclaimed Mary. "Someone to take up for us at last."

"He moved the See to St. Patrick's," said Micah. "Who could have imagined a day such as this? An Irishman the Bishop of Buffalo!"

"And an Irishman a delegate to the Democratic convention," put in James.

"Huzzah for Da, huzzah for Bishop Timon!" yelled the family in unison.

"You'll not be comparing me to a man of God," countered Sean. "That would be Blasphemy, for true."

"It's no Blasphemy," said Micah. "It's a beginning for us all. We are a people to be reckoned with. No longer will we be obliged to others for our livelihood. We have two men who will give bold voice to our people."

"Here, here," affirmed James.

"I thank you for your faith in me," replied Sean. "I only wish I could be as confident."

"And who but the man who built the canal and brought the Dullahan down should we turn to?" asked Katie. "Enough flapping your gobs. It's to home now for a feast of safe journey and celebration."

Early the next morning Sean slept fitfully as the rail car rocked along the tracks bound for the convention in Utica. Anti slavery, anti President Polk and pro Wilmot Proviso, the Democratic Party "Barnburners" had been refused a seat at the Democratic convention in Baltimore. Unwilling to accept Lewis Cass, the party nominee, they were meeting to select a candidate of their own. The institution of slavery had become the central issue of the day and the established political parties were being reshaped by the rival factions.

Sean had fled Ireland to escape the English oppression of Catholics. He felt a special affinity to the plight of the Negro slaves even though in some ways they were "valued" more than the Irish. In America a slave was an investment while an Irishman was an expendable and readily replaceable commodity. Many of his countrymen, who struggled to earn enough to feed their families performing the tasks considered too dangerous to risk valuable slaves on, faced rivalry for these lowest of labors from free Negroes. Freeing the slaves would just bring more competition and lower the paltry wages even further. Though he could sympathize with the predicament of the Irish flooding into Buffalo, Sean could not abide the enslavement of any man. He vowed to push that view to the fore at the convention.

The train stopped to take on water and wood at Batavia and the passengers disembarked to use the privy and stretch their legs. Standing about individually or in small groups they marveled at the complexity of steam engines and the ingenuity of the men who built them. The engineer had brought the iron beast to rest precisely alongside the water tower so the fireman could easily swing the huge spigot over the chugging engine to refill the water tank while others loaded cords of wood onto the tender. The whole operation took only a few minutes and the conductor was crying "All aboard!" before most were ready. The harried passengers climbed aboard and the train was soon racing along the tracks at seventeen miles per hour.

Instead of returning to his seat, Sean stayed on the platform at the rear of the train watching the countryside spin by. He clamped his teeth on the stem of his clay pipe and leaned against the railing. Dense black smoke swirled over the roof of the car and spiraled along behind, marking the passage of man's newest marvel through God's bounty. He felt as though he were speeding through a dark tunnel from the familiar past to a vague and mysterious future.

"Heavy thoughts weighing you down, Sean?" asked Ebenezer Johnson as he stepped onto the platform with a thick cigar protruding from the side of his mouth.

"Aye. It's a powerful, great thing we are attempting, Mr. Johnson, but nigh on impossible."

"The country is divided. Our party is being torn asunder by it. It's no good for business, no good for the party and no good for the People. We must take a stand."

"They're calling us the "barn burners. Say we want to burn down the whole barn just to get rid of a few rats."

"The ones who call us "barn burners" are the rats we are aiming to rid ourselves of. They care naught but for their personal power. They will do or say anything to stay in office. If it takes burning the whole barn to get them out, then so be it."

"To think, we could put an end to slavery in this great land."

"That we will, Sean. That we will. I am just afraid of the cost."

"The cost?"

"Not in riches, but in ideals, in lives, in our better selves. What shall we lose to free our brothers?"

The two men, odd fellows at best, stood on the platform adding the smoke from the pipe and cigar to the clouds belching from the engine, portending the fire and brimstone that would soon ignite the land and forever change the lot of the poor, the privileged, the enslaved and the young nation.

James reached across the table and took Margaret's hand. He smiled and looked deep into her eyes.

"We shall have clear sailing from here on, Margaret," he promised.

"It is a wonderful thing, true, but I don't like that you shall be away so much."

" 'Tis the life of a sailor. I shall be with you every fortnight and all the winter while ice rules the lake."

"Still."

"This is what I know. I cannot spend me life shoveling grain. This is what I was meant for. A vessel of me own. That is where our future lies."

Margaret pulled her hand away when Katie came into the room carrying Timmy.

"The wee one is ready to see you off," said Katie.

"Come here boyo," said James.

He took the laughing boy and tossed him squealing into the air.

"James!" yelled Maragaret.

"Aw we're just funning. He loves it, Don't you Timmy?

Timmy called out, "Again!" and James obligingly tossed him skyward.

"James," warned Margaret.

"Again!" urged Timmy.

"No, boyo. I weathered the great storm on the Julia Palmer, but I'll not risk one of your Mother's."

He put his cap on Timmy and hoisted the boy atop his shoulders. Margaret punched James in the stomach and then kissed him on the cheek.

"All right then," she said. " 'Tis off to the docks and the start of our new life. You come home to me and stay away from the ladies while you're about your business."

"And why would I go out for cabbage when I have roast beef at home?"

Margaret patted his butt and said, "You have a sweet tongue, James. Just be remembering what's waiting for you at home while you be out there with all them cabbages waiting to be picked."

"Enough you two," said Katie rolling her eyes. "My stomach is not as strong as it was,"

"Sorry Ma," said James. "Will you walk to the docks with us?"

"That I will, but we must come straight home. We Reddys have one man going and one man coming this day."

"I will miss hearing all about the convention from Da. We are living in contentious times. Everybody is at odds. We need level headed men like Da to take things in hand or we are in for hard times, sure."

"I am sure that reasonable men will prevail. You just worry about your vessel and returning safely to those who love you, son."

"Ah Ma, will you never stop worrying. I'm a grown man."

"That you are, and I will not."

That night Mary and Micah waited expectantly to hear of Sean's trip. Katie set the roast beef in front of Sean and smiled knowingly at Margaret who laughed out loud at her stepmother's blatant enticement.

The twins huzzahed and Sean said, "I think I should go away more often if this is how I am treated upon my return."

Katie gave him a kiss on the top of his balding head and said, "A feast fit for a man of your position is all. Someday we shall eat this well everyday because of you. Now carve the roast before we perish."

"Hurry Da, before I swallow me tongue!" cried Michael.

"My tongue," corrected Katie.

"Oh, Ma," whined Michael.

"Better carve into it, Sean, before the boyo loses his mind and attacks," laughed Micah.

Sean sliced thick slabs off the roast, laying them on the proffered plates as Katie ladled steaming carrots, potatoes and gravy over all. Sighs and groans of anticipation hung over the table as the beneficiaries of the feast took in the tantalizing aromas while awaiting the blessing from Sean. He looked over the faces of his loved ones and leaned back in his chair.

An impish smile animated him. He clasped his hands in front of his face, bowed his head and closed his eyes. The fidgeting diners followed suit.

He cleared his throat and pronounced, "This reminds me of a tale my Da told me that his Da had told him he had heard from his Da's Da."

"DA!" shouted the anguished diners waiting to dig into the aromatic feast.

Sean laughed and prayed, "Lord, thank you for this bounty and those that are so anxious to be done with it. Dig in!"

Knives and forks flashed. No idle conversation interrupted the frenzied, but deliberate assault on the bountiful table. Occasional sighs of "Oh Ma," and "Praise be," were the only attempts at social discourse until every scrap of food had vanished from the glorious spread. The contented, satiated diners leaned back glorying in the uncommon feast they had just conquered only to shout for joy when Katie brought forth a raspberry pie. Hot coffee, steaming tea and lively conversation took over the happy table.

"Do you have good news to share with us?" asked Micah.

"Yea and Nay I fear," answered Sean.

"How so?"

"The party has gone for Cass and popular sovereignty. They wouldn't even give us a seat at the convention."

"They couldn't," said Katie.

"They could and they did. I can hardly believe it myself. To sell the Negro down the river because businessmen are worried for their profits. 'Tis a disgrace before the Lord."

"Have they no shame?" asked Mary.

James guffawed, "A businessman with shame? Wouldn't that be a new creation on God's good Earth? A good man and a good man of business are not the same animal."

"Then what is the good news in all of this, Da?" asked Micah.

"A new party is to be born right here in Buffalo."

"The Barnburner Party?" asked Micah.

"No, The Free Soil Party. The convention is to be held here to make it easy for all to attend from the East and the West. Barnburners, Liberty Party members, antislavery Democrats and Conscience Whigs are coming together here to build a platform and nominate candidates. It is the first step toward the total abolition of slavery, and Buffalo shall be the center of the struggle!"

"Saints be praised!" exclaimed Katie. "Buffalo, to be the leader of the nation. First an Irish Bishop and now a national party!"

"When is this to happen?" asked Micah.

"In August. True liberty and justice for all begins this August in the year of our Lord, 1848!"

17

THE BIRTH OF MORALITY IN THE DEN OF INEQUITY

The city stood poised, waiting for recognition, the atmosphere charged as before a thunderstorm. For days men from New York, Ohio, Pennsylvania, New England, Maryland, Delaware, New Jersey; eighteen states altogether, had been flowing into Buffalo on trains, steamboats, sailing ships, packet boats, horseback and on foot. The once remote frontier village was about to take center stage in the nation. Marching bands met the esteemed travelers, leading the delegates to the more respectable environs, a short distance, but a world away up from the seedy waterfront. The denizens of the infected district cheered them along, knowing that many would return later to partake of the district's shadier distractions. The ladies of the evening, arrayed in their finest, voiced acclaim and promises of delights to come as the worthy delegates marched past.

Micah and the Watch were on hand to ensure that the "ladies" didn't put too much on display and didn't venture up from the district. Buffalo had been chosen to lead the nation in the fight against slavery, the most vile of practices. Righteous men were gathering there to bring an end to the scourge. At the end of the day some of the righteous would seek release from their sacred but taxing labors. The city fathers recognized the service the fallen women would render, but propriety was to be maintained, and the whores kept in their place.

Lydia Harper sidled up next to Micah and poked him playfully.

"There is many a coin to change hands tonight," said Lydia.

Micah smiled at the pleasing image before him. Lydia was of medium height, with bright blue eyes and auburn hair. Her clear complexion showed no sign of the many diseases infecting the ladies of the district, and her bright expression conveyed impish sensibilities. Micah could not help but admire and pity her. Many was the time he tried to get her to abandon her profession, but she had no one to turn to and no other way to support herself.

Attractive and pleasant to be with though she was, it was her remarkable kindness that made her stand out. During the great cholera epidemic, she had come forward to care for those that no one dared go near. She had fed, bathed and comforted the down trodden, as well as the respectable citizens, who would have nothing to do with her under normal conditions. Micah was baffled by the contradictions she embodied. Lydia lived the life of a whore, but had the soul of a saint.

"Ah Lydia, most of them will end in your purse I am sure. You are a sight to behold."

She genteelly curtsied.

"Thank you kind sir."

"Am I to be kept busy arresting the fine gentlemen fighting over you then?"

"You know me better than that Micah."

She spun around in front of him.

"I just wanted to show you my new dress."

"You are even more lovely than usual."

"Then why don't you ever come around?"

"You know *me* better than that, Lydia."

"The others on the Watch are not so particular."

"You know that's not the reason."

"Still, I wouldn't mind, you know."

"Neither would I, Lydia. Neither would I. But those days are behind me. I am already blessed with a sainted wife and child."

As the band reached their vantage point and the drums, horns and cheers swelled, Lydia leaned in close.

"I have some thing to tell you, Micah. I saw the German just the other night. He and a canaller been making noise about getting even with you."

"Where is he staying?"

"I don't know. Just watch your back. There ain't enough good ones like you to go around as it is."

The marchers came to a halt and all eyes turned to a second story porch overlooking the street where a man pounded an exotic beat on a huge base drum. The savage rhythm caught the attention of the exuberant throng and held them transfixed. A collective gasp escaped from the onlookers when a pale young woman appeared above them. Wrapped in a red silk robe she spun lazily above the enthralled watchers. The robe fanned out exposing brief glimpses of her nubile young body. The quiet groans and sighs were drowned by the crazed shouts of the men below. Acquiescing to their entreaties the woman stopped dancing and stepped onto a platform on the porch. The drum went silent. The crowd followed suit, and the woman slowly, enticingly opened the robe to stand spread eagle above the crowd revealing all of her charms. The crowd sighed as one. The drum took up a slow steady beat and the woman gyrated provocatively drawing the mob closer.

Snapping out of his daze, Micah turned to the Watchmen staring open mouthed at the vision above and shouted, "After her boys!"

The men started pushing their way through the crowd. The drummer stopped beating his primitive tattoo and pointed to the Watchmen coming their way. The woman smiled, closed her robe and bowed to the men below. To no avail, they called out for more, but she swirled about and disappeared into the building. The Watch never found her that afternoon, but many of the throng would return to seek her out after dark.

Micah turned to find that Lydia had melted back into the crowd leaving him to ponder her warning and the task of keeping so many naïve travelers safe in the most perilous city in the world. The doxies and hooligans were out in force, and he feared that before the convention was ended "De Divil would 'ave 'is due."

Sean walked up Delaware with Oliver Dyer, following the marching throng of delegates and onlookers. Shouts of acclamation and affirmation competing with brass bands echoed back and forth as the various delegations converged on the park. A great moment was at hand and the very earth seemed to vibrate in harmony with the Free Soil movement.

"Is Micah about?" asked Oliver.

"He has been everywhere these last few days," replied Sean. "The vultures have been gathering along with the delegates. There's to be no rest for the wicked or the righteous until this gathering is over."

"It baffles my beleaguered brain how these great men of intellect can be led astray as easily as lambs to the slaughter."

"They see the world as they would like it to be and not as it truly is. Micah and the boys will look after them."

"My paper has two chairs reserved on the reporters' platform. Phineas will not be here for the opening day, so you are welcome to take his seat if you wish."

"I should sit with my delegation."

"Suit yourself. Best seat in the park."

"You sure no one will mind?"

"If they do, it is no concern of mine."

"Well thank you, Oliver, don't mind if I do."

When the two men reached the platform, they found all of the seats taken and an argument underway between the squatters and the arriving reporters.

"These seats are set aside for newspapermen," a reporter from the gazette pointed out civilly to the trespassers on the platform.

Not one man budged.

"You have to move along, now." he continued a tad more animated.

"Phhh!" responded one.

"Phhh?" repeated the reporter. "Get your bloated arse outta my chair!"

The man sneered back, "And when is some scribbler more important than a bona fide delegate from the great state of Pennsylvania?"

The reporter lunged and the two men tumbled from the platform, each discussing the other's parentage and reproductive habits. The onlookers took sides and a general melee broke out amongst the lovers of freedom and equality. Chairs and tables were upset and it looked like the Free Soil convention would degenerate into the free donnybrook convention.

Sean and Oliver stood to the side waiting for the combatants to tire.

"Will soon be over," said Sean. "The esteemed delegates are running out of steam."

Oliver laughed and added, "Here comes Micah and the Watch to put out their fires."

There was little left for the Watch to do. The combatants, excepting one or two reporters, were not accustomed to brawling, and the Watchmen merely had to remove a few persistent hands from a few grateful throats. Most were happy to see the Watch finish the day's business. Tables and chairs were restored to their proper spots and the reporters reclaimed the disputed territory. Sean and Oliver took their seats, and Oliver laid out his sheets and pencils. He immediately set about recording a rather unflattering account of the dispute while waiting for the speakers to commence.

"Am I to have trouble with my own Da?" asked Micah when he saw Sean seated at the table.

" 'Tis a guest of the great Commercial Advertiser I am," he replied pompously.

Oliver looked up and nodded.

Micah smiled and said, "I might have known you would find the most comfortable place to rest your aging bones."

"With Age comes Wisdom. With Wisdom comes Privilege and with Privilege comes Comfort."

He leaned back in his chair and smiled magnanimously down on Micah.

"Now go about your business, constable, we men of consequence are full of matters of import."

"A trip to the privy would relieve ye of what you are full of."

The two men laughed and quieted when the Ohio delegation marched into the tent with banners flying. Soon the concourse was filled to overflowing and the speeches began.

Incensed by their exclusion from the Democratic National Convention and the Whig's selection of Zachary Taylor, the speakers launched into pointed character assassinations attacking their opponents' morals, beliefs, motives, heritage, parentage, mental state, Christianity, abilities, integrity, manhood, civilization and fitness for office.

"Why that hatchet-faced Virginian has a face so sharp, he could split an oak by looking at it."

"He calls the Wilmot Proviso 'nothing but an abstraction.'"

A voice from the crowd called, "His face is the abstraction!"

Raucous laughter ensued.

"No, no to a certain extent, I admit that the provision is an abstraction. I am also willing to say what it is not. It is not butter and bread. It is not roast beef and two dollars a day."

More laughter ensued.

"No, the Wilmot Proviso rises above all these considerations. It is an abstraction to be sure, and so was the Magna Charta."

"Yes! Yes! There you have 'em!"

"And so was the Declaration of Independence. So is the idea of Right and Justice and the Truth of God an abstraction. And it is these ABSTRACTIONS that raise mankind above the brutes that perish."

"That's the fact! Go for it!"

"And it is around these abstractions that we rally to put our Government right!"

The crowd that had swollen to almost 40,000 strong, burst into cheers, the horns blared out and the crowd began marching behind the pounding drums.

These demonstrations were soon drowned by the chant picked up by every voice:

"He who'd vote for Zacky Tailor,
Needs a keeper or a jailer.
And he who still for Cass can be,
He is a Cass without the 'C' !

Free Soil!
Free Speech!
Free Labor,
and Free Men!

Free Soil!
Free Speech!
Free Labor,
and Free Men!"

As the chanting died in anticipation of the next speaker, another sound intruded on the celebrations. A crowd of Taylor and Fillmore supporters could be heard coming down the street toward the gathering beating drums and exclaiming:

"Then go it boys, strong and steady,
And raise the shout for Rough and Ready.
Rumadum Dum!

Then go it boys, strong and steady,
And raise the shout for Rough and Ready.
Rumadum Dum!"

Though the rally to form a new party was being hosted by Buffalo, many Buffalonians embraced the ticket of Zachary Taylor and Millard Fillmore since the Queen City of the Lakes was Fillmore's home town. Yet in spite of his favored son status, Fillmore's harsh anti-Catholic and anti-immigrant stances won him few friends among the throngs of immigrants pouring into the growing city. The city like the country was hopelessly divided between the haves and the have nots, the abolitionists and the slavers, the Catholic and the Protestant.

The blatant attempt to disrupt the convention by the local Whigs supporting Taylor did not sit well with the jubilant Free Soilers assembled in the park. A cry of Free Soil rose from the crowd which surged out of the tent to rout the interlopers with a barrage of curses, stones and empty bottles before returning to the business at hand.

Speech followed speech and Sean grew weary of the sound of great men extolling their own virtues without adding anything to the issue at hand. He knew that the real business of the convention was taking place indoors where the party platform was being hammered out by a few determined men, and he was anxious to hear the result of those negotiations.

"I believe I have heard enough for the day," he said to Oliver.

"If only I had the choice," answered Oliver wearily. "Ned Christy brought his minstrels back for the week. Thought I'd see the show tonight. Will you join me?"

"Katie and I are going with Micah, James and the girls."

"James is back in port?"

"Should be docking any time now. The steamers with the new propellers are generally right on time."

"Over 50,000 passengers crossing the lake already this season. When will it ever stop?"

"The country is growing every day. That's why this convention is so important. We want it to grow the right way. Guess I'll be going down to meet him. Perchance we can all have a drink after the show."

"Or maybe one for each of us?"

Sean laughed and pushed back from the table just as an ominous tremble in the platform telegraphed alarm. The overflowing crowd surging back into the tent pressed against the platform, and the flimsy contraption lurched toward the stage, crashing to the ground and spilling the tables, chairs, papers, pencils, water pitchers, hats and bewildered newspapermen to the ground. Sean toppled backward from his chair and tumbled on top of Oliver, followed by three men, who had been seated behind landing on top of them both. Curses and groans dominated discussion for the next few minutes as the men untangled limbs and rubbed bruises before the platform was set right.

Oliver crawled about in the dirt scooping up his scattered notes and cursing himself for not numbering his sheaves. Sean twisted his neck back and forth to work out the kinks and then bent to helped Oliver and the others gather their papers and then, dusting himself off and stretching the muscles in his back and neck one more time, bid his adieus.

He reached the slip of the "Buckeye State" just in time to see James and Margaret coming down the gangplank with Timmy toddling between them. James was talking expansively and pulling Margaret in close, delighting in her presence. Margaret glowed with delight. Her bright eyes shown over an ecstatic, beaming smile. A new dress, a new hat and a touch of face powder completed the picture of a happy homecoming. Stepping ashore James let propriety sail with the wind, took Margaret in his arms and kissed her ardently. Timmy jealously wedged himself between the two and struggled to pry them apart. Sean laughed and Margaret pushed back from James, a crimson blush showing through the powder and coloring her pretty face.

"Do you take me for some Doxie then?" she admonished.

"I'm just a lonely sailor back from the bounding main," teased James.

"And you will stay lonely, if you don't back away and show a little respect."

Sean laughed again and called, "Welcome home. Katie has an early supper waiting and then it is off to Ned Christy's Minstrels."

"They are back in town? I thought they would forget Buffalo and Harrington Hall now they are playing New York and Washington."

"No matter where they roam, Buffalo is always home, and Mrs. Harrington gave Katie tickets to the early show."

"Strange how Ma can be friends to the grandees and saloon keepers alike."

"Your Ma doesn't judge a person by their position in life. She sees them for what they do. Mrs. Harrington has run the hall for these many years, but she runs a clean establishment, and she knows where she came from."

James settled Timmy on his shoulder, Margaret slipped her arm in James' and the family strolled down the slip toward home where Katie was waiting with the twins.

"Take the twins and the four of you out back to clean up," commanded Katie. "Mary and Micah will be here soon, I have set a table fine enough for the Bishop himself, and you hooligans are not setting down to it with one speck o' dirt between the lot of you!"

She hurried Margaret and Timmy in, pushed the twins out with a bit of lye soap and shut the door in Sean's face.

"Now why would she be going on like that?" asked James.

"Doesn't matter. She's got the high ground. Did you get a whiff of that roast mutton? A little soap and water is not too high a price to pay for a plate of Katie's cooking."

He took hold of the twins and they went back to the wash bucket. Katie had filled the bucket with clean water and left linens and clean shirts for each of them. The four males shed their shirts. Sean dunked his head into the laundry tub and came up sputtering. James and the twins followed suit howling like banshees when the cold water ran down their backs. Sean rubbed the lye in his hair working up a lather and made a few quick swipes at the rest of his body before passing the bar on to James. Once they had all washed, they dunked back into the tub to rinse the harsh soap away. Sean inspected the twins and rubbed any evidence of the day's shenanigans clean, before letting them put on the clean shirts. The shivering boys brushed their dripping hair as the men trimmed their facial hair, and after one final inspection all around, they went into the house to face Katie's scrutiny. One by one, they submitted to her inspection. Michael shifted uneasily from foot to foot anxious to get to the source of the enticing aromas enveloping him. Katie passed him through and then pulled him back by the collar.

"Just a minute, Laddie," she called halting him in his tracks.

She bent his head forward, licked her thumb and rubbed out one last smudge behind his ear.

"Always behind the ear," she muttered.

Giving him one more spin and a pat on the rump she sent him on to the table. The rest passed inspection and soon the small home was alive with feasting, laughter and high spirits.

Dressed in their finery the three couples paraded down the street after dinner to Harrington Hall exchanging greetings with those they met along the way. Katie reveled in the admiring glances and comments and smiled magnanimously back at her neighbors. It was a proud day for her family to show off how far they had come since the devastating flood. Washerwomen generally did not go to fine entertainment even on the fringes of the "infected district."

Arriving just as the doors opened, they took their place in line alongside the delegates from the convention and the well-to-do of the city. This was not to be an ordinary night in the Harrington. Ned Christy and his minstrels were just back from touring the great cities to put on a spectacular show where it all started.

The three women chatted nervously in the noisy music hall, surveying the other ladies in the crowd and admiring the latest's dresses and bonnets on display. The men leaned back in their seats sighing through closed eyes and rubbing their overworked stomachs contentedly. Ushers walked down the outer aisles turning down the lanterns and the crowd settled down. A crash followed by a tambourine falling and a graphic curse came from backstage and the crowd laughed at the performer's misfortune. A series of "settle down, ready now, everybody set?" could be heard as the limelight's flared and tambourines and banjos rang out loud and clear.

The minstrels clad in stove top hats, long tail coats and blackface strutted onto the stage singing "Old Susannah" with the audience clapping and singing along. The minstrels spread out on the stage sitting in a semi-circle centered on the minstrel Bones, who danced slow and easy to the rollicking melody. He held two bones in his hands and clicked a complex rhythm to the tune. The song ended and all of the minstrels rose to their feet shaking their tambourines in a wave toward the center of the stage. Mr. Bones sat down and Mr. Interlocutor took a seat in the center with Bones and Brother Tambo on either side of him as the applause quieted in anticipation.

He turned to Bones and asked, "I say Mr. Bones?"

"Yow suh?"

"Were you ever in love?"

"I wasn't nuttin else, ol' hoss."

"What kind of girl was she?"

"She was highly polished. Yes, indeed! Her fadder was a varnish maker."

The audience erupted in guffaws. The loudest coming from Oliver seated a few rows in front of them.

"She must have been a spicy girl."

"You hit de nail on the head o' cabbage dere, Mr. Interlocutor. Dat's de reason she was so fond o' me. She was a poickess, too."

"A poickess?"

"Yowsuh. She used to write verses for de newspaper."

"A poetess you mean?"

"She write me a billy do."

"You mean a Billet-doux, a love letter?"

"I do."

"What did it say?"

"What lub is, if you must be taught,
Thy heart must teach alone!
Two cabbages wid a single stalk,
Two beets that are as one!

"How'd that make you feel?"

"Hongry."

The audience roared.

"You always hungry."

"You say we travel the world n' eat like kings through thick and thin."

"I did."

"The more I travel with you, the thinner I gets."

"Now Mr. Bones."

"I rather eat like a French peasant stead o' a king."

"Why is that?"

"You can't eat much if dey chop off yo' head but da peasants, dey gots to eat cake."

"I see."

"Did you write a verse for your girl?"

"Makes me hongry jus' to think on it."

"Makes you hungry to think about your verse?"

"As I live and die."

"Have at it then."

> "O you sweet and lubly Dinah!
> Dare are nofin any finah;
> Your tongue is sweeter than a parrot's.
> Your hair hangs like a bunch of carrots,
> And though of flattery I'm a hater,
> I lubs you like a sweet potater!

"Beautiful, Mr. Bones. Nothing rings so true as something from the heart."

"Dats right. The way to a man's heart is trew his stomach, an' I'm hongry."

More laughter.

"Won't she feed you?"

"She ain't like dat."

"Was she the one that…?"

"No dat was her sister. You know she had…"

"Did she ever get that fixed?"

"No the doctor he say…"

"You don't say."

"I do say and that ain't all. He tell her..."

"No, he didn't."

"It de trute as Samson is my witless."

"Well, I never. What about her…?

"No one knows."

"I heard…"

"No dat ain't right. You see…"

"Ah, well what can you do?"

The crowd roared as they watched the two blackface comedians roll their eyes and contort their exaggerated mouths. The esteemed delegates to the Free Soil convention were amongst the loudest. It was obvious that a great deal of spirits had been consumed along with their meals. Katie squirmed uneasily as the performance continued and the audience became more and more engaged in the show, shouting out disparaging comments of their own.

"Give that boy some watermelon! Hey Bones you want some cornpone? That boy is as dumb as he is black!"

Katie leaned over to Sean and said, "I want to leave."

"It's all in good fun, Katie."

"I never met a Negro like that. Have you?"

"They are plantation negroes. It's different."

Just then Tambo stood and shook his tambourine in an arc over his head and beat a driving rhythm. Mr. Bones leapt to his feet and danced along with his bone castanet's clicking in counterpoint to Tambo. The chorus joined in shaking their tambourines standing and sitting in unison. The banjos joined in followed by the horns, and the whole company cakewalked behind Bones and Tambone singing loud enough to bring the house down. Mollified by the music and dancing, Katie decided to stay for the rest of the show.

On the way home, everyone was in high spirits. The music and comedy were better than any of them had imagined. Even Katie had succumbed to the exaggerated blackface humor as the show progressed.

"I thought I would die laughing when Mr. Bones did his figuring," laughed Sean.

"It made sense to me," giggled Mary.

"What? Thirteen is one seventh of twenty-eight?"

"When he wrote down seven thirteen's and added up the threes to get twenty-one and then added the ones to get to twenty-eight. It made sense."

"Oh Mary, I worry about you sometimes."

"No look."

She wrote down the numbers.

"You add the first column three, six, nine, twelve, fifteen, eighteen, twenty-one."

1 3
1 3
1 3
1 3
1 3
1 3
1 3
21

"Then you add the first column one, two, three, four, five, six, seven. Add that to 21 and you get 28! So that makes thirteen one seventh of twenty-eight."

1 3
1 3
1 3
1 3
1 3
1 3
1 3
7 + 21 = 28

"You cipher good enough to keeps books for Benjamin Rathburn when he gets out of jail," laughed Sean.

She twisted her mouth sideways, scratched her head and sighed, "I know, but he made it seem right."

They laughed and James said, "Let's not end the night so soon. We should stop off for a drink, I'm buying."

"Those are words I never thought I would hear," said Sean. "Lead on, lad. Lead on!"

They followed the theater crowd to the Gothic Hall and took a table in the dining room. Christopher came over immediately.

"It is so nice to see the whole family out for a change," said Christopher.

"We've been to see Ned Christy's Minstrels," said Mary beaming happily. "The music and the beautiful costumes were more than I could have dreamed. And we laughed so much. It was wonderful."

"I'm happy you enjoyed the show," he replied through a forced smile. "What can I get you?"

"Hey Bones!" shouted one of the convention delegates. "Get your lazy bones over hear. Men want a drink."

The hall echoed with laughter and Christopher's eyes flared. He took a deep breath and turned toward the man.

"I'll be right with you, sir, as soon as I take care of these good people."

"Don't take too long, Bones. Just shuffle along and get our drinks."

Christopher said, "Right away sir," and turned back to the table.

"A bottle of wine is all," said James.

Katie elbowed Sean and said, "Those are the great delegates who are aiming to free the Negroes. You go tell them to show some decency."

"Now, Katie."

"I won't have it. If you won't do something. I will."

Christopher leaned in close, "Thank you kindly, Mrs. Reddy, but it will just make things worse. These men say they love the Negro race, but they don't seem to like the Negro man all that much."

He left to take the order from the men at the other table.

"What will happen at the convention with men like that deciding things?" asked Katie.

"Not all are like that," said Sean. "All of us are opposed to the idea of slavery, but not everyone agrees about the details."

"Details?" asked James.

"What to do with the slaves when we free them," said Sean. "Do we say they are free and leave them to their own devices?"

"No one helps us," said Micah. "Why should they be special?"

"That is one of the main sticking points. How do men raised as slaves, men told what and when to do everything, how do they shift for themselves?"

"Are you talking freeing all the slaves?" asked James.

"No. Not yet anyway. The Free Soil Party just wants to stop the spread of slavery into the new territories. Freeing the slaves in the South will take generations."

"It isn't right that one man should own another," said Katie. "They should all be freed now."

"But what to do with them is what divides the party and the nation," said Sean. "Most want to send them back to Africa."

Christopher returned with their wine and Katie asked, "If the slaves are freed, if you were one of the slaves that might be freed, would you want to go back to Africa?"

"I don't know nothing about Africa. I was born here. Most of us were born here. Why would we want to go live in a jungle somewhere? We are Americans now. Have been for a couple hundred years. We don't know nothing else."

Sean cocked his head and stared curiously at him for a moment. Christopher looked steadily back at him.

"Most of us was born here," continued Christopher. "Most of you all just got here."

Another delegate shouted from the other end of the room, "Boy! Come clean up this mess. I spilled the bottle."

Christopher smiled sadly and went to clean up.

Sean was a different man the next morning at the convention. Katie and Christopher had shown him something that had been right in front of him all along. Negroes were men just like him. They wanted the same things and fought the same battles.

The convention continued with more speakers while a committee of conferees deliberated inside the Second Universalist Church on the corner of Washington and Clinton. The leading delegates maneuvered, compromised and sought equitable solutions behind the scenes. The committee laboriously developed a compromise platform that most could agree to, and it was presented to the assembly for their approval.

When the chairman read, "We accept the issue which the Slave Power has forced upon us, and to their demand for more slave states and more slave territory, our calm, but final answer is, No more Slave States and No more Slave Territory." The delegates erupted in ear splitting cheers.

They nominated former president Martin van Buren for president and Charles Francis Adams for vice-president to a deafening acclamation from the crowd. The banner which proclaimed "Free Soil, Free Speech Free Labor and Free Men" was unfolded and in a tumultuous din, the convention was adjourned. The assembled left the tent in the Park on Courtyard Square and marched through the streets of the city, with torches flaring, drums beating and whiskey flowing. A new party, a new outlook and a new morality focused on individual rights and freedom for all was born in the Queen City of the Lakes that warm summer day.

18

GROWING PAINS

The divisions in the Free Soil Party paled in comparison to the forces tearing at the core of America. Taylor and Fillmore won the three way race for the White House and slavery retained its grip on the nation's psyche. The feudal agrarian society of the South could not continue without slavery and couched in the issue of states rights, the ruling class worked relentlessly to expand slavery and maintain their political power. The Fugitive Slave Act of 1850 extended slavery's reach into free states. The conflicting interests of the North and the South intensified as Buffalo struggled through another cholera epidemic even as the city grew in population, power and prestige.

The three story brick house on Hamburg Street standing in the shadows of the city's commercial expansion still managed to rise above the other homes scattered throughout the burgeoning industrial district. Katie worked tirelessly to make a home for her children, grandchildren, husband and boarders. The family had moved to their new home on Hamburg Street, built on the small remnant of their farm. Cara, Seamus, Honora and Liam were around as much as her own brood since Cara had taken over Katie's laundry contracts. After going through the kidnappings, she never let Seamus and Honora wander far from her sight. Buffalo had too many wicked places and wicked people to ever trust her children to the streets. Mary had left her scullery maid position to help with the general store facing Seneca Street. Deeply involved in the business and the growing Catholic Church, the women were becoming as great a force in the first ward as Sean and Micah. The Reddy family found themselves to be a rickety bridge between the immigrants and the powers that be during the relentless build up to civil war.

Standing by the door with the box lunches she had prepared for her boarders, Katie watched the first rays of the sun strike the roof tops above the dark, quiet street. Muted grunts and clunks could be heard from the dining room as the boarders devoured the breakfast she had spread on the table. At regular intervals the sharp slap of the privy door echoed from the back yard setting off barking dogs and clucking chickens from adjoining yards. The lowing of her three cows waiting to be milked completed the morning symphony and Katie closed her eyes taking in the fresh air and sounds of life in one of the few peaceful moments in her hectic existence.

"Morning Katie," called Cara.

Katie opened her eyes and saw Cara hurrying down the street pulling her sleepy-eyed children along behind.

She smiled and waved hello.

"Thank you missus," said Robby Higgins taking the lunch she held out to him and hurrying down the street.

He was soon followed by the others rushing off to long days of grueling labor. Cara stood aside as the men exited one by one nodding to each in turn. Seamus yawned loudly and he and Honora slid to the ground to lean sleepily against the brick storefront.

"None of that now," said Cara. " Tis time for work. Around back and milk those poor suffering cows, Seamus. Nora, check for eggs, and mind you tell Aunt Katie which hens ain't laying."

"Aw, Ma, give us a minute," moaned Seamus.

"There's a biscuit and some blackberry jam waiting in the kitchen when you're done," said Katie.

The two jumped to their feet and dashed around back. The two women laughed and Mary joined them in the cool morning air.

"Well that's that," said Mary. "The men didn't leave a scrap to clean up."

"Do they ever?" asked Katie. "They need all they can get to make it through the day."

"Will you look at that?" declared Mary nodding down the street.

A barefoot boy no more than five years old came out from behind the iron works carrying a growler. His ragged pants were held up by a bit of rope tied around his waist. The right sleeve of his shirt was torn off and he wore a battered oversized cap atop his curly red hair. Freckles, merged with dark smudges, covered his baby face, and he smiled when he saw the women looking at him.

"Moining goils," he called boldly.

"It's Mrs. Reddy to you, Davey Daugherty."

He tipped his cap rakishly and replied, "Me Da t'inks you are de finest lady in de valley, and so says I."

"Lord save us," sighed Katie.

Davey crossed over to O'Toole's Saloon and rapped at the side door. When no one responded, he picked up a cobblestone and began pounding on the door. The door swung open and O'Toole dressed in his nightshirt made a wild grab for Davey, who skipped nimbly away.

"Wa de feck ya doing breaking down me door afore de sun has got outta bed?"

"Me Da wants a growler," said Davey holding the metal pail up.

"Git outta here, ya pup, or I'll break your arse."

"Fill de growler and I'll be on me way."

"Didn't ye hear me? Do ye t'ink I'm bluffing?"

"I have a lot more to fear if I bring an empty growler home to himself. He'll do me sure."

"Let me see de pennies."

Davey held out his other hand showing the coins.

"All right give me de growler and de coins."

Davey handed over the growler and closed his fingers around the coins.

"When I gets de growler."

O'Toole stomped off and came back with the foaming growler. Davey reached out for it and O'Toole held out his hand for the coins. Davey reached out his hand and dropped the coins in his palm. O'Toole pulled back the growler and stepped back through the door.

"Don't you go cheating the little Hooligan!" yelled Katie.

"Mind your own business, Katie Reddy."

"I'll have Micah send the Watch by, Mr. O'Toole."

O'Toole scowled and surrendered the growler. Davey brushed his fingers off his chin at O'Toole and crossed back over to Katie.

"T'ank ye Miz Reddy. My Da woulda whooped me sure,"

"How's your ma doing Davey?"

"Poorly. She just stays in bed and Da mostly stays away."

"Wait here," she said stepping inside.

Turning to Mary he said, "Your Ma is a fine lady, ain't she?"

"The finest."

Katie came back with a bundle of food and handed it to him.

"Make sure your ma eats some those biscuits and eggs herself. They'll get her better. Don't let her give them all to you."

A tear ran down Davey's cheek and he turned away to hide it.

"T'ank ye Miz Reddy," he sniffed and he trudged away bearing the gift of the devil in one hand and the gift of life in the other.

"Something has to be done for the likes of him or they'll be worse than his Da when they get older," said Mary.

"I'll bring it up again at the St. Patrick's meeting tonight. The Sisters of Charity are doing what they can at St. Vincent's, but with so many left orphaned by the cholera, they can't keep up. We best get busy now or we'll be joining Davey on the streets," replied Katie.

"Liam told me that The Buckeye State was sighted off Sturgeon Point at sunset and would be in port this morning," said Cara.

"That was a fast trip," said Mary. "Margaret will be happy to have James home for a few days."

"Enough of the blather," said Katie, "to work ladies."

The women smiled knowingly back, and Katie eyed them suspiciously. Her eyes went wide and she squealed, "Sean, Ye British pig!" as he grabbed her backside swinging her around to nuzzle her neck.

She pushed him away and turned scarlet as the two women hooted their approval.

"And what should a lass leaning in a doorway expect from a healthy young lad?" asked Sean.

"Dat ain't de belly o' a 'ealthy young lad," taunted Katie punching his paunch and doing her best impression of a doxie.

Letting out a gasp of air, Sean moved in again, but she danced away saying, "Off to work now. This is no time for your foolishness."

"Ah Katie, 'tis always time to be chasing you."

"Go on now. Micah said he was meeting with you this morning."

He smiled, tipped his hat rakishly, said, "G'day goils" and sauntered down the street like the cock of the roost.

"Will they never grow up?" asked Katie. "Five or forty-five, there's no telling them apart."

"Morning, Da," said Micah standing by the door to the warehouse.

A fresh breeze off the lake ruffled Sean's thinning hair as he shook Micah's extended hand. Both men breathed in deeply, savoring the break from the ever-present odor of the canal.

"James is coming in today," announced Sean as he bent to unlock the office door.

"Margaret will be pleased."

"Why did you want to see me so early?"

"It's the Fugitive Slave Law that President Fillmore signed into law. He's been no friend to the Irish, and now we know how he feels about the Negro. I met with his appointee, Commissioner Smith, a few weeks back and he seems a hard case. Now I find that the slaver, name of Rust, has been hanging about, and I am afraid we are in for trouble."

"How so?"

"He as much as told me to stay out of his way. He would handle any fugitives and that the Watch had to follow his orders."

"You are one of the magistrates even if you still work with the Watch."

"He emphasized that Federal authority trumps mine."

"Well that's true, but you know the city and the negroes."

"He won't listen. I'm afraid that if something happens, he'll just act without any consideration. The law is on his side, but I had hoped we could work together."

"I don't get what you're asking me."

"If Negro prisoners are found to be slaves, the Commissioners' fees are greater. There is no trial by jury, they can't even speak on their own behalf, and there is no provision for legal counsel. A $1,000 fine and up to six months imprisonment for those who help fugitive slaves. He stands to profit greatly by denying freedom to as many as he can. All's it takes is for a white man to claim a man is a fugitive slave."

"Do you really think he'd send a man into slavery for profit?"

"I don't know, but he could, and he just brushed away my concerns for fair hearings. You remember what happened with Christopher."

"What do you want me to do?"

"Maybe as a party boss you could get him to see the light."

"Maybe."

"Think about it?"

"Of course."

"Thought you might like to know there's rumors of a dock workers' strike."

"I heard the same at Mooney's. The men deserve more, but the bosses will never go for it. Think there will be trouble?"

"Without a doubt."

"Is the Watch on the alert?"

"Yes, but if it's a general strike, there won't be much we can do about it."

"Can you call for backup?"

"I was hoping I could count on you and some others."

"You know you can if things get out of hand, but don't expect me to take part in strike breaking. I will have to do what Mr. Johnson wants regarding any of our workers who go out, even though the men are in the right. I am caught in the middle here."

"I know. Let's wait and see how it all plays out. I won't call on you unless I have to."

"I'll have that talk with Smith for you."

"Thanks Da."

With the boarders fed and Mary tending to the dishes, Katie knocked on the door of the St. Vincent's Orphan Asylum. The sounds of a battle royale answered her knock, and she stood at the door not sure what to do. The shouts of boys accompanied crashing furniture and the thud of fists. She pounded on the door again and a tiny lass with large brown eyes opened the door.

"Sister is busy just now," she whispered. "Will you have a seat in the parlor?"

Katie crossed the threshold just in time to see two boys roll by with Sister Genevieve striving to separate them.

"Arête! Vit! Vit! Stop it this instant!" shouted Sister Genevieve.

The boys locked in mortal combat ignored her entreaties and continued to thrash each other. Katie stepped in and helped separate the boys, both of whom leaned into their respective referees grateful to safely catch their breath.

"Thank you," said Sister Genevieve who was sitting on the floor trapping one of the combatants in her arms. Katie stood opposite holding the other boy. Blood dripped from his nose and Katie took out her handkerchief to stop the flow of blood. Two sisters wearing damp aprons appeared and dragged the soon to be penitent boys to the back of the residence.

"I'll deal with the two hooligans when I get back from the council meeting," said Sister Genevieve.

"I'd like to accompany you, Sister," said Katie. "I have a thing or two I'd like the Bishop and the good men of the diocese to hear."

"The Bishop won't like it."

"You need help here. There are too many orphans for this home already, and the streets are swarming with so many more. It is time we did something to give the wee ones a chance before they get swept up into the evils of the district."

"The Bishop and I could use the support. He wants to open a trade school for the boys and have separate homes for the boys and the girls. The men are always on about the cost, but what is the cost in lost souls?"

"Sister, can I go back with the others now?" asked the little girl by the door.

"Of course." she answered patting the girl on the head. "Bless you child. You are a good girl, Jenny. Get on with you, and stay clear of le truands."

"Yes, Sister," she answered, skipping away.

The two women went next door to St. Patrick's church and took seats in the pew across from the leaders of the diocese who eyed Katie warily.

"And what is she doing here?" asked Brother Donnelly.

"She asked to address this council about the orphans," answered Sister Genevieve.

"Not that again. Are we to feed every thieving urchin in the city?"

"Is that not what the Lord would have us do?" asked Bishop Timon as he emerged from behind the altar.

"Well yes, your Eminence, but we must be practical. Already we have spent more than we can afford."

"Can we afford not to?" asked Katie.

"It is good to see you, Katie Reddy, but this is a council meeting and not open to others without an invitation."

"Would you let me speak before the meeting starts?"

He paused taken aback by the thought and then smiled.

"I don't think that would violate the rules of order if the meeting hasn't started. Speak your piece."

"Micah Curly tells me that the orphans are easily tempted to criminal ways. The vermin of the district will shelter, feed and clothe the poor souls if they will pick pockets, lead immigrants to them, cut purses and far worse. Their devilish ranks grow day by day."

"They should be put in jail then," said Donnelly.

"To learn even graver crimes from the murderous men kept there?" posed Katie.

"What would you have us do?" asked Bishop Timon.

"Build bigger homes for the boys and the girls. Teach them good trades, and they will become good citizens and more importantly, good Catholics. Are we to let the Devil lead them into crime and prostitution without lifting a hand to lead them to God?"

"We are overrun at St. Vincent's," put in Sister Genevieve. "The City's Orphan Asylum will take no more children and those they have taken in are forced to give up the Faith. So many more of our wee ones are still on the streets. We must help them. The Sisters of Charity will send others to help if we give them the means."

Bishop Timon turned to the men.

"The time to save money will come someday, but our first duty is to save souls. These are not street urchins and hooligans. These are the children of the faithful and our future. What shall that future be? Shall Fillmore and the Know Nothing Party undermine The Church?"

He paused and looked directly at the men. One by one they lowered their eyes before his soul-searching gaze. He bowed his head and murmured a short prayer before turning back to the women.

"Sister Genevieve, Mrs. Reddy, thank you for coming tonight. You have given us our topic for the evening. I know we can count on you to help us in our mission of Faith. We will keep your comments in our hearts and please keep us in your prayers."

"Thank you, your Eminence," they said in unison as they stood and left the church.

"Do you think they listened?" asked Katie.

"He listened to us and they will listen to him."

"I pray you are right."

"Amen."

James was weary from the midnight watch, and the dock workers on the ship seemed to be deliberately slowing the unloading despite the foreman's curses. The ship's cook, Daniel Davis brought him a cup of tea and leaned against the rail alongside him to watch the last of the passengers disembark.

"Mus' a been a rough night on de street," he drawled. "De boys is moving mighty slow."

"Something has got 'em," said James. "Lord help us if it is the cholera again."

"Dey doan look sick, jus' kinda ornery."

James drained the mug and held it out for more.

Daniel poured another cup and commented, "Be good for you to see de missus again. Hardly had more'n a day las trip."

"Engines need maintenance this trip. Give us a few days at least. What you got in mind?"

"Mos'ly stay on board. Nothing but trouble for me our dere. Got beat bad las' time at Dug's Dive. Had a good time 'til dose Canallers laid inta me. An' nowadays de slavers is gittin' mighty bold. Well looky dere."

The foreman was shoving a huge sullen worker backward and calling him every name in the book.

"Pick dat up ye dumb arse Irish piece o' shite!"

"Shove it up your bleedin' arse, ye blackguard!" growled the worker slashing out with a rusty blade.

Red rage colored the foreman's face as he barely dodged the thrust. The dock workers stopped working and shouted encouragement to the knife wielding man. Laughing madly he charged at the foreman again, but he was ready this time. He jumped back pushing a stack of crates over. The worker ducked to avoid the falling boxes. The smaller, nimbler foreman pulled a lead sap from his pocket and leapt over the tumbling crates and slammed the sap into the larger man's temple. The knife clattered to the wharf. The man's eyes rolled back in his head and he collapsed on the spot.

"Get dat sack 'o Irish shite offa me dock and clean up dis mess ye poxie Irish pigs!"

A couple of men dragged the man off the wharf leaving him unconscious alongside the canal while the crates were restacked. The dock workers went back to the task at hand moving much faster with the feisty, scowling foreman ready for all comers.

"Dat be why I doan need to go ashore in dis hell hole," commented Daniel.

"Amen to that," replied James. "They are an evil lot."

"Mo' tea?"

"Nah, that'll do. Looks like we'll be done here in an hour or two."

A little after ten that morning Sean hung up a note stating "back in the afternoon" on the door to his office and made his way to Commissioner Smith's office in the Spaulding Exchange. Leaving the bustling waterfront behind he crossed over to another world. The Irish generally stayed in the First Ward left to their own devices and generally invisible to the grandees of the Queen City. Sean's dual role as Johnson's chief clerk and as party boss saw him cross over on a regular basis. Though Buffalo's elite couldn't care less about the Irish Catholics, they were needed to do the heavy work of the "crossroads of America," allowing the scions of industry to reap the spoils.

The streets above the waterfront buzzed with a hectic frenzy of their own. The business district lent a more genteel nature to the bustling commotion. Carriages bearing the grandees weaved past the tradesmen, the delivery wagons and the omnibuses bearing managers and clerks conducting the financial business of America's link to the West. Street cleaners moved up and down the street shoveling the deposits of the horses while the bankers manipulated deposits of a more refined sort. Maids and housekeepers ran errands for their tea sipping mistresses, and members of the Watch kept an eye out for any that did not belong.

"Good day to ye, Mr. Reddy," said O'Malley

"Haven't seen you in a while, Hugh. How's the family?"

"Good, de missus is feeling her ol' self agin."

"That's good to hear. I see you have a quiet duty today."

" 'Tis nice to get away from the district now an den. Might be trouble brewing dere I hear."

"The strike?"

"Aye an' dat slaver has been makin' noises all week."

"I'm here to see Commissioner Smith about that."

"Don't know if it'll do much good," answered O'Malley nodding toward the office.

The slave catcher Rust with an evil smile plastered across his face came out of the office followed by Deputy Marshall Gates, a small posse and Watchman Jamie Tyler who was stuffing a paper into his breast pocket.

"What's going on?" asked Sean as they hurried by.

"Don't butt your nose where it don't belong," answered Rust brushing past him.

"Official business," Tyler muttered rolling his eyes skyward.

Sean watched them hurry toward the waterfront curiously and O'Malley said, "Dat's looks ill for some un'."

"Hmph," sighed Sean. "I guess I'm a little late."

Remaining on the wharf, Marshall Gates dispatched Tyler and Rust onto the deck of the Buckeye State. James hailed Tyler and Rust as they made their way up the gangplank. The two men ignored him and went into the forward cabin proceeding below deck to the kitchen. Realizing something was amiss he called for the captain and hurried after them. He was right behind when the two entered the ship's galley. Davis and four of his friends jumped to their feet and stood glaring darkly at the men.

"Daniel Davis?" asked Tyler pointing at Davis.

Tyler pulled out his paper and announced, "I have a warrant for your arrest. You'll have to come with me."

Davis and the four men picked up knives and Davis snarled, "We be walkin' o'er corpses if'n you try an' take me, constable."

Rust stepped back warily bumping into James and retreating to the deck.

"What is this all about?" asked James.

"I have a warrant for the arrest of the fugitive slave Daniel Davis," replied Tyler.

"What? He ain't no slave. He's been cook since before I came on crew."

"That's him all right," called down Rust nervously.

Davis moved toward Tyler with his knife held out threateningly.

"Hold on there, Daniel. There's no call for blood."

"I ain't no slave and dey cain't make me one. I die 'fore dat happen."

"I'm bound to satisfy the warrant. Put down those knives. You don't think I came here alone do you?"

A look of alarm crossed Davis's face when they heard Rust screaming, "Marshall Gates! Hurry, they'll kill us all!"

The thudding of feet up the gangplank and across the deck panicked the men behind Davis and they put down their knives when the Marshal pushed into the galley followed by a half dozen of the watch. Davis nervously put his knife on the table.

"That's better, now put out your hands," ordered Tyler, holding up a pair of manacles.

Davis darted for the small hatch behind the stove. As he climbed up there was a sickening crunch, and he tumbled senseless onto the stove where his skin sizzled as he lay on the searing iron surface. Rust peered through the hatch at Davis's limp form, smiled and disappeared from sight. James pushed past and pulled Davis onto the floor where he lay moaning. James wrinkled his nose and gagged from the putrid smell of burning flesh filling the tiny cabin.

Tyler handcuffed Davis' hands behind his back and the constables picked him up and dragged him on deck. They half carried him down the gangplank and tossed him into a cart to take him to the Fugitive Commissioner's office.

Rust put his arm around Tyler and declared, "That was a fine job officer. He is a bad one and when his master gets his property back he'll set him to rights!"

Tyler twisted out from under Rust's arm and snapped, "I did what I was sworn to do, but I don't have to have anything to do with the likes of you."

Rust shrugged his shoulders, put his hands in his pockets and walked off whistling "Soldier's Joy" toward the Spaulding Exchange.

Word spread quickly through the community and a large, mainly Negro crowd gathered outside the Exchange. Strangely enough the crowd was quiet and orderly. Commissioner Smith appeared about 2 o'clock and adjourned the proceedings to the Court House. When the officers led Davis to the waiting carriage, the crowd turned ugly and rushed them. The men of the watch held them off and the wagon started down Main Street. The crowd, now a mob, followed along, tossing cobblestones at the carriage and shouting violent threats. One man grabbed the horse's bridle while others grabbed the wheels briefly bringing the wagon to a halt, but effected nothing further before the Watch intervened. The mob turned their anger to their surroundings. Shop windows were broken and most of the idle bystanders scurried inside to evade the impending riot.

The Negroes in the crowd were enraged, and a few of the white men tried to incite them further. Cries of "Burn the Nigger!" and "Hang 'im" rang out and rocks were tossed into the crowd while still other white men shouted to free the poor man. The situation was ready to explode. Mayor Wadsworth came out with an aide and walked calmly alongside the carriage standing in the way when several men tried to open the door of the carriage to free Davis. In the end the bulk of the people were ready to stand by the officers, in case of need, and preserve the peace. Still hopeful after the Free Soil Party's stand in Buffalo a few years past, they trusted he would be vindicated in the courts. But other forces were at work in the city.

19

MORE OF THE SAME

The next evening Micah came by with Malachi and Christopher to see Sean and James concerning the arrest. Christopher produced a jug and the men settled on the stoop in front of the Reddy home to enjoy the cool breeze blowing up the creek from the lake.

"Thought this might help ease things a little," said Christopher pouring for the others. "We need to see what can be done. Most of the men on the committee are being calm for now, but I don't know how long they will just sit by and watch a free man taken away in chains."

"The news isn't good. I met with Commissioner Smith, and while he is sympathetic, he is bound to follow the letter of the law."

"Some is talking of breaking him out," said Malachi.

"Och, that would just make it worse for everyone," said Micah. "If we don't have the law, what do we have?"

"Free men," countered Christopher.

"You know what I mean. We have got on well for the most part. Are we to let this cursed law tear our city apart? Anti-slavery feelings are pretty strong among the whites too, but we got to do this right."

"Daniel is a good man and there was no reason to do him that way," said James.

"He threatened to kill Tyler, pulled a knife and then tried to escape," said Micah. "In my book that was reason enough."

"Would you let some man take you for a slave?" asked Malachi. "Ain't dat why you Irish come heah?"

Micah shook his head indecisively and looked to Sean for support.

"Let's have another," said Sean draining his glass and pouring one for Christopher.

Christopher smiled at the courtesy and raised his glass to Sean.

"I tried to get Smith to see reason," offered Sean. "And I truly believe he is a good man, but he's torn between his duty to the law and his personal feelings, just like Micah."

The men nodded gravely and Malachi rested his hand on Micah's shoulder as Sean continued, "The whole country is torn by this damned evil. We have to think on it and not do anything too rash. We have to wait for tomorrow's hearing. Mayhap the Commissioner will set him free."

"And mebbe Jonah will swallow de whale," said Malachi.

"Have another," said Christopher pouring the last of the jug into their glasses. "We will see what tomorrow brings."

The hearing did not go well for Daniel. The people in the gallery gasped when the court officer led Daniel into the room. They were unaccustomed to the ways of southern slaveholders. Daniel shuffled in to the packed courtroom led by a chain affixed to an iron collar around his neck. His hands and legs were manacled, and he looked around vacantly at the people assembled for his hearing. Micah was enraged that no attempt had been made to treat Daniel's injuries. A great festering burn scarred the prisoner's face and dried blood ran from several contusions and flesh wounds on his head. Appearing dazed, confused and frightened, he swayed unsteadily as the charges against him were read.

Opening for the defense Mr. Talcott and Mr. Hawley moved for dismissal claiming that the papers were insufficient, because the record of the court in Kentucky was not properly sealed.

Commissioner Smith ruled against the defense, and then Mr. Bowen opened the proceedings for the claimant stating, "The evidence against the fugitive is irrefutable. He is a fugitive from his rightful owner. He is a fine athletic Negro. As such he is of great value to his master, who suffered a great loss at the hands of this ungrateful slave. Daniel had been treated most fairly, clothed and fed at great expense, yet he saw fit to steal himself from his kind and rightful owner."

He then called the first witness, who stated under oath, "I am Geo. H. Moore of Louisville, KY. I knew the negro, Daniel, in Louisville, Ky. Knew him first when I was very small. I don't recall his master's name at the time. I think it was Fraser, my father purchased him of – Fraser, I'm pretty sure that was his name -- in 1850 and he -- he ran away four months later in August, 1850. I have no doubt of his being the person."

"Daniel was hired out by my father as cook part of the time as a steward on the steamboat, 'Anna Lennington'. He was at my father's house the rest of the time. My father paid seven hundred dollars for the nigger, and that nigger robbed my father of his rightful property!"

In response to the damning testimony, Mr. Hawley claimed that the act of taking the slave to a free state enfranchised him, "He is now a free man living in a free state. No man can lay a claim to him here."

The Commissioner disagreed, "The slave, Daniel, was not taken into a free state by his master. Even if he had been, that act could not have the effect to enfranchise him, as any master has a right to take his property through or into a free state. Would you take a man's horse because he rode it into another state?"

The Commissioner then made and signed the certificate, required by the act of Congress, authorizing the agent of the claimant to take the slave back to his master.

The Commissioner remarked to the colored people in the gallery, "Mark my words and mark them well. The law will be executed at all hazards, and any attempt at rescue will be met in a summary manner. Whatever we might think of slavery in this section of the country, the law must be executed. The slave Daniel must be sent back to his master. It has been shown that he was purchased for $700, and I don't know what others might do, for the purpose of securing his freedom, but I will give here and now, twenty-five dollars toward that end."

Daniel was led from the room with no more than a few muttered objections and many more expressions of surprise from the gallery.

"This isn't over, Daniel," said Micah. "We'll find a way to help you."

A few days later James barged into Sean's office and threw a letter torn out of the Buffalo Morning Express on his desk.

"Do they expect anyone to believe this? How many colored boys working on a ship do you know who can write or even talk like this? Daniel never could."

BUFFALO MORNING EXPRESS.

VOL. X WEDNESDAY MORNING,

Sean picked up the scrap and read the letter.

To the Colored Population of Buffalo:

I thank you for what you have tried to do for me. You meant it for good but it is of no use. -- We colored people of Kentucky are about as well off as you are. I am going back-- I had rather go than stay here. I hope you will not interfere with my going. My master, Mr. Moore, has always treated me well; I feel that I did wrong in running away-- he bought me at my urgent request; he placed confidence in me, and I do not feel that I ought to deceive him.-- If he had treated me ill I should feel differently about it. He never did. I was advised to run away and come to a free State, or I should not have done so; the advice was bad, though I reckon it was not so meant. We are about as well off in

Kentucky as you are here, and some of us better. I shall advise the Kentucky boys, when I get home, to stay where they are. We have plenty to eat and to wear, and are not so badly worked-- this every body knows who has been in Kentucky.

Again, my colored brethren, I thank you for your kind sympathies, and to my white Abolition brethren in Buffalo, I wish you the same, but I do not want you to do any more for me.

Daniel Davis, his X mark
August 28, 1851

"My colored brethren?" said Sean. "They have to be kidding."

"The Express at least calls them on it," said James. "Our friends at the Advertiser praise Daniel for being a truthful and literate man. It turns me stomach that money can buy a Congress to pass an unjust law and a so called 'free press' to lie about it. The Divil take 'em all."

"The committee still hasn't raised enough to buy Daniel's freedom. Most are for it, but when it comes time to back up your beliefs with cold hard cash, those beliefs tend to dissolve into mist."

"Malachi and some of his friends are talking about taking Daniel by force."

"They have to show restraint or they will lose their freedom along with Daniel or worse. Rust appeared before Micah last night in Police Court and was fined the maximum for the Assault and Battery on Daniel, and we started a civil suit against him. Things are moving in the right direction."

"And if we win the suit and Daniel is sent back to his master, who will profit from the damages? It'll be his master, because his property, Daniel, is what was damaged."

"True, but Judge Conklin is reviewing the case today. I think he will go free."

Daniel, his wounds healed after weeks in jail stood before Judge Conklin as he announced, "I find no merit in the claim brought forth by Mr. Rust. Mr. Davis you are free to go. Bailiff remove the prisoner's bonds."

A cheer went up from the gallery as the bailiff unshackled Daniel. Mr. Talcott handed him some coins and patted him on the back. A broad smile illuminating his face, Daniel hugged Mr. Talcott and Mr. Hawley. He rubbed his raw wrists, waved to the people then walked spritely out of the courthouse. Without a backward glance at his latest place of captivity, he proceeded straight to the ferry and crossed the Niagara River to disappear in Canada.

As summer faded into fall the Davis case faded into memory. The shipping season was at its peak as the sailors raced to beat the coming winter. Steam and sailing ships arrived daily to offload their cargo in the ever bustling port. The bountiful harvest from the West was pouring into the harbor, filling the elevators, canal boats and rail cars to supply the burgeoning needs of the growing country.

The Irish dock workers watched the wealth of the country slip through their fingers to line the pockets of a few captains of industry while the workers struggled to feed and clothe their families. All summer discontent seethed below the surface and the Watch was kept busy keeping the peace. Egalitarian concerns were put aside as the threat of violence infected both sides of the canal.

With the port at its most vulnerable time of year and completely dependent on Irish labor, the workers saw an opportunity to claim a share in the enormous profits. Calls for a work stoppage had been circulating along the waterfront and in the hundreds of saloons along Canal Street and throughout the First Ward. Surly workers challenged their foremen daily. Workers were fired and their fellow workers slowed the unloading, leaving the foremen unable, and some secretly unwilling, to keep the work going.

Micah was forced to go on patrol with the Watch on a daily basis and hold police court at night to handle the increased assault cases. As the slowdown impacted the transfer of goods and started affecting profits, Sean was called to Mr. Johnson's mansion on Delaware. Hopping aboard the horse drawn trolley and handing the conductor the coin, he sat lost in thought, glumly looking at the fine homes slowly passing by. He was sure that nothing good would come of this meeting. Reaching the mansion, he stepped off the trolley and walked up the long curved driveway to the magnificent home. Mounting the expansive porch, he removed his hat and rang the bell. A moment later, the butler appeared.

"State your business," sneered the Butler as he took in Sean's cheap suit.

"Chief Clerk, Sean Reddy to see Mr. Johnson, if you please."

The butler sighed and opened the door wider.

"Wait here," he commanded indicating a bench in the hallway before turning his back and strutting away.

The minutes ticked by as he waited on the bench. Voices were raised in the library and he heard someone pounding on a table. The voices returned to a low murmur, and a rough looking man emerged from the library off to his right and hurried past him to the street.

The butler returned and said, "The master will see you now."

He led Sean into the library where Mr. Johnson sat pouring himself a glass of whiskey and smoking a big cigar. Mr. Bowen, the attorney who prosecuted the case against Daniel, was there along with a man he had never seen.

"Good morning, sir," said Sean.

Mr. Johnson sipped his whiskey, leaned back in his chair and puffed on his cigar staring idly at Sean, sizing him up for a moment. Sean shifted uneasily.

Johnson leaned forward in his chair and said, "This has to end now."

"Yes sir."

"You're Irish. What is the Hell is wrong with your race?"

"Sir?"

"I gave you a position! Raised you up. You were supposed to keep those Papists doing their duty, What happened."

"It's wages. The men cannot buy bread for their families."

"They seem to find whiskey a plenty, don't they?"

"Well."

"You are a low race. Worse than the colored boys."

"I don't see."

"I'm sending in the coloreds. O'Connell just went to round up the darkies. They will get the jobs that you Irish don't seem to want."

"That will cause a riot. People will get killed."

"People?"

"The lads won't stand for it. They'll kill the men you send to take their jobs, and the Negroes will fight."

"A few less coloreds and Papists? What's not to like?"

"Mr. Johnson, you hired me to help you understand the Irish."

"I don't need to understand the drunken sots. I hired you to make them work. The coloreds are going in later today. You are to choose foremen who can show them what to do and make sure the boats are unloaded."

"But sir."

"Do I need find another?"

"No sir, but just a small increase and a kind word would set things right."

"The lazy sots are not worth the money I pay them. You can say all the kind words you want, but the Watch will be on hand to keep things under control. A man gets more with a kind word and a club than with just a kind word."

Micah and James were standing by the bridge over the commercial slip when Sean returned. Douglas and a few other colored men stood outside Dug's Dive passing a jug around and staring up at the three men on the bridge suspiciously.

"I see you're here already," said Sean.

"They must have heard something," said Micah nodding toward the men below. "What did you hear from Johnson? The Watch was told to stand by for trouble."

"They aren't going to wait for a strike. They are hiring Negro men to unload."

"The bloody fools. The whole place is going to explode. The jail is already overflowing. We won't be able to deal with this. What are we to do?"

"This is about our duty. What choice do we have? Shall we both lose our positions? I must try to keep the port going with the Negros, and you must try to keep things calm. We have our own to worry about, Micah. We cannot afford to take a stand."

"How can you say that, Da?" asked James. "You who always said a man stands for the right, come what may."

"Many times I risked my life for my beliefs, but am I to risk my family for ignorant men, who would kill any who get in their way?"

"Aye, they will kill all right, but it will be to protect families of their own."

Father and son glared at each other on the bridge over the foul waters of the canal that united a country but now divided the workers.

Micah shook his head sadly not knowing what to say or do. The men outside Dug's Dive watched and listened to these men, who had done their best to make Buffalo a city open to all who came there, as they wrestled with the eternal struggle of the classes.

"So what shall it be, Da? Betray your own kind to please the bosses or stand with those you know are in the right? When does your duty to your boss, to your family, to your comfortable position, trump your duty to the basic rights of others?"

"Is there no other way, Da?" asked Micah. "Must it be one or the other?"

"Mayhap," offered Sean. "We are only looking at the problem. It is the cause we need address."

"How so?" asked Micah.

"The problem is the coming battle between the workers. The bosses are the cause. They are pitting us against each other. Are we too stupid to see that? We must find a way to get the workers together. Then the bosses will have to deal with us."

"There is no time. The colored workers will be here before long."

"You know them well," said Sean. "Head them off. They know you for a fair man. You can get them to see reason. I'll do the same with the Irish on the docks."

"I don't know. How does this help with the bosses?"

"If we get the men working and the goods flowing again, they'll let things be."

"Maybe."

"He's right, Micah, we can do this," added James. "We at least have to try. Malachi can help."

Sean crossed to the docks and Micah and James hurried down the street to Malachi's smithy, where a wiry young boy almost as dark as Malachi was shoveling coal into the fire. The thickly muscled Malachi worked the bellows one handed breathing life into the added coals.

"Thought I might be seeing you," said Malachi setting the iron aside. "Trouble is coming sure."

"You can help us avoid it," said James.

"An' why would I want to? All you Irish pourin' down de canal an' ridin' de rails took de jobs. Hardly no one let a colored man work de docks."

"You know that isn't true," interrupted James. "You know Daniel was cook on my ship, along with other Negro stokers and deckhands. And how many others are working the canal and the lake?"

"Dem jobs is for men widout family. A man be on de water all de time."

"Like me."

"You know how it is."

"Help us avoid blood," pleaded Micah. "White and colored blood."

Malachi scratched behind his ear and screwed up his face. He looked past the rancid waters of the canal out toward the clear, peaceful waters of Lake Erie.

"Will dere ever be a time or place where color doan make no difference?"

"It has to start somewhere," reasoned Micah. "Why not here? Why not now? Will you join us?"

Malachi wiped the beads of sweat from his brow and hung his leather apron on a peg in the wall.

"Dat 'nough fo' now, son" he told his helper. "Go get some cold water and come back tomorrah."

He stepped into the sunshine and said, "What we waitin' on?"

That day in that place the men were able to dissipate the rising tensions. Sean promised the dock workers a meeting with the bosses and Malachi, James and Micah talked the Negro men into waiting for a chance at permanent jobs that would remove the unceasing threat of violence. But it was a temporary truce and the four men knew that if they didn't address the underlying injustices, the Queen City of the Lakes would soon be wracked by racial violence.

That evening Katie listened uneasily as Sean related the events of the day.

"Micah and James handled things well. If they hadn't been able to sway Malachi, there was no way they could have stopped the Negroes from marching on the docks. They are hungry too. 'Tis a hard thing for us all."

"And our lads on the docks, they listened to you?" she asked.

"For now. I am afraid I have only bought some time. Johnson and the others aren't going to give on the wages. Not when they can play the men against each other and keep the profits to themselves."

"What will you do?"

"I have to think about us, Katie. If I don't do what I am told, I will lose my position and never get another. We would lose everything."

"What of the men? What of their families? Do their children deserve to starve and die?"

"We have to think of our own. What else can I do? I've nothing more to say. I'm off for a pint."

Katie stared in stony silence as he left without another word. What had happened to the man who had seen them through so many trials? Lately he had taken to the drink more and more. Hadn't he learned anything from her battles with the demon rum, and the misery the brew bred around them? Why should success make him less of a man? When they had nothing, he was ready to take on the world. Now that he was a man of import, a man with respect, did he fear the loss of his position more than the loss of his dignity?

She lay awake into the early morning hours waiting for him to come home. Her mind would not give her rest. Her thoughts were spinning, the whole country was spinning out of control, and her family was spinning along with it. There had to be another way. They had always found a way before. Why should this be any different?

"Daughter. Daughter. We must talk."

Katie opened her eyes. She was back in the forest. Moon shed his blue light on the sparkling shroud of snow even as sinister shadows moved in the dark woods bordering the path. Sitting up she rubbed her eyes and then brushed away the snowy blanket surprised by the warmth of the snow on her smooth, youthful hands. Gazing through old eyes at her rejuvenated child's body raised only a slight inkling of curiosity, as she took in her surroundings.

Moon slipped behind a cloud and the bright path faded to shadow. She shivered in spite of the warm snow, when a high-pitched keening roared through the treetops. The wail of the Banshee shattered the stillness and then lowered tone and pitch to be supplanted by the snarling and howling of wolves. Physical and supernatural fear brought her to hyper-vigilance, and she peered apprehensively into the sinister woods trying to bring substance to the shadows. Trembling fearfully, Katie closed her eyes and prayed for deliverance as the pack of wolves closed in on her tiny body.

The soft voice of Wings Spread Wide muted the frightening howls and Katie opened her eyes.

"Remember daughter, there are two spirit tribes at war for our hearts. The evil tribe is Fear, Anger, Lies and Hate. The good tribe is Courage, Serenity, Love and Truth. The evil tribe is fed by lies, the good by Truth. It is the one you feed that grows and triumphs."

Moon came from behind the clouds brilliantly lighting the path. The snow sparkled with a million diamonds illuminating the forms of Wings Spread Wide and two white deer treading so lightly upon the path, that they left no tracks in the mid-winter snow.

The two deer trotted over to her and rubbed their muzzles against her cheeks, sniffing and licking her until she laughed from the playful tickling. A feeling of comfort and peace spread throughout Katie's being, and she hugged the animals with tears of joy streaming down her face. The deer shifted shape, and she found herself embracing her parents. Her mother, Maureen, gently rocked Katie and hummed the tender forgotten lullaby from so long ago.

"It has been so hard, Ma. So hard. Will it never end?"

Her mother hugged her tighter as Wings Spread Wide, or was it another who spoke?

She spoke strangely, gently, "Your path stretches on, though many will veer off or falter along the way."

Wings Spread Wide shimmered in the moonlight. Her blankets took on a blue hue, altering into a long flowing robe glistening with a thousand stars. The woman's loving, tranquil gaze calmed Katie's troubled mind.

"It is not an easy path, but it is the righteous one, the path to peace and justice. Your men face a dangerous turning point, and you must guide them safely on. The spirits rage differently in men. It is for the women to help them see beyond the forest gloom. Battles may be won by the strong, but final victory resides with the wise."

Confused, Katie stared back, unsure of how to phrase her questions. She felt her mother pull away, and when she looked, her parents had shifted back into white deer. The Lady who was or was not Wings Spread Wide was gone. Moon set in the West and the forest dimmed.

As the deer walked down the path the buck turned to her, shook a light dusting of snow from his antlers and spoke in her Da's firm voice, "You will find the way, Katie. 'Tis not a way for the Irish alone, nor the British, nor the Seneca nor the Negro. 'Tis a way for all men that must be followed."

"Will you be lying abed all day, Katie dear?" asked Sean as he brushed back her hair and kissed her forehead. "James shipped out hours ago."

A wistful smile brightened her sleepy face, but it faded into a frown when she smelled the whiskey on his breath and remembered the dream.

"Get away from me," she flared. "You breath would make a boulder weep."

"I was out late," he apologized.

"And that is an excuse?"

Chastened he backed away from their marriage bed.

"I needed a drink. You don't understand how hard it has been."

"We needed to talk things through. The drink will do you no good."

"Katie, I tries me best."

"Don't go thinking a little brogue will make me go easy on you, Sean Reddy!"

"But, Katie, I'm making a life for you and the children. You have to give me credit for that."

"If you want praise, die. If you want to fool yourself into thinking you know all, drink. If you want the truth, listen to the one who loves you true."

"What can I do? Mr. Johnson won't listen to me. The men will turn as soon as they know that. What's to be done?"

"I don't know, Sean. I just know that if you lie down with dogs you come up with fleas. We can't lose ourselves for naught but a job. You can find work somewhere. We could go back on the canal. We don't have to lose our souls for the leavings of Johnson's kind. We can get by."

"When I think of Erin, Bernadette and the twins…"

"They are grown. They can do for themselves. We don't have to, and shouldn't try to, keep them with us forever. They need to make lives of their own. They will have a better chance if we do what is right. You know that."

"How Katie? How will we make it right?"

"Maybe the Bishop could help. He could talk to Mr. Johnson and the others and to the workers. They would listen to the likes of him, sure."

Two nights later Sean and a few of the dock workers went to St. Patrick's to meet with Bishop Timon. A more sympathetic ear couldn't be found.

"It is my mission," said the Bishop. "That is all there is to it. The Know Nothings would expel every Catholic from this great land, and the bosses would help them do it if they didn't need the sweat of our brows. There is a chance here to make things better for all of us."

"Thank you, Your Excellency," replied Sean. "They will listen to you, sure. The Faith is strong among the men, and surely God will lend His strength to your entreaty on their behalf."

"God will prevail, though He works in His own way in His own time. We must strive to do His work though we never may understand His means."

The Bishop rose from his chair and gave the men his blessing.

"May Almighty God Bless you in the name of The Father, The Son and The Holy Ghost. Tell the men on the docks to be patient. We will find a way to peace and justice for all."

Peace and justice for all reigned until sunrise.

When the first of the Irish laborers arrived on the docks, they found Mose Richards, a Black sailor from a steamer, seeking to find work on the docks. Sitting on a barrel amidst the refuse of the night's carousing, he glanced anxiously at the approaching men.

He smiled broadly and greeted the sleepy-eyed laborers, "G'mornin' gentmen, Look like it goan be a fine day! Any hiring hereabouts? I longs to feel solid ground 'neath my feets from here on."

"What's dis den?" asked Aidan Foley frowning at the affable sailor.

"Goin' be a fine day in dis fine city," he answered cheerfully.

"And dis is what we can 'spect from Mr. Reddy? Sure as I am Mother Foley's son, I told you as much. Git your black arse outta here, boy!"

"Jus' lookin' to git off de boats and find some work is all."

Foley grabbed a cast off jug and smashed it into Mose's face. He tumbled backward off the barrel crashing into the pile of debris.

"Ye won't be takin' no White man's wages this day," cried Foley picking up a broken carriage spoke.

Mose backed away, delicately pulling a shard of the jug out of his forehead. Blood gushed into his eyes and he dashed down the street with the men in hot pursuit. As the mob chased the man past Dug's Dive another colored man stumbled from the dingy saloon.

"Here's another!" cried one of the pursuers.

A huge Irish worker latched onto the bewildered man and slammed him head first into the wall. The dull thump of his skull against the stone was greeted by cheers from the rest of the mob. The dock worker hoisted the man's limp body high over his head and tossed him into the canal where he disappeared from sight.

Mose ran on looking desperately for a place to hide, with five of the mob right on his heels. The rest of the mob took up the pursuit and the cries of hate interspersed with curses and threats woke even the soundest sleepers in the district, finally catching the attention of the morning patrol.

Mose sprinted to the two watchmen pushing their cart along the canal.

"Save me, boss!" he pleaded. "Dey is crazy."

"What now?" demanded O'Malley.

"Don't be gittin' in our way, O'Malley!" warned Foley.

"Back off, boys," said O'Malley taking Mose by the arm.

"He kilt a man," lied Foley.

"The Watch will handle it. I have him now and will run him over to de jail."

"Ye will do no such t'ing," barked Foley. "We mean ta settle it here."

The mob edged around cutting off all avenues of escape. O'Malley nodded to his fellow officer to go for backup and said, "'Tis a matter for de law, Aidan. I am taking him in."

He pushed past the shouting men pulling Mose behind him. The thud of fists and clubs replaced the shouts and Mose went down. O'Malley frantically tried to intervene and get Mose back to his feet. He was struck several times himself, then grabbed from behind and pulled away. The mob pummeled Mose mercilessly until four members of the Watch dove into the melee with clubs flying. They beat back the mob enabling O'Malley and another to latch onto Mose and drag him up the street toward the jail. The crowd followed along throwing stones and punches at the men of the Watch. Once the battered Watchmen and Mose were safe within the jail, the rabble headed off to find other victims. O'Malley sent out the call for help and went to find Micah at his home still sleeping after a late night court session.

"Turn out Micah!" he yelled as he pounded on the door. "It has come to pass."

Mary came to the door rubbing the sleep from her eyes and asked, "What is it, Hugh? Micah is worn to the bone."

"A pack of bloodthirsty Irishmen from the docks are making for dark town. They be Hell bent on killing every last one."

When she saw his bloodied face she sighed, "Oh Hugh, come in and let me tend to you.

" 'Tis no time. We need Micah."

"Has it truly come to this?"

Micah appeared in the doorway pulling on his boots.

"Call out the guard and send to Fort Porter for soldiers," ordered Micah.

"I sent runners. The men on duty are beat bad, but most should be able. We need to hurry or 'twill be too late."

Micah checked the loads in his Colt revolver, and Mary reached over and stayed his hand.

"Micah, you can't."

He gently pushed her aside and strapped on the holster.

"It is only for show, Mary, only for show."

He stepped into the early morning air shivering a bit from the cold or possibly the adrenalin.

"Which way?"

As if in reply a deep throated roar echoed down the street before O'Malley could answer, and the two men broke into a trot toward the

Commercial Slip. They could see that the mob had swelled along the way as word of the riot spread. The disorganized band of hooligans was rampaging through the street overturning carts, smashing windows and scouring the area for more victims. Micah saw William Douglas and two other men rowing frantically across the river, fleeing a rain of cobblestones and foul curses.

They heard a woman's screams and spotted Sadie and Malachi holding back a knot of men in front of the blacksmith shop. Shouts from the crowd soon drowned out her cries for help.

"Fecking whore!"

"Abomination!"

"Lying down wid dat fecking animal!"

A man lunged at her brandishing a stout club. Malachi swung his hammer, crushing the man's shoulder and sending him sprawling.

The crowd roared and a man screamed, "Stone the unholy fornicators!"

Cobblestones pelted the besieged couple, and they retreated into the smithy, slamming shut the door behind them. The mob surged forward battering the door. Micah and O'Malley sprinted toward the shop just as a cry of, "There goes one!" sidetracked the fickle mob which dashed off after the hapless man fleeing at break neck speed for his life. A gunshot rang out and the man collapsed. The vicious horde moved in and stomped the wounded man to death.

The men of the Watch were staring fearfully at the rioters from down the street, not sure what to do when Micah and O'Malley showed up. Murmurs of " 'Tis not our concern," and "Are we to go against our own for de likes o' dem?" were met with nodding assents.

"Easy men," said Micah. "We can handle this. Those lads have just let themselves get out of hand. They know us. A little show of force and they will go there own way."

"Dey will kill us sure," said Griffin.

"We make a stand on the bridge and cut off the bulk of the mob. They won't be able to get behind. We are rough and ready, and they'll soon find that out if they try us. Are you with me?"

"Aye, Cap'n."

They marched to the center of the bridge and stood abreast of each other blocking the way as the mob reached them.

"Out of the way, Micah!" shouted Corky O'Day. "We aim ta run dere black arses outta our town."

Micah stepped forward, hand on his revolver, with O'Malley at his side.

"You will be going no place but the jailhouse if you try to cross this bridge, Corky."

"Stand aside. Our trouble is not wid you. 'Tis wid de darkies what want our jobs."

"We stand for the law and cannot let you pass. Now go back to work or back to your homes. You will not pass this way."

"Ye be a traitor to yer own. C'mon, lads. Git de fecking Black an' Tans!"

The crowd surged forward and crashed against the line of Watchmen. The men of the force wielded their clubs skillfully and the first of the men fell at their feet, but the throng pressed on relentlessly and drove the outnumbered men back across the bridge. Men went down and their bodies were trampled by the press of the angry mob. Micah stumbled backwards over a fallen comrade and tumbled into the street beyond. A squad of rioters broke off to stomp him when he tried to scramble back to his feet. They knocked him down again as the Watch was beaten aside by the onrushing wave of crazed men. The throng flooded into the streets beyond leaving behind a battered police force retreating from their fury.

Abandoned by the beaten Watch, Micah rolled into a ball trying to shield himself from his attackers. He was sure he was done for. Thudding boots slammed into him cracking ribs and pummeling him into jelly. A man fell over him and the beating slowed and then stopped. He pushed the body aside and looked up to see his father-in-law, Sean, in his prize fighter's stance, battering his attackers. Two more went down and the rest ran off with the mob.

Sean bent down and examined Micah's injuries. When he tried to lift Micah to his feet, the battered man cried out in pain. O'Malley came over to help and ended settling to his knees and staring incoherently at them. A cobble stone had found its mark bounding off his head and onto the ground. Blood poured from a gash in his head, and he keeled over next to Micah. Others were stirring in the remains of the melee and a Watchman came up with the Death Cart.

"We can load them and take them to the hospital," said the man.

He and Sean, assisted by a bystander, placed O'Malley and two others onto the cart and then lifted Micah screaming piteously on beside them. A gunshot rang out down the street, and Sean, noting Micah's empty holster, knew more would be needing help that day. They rushed toward the hospital as the first unit of soldiers arrived on the scene.

Order was restored by the soldiers, but not before three more Negro men and one woman were murdered. The rioters, weary from the battle and facing soldiers armed with muskets, scattered to dozens of saloons to regale one another with epic tales of the day. With the threat of Negro replacements beaten back, the rioters returned to the docks the next day for the same wages and conditions with no further strike talk.

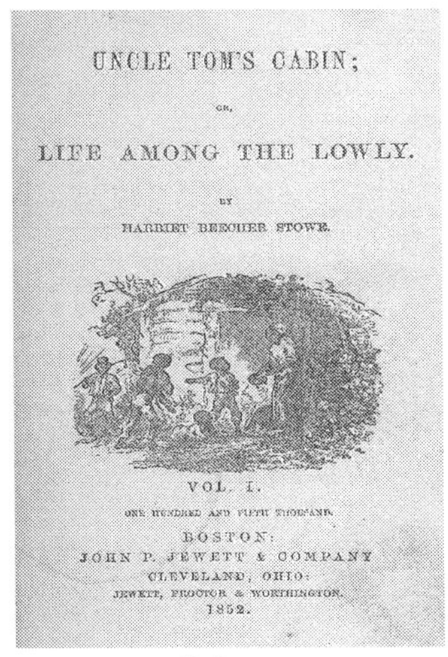
UNCLE TOM'S CABIN;

OR,

LIFE AMONG THE LOWLY.

BY

HARRIET BEECHER STOWE.

VOL. I.

ONE HUNDRED AND FIFTH THOUSAND.

BOSTON:

JOHN P. JEWETT & COMPANY

CLEVELAND, OHIO:

JEWETT, PROCTOR & WORTHINGTON.

1852.

20

THE PATH TO WAR

Malachi and Sadie crossed into Canada the next night. Soon other Negroes joined them not to flee slavery but to escape the bigotry and hatred of those who would set them free. Arrests were made for the assault on Micah and other officers, but none for the Negroes slaughtered by the mob. The small but strong African American community of earlier times retreated unto itself with many abandoning the city for safer environs with only transients left to fill their place. Escaped slaves still made their way to the city, but only as a stop on the way to Canada. Professional men of color became a rarity in the city, and the promise of equality faded from view. Like the Seneca before them, the Negroes of The Niagara Frontier were swept aside by a wave of White immigrants.

The march toward freedom in the city, and the country as a whole, was slowed by many pitfalls and snares along the way. Noble Northern sentiments were riddled with dark prejudices. The same reformers, who prattled sanctimoniously against the evils of slavery, declared the natural superiority of the White Race, sought a permanent solution to the Indians impeding the Westward expansion and called for keeping the Black man in his place.

As the country and its troubles expanded, so also did the Reddy Clan expand. Bernadette married Tommy Hennessy in the spring of 1858 and sailed on James' ship to Cleveland where the newlyweds disembarked to join a wagon train bound for the new state of California. It was months before Katie heard that they had arrived safely, were settled by the port of San Francisco and expecting their first child.

Late on a Saturday afternoon in August of the following year, Micah and Mary showed up at the Reddy home with Micah's young cousin fresh from New York after a long perilous journey from Ireland the previous autumn. Katie, Margaret, Cara and Erin were outside washing clothes in the warm afternoon sun chatting amiably as they beat and scrubbed the week's laundry, oblivious to the approach of the others amidst the bustle of the busy city street.

"And don't you two look a sight," laughed Mary.

Katie straightened up and frowned at her eldest daughter.

"And what is wrong with honest women doing a little honest work by the light of the day?" she asked pointedly.

"Micah's cousin has come at last, Ma."

Katie noticed the young man smiling at her. She brushed a stray wisp of her silver hair from her forehead and smiled at the young man.

"Oh my," said Erin untying her apron, wiping soap suds from her reddened hands and straightening her gingham dress.

Micah stepped forward and said formally, "Mrs. Reddy may I present my cousin Johnny Curly."

"It is a pleasure to meet you Mrs. Reddy," said Johnny with a slight bow.

"Now none of that," said Katie. "Any family of Micah's is family of ours. This is my friend Mrs. O'Connor, my daughter-in-law Margaret and my daughter Erin."

The women nodded and curtsied slightly and said "A pleasure, sir," as each was introduced.

Johnny Curly, standing a half a foot taller than Erin, returned the women's nods and, staring into Erin's eyes and flashing a brilliant smile said, "You never told me they were so lovely, Micah."

Erin blushed and stammered, "Ah go on with your blarney."

"Would you step out with us, Erin?" asked Micah. "We thought we would take in the new play."

"And what play is that?" asked Katie.

"The one everyone is talking about, Ma. 'Uncle Tom's Cabin'. The traveling company has played in New York, Boston and across the state."

"We should all go," said Katie. "Sean has been promising to take me and today is as good a day as any. We can finish up here and be ready by seven."

"It is agreed then," said Micah. "We will be back at seven to pick you up."

Johnny looked directly at Erin tipped his hat and said, "I look forward to seeing you this evening."

As the women turned back to the task at hand, Cara said, "Nice looking lad. We must be getting old, Katie. Seems he only had eyes for the bonnie Erin."

"So I noticed," said Katie eyeing Erin appraisingly.

Margaret teased, "Now what would a fine young man like Johnny see in such a plain thing as Erin?"

"Those eyes had the divil in them," sighed Erin watching his cocky walk down the street. "They could peer into your very soul."

The other women exchanged knowing looks.

"Back to work," said Katie. "We will need time to wash the day out of our hair and put the rose back in our cheeks."

Erin wrung out a shirt and hung it on the line absently humming a lively tune under her breath and danced a few steps. Katie laughed, took her arm and soon all of the women were singing and dancing in the warm sun.

The family filled two short rows up front along the side of the theater and talked excitedly as they waited for the performance to begin. Johnny regaled the group with tales of his voyage and long cold winter in New York.

"It were pouring rain on the wharf, and I was afraid me harp would get ruined so I made for a open door to check the bag. A small man with a tall hat was standing in the doorway smoking a cigar big enough to tip him forward in a stiff wind.

"I dashed in and he pointed his cigar at me and asks, "Just off the boat?"

"I nods and the water pouring off me hat douses dat huge cigar."

The party laughed boisterously.

"What did he do?" gasped Erin.

He licked his lips, stared at de soaked cigar and den looked me in de eye and says calm as you like, "Ye ain't 'spozed to bring the ocean ashore. Dere's laws agin it."

Erin stared at him wide-eyed saying, "No?"

"As God is my witness," he swore blessing himself.

"Well, what did you say?"

"I tried to brush de water from his coat and sputtered how sorry I was."

Erin started giggling uncontrollably.

"The man rolls his eyes and looks up at me like I was taken by de fairies. I saw I wasn't doing no good, so I just backed away into de rain."

"Not a grand start you're havin' in Amerikay, are ye lad?" says he. "Do ye have work?"

"No, sir," says I. "I'm for de west to find me family."

"Can you play that?" he asks pointing at me harp.

"As good as any," says I. "This was me fahder's fahder. He hid it under the thatch during the day so de Black and Tans wouldna' find it and brought it out at night to teach me the old songs."

"Then you have found work," says he.

"During de cold winter I slept in back o' de saloon during de day and played every night earning me fare to Buffalo and a little to spare to keep me 'til I find work here."

"Erin has a fine voice," said Sean. "You should bring the harp over after, and we can hear a little music from the old sod."

"I'd be proud," said Johnny earnestly.

The ushers walked down the aisle dimming the lanterns and the Reddy's joined the rest of the audience applauding the rise of the curtain. The applause died down to be replaced by gasps of wonder and delight as the stage lights rose revealing an idyllic plantation home. Uncle Tom and other slaves sang happily as they went about their chores. The slaves broke into cheers when a carriage drawn by two white horses bearing the master, Mr. Shelby and his wife, drove onto the stage.

"Oh my," gasped Erin.

"Will you look at that," said Johnny.

Completely engrossed in the melodrama, the audience cheered and booed throughout the play. Only Johnny noticed when Erin hid her face in his shoulder as Eliza escaped across the Ohio River by jumping from one ice flow to another. He took in the scent of her perfumed hair and lightly put his arm around her. A tap on the back of his head from Katie showed that someone had been paying attention after all, and he sheepishly withdrew his arm.

Katie pulled back from him, leaned forward in her seat and watched transfixed as the plot thickened. She sat upright, shocked, when the slave owner, Mrs. Sinclair, denied Uncle Tom's freedom saying:

"Now, I'm principled against emancipating, in any case. Keep a negro under the care of a master, and he does well enough, and is respectable; but set them free, and they get lazy, and won't work, and take to drinking, and go all down to be mean, worthless fellows. I've seen it tried, hundreds of times. It's no favor to set them free."

Astonished by the number of affirming nods and comments from the audiences, she hissed to Johnny, "What a horrid thing to say. I can't believe there are so many who could agree with her."

"Maybe 'tis true. I never met a colored."

"What?"

"Don't get your Irish up. I am just saying I do na' have ha' anyt'ing to go on, but what others say."

She leaned away from him, muttering, " 'Tis what the British say about us. Do you think that is the truth?"

"Some I've met do na' take to de work but take to de drink, sure enough."

"You are impossible!"

They sat in silence amidst the gasps and sobs of the audience as the tragedy unfolded before their eyes. Johnny stole sideways glances at Erin trying to think of a way to recover from his blunder. His response to the question of slavery was ill-informed but honest. He had seen Negroes in New York, but never paid any attention to them. He truly did not know them at all. In fact he did not know any but the Irish. He had been met by an Irishman at the dock, had worked in an

Irish saloon, lived in an Irish slum and booked passage on the canal with an Irish crew.

Erin started weeping quietly as Uncle Tom, beaten senseless by Simon Legree, lay dying on stage. When the next scene revealed little Eva, robed in white, soaring upward toward sun-tinted clouds on the back of a white dove with her hands extended in benediction over the kneeling St. Clare and Uncle Tom, Erin burst into loud uncontrolled bawling. Wracked by sobs she leaned on Johnny's shoulder, withdrew her handkerchief from her sleeve and blew her nose, blubbering the whole time. Johnny turned around nervously to see if Katie was watching and saw that she was weeping on Sean's shoulder. He smiled and slipped his arm around Erin brushing her hair away from her tear streaked face with his other hand.

"Dere, dere. 'Tis only a make believe."

"I, know," she whimpered. "You have to understand, you have to know now."

"I do."

She smiled up at him, and smiling happily back he drew her close.

"Ow!" he exclaimed as Katie rapped him on the back of the head with her knuckle.

Katie smiled as she cut up a banger and arranged it on the tray alongside the cheddar slices. The aroma of the sausage and cheese drew Sean to the table and Katie slapped his hand when he reached for a piece.

"Enough of that! You will wait for the Curlys."

"Am I not the master of this house?"

"Aye, that you are, and I am the mistress. You'll do as you are told for you ain't de massuh an' I ain't l'il Topsy!"

"Yowzum," he replied shuffling away like Uncle Tom.

"Wasn't that a wonder?"

"It was something to see."

"They spared no expense. The scenery, the gunfire, the bloodhounds. Why it was just as though we were there."

"Every man, woman and child should see it. Then they would know what an Evil infects this great land."

Erin came into the kitchen and spun around.

"How do I look?"

"I've never seen you prettier," beamed Sean.

She stood on tiptoes and kissed his balding head, ran over to give Katie a hug and hurried over to peer out the window.

"Oh, my!" she exclaimed jumping back from the window.

Johnny stood outside staring whimsically back at her. She hurried back through the kitchen, pursued by a loud banging on the front door, cradling her head in her hands and muttering incomprehensively .

"And what is that all about?" asked Sean as he went to welcome their guests.

Katie rolled her eyes and tapped her forehead.

"How can you be so blind?"

He stopped in his tracks and asked, "What?"

"Erin - Fancies – Johnny - you eedjit!"

"For true? I didn't think she'd ever fancy anyone."

"Get the door, you old fool," she sighed wiping her hands on her apron and hanging it on a nail.

Micah, Mary, Terence and Johnny came in nosily and exchanged greetings once again.

"We brought Terence along to hear Johnny," said Mary. "No school for him in the morning."

Johnny set his harp down and absently thanked Katie for inviting him while he looked around for Erin. The door crashed open once more and Danny and Michael barged in brandishing a jug and a couple of growlers.

"A drink all around," called Michael pouring out the beer and raising his glass.

"Wait, where is Erin?" asked Mary.

"Come show yourself, Lass," said Michael. "No point in fussing over your homely self!"

"Michael!" hissed Katie.

"I'm just thirsty is all. She's my own dear sister and I love her and her giant's feet. I don't think ol' Johnny Curly cares much about her big feet."

Erin flew red-faced out of the back and planted her foot squarely on his bottom.

"There's a big foot for ye!" she yelled.

"Careful. Lass. I almost spilled me beer!"

She kicked wildly at him again and he dodged to the side.

"That's enough you two," warned Sean. "Now a toast."

"Let me Da," cut in Michael. "Here's to a long life and a merry one. A quick death and an easy one.

He smiled at Erin and continued, "A pretty girl and an honest one. A cold pint and another one!"

Erin sighed in exasperation and the room erupted in laughter. The thirsty company drained their glasses holding them out for more.

A few more drinks and a few bites to eat enlivened the happy home. Sean looked contentedly around the room and spied the harp leaning against the wall.

" 'Tis time for a tune from the old sod I'm thinking. Something gentle and nice. Show us what you can do Johnny."

"Yes, please," put in the others.

Johnny cradled the harp in his lap and gently drew his fingers across the strings. A heavenly sound filled the quiet and everyone waited expectantly. Johnny caressed the strings again, looked up impishly and stamped his feet in quick time and sang out:

Haavvvve yuh evah bin out te an Irishman's shanty?
Where de water is scarce and de whiskey is plenty,
A t'ree legged stool and a table ta match
An' a hole in de floor for de chickens to scratch!

Laughter broke out and Erin shoved his shoulder.

"Get on with you. Play us something sweet."

He shrugged his shoulders and took up the harp once again.

In the merry month of June
from my home I started
left the girls in Taum
nearly brokenhearted
saluted me father dear,
kissed me darling mother
drank a pint of beer,
me grief and tears to smother
then off to reap the corn,
leave where I was born
cut a stout blackthorn
to banish ghost and goblin,

brand-new pair of brogues,
rattling over the bogs
frightening all the dogs
on the rocky road to Dublin.

Erin stared openly at him as he brought forth first lively, then angelic tunes from the harp. Her infatuation became evident to all in the room save Johnny who played with eyes closed as if listening to a celestial choir.

"Not bad for a harp," said Michael. "But a banjo, now that's an instrument can bring the dead back to life!"

"They say a banjo is the divil's instrument," said Cara gravely.

"Just so," beamed Michael. "Brings out all the urges in the dancing gals."

Johnny laughed spraying a mouthful of beer.

"Ugh, men are disgusting," said Erin.

"Don't I know it, then?" agreed Michael.

"How about Johnny has gone for a Soldier? Erin knows that one," asked Danny.

"I don't think I know that one," said Johnny

" 'Tis the same as Shule Gras," said Sean.

He plucked the opening melody line, asking "This it?"

"You have it true."

He played it again and nodded to Erin who shut her eyes letting the melody sweep over her. She raised her head, eyes still closed, and joined in the second time through, her clear gentle voice starting low and rising gently to a crescendo. Dancing plaintively through the ballad, Erin's sweet voice evoked tender memories for Katie. She shed quiet tears for the long ago loss of her Ma and Da at the burning of Buffalo.

Here I sit on Buttermilk Hill
Who can blame me, cryin' my fill
And ev'ry tear would turn a mill
Johnny has gone for a soldier
Me, oh my, I loved him so
Broke my heart to see him go
And only time will heal my woe

Johnny has gone for a soldier

Shule, shule, shule agra
Time can only heal my woe
Since the lad of my heart from me did go
Johnny has gone for a soldier.

Long into the night, the company drank and sang as Johnny worked his magic on the harp and on Erin. Michael and Danny went for more growlers and another jug to fuel the gaiety, and ensure that more laughter and music filled the happy home. As the night lengthened and the dawn approached, Mary lay fast asleep cradled against Micah's shoulder with the two of them snoring quietly. Erin listened sleepily as Johnny gently plucked another lonesome ballad and gazed longingly at her. The revelers quieted with only Michael calling for more drink and more song.

"I have to stop or me fingers will bleed," said Johnny reaching for the canvas cover for his harp.

"Past time for bed," announced Sean standing shakily and pulling the groggy Katie to her feet. "Bishop Timon was in the front row at the play, and he is sure to go on at Mass tomorrow."

Micah gently shook Mary and said, "Wake up, time for bed."

She mumbled sleepily and stretched emitting a loud, protracted yawn.

" 'Twas a lovely evening. How about one more song?"

"Almost morning," replied Micah pointing to the morning star. "We will have only a few hours rest before Mass."

Prognostication is an uncertain calling at best. Predicting the weather garnered high interest in the Almanac, but that often proved a poor guide to spring planting. Many is the farmer who watched as his tender seedlings expired and gave up the ghost to a late freeze. Foretelling the scope and length of one of Bishop Timon's sermons, however, was an exact science.

Micah, Mary, Terence and Johnny arrived just in time for Mass looking pathetically worn from the late night. They tiptoed up the outer aisle to slip unobtrusively into the Reddy family pew. Erin was seated by the aisle and Johnny stepped in front of Mary, genuflected and pushed in beside Erin. She blushed and moved over to make room for the late arrivals. Johnny knelt, hurriedly blessed himself once more and sat next to Erin brushing his shoulder against her.

A thrill shot through Erin, and she smiled shyly up at him. He grinned foolishly back as everyone of the Reddy's took in his rash display just as the Bishop processed to the altar.

He turned to the congregation intoning, "In Nomine Patria, et Filia, et Spiritu Sancti. Amen."

Johnny sat quietly stealing glances at Erin as the Mass progressed. He watched as her gentle lips repeated the responses in her soft purposeful voice. A shaft of red light from the stained glass window lit the tips of her light hair forming a subtle halo around her delicate features. He wondered at finding such an Irish beauty in the wilds of Amerikay. Erin slid her hand over and laid it atop his, and the thrill ran through him this time. She withdrew her hand a moment later leaving a smile on each others lips in its place.

By the Confiteor a reminder of the night's excesses gurgled in his stomach, and Erin looked at him warily. He smiled self-consciously and swallowing a burp, turned his attention back to the Bishop. By the Gospel he was sweating and changing hues from flushed to pale to a sickly green. More ominous rumblings left him weaving on his feet and struggling to control his stomach.

Erin turned in horror when he hiccoughed and the Bishop paused mid-sentence to stare at him.

"Out with you!" hissed Erin pushing him toward the aisle.

He edged past Mary, Micah and Terence and dashed for the door just making it outside in time but not far enough away to cover the sounds of his distress. Katie shot an annoyed glance at Erin who looked back, innocently shrugging her shoulders as the Bishop finished the Gospel.

"Per evangelica dicta deleantur nostra delicta," said Bishop Timon.

Katie leaned over to Erin and nodding toward the Bishop whispered, "You better hope your sins are taken away. Holding hands during the Gospel, Lass? May God forgive you."

Chastened, Erin lowered her eyes and fervently murmured a quick "Ave" for Johnny and herself. Satisfied, Katie turned her attention back to Bishop Timon and a slight smile crossed Erin's lips.

The congregation took their seats and the Bishop launched into his sermon, extolling the virtues of Uncle Tom and Little Eva and contrasting them to the evils of slavery and the slavish treatment of the Irish in America. Sean closed his eyes and tried to listen as the Bishop droned on but soon found himself wavering in the seat until Katie planted an elbow in his ribs.

Johnny, wearing a suitable hangdog expression on his ashen face, was waiting outside when the Mass ended. He approached them sheepishly stammering apologies.

A bleary eyed Michael cut him off, "You should be ashamed of yourself. You'll never catch me wasting good whiskey that way."

Micah laughed in spite of himself, and Mary, following her mothers lead, planted a sharp elbow in his ribs saying, "Don't encourage them."

"Mrs. Reddy," said Johnny. "Please accept my heartfelt apology for embarrassing you and your family."

She smiled at him and replied, "I will accept your apology though the Lord knows 'tis Michael and the drink should be apologizing. We would be pleased to have you visit for tea after you have had time to rest."

"Thank you. I would be honored!"

Micah, Mary, Terence and Johnny parted for home stopping to introduce Johnny to Caroline Baker and her son Nelson, who had only recently converted to Catholicism.

As the Reddy clan strolled home, Erin clutched her mother's arm and exclaimed, "Oh thank you Ma! Isn't he beautiful?"

"Better good manners than good looks," answered Katie.

She paused, smiled and conceded, "He is a handsome lad, though."

"And he sings like the seraphim!"

"He does."

"And he has such kind eyes. Do you think he fancies me?"

"He does."

"But what he would ever see in the likes o' you baffles the mind," teased Michael.

Ignoring him she continued, "And so tall and strong and."

"Give it a rest, Lass," said Sean. "We get the drift."

The weeks slid by and Johnny had become a regular at the Reddy household. Katie would turn around and Johnny would be standing there asking if he could help with the chores. As if by magic, Erin would appear and after a few awkward moments the two would wander off together. More and more, Katie would find herself alone with the chores. She didn't mind too much. She missed Erin's help and company, but she decided she might as well get used to the idea that Erin would be doing Johnny's washing before too long.

Michael and Danny had left their days of schooling and shoveling grain behind. Choosing divergent paths suited to their talents the young men were making a place for themselves in the young city. Michael ever on the lookout for adventure joined the Watch proudly displaying his symbols of office, the tin star and billy club. Katie gave him Da's shillelagh in place of the billy, and Sean had passed on the prize fighting training McShane had given him so long ago. Micah demonstrated the superiority of the shillelagh over the billy club and Michael soon became a welcome fixture in the district.

Danny's academic propensity led him down a different path. He and Katie spent a great deal of time with Father Hines at St. Joseph's Male Orphan Asylum and St. Vincent's with Sister Genevieve. Katie and Sister Genevieve had helped the Bishop convince the community to build the asylum to provide a home and trade school for the orphans of Buffalo. She and Danny taught reading, writing and ciphering in the evenings to the orphans in the financially strapped institutions. During the days they were both occupied with the mundane pursuits of life in the city, she at the boarding house and he studying medicine at The Buffalo Medical College.

Michael studied the fine art of police work, tracking down and subduing miscreants while Danny studied the art of reassembling the subdued. Both choosing skills that would soon be called upon as the decade ebbed and the march toward war accelerated. Erin and Johnny spent every spare moment together and everyone sensed a wedding looming on the horizon for the Reddy family.

21

THINGS FALL APART

"Did you ever hear of such a thing?" Sean asked setting the paper aside and looking across at Katie.

"It had to be expected."

"Attacking a federal arsenal? Planning to arm the slaves? 'Tis madness."

"Just the same."

"No, 'tis not just the same. Soldiers were killed over this."

"And what of Bloody Kansas? How many people died there?"

"Fools. We elect fools. Three years since Sumner was almost clubbed to death with a cane on the very floor of the United States Senate, and still no one will come to their senses?"

"Keeping men in slavery is a sin and it must be done away with."

"Aye, but at what cost? The boys on the docks don't want to see more free Negroes competing for their jobs, bad as those jobs are."

"Who is this John Brown? I never heard of him."

"Some crazy farmer from the Adirondack Mountains who fancies himself the next Messiah. His men raided a town in Kansas a while back and killed a lot of the southern town folk that had sacked Lawrence, Kansas. Now each side is trying to outdo the other. Bloody Kansas is what they started calling it."

"So he's to hang for trying to free the slaves."

"No, for the killings. Something has to be done to stop this mad march to war. The rule of law is the only way."

"And when the laws are wrong, what then?"

"I don't know, Katie. I don't know, but I worry for our children and the trials they will face."

"Maybe the new President will be able to bring some sense to it all."

"Mayhap, but the South says they will leave the Union if Lincoln shows up to take the oath of office."

"What is wrong with that? Wouldn't that settle the matter?"

"The country would be weak enough for the British or some other country to take over, and the slaves would still be slaves."

"But to go to war with ourselves? Surely God would never let that happen. I will add that to my prayers."

"I don't know how God can keep up," said Sean cocking his head to the side. "He surely has His hands full with all your prayers for the family. We have Sunday, but when is His day of rest?"

"Don't be tempting Him with your blasphemous ways. The children need His help in this veil of tears."

"Ye sound like the Bishop."

"You know what I am meaning. I worry about each of them in their own way."

"Aye, 'tis strange how different they are, and how alike. James lives on the waves, Mary is raising a family, Bernadette marries and walks thousands of miles to a new wilderness, Erin lives the life of a nun and then falls head over bum for Johnny. Then there's the twins. Could two peas from the same pod be any different?"

"True, how could fruit from the same tree be so unlike?"

"Aye, 'tis as if God picked a soul at random, laughed and said, "See what you can do with this one."

"You call yourself a Catholic? You better go to Confession early, for you will surely be spending the whole day with the Penance you are given for your Blasphemy."

On Sunday afternoons Erin and Michael would stroll down to the river to watch Johnny compete in the rowing races. Johnny had grown up fishing along the Galway coast and had been rowing a boat with his father ever since he was a wee lad. His strong back and tireless arms made him a natural oarsman, one to be contended with. He soon found that he was able to turn his skill and strength into ready cash in the weekly races. Cash that a prospective husband would need to start a family.

Johnny was standing by his boat stretching his back with an oar and talking animatedly to a couple other lads from his club. The day was warm for so late in the season, but a stiff breeze blew down the Buffalo Creek from the lake. The wind carried their voices to Erin and Michael approaching along the riverfront walk.

"You're daft, Johnny."

"No 'tis you who knows nothing. Do you not t'ink I rowed against de breeze in Galway?"

"But to bet all of your winnings?"

"I can wait no more. De whores in de saloon tempt me sorely, but I'll ha' no other dan Erin. If I win I can ask her father tonight."

"And if you lose?"

"De breeze blows on every boat in de water. I will win."

"Did you hear that?" asked Michael unnecessarily.

Erin was stopped in her tracks staring wide-eyed up at him. She nodded slightly and shyly turned her red face away.

"Well did you?"

"Give me a moment to compose myself. He mustn't know I heard."

Michael whistled and clicked his tongue rocking back on his heels as he waited.

"The poor lad must have lost his senses."

She spun around and snapped, "Don't you spoil it, Michael!"

He raised his hands and backed away, "All right, all right. Don't get your Irish up. There is just no explaining what would turn a good man's eye."

"Behave and don't go saying anything or you'll be sorry."

Johnny noticed them standing there and called out, "Come ta cheer me on ta victory?"

"Of course," said Erin.

"And to put down a coin or two," added Michael.

Johnny put his arm around Erin and she kissed him lightly on his cheek.

"That's for good luck!"

"I might be needing it," he admitted. "Dey have a lad down from Niagara Falls who is supposed ta be good."

"So should I lay my money on him?" asked Michael.

"You will do no such thing," said Erin. "Here's a dime to put down for me."

"On Johnny or the lad from the Falls?"

She launched a swift kick at him which he easily side stepped.

"You're losing your touch, Erin," he laughed.

"You are impossible!" she returned.

"We will be going against de wind at first but then we make de turn and come back here," said Johnny. "I'll be listening for you."

"They will hear me cheering down the canal to Albany."

A bell sounded and Johnny stepped into the boat to set the oars in the locks.

"Wish me luck," he said as he rowed to the start.

Six boats lined up across the river and back paddled against the current to stay in place. The starter waited until all of the boats were resting behind the start and raised his gun.

"Ready, set…"

He fired the starting gun and the rowers dug their oars in and were off. They stayed relatively even for the first fifty yards, but then Johnny and the man from Niagara Falls pulled ahead of the pack with Johnny ahead by half a boat length. His lead increased as the stiff wind took its toll on the other boaters. He rowed with the strength and precision of a steam piston seemingly unaffected by the wind. Rounding the buoy he had three boat lengths on the man from the Falls, but his back was tiring from the frenetic pace. Erin was screaming herself hoarse as the boats bore down on the return course with Johnny steadily losing his lead. With a hundred yards to go the two boats were even.

Erin terrified that her marriage prospects were vanishing jumped up and down screaming, "Faster Johnny! Faster, for me, ye slacker! Bust yer arse, damn you!"

Michael burst out laughing and then joined in to root Johnny on as the man from the Falls started pulling ahead with only ten yards to go.

"Oh Johnny," cried Erin.

At the last moment, the starboard oar of the man from the Falls skipped across the water's surface causing the boat to veer off course and Johnny glided past him across the finish line. He rowed to shore amidst the cheers of the onlookers and instead of getting out to collect his ribbon, he motioned Erin aboard. She smiled and sat in the rear of the boat while he rowed to the center of the river. Out of hearing from the watchers on the shore, he idled the oars and took her hands.

"Would you like to hang your washing next to mine?"

"What's that you say?"

"Will you have me for your husband? I will cherish you forever."

She looked down at his sore blistered hands and raised them to her lips.

"Of course I will. What took you so long?"

"When? Please say right away. I can wait no longer."

"No, I need time to prepare. In the spring."

"Prepare what? I am ready now."

"The dress for one. I need time to make it."

"Then next month."

"No, no, no. For good luck, the soonest will be April."

"I canna wait any longer."

"You know the saying:

"What saying?"

If you wed when March winds blow,
Joy and sorrow both you'll know.
Marry in April when you can,
Joy for maiden and for man.
Marry in the month of May,
You will surely rue the day."

"April? How am I to wait so long?"

"We shall have a lifetime together."

"Life is short. Forget the dress. We shall marry tomorrow."

"April."

"April?"

"April."

Michael cracked a broad grin and huzzahed when he saw Johnny lean over and kiss his favorite sister. Erin heard him and pulled back shyly from Johnny's embrace.

"Row around the bend, Johnny dearest," she said demurely. "Mayhap you'll get a taste of what you'll be waiting for."

Erin hurried home and found Katie preparing dinner for the boarders.

"What?" asked Katie noting Erin's flushed face and shortness of breath.

Erin blurted, "He asked me! I am to be Mrs. John Curly!"

"What took him so long?"

"Oh Ma. We will marry in April. I am going to start making a dress right away. Will you help me?"

Katie beamed and softly replied, "I would be honored. I'm so happy for you, Erin. He is a fine lad."

"We can pick out the cloth on Monday. I want a lace collar and something bright green or red for the dress."

"What are you thinking? Green will bring the fairies! You can't wear red either, Lass. The dress has to be blue."

"Blue?"

"Like the virgin Mary, for good luck."

"But red catches a man's eye."

"Whores wear red. You've already caught your man's eye. You don't need to be catching any others."

"Yes Ma."

"Remember the proverb:

Marry in green ashamed to be seen.
Marry in red, wish you were dead.
Marry in blue. Lover be true!"

"Oh he will be, Ma. I know he will."

"Aye, he is a good lad and true. I can help you with the dress, but we'll have to ask Cara to help with the collar. I don't know how to tat, and her lacework is the envy of the ward."

"I'll go ask her now. Oh and I have to tell Mary. She will be so surprised!"

"I don't think you'll be surprising anyone with this news, Erin dear."

Winter ice closed in on the port stranding sailors and canallers alike with a season's wages weighing heavily on their pockets and a season's monotony weighing heavily on their minds. Canal Street provided the perfect outlet to relieve the men of both burdens. Hundreds of saloons, dance halls and more disreputable places of business awaited them throughout the city with the rowdiest, vilest and depraved of the lot lining Canal Street. Johnny Curly and Michael Reddy chose to make their living in the midst of it all.

Michael ambled down the dimly lit street listening to the muffled sounds of music and drunken revelry leaking from the shuttered saloons and dance halls. He cupped his hands blowing into his wool mittens to warm his stiffening fingers. Looking over the high piles of snow toward the lake he gazed into the clear black skies studded with the cold brilliant stars keeping watch over the World below. It was strangely peaceful to pause on the quiet street in the midwinter stillness knowing what would come when enough liquor coursed through the blood of the men gathered inside the saloons.

The frigid air seeped down his collar sending a shiver down his spine. One of the greenest of the rookies on the Watch, Michael was given the cold, lonely duty patrolling the dark streets of the district. It was early in his shift. He had made his first rounds and the action wouldn't start until later, so he decided to stop in to warm himself in Hoyt's Saloon and Brothel on Evans Street and catch a little of Johnny's singing.

The door to Hoyt's banged open and two whores stumbled out leading a pair of drunken canallers toward the side door to the upper rooms.

"Damn, 'tis cold enough to freeze off me privates," cursed one of the men turning back to the saloon.

"Now, and don't I have just de place to warm dem for ye?" cackled the aging whore grabbing his crotch.

The man's eyes went wide and he exclaimed, "Lead on, woman!"

The two couples started up the stairs and Michael heard them laughing and falling and crashing on the stairs as they made there besotted way to the exchange of favors.

Stepping into Hoyt's he unbuttoned his overcoat letting the steamy warmth soak into his core. The saloon was dimly lit by lanterns hanging in the smoke filled room. Johnny and a fiddler sat on a raised platform in the rear of the bar playing a lively tune just barely audible above the din. Men lined the long bar, pounding their empty glasses as five bartenders ran back and forth trying to keep the glasses filled. Michael edged his way through the tightly packed tables to the bar and ordered a hot toddy which he downed in one draught. He waved to Johnny who nodded back and spoke to the fiddler. The musicians finished the tune and set aside their instruments.

As Johnny stepped off the platform an attractive woman grabbed his hand and pulled him down kissing him ardently. Johnny disengaged himself and backed away from her, holding up his hands and shaking his head. She looked angrily at him, spit on the floor and dismissed him with an obscene gesture.

"You have an admirer I see," said Michael.

Johnny looked back toward the woman staring angrily back at him.

"Not anymore, I'm guessing. Some o' the lasses get the idée dat I'm singing to dem. Gets pretty warm in here at times."

"I could use a little of that warmth tonight, but the lasses don't seem to take to the tunes of a Watchman."

"Believe me. 'Tis not worth it. The lasses ye see in here are daft even widout de drink."

"Speaking of daft my pixilated sister is like to drive us daft with all her wedding plans. Will you run off with her tonight and give us some peace?"

"Leave off on her. She's an angel and will be my concern soon enough."

"Well Lord bless you, Johnny. She may be an angel to you but she's just a sister to me."

"Ah you and all your talk. You know you love her too."

"Aye that I do," said Michael nodding toward the woman who had kissed Johnny and fingering his shillelagh. "And I wouldn't take kindly to any as would hurt her. She is as innocent as a new born babe."

Johnny leaned forward.

"I will never hurt Erin. For now dis is where I work, but dis is not where my heart lies. It lies with Erin. Don't t'ink your t'rets are worth a damn. Your little twig means nothing to me. Erin means evert'ing."

"Let's drink on it then!" said Michael slapping him on the back and waving the bartender over.

Later that night Michael met Doyle and Daugherty wheeling the cart down the street. A deep freeze had settled on the city and a light snow was falling covering the rooftops, the litter in the street and the piles of trash in the alleys. Only the stinking manure pile by the stables stood in stark contrast to the white blanket, the snow melting in the foul dark mass steamed in the cold arctic air. The men had already loaded one unconscious man they had found lying in the snow.

"Dead or dead drunk?" asked Michael.

" 'Tis Dugan again."

"He will never survive this winter. One of these nights we will not find him in time. Where does he find the money?"

"He works de docks days and his wife works de dock workers nights."

The three men continued down the street and pulled another man from a drift. He stood up, buttoned his trousers and smiled broadly at the men.

"Thank ye kindly lads. Stepped out to refresh meself and musta dozed off."

He staggered down the street and turned into the first saloon.

"Wouldna be inside his head in de morn for anyt'ing," said Doyle.

The men laughed and continued on.

Three watchmen wielding their clubs ran down the street toward them shouting, "Leave the cart and come wid us!"

They left the cart and followed the men to Brennan's Dance Hall where a battle between sailors and canallers was in full swing. A caller, Jacob Murtagh, stumbled out of the dance hall clutching his blood soaked stomach.

"Hep me," he moaned collapsing at their feet.

Michael knelt to aid him and the Captain barked, "Leave him 'til after!"

The officers beat their way into the melee cracking heads and breaking noses to separate the warring sailors and boatmen who turned their anger on them. Soon the men of the watch were fighting a battle on two fronts. Women standing on the fringes laughed and taunted them as they struggled to gain the upper hand. The Watchmen were fresh and beat back the rapidly tiring combatants. Most of the rioters fell back, too exhausted to continue fighting. The captain led the detachment into a determined group ranged along the bar still resisting the calls for order. He raised his club to strike and dodged sideways as a blade flashed in the dim light. He cried out clutching his side and fell to the ground. Michael stepped forward and laid the assailant low with a crushing blow to the man's temple. The remaining rioters scattered and broke for the door leaving the men of the Watch to survey the damage.

Four bodies in addition to the captain lay on the floor with a few dazed men left staggering aimlessly about the almost empty room. Broken glass and shards of bottles littered the floor, but no major damage was evident. Brennan knew his customers well and was wise enough not to have anything breakable in his establishment. Whiskey fueled combat of varying degrees was a nightly occurrence along the canal. He saw no reason to provide chair legs or anything else to use as weapons. Usually the men let off a little steam leaving behind bruises and a few broken bones, with the victors drinking into the wee hours and the losers retreating to other locales to nurse their wounds. The next night would find them all back together laying their money down on the bar and their curses on each other. It was a rowdy but satisfactory arrangement that all considered proper and fair.

Tonight was different. The captain lay wounded propped against the bar while another man lay bleeding out his life blood into the snow.

"Send the girls home and shut your door, Brennan," ordered the captain through gritted teeth. "You are closed until further notice."

"Ye canna do dat!" protested Brennan. "How am I s'posed te make me living?"

Michael grabbed Brennan by scruff of his neck and cast him to the floor.

"Out!" he shouted at the ladies of the evening still drinking by the stage.

"Feck off, 'tis too cold to be leaving," muttered one.

"Out with 'em, lads," ordered the captain.

The men moved in lecherously and evicted the cursing women with roaming hands and well placed kicks.

"Watch ye hands!"

"And after what I done for ye!!"

"See if ye evah get a free ride agin!"

When they brought the captain out, the crowd had already dispersed to other watering holes. Friends of the wounded man had taken him away leaving only blood soaked snow as a reminder. Michael stood catching his breath and calming his beating heart in the gentle snow and stillness that settled on the street as his comrades carried the captain to the cart and drew it away. He glanced at his watch and sighed wearily, realizing he had a long time to go before his shift ended.

The warring parties had gone their separate ways with the canallers drifting down Evans Street to Hoyt's. Johnny had developed quite a reputation as a balladeer and the combat weary men and women were ready for less boisterous entertainment. They crowded into Hoyt's to listen to the heart rending ballads and drink their troubles away.

The men grew surly as the women exhibited their customary reaction to Johnny's soaring voice and gentle harp accompaniment. Pronouncements of praise came from the ladies in the audience.

"Sing it Lad."

"He sings like the Angels."

"A voice to make Heaven sing."

Less refined praise was also sent his way. He artfully deflected the longing gazes and promises of delight that were thrown his way by the drunkenly amorous ladies who danced provocatively in front of him. One had to be pulled away after she bared her chest and pulled his face into her ample bosom. The room erupted into cheers which she acknowledged by lifting her skirt and flashing her bare bottom to the appreciative audience. Her husband slapped her face and dragged her off to more cheers from the inebriated crowd.

The din subsided and the saloon stilled when Johnny closed his eyes and began to croon "Barbara Allen." The effect on the listeners was unprecedented. A few sniffles were all that challenged his sweet voice as eyes filled with tears and hearts filled with longings.

An argument erupted between an overly demonstrative woman and her husband. Shss's and comments of "Shut ye gob." and "Quiet!" silenced them momentarily. Johnny again became the focus of the audience's attention, and the couple was soon forgotten. A loud slap shattered the spell and everyone turned in time to see the man smash his fist into his wife's face. She toppled over backward out of her chair and cupped her face in her hands. She screamed when she drew her blood soaked hands back.

"Ye bloodied me nose, ye fecking gobshite!" shouted the battered woman.

"Bitch, Whore!," her husband screamed. "I'll show ye what a man is!"

He ran across the room and leaped onto the stage catching Johnny, who was still singing with his eyes closed, unawares. He knocked Johnny down and grabbed him by his long hair.

He pounded Johnny's head against the brick wall over and over raging, "I'll teach ye to fool with the affections of a man's sainted wife, ye blackguard!"

Johnny never had a chance to offer any resistance and his head was a bloody pulp before the men in the audience could pull the man off. Johnny lay in a spreading pool of his own blood, his breath coming in shallow gasps. A crowd gathered around him, but none could rouse him.

"I'm going for de Watch," blurted a woman as she ran into the street.

She found Michael talking to Doyle and Daugherty who were back with the cart at the corner of Canal Street and told them to come quick. When Michael saw Johnny lying motionless in the enormous pool of blood his heart skipped a beat. Throwing Johnny over his shoulder, he ran out the door. He gently set Johnny down in the cart, and the three Watchmen dashed recklessly through the deepening snow toward the hospital, almost dumping Johnny in the process.

Erin woke in the cold room. Michael was standing by her bedside shaking her rudely awake.

"Leave off, Michael. It is too cold for your foolishness."

"Get up girl," he said pulling the blanket away.

"Michael," she whined. "Ma! Michael is tormenting me again!"

"'Get up. 'Tis Johnny."

She sat up fear etched across her face in the soft lantern light.

"What is it? Is he dead?"

"He is hurt bad. Come quick!"

She leapt from the bed throwing her nightgown to the floor and reaching naked for her dress. Michael looked away.

"We will be waiting at the door," he said stepping out of the room.

Katie and Sean were interrogating Michael when Erin came out of her room.

"I'll tell you on the way," said Michael as he helped Erin into her coat. "None of it makes any sense."

The family hastened into the frigid night air trudging through knee deep snow toward the hospital, as Michael relayed all that he knew. Erin listened intently unable to ask the dreaded question. She prayed silently all the way to the hospital, begging fervently for a miracle.

Sister Mary Ellen met them at the door and, lighting the way with a candle, led them into the ward. Fifteen of the twenty beds were occupied in the long narrow room. By the window at the other end, Sister Clarice and the doctor were administering to Johnny, the pale kerosene lantern light casting ominous shadows against the wall. Erin ran over, staring helplessly in the dim light, as the doctor sewed Johnny's scalp together with rough stitches while Sister Mary Clarice blotted the blood so the doctor could see what he was doing.

"That should do," said the doctor when he tied off the last stitch. "You can bandage him now, sister."

"How, how is he?" asked Katie brushing back her hair nervously.

"He lost a lot of blood, but I've stopped the bleeding. I can't tell how bad he is hurt inside. The skull was cracked. I've done all that I can. He has a chance if he survives until morning. It's anybody's guess."

"Oh God," moaned Erin.

The doctor put on his hat and coat and said, "I am going back to bed. I'll check on him tomorrow morning."

When he left the ward guided by Sister Ellen's candle, Michael put his arm around Erin, and she broke down, crying into his shoulder.

"It will be all right," he said as he uneasily watched the good sister finish the bandaging.

"You two men help me move him to the bed," said Sister Clarice brusquely.

Michael grabbed Johnny under the armpits and Sean took his legs. They lifted him off the table and carefully laid him in a nearby bed. Johnny was as pale as the bandages and a little blood was already seeping through the wrapping when they laid him down. Michael looked at the sister anxiously.

"A little bleeding is normal," she explained. "The stitching and bandage will soon stop it. There is nothing you can do but wait. You might as well come back in the morning."

"I am not leaving," declared Erin.

"Very well. You can pull that chair over. I'll check back after my rounds."

She took the lantern, leaving them standing in the darkness silhouetted against the window. Erin turned to Katie and whimpered, "Oh, Ma. How could this happen?"

Katie enveloped her in her arms and rocked her tenderly, smoothing and petting her long hair. They stood together rocking back and forth sadly as Sean and Michael looked on. Finally Erin stepped back.

"You better go now. The boarders will be expecting their breakfast."

"They can go without for one time."

"No they can't. I'll be all right. I can't leave him like this. What if he should wake and I wasn't here?"

"You're sure?"

Erin sniffed and wiped her nose on her sleeve.

"I'm sure."

"We love you," muttered Michael.

"I know," she sighed. "I know."

"I will be back in the morning, child," said Katie. "Be brave."

Erin watched as they carefully made their way across the dark ward to the door. When they opened the door a draft swept through and the light from the hall illuminated the sleeping forms of the suffering men. A man groaned, and muttering unintelligibly, turned away from the light. Erin shivered in the drafty room and pulled her coat tight. She leaned down, adjusted the covers on Johnny and then settled in for the night watch.

Slowly her eyes adjusted to the dim light sifting through the window and she knelt beside his bed. Clasping her hands together she prayed to a merciful God to spare him. Johnny lay still in the darkness, his breathing barely audible, oblivious to her prayers. Erin's knees started to ache, but she refused to change position, hoping that her sacrifice would tip the balance in Johnny's favor. Eventually her head drooped onto the bed and she drifted off to sleep.

A plaintive voice woke her, "Miss, Miss, please."

She raised her head and saw a shadowy figure in a bed across the room propped on his elbow looking her way.

"Water, please. I'm burning up."

She rubbed her eyes and peered nervously into the darkness.

"Please, Miss," groaned the man.

She rose shakily to her feet and caught herself against the wall when her tortured knees buckled beneath her.

"By the door," said the man.

She straightened her legs and hobbled to the bucket by the door. Taking a dipper full, she returned to the man and held it to his lips while he greedily lapped it up.

He laid back down and sighed.

She felt his head and saw that he was burning with fever. She took a cloth from the table and soaked it in the water bucket. She returned and mopped the man's head and neck with the cool water. She refilled the dipper and held the man's head while he sipped the cool liquid. When she laid him back down, she placed the damp cloth on his forehead and adjusted his covering.

Closing his eyes his murmured, "Thank ye, Lass. I will tell the Lord of your mercy."

She gazed sadly at the failing man who was so resigned to his fate and petted his feverish head. Released from the mission of mercy by his snores, she looked around at the afflicted who crowded the room wondering at the extent of suffering in the world. She had given no thought to the torments so many endured alone in the dark. Still, it was a blessing that the Sisters opened their doors to them and tried to ease their misery.

Returning to the small wooden chair and propping her elbows on her knees, Erin leaned forward looking for any signs of life in Johnny. Sister Clarice returned with her lantern and moved down the row of cots examining the sleeping men. When she reached the man Erin had helped, she paused and bent low over his chest listening. She felt along his neck then bringing the lantern close lifted his eyelid. She pulled the covers over the man's head and drew a screen around his bed.

Seeing Erin watching, she nodded solemnly and left the room. Erin was surprised that her eyes teared again. She was sure that she could have no tears left. Then, strangely, she smiled. Thinking of the man standing before the Lord and telling of her mercies gave her hope that the Lord would heed her prayers and show Johnny mercy.

Sister Clarice returned and set her lantern on the floor.

"Shall we pray together?" she asked.

Erin nodded enthusiastically and the two of them knelt by Johnny's cot. Sister Clarice led Erin through a few "Hail Marys" and the "Our Father" before asking for God's intercession. Erin recited the prayers optimistically, sure that the Lord would listen to the good Sister and the man who stood before Him testifying on her behalf.

Sister Clarice stood and said, "I see you've been tending to Mr. Kelly. He was a lonely man stricken with a fever from his wounds."

"I didn't see any wounds."

"The horse bolted while he was loading coal and his chest was crushed by the wagon. I didn't expect him to live this long, poor man."

"What of Johnny?"

"He hasn't gotten any worse. There is always hope, Lass. Especially in the Lord."

Erin blessed herself.

"You should go home and get some rest."

"I can't leave him."

"How long have you been married?"

"We were to be married in the spring."

"I am sorry, my child. Stay as long as you wish. Actually having you here can be a big help. There are so few of us and so many of them. I must be off to the ladies ward."

"I will do all I can."

"Bless you child and may God bless your man."

With the dawn came the porters. Erin awoke to the sound of the noisy cart rolling into the room. The men removed the screen from around Mr. Kelly's bed and grunted as they lifted the corpse onto the cart. The body almost tumbled onto the floor but one of the porters caught an arm just in time and pulled the limp form to the center of the cart. He turned and grinned lecherously at Erin.

"'Tis a joy to find a li'l life in dis death hall," he smirked.

"Go on about your business!" barked the sister standing in the doorway. "There are two of the women to take out."

The man frowned at her and muttered under his breath, "Bloody waste of a woman."

They left the ward banging the cart into the door frame on the way past the nun. Erin exchanged glances with the nun who turned and went down the hall. When she looked back to Johnny, he still lay breathing shallowly.

"Thank you dear God," she prayed.

She rose from her chair and stretched her aching back. Creaking cots and low moans announced the waking of the men.

"I needs de chamber pot," said one man.

Erin picked up the pot and turning away handed it to him. Though she couldn't see, the sounds of the man relieving himself colored her face.

"Me next, Lass," said another as she emptied the pot into a barrel in the hallway.

She made the rounds of the conscious men in the ward losing her timidity after the first few. At least half of the men never stirred and many a bed sheet was soiled adding another layer to the stench of putrid flesh and death hanging in the ward. A man began thrashing about and fell to the floor crying out in agony. She ran to the door and called out for help.

The sister looked in and called for the porters who put the man back on his cot where he lie moaning piteously.

"Ye de new lass?" asked one of the men.

"No, my man is lying yonder."

"At least he's a quiet one," he replied rolling onto his side.

About an hour later Katie and Mary came by with tea and biscuits.

"How is he?" asked Mary.

"The same," answered Erin.

"Praise God for that," said Katie. "The doctor said if he made it until morning, he'd have a good chance."

"A chance," corrected Erin.

"You look terrible," said Katie. "You need to come home to rest."

"I can't leave him."

"Well lie down on that empty bed, and I'll keep watch while you sleep."

"But."

"I'll wake you if anything happens. Now lie down."

She went to Mr. Kelly's bed and the two of them wearily turned the mattress over before she laid down. Katie covered her with the blanket and kissed her forehead.

"Rest easy child. "We have done all that we can. 'Tis in God's hands now."

Erin smiled weakly back and closed her puffy eyes.

She murmured, "Yes, Mama," and fell to sleep with a half spoken prayer on her lips.

Sister Clarice came back and smiled at Katie.

"I don't know how you did it, but it is good to see her at peace," said Sister Clarice. "She is a good one. Even in her grief she has found the strength to care for the needs of others. She has been a gift from God this night. I would keep her if I could."

"She has always been a kind soul," agreed Katie. "God has given her a big heart. I just hope it is hearty enough to bear the trials he has put upon her."

"God works in mysterious ways."

"Aye, very mysterious."

Over the next few days Johnny seemed to shrink before her eyes. His skin dried and paled to translucence revealing the blue veins beneath. Every time Erin tried to give him food and water he choked and she had to stop. She gave him sponge baths to moisten his drying skin, but despite all of her ministrations he faded before her eyes. As Johnny lay insensible in bed, Erin turned her attention to the other poor souls in the ward helping Sister Clarice bring comfort and ease their suffering. She washed and fed the men listening to their tales of woe and praying with them when they asked in the cold, lonely dark of night. Many never lived to see the dawn, and she tried to fill their last hours on earth with a sense of peace and purpose.

Katie came every day stealing hours from her hectic life to bring Erin some comfort and rest. At the end of the sixth day, Erin saw Sister Clarice stop Katie in the hall as she was leaving. The two held hands as Sister talked earnestly to her. Katie nodded and looked back into the ward and smiled weakly at her. The west wind blew hard off the lake that night bringing a howling blizzard to buffet the hospital. A chill descended on the ward and only Johnny and another critical patient managed to sleep through the tempest.

The next morning, Katie brought an exhausted Erin a clean dress and talked her into a bath in the sister's private quarters. Soaking in the steaming bath Erin closed her eyes, momentarily forgetting her woe, as she enjoyed the guilty pleasure of hot soothing water. She was surprised to see two white deer come to drink from the tub.

She laughed watching them lap the warm water at her feet. She leaned forward and reached out to pet them. They raised their heads and stared quietly at her. Gazing into their eyes she felt a calm sadness settle on her. The buck tilted his head as if listening to something and left the room. The doe lingered and nuzzled Erin lovingly before leaving.

"Strange," wondered Erin. "I wonder how they got in."

"Come quickly," said Sister Ellen.

Erin opened her eyes to see Sister Ellen standing in the doorway, her face etched with sadness and anxiety.

Erin took her head in her hands and screamed, "Oh Lord, please, no!"

She climbed out of the tub and ran naked to the ward. The doctor was pulling a rubber tube from Johnny's throat. He set the tube on the bed and wiped his bloody hands on a towel. Katie was kneeling by Johnny's bed crying, with Sister Clarice standing next to her with her hand resting on Katie's heaving shoulders. Erin threw herself on top of Johnny hugging and kissing him.

"What? Why?" she moaned.

"The feeding tube ruptured his esophagus and he choked," explained the doctor impersonally. "We had to try. He was slowly perishing from hunger and thirst. He would not have survived another night."

He dropped the towel on the floor and turned to Sister Clarice.

"I'll send the porters," he said.

"Give her some time with him."

Erin would not be comforted. She sat unresponsive at the wake and frostily stared at the priest when he told her Johnny was happy with Christ. She didn't cry again. She didn't hear. She didn't speak. She didn't eat. She didn't care. For two weeks she languished mutely in her grief. Katie was at a loss. Her darling girl had given up on life, and she didn't know how to bring her back.

"I can't reach her," said Katie. "The priest cannot. No one can. What are we to do?"

"I do na know," admitted Sean.

"Tell me what to do! We shall lose her!"

"Bring her to me."

"What are you going to do?"

"She cannot go on like this. "Tis time to bring it to an end. Bring her."

Katie looked at him warily.

"Now, woman."

She went to Erin's room and found her still lying in bed.

"Get up, Erin. Da wants to talk with you."

Erin ignored her and continued staring at the ceiling.

"Up!" commanded Katie pulling her off the bed.

Erin allowed herself to be led meekly from the room to the kitchen where Sean waited.

"The time for mourning is past," said Sean. "You are still of this world and you have duties. Now, no more of this nonsense."

She stared blankly back.

"Do you not hear me, Lass!" screamed Sean.

She stood unhearing and defiant.

He slapped her violently.

"I will not be ignored!"

Katie stepped between them holding Sean back. Erin rubbed her cheek and glared back hostilely at the two of them.

"What life is there left to me now?" she snarled. "What duty calls me? I've given myself to Johnny. Who in this world would want me now?"

"You are still my daughter," he panted trying to control his anger.

"I am nothing!" she cried. "I died on that table alongside Johnny."

Tears filled Erin's eyes for the first time since her lover's death.

"You don't know, you don't know you don't know," she sobbed convulsively and ran into the busy street, not to be seen by them again.

Sean turned to Katie and raised his hands helplessly.

"I just thought I could bring her to her senses."

Oh, Sean, you had to try something."

22

CAUGHT IN THE WHIRLWIND

Sorrow was Katie's constant companion. She couldn't tend to the cleaning, cooking, washing or gardening without feeling the emptiness in her heart that Erin had left behind. Erin had been the most loving of all her children. She had always been a steadfast shadow following Katie about basking in the glow of her mother's love. The arduous housekeeping chores were a joyful burden that provided Erin the opportunity to be with her mother.

As a child, Erin's gentle compassion had brought in stray cats, dogs and children to share the Reddy's meager resources and fill the household with unceasing noise and activity. Her earthly connection, though, lay mainly with Katie. She loved her Da, her sisters and the twins, but Katie was the center, the anchor, the meaning to her life.

There was a distinct fragility to Erin. Despite her loving nature, she had been unable to make a meaningful connection with those around her. Empathy came easily to her, lasting relationships did not. Once fed, the cats and dogs wandered away to other homes and the children ran off to play, leaving Erin to work alongside Katie. Erin didn't mind their fickle nature. She had her mother and the attention of others didn't matter, until Johnny Curly had found his way to her.

Johnny had been the missing connection, the doorway to the world at large. She loved his music, his facile demeanor, his keen perception, his strength, and his handsome Irish face. All this Erin had told her mother, blathering happily as they did the household chores. Katie had listened knowingly as Erin prattled on, and then related the thrill she had felt when she had met Sean so long ago. Mother and daughter had shared the joy of love's discovery and then the tragic loss had severed their bond. Katie had done all she could to reach Erin, but their connection was lost, leaving Katie to wonder what more she could have done. She feared she might easily lose herself to the bottle. If she gave in, she knew she would never break free of it's blessed forgetfulness.

The Christmas of 1861 had been especially bleak. Erin, Katie's loving shadow, had vanished, and the threat of war now ominously cast its darkness over the country and her family. Since Lincoln's election, everyone was speculating how the South would react. Finally, just before Christmas, South Carolina passed the Ordinance of Secession, officially breaking ties with the Union and demanding the surrender of all federal facilities in Charleston Harbor. Shortly after, U.S. Major-General Robert Anderson had surreptitiously moved his troops from Ft. Moultrie, in Charleston, South Carolina, to the more defensible Ft. Sumter. Katie feared it would mean war, and her men would be swept up in the maelstrom.

Her grandson, Terence was the first to bring her the dreaded news.

"It's War!" he yelled joyously bursting into the kitchen.

"What has happened?" asked Katie anxiously.

"It is in the papers. President Buchanan sent the "Star of the West" to bring General Anderson supplies and the secesses opened fire on her and drove her off."

"Secesses?"

"That's what they're calling the southern boys now. Florida and Alabama have gone with 'em and they expect more to go over any day now."

"Lord save us."

"I'm joining up!"

"You will do no such thing!"

"All the boys are joining. We'll thrash 'em good."

"You are too young. Stay in school."

"School? The boys would know me for a coward, sure. You sound just like Ma. I thought you would understand. Your Da gave his life for this great land."

"War is a terrible thing, Terence. You canna go."

He frowned darkly, threw his hands in the air and declared, "Da will let me. He will understand."

Katie watched him storm out of the house and stood frozen by dread. She hung her apron on the nail and hurried toward the harbor to get Sean to stop Terence. She found Michael, Danny and Micah gathered in Sean's office heatedly debating the news.

"Doctors will be needed here as well," said Sean.

"But the boys will need me more," said Danny. "I have studied to be of use to this country. I can think of no better way to do that."

"He will be safe, Da," bragged Michael. "He will be far from the action. I'm the one will be in the front lines winning the war."

"Aye," said Katie angrily. "He will be at the sister's hospital examining your head and tending to the sick of Buffalo. What is wrong with men? Don't you know what it means to go to war? War killed my Da *and* my Ma. You are all staying out of this one."

"Ma," said Michael.

"I won't allow it!"

"Katie, dear," said Sean. "No one is doing anything just yet, but if there is a war, it will be our duty to go."

"And Terence? Do I send my grandbabies to be butchered along with you?"

"Terence?" questioned Micah.

"He came by just now to tell me he was joining up."

"He will do no such thing," declared Micah.

"You better go find him and have it out with him, I'm thinking."

"And what do you mean by 'tis our duty, Sean? You are an old man."

"I can still hold my own."

"Then why do you need me to rub your back before you can get out of bed in the mornings?"

"Now, Katie."

"Will you be having a valet with you in the tents, then?"

"Katie."

"No one is going to war, and that's final!"

She slammed the door on the way out into another storm blowing in from the lake. The four men shivered from the blast of cold air and the blast from Katie and exchanged sheepish looks.

"Old man," muttered Sean. "We shall see about that."

Despite her reservations, Katie was as anxious as any to see Mr. Lincoln speak when he stopped in Buffalo on his way to the inauguration. She brushed her long hair, sighing dismally at the silver streaks that were winning out over the rest. She smiled sadly at her reflection and frowned at the wrinkles brought out by the smile. The years with all their hard work, worry and trials had etched themselves in her beautiful face. Matronly, was the kindest word she could come up with.

"Time will have its due," she sighed setting the brush aside.

She felt Sean put his hands on her shoulders, and she glanced up in the mirror to see him staring lovingly at her reflection.

"You've never looked lovelier," he said.

"You're full of Blarney," she replied.

Leaning down to kiss her neck he said, "And who would waste time kissing a cold gray stone when such a lovely neck is waiting?"

"Get on with you. The others will be waiting."

He took her hand as she rose to her feet and kissed her softly. She sniffed and threw her arms around him.

"What have I done to deserve the likes of you?"

"Must be the luck o' the Irish, Lass."

"The older the fiddle the sweeter the tune," she said patting his butt.

She stepped back and looked him over carefully. She adjusted his collar then spit in her hand and tamped down a cowlick on the back edge of his crown.

"There, we are fit to meet the President!"

The streets were crowded with people on their way to the Exchange Street station. Others were gathering along Main Street hoping to get a close up glimpse of the President-elect as he rode by. Sean had decided they could meet the train and still have time to make their way to the American Hotel to hear him speak. The crowd gathered about the station filled the street, offering no way to get any closer.

"We shall never get close enough to see him," said Mary. "Is no one going about their business this day? Where did all these people come from?"

They stood at the edge of the crowd wondering what to do as more people came up from behind.

"Follow me," said Michael.

They walked back the way they had come and he led them single file down a narrow alley between two buildings. They emerged amidst enormous piles of accumulated trash stacked along the tracks.

Katie put her handkerchief to her nose and asked nasally, "Where are you leading us?"

"Danny and I spent a lot of hours wandering here when we were young. We know what we are about."

They wound through the mountains of trash and stepped onto the tracks a hundred yards from the station where they could see the throng standing in front of the locked and barred doors. Dozens of others already lined the tracks, but Michael led them past to the train side of the depot and into the station. When others saw the Reddys get into the station they crowded in behind. Soon the room was packed way beyond capacity and the Reddys struggled to keep the children safe in the crush of onlookers.

A train whistle blew and a huge cheer rang out as the train chugged into the station. As the train slowly came to a halt, President-elect, Abraham Lincoln, stepped onto the platform to be met by ex-president, Millard Fillmore and acting Buffalo Mayor Bemis.

The artillery brigade loosed a blazing cannonade saluting the President-elect, and the excited well-wishers pressed forward cheering wildly. The official cortege lined up to march between the ranks of military personnel assigned to protect the dignitaries. The crush of the crowd was tremendous, necessitating a squad from Company "D" to throw themselves around Mr. Lincoln and his party to protect them from the enthused mob. The soldiers were forced to press bayonets to the crowd, but soon found they had to raise them because the people in the front ranks were being pushed into the sharp bayonets by those crowding in to get a closer look. The soldiers brought their muskets to present arms and used them to push their way through the crowd, enabling Mr. Lincoln to safely enter his carriage. Others in the crowd weren't so fortunate. Women fainted, and men were knocked down and trampled, suffering bruises, abrasions and broken bones as the irresistible mass surged forward.

The Reddys were barely able to maintain their protective ring around the children, and Micah's shoulder was wrenched out of its socket during the struggle. With Mr. Lincoln in his carriage, the crowd flowed into the street to follow along. Once out of the depot The Reddys stepped aside to look after Micah. A few other people with personal injuries were carried away and some faint-hearted women were being doused under the water hydrant.

"This might hurt a mite," said Danny. "Couldn't hurt any worse than it does now," moaned Micah.

"Might," said Danny as he grabbed Micah's arm, twisted it and pulled it forward.

Micah fell to his knees and screamed, "For the love of God!"

Danny examined the wounded shoulder and said, "I told you it might hurt a bit."

Micah panted through clenched teeth and tried to grab Danny with his good arm. Danny jumped back out of reach. Micah began rubbing his shoulder.

He grimaced and muttered, "' Gawd, were you trying to pull it off?"

"Just a little loving care."

" 'Tis starting to feel better," he said rotating his shoulder.

"Good," said Danny.

"And when it gets back to normal, I am going to tear both your bloody arms off."

The family that had been gathered around the two men burst into relieved laughter.

"I'll take you home now," said Mary.

"Give him a few drams to ease the pain," said Danny.

"A few bottles," insisted Micah.

The rest of the family followed the mob from a safe distance. The brief route that Lincoln's carriage took went directly to the American Hotel on Main Street. The scene outside the hotel was inspiring. The surging rush of the crowd was both frightening and compelling. A fine sight was presented from the lofty unfinished buildings. Cheering echoed from the surrounding roofs and windows of buildings that were filled with men and women gaily attired in heavy winter furs waving handkerchiefs and flags as the carriages passed. Most buildings were decorated with banners and the stars and stripes hung from flag-staffs lining the route. On the corner of Main and South Division streets, the windows of a building under construction were filled with the proud workmen waving American flags. An unbroken mass of Western New Yorkers stretched from Eagle to Court Street. Standing on the edge of the crowd, the Reddys could neither see nor hear anymore of the President-elect. But even louder cheering accompanied by the salute of more cannons announced his appearance before the crowd.

Turning to Katie, Sean shouted over the roar of the crowd, "I don't envy the man."

"He faces a terrible burden," agreed Katie.

"I read that more southern states voted for secession. The hypocrites in Texas even had the nerve to say equality of the races is a violation of Divine Law."

"Twisting God's Word to keep men slaves? 'Tis blasphemy."

"And, they elected a President of their own!"

"What will come of it all?"

"Mr. Lincoln will be obliged to sort it out."

"May God grant him Wisdom."

"Aye, and the Will to use it. We might as well go home. We'll not be seeing anymore of him with this crowd. Mr. Lincoln will have to find his way to Washington without our help."

Disappointed, they turned for home planning to read Mr. Lincoln's speech the next morning.

"I pray he is a good man," said Katie.

"What we need is a great man," said Sean.

"No, said Katie, what we need is a good man who will bring out the greatness in us."

Unlike the adoring crowds that met Mr. Lincoln in Buffalo, the crowd in Baltimore was hostile and intent on causing the new Commander-in-Chief harm. His handlers had him surreptitiously slip into Washington to avoid the threatened assassination. Just eight days after his inauguration on the steps of the U.S. Capitol, the Confederates commenced the bombardment of Fort Sumter and the bloodiest war in U.S. history was underway.

23

WAR!

Michael was the first of the family to sign up when the call for volunteers was issued. He and O'Malley had spent many a night drinking with Fenians at Hugh Mooney's saloon on Ohio Street. Some were for forming an army to attack Ireland but most of the local brotherhood advocated an attack on Canada. Thinking it would be easier to arm the Irish immigrants in America instead of smuggling weapons to Ireland, they hoped to capture Canada and force Britain to leave Ireland in exchange for its return. The War Between the States became the deciding factor.

The Fenian recruiter from New York had finished his call to arms and Michael ordered two more beers while O'Malley stepped out to the privy to make room for it. It was a warm, sultry night and the room was heavy with smoke and the stench of hard working men. The beers went down easily.

O'Malley came back and suggested, "Let's take these outside. There is a fine breeze coming off the lake."

Michael drained his beer and asked "And why would we take empty mugs outside?"

O'Malley laughed and drained his, slamming the empty mug on the bar and belching, "Fill 'er up Mooney!"

The two men took their drinks out front and leaned contentedly against the wall of the saloon.

"We are good policemen," said O'Malley. "Or at least I am. But we are not soldiers."

"An Irishman can lick ten British any day of the week," bragged Michael.

"If that were so, why are we in Amerikay with the bloody British bleeding the life out of Ireland?"

"They don't fight fair."

"That they don't," agreed O'Malley. "They fight like soldiers. If we are to win back Ireland, we must learn to fight like soldiers not brawl like drunken Canallers."

"How do you propose we do that?"

"I'm for volunteering."

"For the Union?"

"The Union must stand. Where else can out people go to escape the tyranny of Britain? Jack McAnally wants to form an Irish brigade. We train together, fight together, and when it's over, we use what we learned to fight for Ireland as professional soldiers. "

"An all Irish brigade?"

"Brothers in arms fighting to free the slave and free Ireland. God surely will stand with us."

"When would we go?"

"Lincoln has called for seventy-five thousand volunteers to fight for ninety days. We sign up at Fort Porter tomorrow, and we'll put down the rebels and be back before the first snow of winter."

"Who wants to be back for a Buffalo winter? It is a mite warmer in Georgia."

The train from Niagara Falls passing along the river blew its whistle and Michael looked up. Standing in the early morning sun with O'Malley, had given him a queasy stomach after the previous night's excesses, and the oily smoke belching from the engine didn't help matters. The train rumbled across the canal and he turned his gaze across the turbulent river to Fort Erie. Ninety days in the union army to learn the trade and then a march on Canada. The Canadians he knew didn't seem a bad lot, but if it meant winning freedom for Ireland, he would do it. It was a good plan. That is, if the rebels or more likely his Ma, didn't kill him first. He was pretty sure he could handle the rebels.

That evening when he told Katie and Sean that he had volunteered, Katie glared at him mute and coldly detached. Danny and Mary sadly wished him well.

Sean shook his head back and forth then took both his hands in his and said, "Well 'tis done now, so it is. Remember what I taught you of prize fighting, be wary, be patient and when you strike don't stop until you have your man down."

"God be with you," said Mary.

Danny said, "I'll be volunteering when I finish school. I am afraid they'll be needing doctors as well as soldiers.

"Ma?" asked Michael.

Her piercing stare left him hurt and confused.

"But Ma."

"There was no need. It is not our fight. They hate us. They knock down any of us who tries to rise up and get ahead. We are less than slaves in their eyes. We are only beasts of burden to them, animals to do their dirt and fight their war. My Da died to save his family from the British. Who will you die for? Them that despise you and the air that you breathe?"

She left her stunned family standing in silence and returned to her wash tub.

24

HARDTACK AND DRILL

The accolades and honor were missing at Fort Porter. Danny had expected a quick trip to Washington, a lively fight and a rapid return covered in medals and glory. In their stead he had found poor food, poor quarters, and poor hygiene abounding. Drill and tedium was the order of the day and cold, broken sleep surrounded by loud, foul smelling companions the order of the night.

Fort Porter could not accommodate the influx of so many recruits, so tents were erected to house the first to volunteer. The men endured the wind and storms blowing off the lake as they drilled and were assigned "fatigue" duty during the day. In the beginning fatigue duty centered on the expansion of the camp. Fields were cleared, foundations were laid and barracks were constructed for those to come later. Situated along the Niagara River on the edge of the city, it was an easy matter for the new soldiers to slip away to the more hospitable canal district where many helpful souls willingly relieved the young men of their money and their virtue. Most of the recruits, having exhausted their scant resources, would come wandering back to the fort, but a substantial number deserted and tried to lose themselves in the crowded city or headed west for safer pastures. Fort Porter became just one more source of problems for the Watch. The bored soldiers regularly walked off the post to create havoc along Canal Street, adding another powder keg to the already volatile mix of sailors, canallers, whores and hooligans.

Desertions plagued the units stationed so near the delights of Canal Street. Some men planned to collect their bounties and desert, while others lost in a fog of bad whiskey and judgment, absconded on the spur of the moment, trying to hide amongst the denizens of the street. It became the primary duty of Sergeant Donnelly, who led the daily patrols of the district to bring the AWOL soldiers back to the guardhouse bloodied but peaceful, at least until they regained consciousness after their interaction with Donnelly. The mix of naïve young men, whiskey, harlots, and murderous hooligans inevitably erupted into a bloody confrontation between the soldiers and the city.

With a tip from a young pickpocket who had seen a runaway private with Eliza Flynn, Sergeant Donnelly staked out Hoyt's Saloon on Evans Street where Eliza's common law husband, George Hoyt ran a brothel above the saloon. After a short wait, he saw Eliza and the private come down the stairs and enter the saloon. Donnelly hurried across the street and confronted the private standing at the bar with Eliza.

"You'll be coming wid me, lad," said Donnelly calmly.

"Sure and I will not be going nowhere," sneered the private.

Eliza laughed and said, "Be off wid ya Donnelly. De lad owes me fer me services."

"He owes de army, and dat's all I cares about."

He stepped forward and put his hand on the private's shoulder.

"Las' chance ta come peaceable."

The private knocked his hand away and threw a punch. Donnelly ducked and laid the man low with a rabbit punch to the back of his neck. He bent down and grabbed the boy by the collar and dragged him through the beer soaked sawdust toward the door.

"What about me money?" screamed Eliza.

"Take it up wid de President. Dis boy is mine."

Eliza's husband, George Hoyt, stepped up behind Donnelly and without warning slashed his face, tearing his nose off and leaving a gash along the jaw to his ear. Donnelly fell to the floor, blood pouring from the ghastly wound. Hoyt rifled the privates pocket, and he and

Eliza fled when other soldiers in the saloon leapt to the defense of their fallen comrade.

The soldiers put together a makeshift litter and carried Donnelly to the Sisters of Charity Hospital where he lay on the brink of death. The private was taken back to the guard house and Hoyt and Flynn were apprehended later that night trying to board a steamer, and were taken directly to the city jail.

When word reached the men of the Irish regiment, they vowed to take their revenge on the murderous thugs of the district who preyed on them. Michael was astounded that the regimental officers were able to contain the men's anger and keep things in check when news of the attack spread through the fort. The officers notified the Buffalo Watch that they had pacified the men for the time being, but feelings were running high and they were not sure they could keep things under control. The next night their fears were justified.

During mess the men of the Irish Regiment were restless. The evening meal was a thin stew and an uproar ensued when one of the men found maggots floating in his bowl.

"Fecking maggots?" screamed the man flinging the bowl, bouncing it off the head of the hapless private scooping the unappetizing gruel into the soldiers bowls.

The private stepped back dazed and the rest of the mess hall staff took to their heels when three hundred bowls of the tainted stew rained down upon the serving line.

"What do dey t'ink we are?" yelled the soldier. "Pigs ta be fed slop?"

"An poor Donnelly lies on is deathbed wid de murdering Hoyt on de loose."

"I heared he died!" shouted another.

"Dey canna get away wid it dis time!" shouted the first.

"As one man, they stood and emptied the mess hall. Captain Byrne called for the guard, but the angry men pushed past the frightened soldiers and stormed off the post en masse, calling for the blood of Hoyt and the rest of the thieving hooligans in the district. The mob of soldiers stormed Hoyt's saloon, and not finding the perpetrator, George Hoyt who was safely ensconced in the city jail, proceeded to smash the saloon's windows and furniture while grabbing jugs of whiskey to fuel the riot. They moved down the street, smashing windows and setting fires, sending the proprietors, pimps and prostitutes running for their lives. After venting their frustration on a few of the divil's emporiums, the men tired and their officers, with a little prompting from the Buffalo Watch, were able to get the men back to the fort. For the next few weeks, the guard was doubled and the soldiers were confined to camp until the saloon owners demanded they be allowed back. Soldiers could be trouble, but a little trouble could be overlooked in the purposeful pursuit of profits.

After many weeks of drill and discomfort, Michael was granted leave to say farewell to his family. Dressed in his scratchy, ill-fitting wool uniform he passed along the canal and through the city to his parents' home. Little notice was paid to him as he made his way through the masses going about their business on the crowded streets. Soldiers had already become a common sight in Buffalo and throughout the country. Camp soldiers were considered more of a nuisance than anything else, even after the sporadic riots fueled by alcohol and boredom.

Micah and his Da had come to visit Michael at the fort, but Katie never came by. This final farewell filled Michael with trepidation. He didn't want to leave his Ma with bitter feelings. He knew he would return unharmed from the fight, but there was always the possibility that something could happen to him.

His worst fears were realized. The family had been surprised when he came home unexpectedly. They were gathered around the table and he saw that a place had been set for him.

"You were expecting me?" he asked surprised to see the empty chair and place at the table.

"There will always be a place set for you, son," said Sean.

He sat down and Margaret took up his empty plate spooning piles of potatoes, carrots and chunks of beef smothered in gravy on it. She set the heavily laden plate down in front of him and bent over to hug him to her breast.

"You'll smother the lad," said Danny.

She stood up and wiped a tear from her eye.

"He looks so skinny and it has been only a few weeks."

"We leave tomorrow morning," announced Michael. "We go to the defense of Washington."

Katie stared unflinchingly at her plate.

"So soon?" asked Sean.

"The rebels are gathering across the river from Washington and brag that they will fly their flag over the Capitol by the end of the month."

Silence filled the room and Michael awkwardly turned his attention to his plate. The family stared at him as he sat at the table greedily devouring the meal Katie had laid out.

"How are the other lads?" asked Danny.

"Most are itching to get at the Rebs. Some has run off though."

"Deserted?" asked Sean.

"The life of a soldier is not easy, and a lot of men are heavy on the bragging but light on the doing. 'Tis best they leave before the fighting. I wouldn't want to depend on the likes of them."

"No, I wouldn't expect so," said Sean.

Michael picked up his plate and licked it clean.

"I best be getting on. They only gave us until seven, and I wanted to stop by to say goodbye to Beth."

"She'd be expecting you to say goodbye before you leave," said Margaret. "She's pretty sweet on you."

"Aye, the Gentiles are good people," said Sean. "They took care of me after the flood."

"Every time I stop by Joe has a good laugh about pulling you naked outta that tree," laughed Michael.

"That's how I came into this world and when the Lord snatched me back from the waters, that's how he saw fit to send me back."

Everyone but Katie laughed. She sat with her head down frowning at her uneaten dinner.

"Ma," said Michael. "I'm sorry to hurt you this way. I have to do this. I'll be back."

She sat silent her head still bowed.

"I love you Ma."

He sighed when she failed to answer and started for the door.

"Make us proud," said Sean slapping him on the back.

"I will be back," declared Michael stepping into the street.

He heard the front door slam after he had walked a half block down the street. Turning at the sound he saw his mother running toward him. She threw her arms around him burying her face in his shoulder and sobbed bitterly. He pulled her face up to look her in the eyes.

"I am so sorry, Ma, but I will be back. I am doing this for us, for our people. You'll see."

She nodded and sniffed, "I know, I know. Be careful. I can't bear any more, Michael. Just come home safe. "

She disengaged herself and before turning to walk home, said, "I love you, Michael, and I will pray for you every waking moment. God be always at your side."

The regiment assembled at Fort Porter, formed ranks and marched through the city to the Exchange Street station. A German band played as they marched proudly past the cheering throngs lining the route. Micah ran alongside Company K shouting to be heard above the tumultuous sendoff.

"Terence and Seamus have gone missing! Keep a look out for them. They may try to join up."

Michael glanced at the drummer boy Newell Smith who was the same age as his nephew. Many a young lad had signed on, some for glory, some for the promise of regular meals, some to escape brutal homes and brutal lives. Naïve as they were, it was likely that Terence and Seamus caught the war fever and had joined as well.

Michael cupped his free hand and shouted back, "If I come across the lads, I will take care of them, for true."

"Keep them safe Michael; keep them safe," he answered slowing to a standstill and waving farewell.

At the station the regiment was crowded onto the waiting train and as the train slowly chugged away, Michael saw his parents looking around desperately for him and the missing boys. He waved, but they didn't spot him in the over crowded car, and his heart grew heavy as he watched them fade from sight.

Traveling faster than Michael ever imagined possible, the train rolled on through the countryside past slow moving wagons and walkers and eventually past even slower canal boats. The hours dragged by, broken only when the train stopped to replenish the wood or refill the boiler. The men talked of the brave deeds they would do, of what some fine lass had done to see them off proper, of mothers and fathers and how they'd send the Rebs a running. The novelty of their first train ride wore off and monotony and apprehension took their toll. Most turned to sleep while a few still droned on quietly as the dark of night settled on the war bound train. Michael found sleep impossible and the nervous conversations did not interest him. His thoughts were troubled, dark and unrelenting. Doubt was his sole companion that night.

Michael was startled awake when the train jerked to a halt once again. The sun was up and he opened his eyes, anxious to return to the sleep that had finally brought him ease.

"Off yer bloody Irish arses!" screamed Sergeant Coughlin.

Michael looked out the window. The officers were lined up facing the train and the men were climbing wearily down from the cars with sergeants and corporals bellowing commands. The men of K company were shuffling through the aisle to join their comrades in line at the Camp Scott depot on Staten Island.

Climbing down from the railroad car, he saw the men of the155th assembling in two ranks along the tracks. The men stretched their stiff muscles and readjusted their packs trying to work out the kinks from the tedious trip across the state. The non-commissioned officers moved through the ranks getting the men in order for the march into camp. There was some momentary confusion when the regiment was ordered to stand down and Company B, C and D were separated and marched from the station. Michael thought he saw Seamus down the line with Company D but he couldn't be sure.

The men in K company milled about wondering why they had been separated from their comrades from Buffalo.

"We was ta train and fight tagedder," complained O'Brien.

"What are dey up ta now?" asked Finn.

O'Malley said, "No reason ta blather about it amongst ourselves."

He walked over to Sergeant Coughlin and asked, "Why were we told to stand down while the rest went on, and what's going to happen with da rest of da boys from home? We signed on ta fight as one."

The sergeant put off his questions with, " 'Tis the fool army yer in ye bloody eedjit! Do ye t'ink dey would be letting a bloody sergeant know what's going on."

The sergeant gave a dismissive wave toward Captains Mc Anally and Byrne who were talking to a colonel in front of the depot and shaking their heads in resignation. The two captains saluted the colonel perfunctorily then returned to their units signaling the non-coms to assemble the men. Without a word of explanation the remaining companies were assembled and marched down the road to camp Scott with a cold drizzle coming down to add to the misery of cramped legs and overloaded backs..

The regiment was directed past the neat rows of long, narrow barracks already occupied by other units of Corcoran's Irish Legion to a line of Sibley tents in the fields beyond. The men eyed the smoke drifting from the barracks' chimneys enviously as they shivered in the cold offshore wind. The autumnal rains had turned the heavily trodden campground into a muddy bog. Glutinous muck tore at boots with every step, and the men struggled to make their way through the mire to the tents assigned to the hapless latecomers.

"Company K, dese be your Sibleys," said Sergeant Coughlin. Make your own selves ta home lads!"

Michael looked at O'Malley and the two men eyed the cone shaped tent rising a good twelve feet high providing more head room than the barracks. Michael lifted the flap and stepped into the slightly drier interior. His eyes adjusted to the dim light. The ground was damp around the edges of the tent, but the majority of the space was dry. An iron tripod supported the single pole that held the canvas. A rusted stove pipe rose from a cone shaped stove along the pole and poked through a circular opening at the peak. Eleven other men crowded in behind him and laid their packs on the dirt floor. With the stove at the center of the tent, there was enough room for each to lay out rubber ground cloths providing a dry spot to spread their blankets out for sleeping. No bunks or other furnishings were provided, and the accommodations promised a miserably Spartan shelter.

Seeing his breath in the cold interior, Michael said, "We best find some wood or we'll freeze our arses tonight."

"Best get to foraging before the other lads, or there will be nary a thing for the finding," declared O'Malley.

Two hours later and the tent was crowded with branches, empty hardtack boxes and a pile of broken bricks. The stove was glowing and the men were huddled close trying to dry their clothes and vanquish the chills.

The miserable men groused as one when the flap was pulled back letting a cold blast from the raw October day into their midst. Curses and promises of bloody murder were flung at the interloper.

Sergeant Coughlin stepped inside and asked, "An is dat how you should be speaking' ta your own Sergeant?"

The men quieted.

"Hot grub in the mess in 'alf an hour. Eat hardy. You've pulled guard duty and 'tis a cold, wet night ahead."

"Why us?" whined Comerford. "We just got off da train."

"Ye kin ast da Lord on de midnight watch."

"Blast de army," sighed Comerford.

"What is to happen to the other boys from Buffalo?" asked Michael.

The sergeant ignored Comerford and replied to Michael, "We are all ta be with Corcoran's Irish Legion, but de udder lads are filling out de ranks o' da 164th. Company I and Company K will be the only all Buffalo units. We won't be seeing much o' de udders 'cept mebbe tamorraw at de outfitting."

"Can I get some time then to look for my nephew? He run off the night before we left Buffalo. I'm thinking he may have signed up."

"We all have ta take care o' our own selves in dis man's army."

"He's just a boy."

"You kin be first wid de quartermaster and den have a look see."

"Bless you sergeant."

"Lay off wid dat. You'll be bringing the bad cess on me."

After receiving his government issue kit, Michael hurried back and dumped them on his bunk and rushed back to the units milling about the quartermaster's hut. He spotted a cluster of Buffalo men from the 164th gabbing with O'Malley and a few others from the 155th.

"Here's Michael now," said O'Malley.

The men broke into grins and greeted him warmly.

"Looks to be we won't be seeing much of each other until the fighting's done with," said Delaney. "Least you boys are all in the same company. We been parceled out like beef at a church supper."

"Have any of you seen my wee nephew, Terence Curly?" asked Michael.

"No, I don't recall seeing him about," said Delaney. "Mostly we been kept to our own company. Haven't talked to many other Buffalo lads until this morning."

"How about Seamus O'Connor?"

"Don't know the lad."

"Isn't he the lad that Engel's men kidnapped a while back," asked Bailey.

"The same," replied Michael.

"Try company C over yonder. They had a couple of younguns. Mebbe he be one."

"Thankee," Michael called back as he trotted toward Company C."

The men from Company C were sitting in the shade of the commissary smoking clay pipes and grousing about the hurry up and wait army.

"Morning boys," said Michael.

"Well looky here," said Madigan. "De grand constable hisself. Broken any heads of late."

"Can't say as I have since I broke my billy on that thick skull of yours out side of Mooney's."

"Aye, ya walloped me good dat night."

"What would you expect after pulling a mean looking pig sticker on me."

"Ah, I din't mean no harm."

"I knew that and so it was just a wee tap I give you to put you to sleep."

The men laughed and Billy May gave Madigan a friendly shove.

"You're always pulling out that blade and saying how you'll trim ol' Jeff Davis' beard, and now we find wee Mikey Reddy had your goat."

The men teased the bejeezus out of Madigan until Michael interrupted, "I'm looking for my nephew, Terence Curly. Any of you seen him or his friend Seamus O'Connor?"

"Haven't laid eyes on Terence but dere be Seamus by de creek filling our canteens like a good lad," said Billy pointing to the creek.

"Thank ye Billy," he replied hurrying toward Seamus.

"Seamus, my lad, 'tis good to find you. You're mother is worried sick over you. I said I'd keep an eye on you and Terence."

The boy stood up capping the last canteen and slinging it over his shoulder. The load of the canteens bent his small frame over, and he raised his head to look at Michael.

"Ah, I'm not a baby anymore, Mr. Reddy. I'm a soldier now."

"That you are, lad. Once you put your mark on the papers you belong to the army until they see fit to let go of you. Where is Terence?"

"He knew you or O'Malley would come after him, so he signed with the 1st Light Artillery in Lancaster. He shipped out for Newport News last week."

"He is already in the fighting?"

"They are where the fighting is in Virginia ."

"God save the lad," sighed Michael.

After two months of training, drilling and tedium at Camp Scott, the regiment shipped out on the steamship "United States" for Newport News where they settled in more substantial quarters at the Union camp outside Suffolk, Virginia where life danced to the strident call of the bugle.

The first inkling of the camp coming to life was sounded at five in the morning. The short Assembly of Buglers tore at the edges of Michael's dreams. He grunted and rolled over to curse K company's bugler, Barry Hanlon, for knocking over his kit on the way past his bunk.

"Watch your bloody clodhoppers, ye blasted Jonah," growled Michael.

"I swear by the Almighty that I'm going to slit your skinny throat some night, and we'll see if ye blow dat damn bugle with your pipes cut ear to ear," chimed in O'Malley.

"I'll blow sweet and low to ease you out o' yer grayback infested bunk, Hugh darling," purred Hanlon. "A fine gentleman de likes o' you deserves special treatment from de bugs and de bugler."

"Dat's better. A nice soft ballad would be nice. Don't want the lice feeling abandoned."

Before stepping into the cold morning air, Hanlon looked over the men huddled under their blankets and shouted, "Yer all a bunch o' shirking lay abouts. When ye hear me call 'tis all hands off your privates and on deck!"

Hanlon laughed and ducked a poorly aimed boot on the way out the door.

"Damn dis man's army," sighed O'Malley.

A few moments of sleep later and the braying sound of Reveille brought all of the men to the bleary eyed reality of another day of drill, fatigue duty, training and boredom. Most of the men tumbled out of their bunks and made their way to the latrine. A few with hardier bladders who slept in their uniforms skipped the washing to steal an extra few moments of rest before Assembly was sounded. Their lack of grooming added a special bouquet to the roll call every morning.

Men arrived at roll call in various stages of dress. A select few arrived with hair groomed, faces washed and brass buttons shined. Others hopped to the assembly with one boot on and one in hand. Coats were half buttoned or buttoned out of order or still being donned as the men fell in for the roll. As the roll call was dragged out by sadistic sergeants, late risers pranced from foot to foot wishing they had taken care of business when they had the chance. As each of the duty sergeants reported, "All present and accounted for," the officer of the day issued fatigue duty orders and the men were dismissed. The shirkers made a dash for the latrines as the rest of the men made their way leisurely back to the barracks to await breakfast call.

Stable Call sounded and the cavalry artillery and teamsters assembled at the grain pile to fill the canvas nosebags for their charges. The men attached the feed bags and used curry combs to groom the horses and clean the stalls. While their compatriots were engaged in fulfilling the needs of the horses, the rest of the men had time to tidy the barracks and grounds or themselves. The most anticipated call, Breakfast Call sounded next and the whole camp descended on the mess halls ready, willing and able to the duty.

Sick Call, Water Call, Fatigue Call, Drill Call, Dinner Call, Retreat and Taps brought order and monotonous routine their lives. Settled in after a few weeks of camp life, Michael and O'Malley hurried through a sudden snow shower back to the barracks. They stomped their feet and brushed the snow from their shoulders before firing up their clay pipes and taking seats on a rickety log bench around the stove.

"Much more of dis and I t'ink I'll go daft," said O'Malley. "Is dere no fighting ta be done?"

"Donegal from I Company says the Rebs is hiding out in Richmond," offered O'Brien.

"Nate told me dey was moving on West Virginny," countered Finn.

"If all de rumors be true, dem Rebs is ever'ware," said O'Malley. "We should be about findin' dem and sendin' de whole lot to de divil. Right, Michael, me laddie?"

"I figure we'll be waiting it out 'til spring in this sorry backwater."

"'Fraid so," said Sgt. Coughlin. "And you, me laddie, got first watch dis fine night."

25

THE HOME FRONT

The winter months had dragged on for Katie and Sean. Every foray into the streets was made beating against wailing winds, wading through driving snow or sloshing through muddy bogs called streets. They were always cold with little sun come to warm their bodies or their spirits. It had been over a year since President Lincoln lost his son to fever and the two of them mourned along with him, feeling the pang of the great man's loss as they worried about their own. No word of Erin or Terence had reached them. Michael had written once from Camp Scott with little to tell other than that he, Seamus and O'Malley were fine and that the regiment was expecting orders to embark for the South. He offered no intelligence on the rest of the family. Little good was happening on the war front. The Federals had been soundly routed at Bull Run for a second time, 13,000 Union men were killed at Shiloh, 26,000 at Antietam and another 13,000 at Fredericksburg.

Regardless of Winter's whims, every morning after the tenants were fed Katie found her way to Mass to pray for her children and an end to the brutal slaughter of the nation's children. Most days she was joined by Mary and Cara for the Mass and the Rosary afterwards. The women would stop for tea, a biscuit and support with Katie before going about the day's business.

Katie poured out the tea and asked Mary, "Would ye check the biscuits before they burn?"

Mary reached in the oven and drew out the warming treasures set aside from the morning's breakfast.

"They look fine, Ma."

"I brought us a treat," said Cara laying a jar of blackberry jam on the table.

"Where did you come by that this time of year?" asked Katie.

"I kept it hidden from himself to share when spring was upon us."

"Well here's the biscuits, here's the butter and here's the women willing to share," laughed Mary. "No sense waiting for Spring to find her way here."

The women buttered the biscuits, spread the jam and savored each bite as they shared the news of the day. Mary recounted the testimony in the murder trial that Micah was hearing and the women shuddered at the gruesome details.

" 'Tis a shame the way them hooligans on the street prey on the immigrants passing through," commented Katie.

"They care not for any but themselves," added Cara. "If it hadn't been for Micah, my whole family would have been lost. They are worse than the divil himself."

The door crashed open and Sean shouted, "Katie! Mary! Are you about?"

"In here," answered Katie.

Micah and Sean stormed into the kitchen and threw a letter down on the table.

" 'Tis Terence!" exclaimed Micah. "He is OK! He's with the boys from Lancaster."

Mary picked up the letter and read:

Feb. 14, 1863

Dear Ma and Da,

I signed up with the boys from Lancaster and Alden and after a bit of training was sent directly to join the unit outside of Washington. They lost a number of men at Bull Run, and I was assigned to Company I as a replacement. These boys is mostly German and they don't care much for us Irish replacements. They is Catholic, though, so we have the priest and the Mass in common.

Camp life is all right. The food is mostly fit to be eaten, but I sure miss your cooking, Ma. Spend most of my time training and I think I know my way around the Napoleon as well as any. Mostly I am a number 1. I ram the charge as we prepare to fire, but I have worked every position. There are seven of us in the crew and we load and fire as fast as any. We marched to Fredericksburg but missed the fighting there.

"Thank the Lord," interjected Katie.

"Amen to that," added Sean.

Mary continued:

We went with General Burnside, on the Mud March. On January 21, the engineers pushed five bridges across the Rappahannock south of Fredericksburg. The night of the 20th, the rain began, and by the morning of the 21st, the earth was soaked and the river banks had the appearance of a bog. Already, fifteen pontoons were on the river and five more were at the ready. The artillery was brought up to the area around the ford. We worked in the rain but to little purpose. Quite a number of cannon were in place, but the next day the storm continued, and the artillery, caissons and even wagons were swamped in the mud. In the meantime Lee lined the opposite shore with his army. His sharpshooters peppered us all day. We lost a lot of horses to the sharpshooters, but no men. General Burnside saw there weren't no point crossing the swollen river and ordered us to retire. We slogged back through the mud with nothing to show but dead horses, ruined boots and mud soaked uniforms. We are back in camp waiting on spring.

I'm sorry I left without saying goodbye, but I knew you would have tried to stop me. I love you both and aim to make you proud.

Your loving son,
Terence

Mary put down the letter and wiped her eyes.

"He's just a wee lad," she sobbed. "What will become of him?"

"The mayor arranged a commission for me with his unit, the 1st. Light Artillery, and I will be joining him soon," said Micah. "I'll keep an eye on the lad."

"And I shall lose the two of you to this madness? I forbid it!"

"I know what I am about, Mary."

"And do the Rebel cannonballs know that as well?"

Micah lowered his head and sighed in exasperation.

"This is a man's world, and a man must do what he must."

"Can't I have a moment of peace knowing Terence is alive without having to start worrying on you?"

"He's me boyo. It's me duty to him and the Union."

"He's my son too! Feck yer duty and the Union! What about your duty to me? Is there no man alive with the sense to stop the killing and dying?"

"Mary."

"With over 60,000 already gone, how can I expect both of you to survive?"

Katie took Mary's hand and said, "Join me in a prayer. It is in God's hands now."

Mary bowed her head and muttered, "Is this war God's will then? Who should we pray to? Who will be left to pray for? What will be left to live for?"

"You've gone too far. I won't hear it!"

"Why does he let this happen?"

"Mary, stop. I went down this road and it leads to Hell."

"Then it's to Hell for me. Who could worship a God who Kills 26,000 boys in one day?"

"That was the Divil's doing," said Cara. "Terence and Seamus are good boys, and Micah is a good father. If they should fall in battle, 'tis the cost of doing the Lord's work."

Mary stood and glared at Cara who stared back defiantly.

"The good Lord is all we have in the end," said Cara. "Don't cast him aside."

Sean enveloped Mary in his arms and hugged her close.

"Sometimes it seems the Lord asks too much of us, but we Reddy's are a strong lot. We shall get through whatever comes our way as a family."

She buried her face in his shoulder broke down convulsively. Micah put his hand on her shoulder and took her in his arms.

"He's our lad. We must help him."

She pushed back slightly and raised her tear streaked face to him.

"Don't you think I know that? Hearing that he was alive was such a relief. I've held back all these months, and then you have to tell me you're leaving me. 'Tis way too much on my poor breaking heart."

"I'll always keep you in mine. We shall weather this storm. Our boy needs us to be strong."

"Mary," said Katie gently. "Life is hard, sometimes bitterly so. When it is, all we can do is try to smooth the way for those around us. We love you and share your fears for Micah and Terence. We will do all within our power for all of you."

"I know," sniffed Mary. "I know."

The door slammed open and Danny stormed into the kitchen.

"What are you all doing here at this time of day?"

He missed the tension of the crowded kitchen and burst out, " 'Tis just as well, I've good news to share with the lot of you. Me and Nelson Baker just signed on with the 74th. I'm to be the surgeon!"

Mary cried out and Katie collapsed in her seat.

Sean glanced to the heavens and shook his head incredulously.

With O'Malley and other men of the watch gone, Micah had to fill the ranks before he left for the war. Winter had the sailors and canallers idled by the ice and the infected district was in a constant state of chaos. Since the immigrant tide had been frozen out by the winter, there was no one for the muggers and prostitutes to prey upon. The marooned sailors, boatmen and harlots turned on each other often killing out of sheer boredom. Every night the dens of iniquity erupted in murder and mayhem and the Watch could do little to control the bedlam. In late September, Micah turned to one of the sources of the anarchy to recruit men for the Watch.

He turned first to James, who together with his first mate and two of his crew signed on as temporary officers who were dry docked for repairs on their ship. At first, James and his men added to the trouble. The canallers and sailors had become arch rivals over the years, brawling whenever they crossed paths and the canal boatmen openly challenged James and his crew of sailors at every opportunity. Micah had Liam recruit Captain Brennan his canal boatman friend, and he brought a few of his colleagues along with him. Both James and Brennan jumped at the chance to escape the boredom of the winter layover and make a little money to boot.

He and Liam had talked over who should go after Terence and Seamus when they disappeared in August, but until now they had no idea where the boys were. After Michael's letter came they knew that

Seamus was ok for now and under the watchful eye of Michael. They decided that Liam would be more use staying with the Watch and keeping things under control on the home front while Micah went in search of Terence.

A familiar face had reappeared on the Buffalo scene, Emil Engel, aka, the German. Unknown to Micah he returned with a company of thirty volunteers from Ohio. The men collected enlistment bounties with the Ohio State Militia and absconded in the middle of the night only to reappear at Fort Porter anxious to enlist with the NY 74th and collect the bounty before word of the mass desertion reached Buffalo.

Captain Byrne, the regiment's recruiter, couldn't believe his luck when Engel marched his unit into the fort.

"Where are you boys from?" asked Byrne.

"I'm Captain Heinkle from Forestville," lied Engel. "Heard the 74th was paying the best bounty and raised this company of good Union men wanting to get in before the fighting's done."

Byrne almost jumped up and kissed the man. With the thirty volunteers from Forestville, his share of the bounty would equal three months' wages.

"What happened to your arm? How will you manage in the army?"

"Lost it to a Reb mini ball at Bull Run. I can lead men with a sabre held high. I owe those Johnny Rebs payback and my boys will follow me to Hell and back."

"You're just in time," Byrne informed him. "We ship out at the end of the month. The 74th will be on to Pennsylvania and from there wherever the Rebs run to"

"Thank the Lord for that," said Engel. "The men are itching for action. When do we get the bounty? The men will be wanting to send the money home before we embark."

"Sign up today, and I can have the cash ready by tomorrow night. Plenty of time to make arrangements."

"Ach, that's good, that's good. These are good men, but most have families who will be needing the money while they are off fighting for the Union."

"Have the men line up and I'll take down their names. Then Sergeant Higgins will take you to your barracks when we're finished making the roster. We'll swear the men in tomorrow morning.

Afterwards we'll issue uniforms and assign fatigue and guard duties while you are billeted here."

"We want to do our bit."

"Good man. Assemble the men and let's get started."

Engel saluted sharply and snapped, "Yes sir!"

Captain Byrne turned to Sergeant Higgins and commented, "How do the Rebs think they can make a stand against men like him?"

" 'Tis a puzzlement sir," agreed the sergeant.

Engel collected the bounties the next day and keeping the lion's share for himself, distributed the men's share the next morning. Two weeks later, his company drew guard duty on Saturday night. As the newest recruits, they were given the duty to allow the others in the fort one more night on the town before they left for the war.

The camp emptied early as the pent up soldiers descended on the infected district for one last night of riotous revelry. Few were expected to make it back by curfew, but the officers were willing to overlook the infraction. They were planning to celebrate themselves. It would be a long night for the district's saloons, muggers, whores and men of the Buffalo Watch, but a quiet one for Engel and his "volunteers" at Fort Porter. They slipped away surreptitiously in the night, taking horses, arms and supplies with them.

26

TERENCE

Along with forty other recruits, Terence joined the unit which had been all but destroyed at Bull Run. The recruits were assigned to the defense of Washington, where they underwent the brief but intensive training with the gun crews. He found himself excluded from the easy camaraderie of the other men of the battery. They didn't deliberately ostracize him, but the soldiers from Company I were mostly German farm boys from communities a little east of Buffalo from Lancaster and Alden near the Seneca reservation. Loyalties and emotions were mixed with pockets of Copperhead sentiments and ethnic enclaves scattered throughout the area. The hamlet of Townline had even voted to secede from the Union. The boys from Company I, however, were out to prove their loyalty and bravery.

For Terence, the unit was a confusing Babel of languages where military matters were conducted in English with the help of sergeants and corporals barking commands and then translating for the men who spoke only a smattering of English. When the men were at ease they fell back on their native tongue, unconsciously excluding the few English speakers. It was disconcerting to listen to the men joke or argue in a foreign tongue and have no idea what was so amusing or aggravating. He couldn't join in what he didn't understand. At fifteen a boy wants to blend into the flock, but in the First Light Artillery, Terence was a bird of a different feather.

When he found himself with one or two of the men, they would speak in English for the most part, but occasionally a phrase of German would be followed by laughter, and it was clear that they didn't consider him one of their own or worse, he was the butt of the joke. He stay focused on his training and soon was adept at every job of the seven man gun crew. At night though, in the gloom of the tent homesickness would sweep over him and he would struggle to keep the others from hearing him weeping in the dark. He missed his mother, his Da, his schoolmates and the cool breezes off Lake Erie.

Burnside was replaced by Hooker after Fredericksburg and the First Light Artillery was attached to the XI Army Corps under General Howard. Catholic and speaking a foreign tongue, the Lancaster Germans were treated with disdain by the rest of the Corps. Little faith was placed in their fighting abilities.

After a long, cold winter subject to poor food, mud and boredom, the men were heartened to receive orders to march for a sparsely populated part of Virginia to take on General Lee once again. General Hooker had little faith in the XI corps so he had them take the extreme right of his position.

The corps' battle line ran more than one and a half miles, first along the Orange Plank Road then, where the road turned to the southwest, it continued westward along the Orange Turnpike, ending about three-quarters of a mile west of the Talley farm. The terrain was a soldier's nightmare, overgrown with stunted trees and impenetrable undergrowth. Only Dowdall's Tavern, Wilderness Church and Talley's farm had open clearings suitable for artillery. Terence and his crew set up by Talley's farm in the eerie Virginia wilderness with III, XII, II and V Corps ranging left toward Chancellorsville. Gazing into the jumbled woods surrounding them raised the hackles on his neck and a superstitious dread settled on him and the rest of the crew as they prepared for battle. The stunted trees and tangled brambles seemed haunted by lost souls searching for the way home.

Ignoring orders, the men lazed about most of the day neglecting to adequately prepare defenses. Rumors of Confederates moving to the west trickled through the ranks, but the general consensus was that the Rebs were withdrawing. Terence was dispatched to find water, and he carried the crews' canteens and buckets to a small creek that fed into the Rapidan River. He found Adolphus Lanz, one of the Altar boys from St. Louis church on Main Street. The two had met during the Palm Sunday procession the year before with Bishop Timon. He was a year younger than Terence, but he looked even younger than that.

"Adolphus," said Terence. "I didn't know you had signed on. When did you get here?"

"I been wit de boys from de start. Saw me first action at Cross Keys."

"Were you at Bull Run?"

"I'll say. I was de only lad in my squad wasn't kilt or wounded dat day. I'm wit de second corps now."

"I hope I don't run when the Rebs come at my battery."

"Aw you won't have time ta run. You'll be too busy ta t'ink of it when dey come at ya. Sides, de Rebs is running. We didn't bother building no defenses at all. Ye can see 'em pulling back from our position."

"You really think so?"

"You can bet your life on it," teased Adolphus as he capped the last canteen.

Terence laughed and said, " 'Tis what we'll be doing all right. Take care, Adolphus."

"Always do, always do."

Terence took Adolphus' spot balancing on the moss covered rocks to fill the bucket and canteens in the water pouring over a small ledge in the creek. The gurgling water and call of a mocking bird were the only sounds to disturb the ghostly silence of the woods. Cheered by Adolphus' account of the retreating Rebs, Terence was anxious to get back to the boys and tell them the good news. They could take their time making a good dinner and get a good night's sleep to boot!

He returned to the gun emplacement and lazed the afternoon away with the crew. The sound of skirmishes could be heard in the distance, but the encounters were brief and inconsistent. It sounded as though the Rebs were being harassed as they retreated. Meier and Lutz strolled into camp leading a small pig and carrying a bunch of carrots they had liberated from Talley's farm. The rest of the men scrambled to gather firewood and soon the pig was roasting on a spit over a pile of glowing coals. The aroma of the roasting pork awakened a hunger in Terence's belly that could not be ignored. He sat next to the fire warming himself and greedily eying the fat dripping and igniting in the coals. Terence was surprised to see the Second Brigade under General Barlow pull out and march down the line effectively leaving the artillery unprotected.

He pointed at the 3,000 men marching away and said, "Looks as though they think nothing much is going to happen around here."

"Ach dey better not pull us out before the pig is resting in my stomach."

"Does kinda leave us out here on our own though," mused Terence.

"No way anyone could get through that mess of woods," said Lutz. "Just smell that roast."

Terence saw a group of officers ride past talking excitedly amongst themselves. Unknown to the men of the XI Corps the agitated officers were heading back to their units unsure of what to do now that more troops were pulled out of the line leaving a two mile gap between them and the rest of the army.

The pig was finally done around 5:30 PM and the hungry men stood by as Lutz cut slices from the simmering roast. Terence took his plate and started eating the pork before he had even taken a seat by the fire. He closed his eyes in ecstasy as the hot salty meat seemed to dissolve in his mouth. He savored each bite and no one spoke as they devoured the unexpected bounty. A scattering of gunfire sounded to the west and then all grew silent. A frightened rabbit startled him when it flashed past the fire. Terence glanced toward the woods in time to see deer bounding out of the woods and fleeing in all directions. A fox emerged fleeing at top speed and more rabbits could be seen charging across the open field.

"What the hell?" asked Terence.

Bugles sounded and a mighty roar of Rebel voices split the stillness of the evening. Muskets roared and 18,000 Rebs charged out of the woods. His mates dropped their plates and leapt to their feet staring in disbelief at the swarm rushing toward them. Two gun crews to their right tried to fire, but were overrun before they could mount an effective defense.

"Hitch the horses!" screamed Corporal Dietz.

The men broke out of their trance and hitched the gun and caisson to the horses and sped toward the safety of the Union line to the south. The Confederates stormed after them rolling up the flank behind. Terence rode the caisson clinging for life as it careened along the rutted road. Bullets whizzed past and soon the clouds of drifting smoke obscured the battle leaving everyone lost and confused They came upon a Confederate unit crossing the road and crashed through the startled rebels before any had time to fire. The whole Union line was crumbling and the Corporal did not know which way to go. They broke through the smoke and found themselves bouncing over the bodies of Union soldiers littering the road. The horses reared and Terence was thrown from the caisson. He landed hard rolling and sliding down the muddy lane. He came to rest against a battered body. He screamed and lurched back in fear from the frightful sight before him. Adolphus lay staring back at him, a look of terror and surprise frozen on his blood soaked face.

"Right the caisson!" screamed the Corporal. "We have to get to our lines."

They hurriedly righted the wagon and climbed back on board. The Corporal guided the horses past the bodies and they pushed on further toward their lines. Everywhere they went was chaos. The Union flank had been turned and the Rebels' frontal assault was driving the corps from the field. Officers were trying to rally the troops, but they could do little to stem the panicked flight. The army had collapsed and the rout was complete.

Some of the fleeing men stopped and rallied on the 75th. Most, however, continued their flight to the rear, followed by horses, mules, stragglers and a few wagons, Terence's crew along with them. The 75th slowed the charge, but soon they were enfiladed with flanking fire from two sides and forced to retreat with the rest toward Talley's farm.

"Prepare the gun for firing!" screamed the corporal when they reached the clearing by the farm.

The men dismounted and began to set up when the 75th collapsed and the Rebels pressed forward.

"Prepare the charge!" ordered the corporal.

"Number two! Number one!"

The men fell back on their training and fired a canister charge into the advancing rebels. Confederate artillery returned fire with canister at short range, and every mounted officer fell from his horse. Two Rebel infantry brigades enveloped the division's front and right. After momentarily stopping the advance with three volleys, the 25th broke and ran. The 55th fired two more rounds and followed. Terence and his crew were able to fire again before the line was completely destroyed and the corporal ordered them to the rear once again. They took flight with the remnants of the corps and fled toward Wilderness Church. They dashed past General Howard who was trying to rally the fleeing men. Holding a flag in the stump of his right arm he tried to bring the routed men into line. Like Terence and his crew, most ran past the general without giving him a second glance.

Terence and his crew joined up with Colonel Brushbeck's brigade near Dowdall's tavern to face off against the advancing rebels once more. The Confederate line was now a semicircle with both ends past Bushbeck's flanks. Outnumbered and almost surrounded, the situation was desperate and Terence expected to die before nightfall. He couldn't keep from crying as he went through the firing sequence again and again pouring canister fire into the Rebel lines for the next hour.

"Number one!" cried the corporal.

Blinded by tears and the thick smoke, Terence rammed the charge.

"Fire!"

Terence dropped the rammer, plugged his ears and turned away from the gun.

"Prepare the charge!"

Terence drove the rammer down the barrel and extracted a smoldering bit of cloth. He picked up the rammer and soaked the sponge end in the bucket and sponged the barrel to douse any remaining embers.

"Bring the charge forward!"

Terence rammed the charge.

Over and over, he went mindlessly through the drill becoming oblivious to the incoming rounds and losing himself in the familiar routine as the day faded to twilight. A Rebel shell hit beside the gun blowing off the wheel and taking out Lutz and Schwabel. The blast knocked Terence off his feet and deafened him. He saw the Corporal shouting commands, but he couldn't hear him. Terence put his hand to his ear and was shocked to find blood seeping from it. The Corporal staggered and Terence saw a chunk of the undercarriage protruding from the man's side as he fell to the ground.

Terence passed out as the sky darkened and the Rebel advance halted allowing the remaining Union soldiers to slip away in the darkness. He awoke cold and disoriented in total darkness. A light rain was falling with only the faint glow from the dying embers of a smoldering wagon and a raging headache to let him know he was still alive. Acrid smoke still hung in the air and he wiped the rain from his eyes straining to penetrate the gloom. His ears were ringing and he could barely hear the sounds of men groaning and wounded horses whinnying in the still of the night. He shivered from the cold and pulled himself to his feet. He saw the shadowy bodies of Schwabel, Lutz and the Corporal next to the ruined cannon, but was able to discern little else in the blackness.

"Jesus, Lord Almighty," cried a voice from the edge of the woods.

Terence turned and saw a torch moving slowly toward the sound.

A voice with a thick southern drawl called out, "Ovah heah, it's the Colonel."

The crack of a musket split the night and the torch fell to the ground. Terence squinted and watched the wounded man struggle to extinguish the light. Darkness returned and Terence bent low and ran into the woods heading for the Union lines.

He struggled through the tangled underbrush tearing his pants on the brambles and falling headlong into the briars more than once. Mud sucked off his boot and he clawed at the glutinous muck in the darkness. His breath came in ragged gasps as the fear and cold drained his last reserves of energy. He took hold of a sapling, pulled himself up once again and staggered forward. A few minutes later he stumbled over a body and crashed to the ground.

"Watch where you stomping about wid those clodhoppers," whispered the body. "You like ta broke de res a my ribs."

"Sorry," murmured Terence.

"You a Yankee?" asked the body.

"A damn scared one."

"Well whaddaya know, Ahm a damned scared Confederate."

Terence reached for his knife, and remembered he'd left it on his plate of roast pork when the attack began.

"No need for any a that me boy. I've already enough holes to suit me. I was hopin' ye would hep me get ta a sawbones."

"I'm not about to surrender to the Rebs if that's what you're thinking. I aim to get out of this alive."

"A Yankee doc will do to plug me up. After all it was Yankee bullets done the damage."

"How far is it to my lines?"

"Not far. I can hear the pickets talking when the wind is right."

"Can you stand?"

"With a little hep."

"My names Terence. What's yours?

"Patrick Houlihan at your service."

"Irish?"

"Bred and born."

"Me too."

"Soons you opened your gob, I picked up on the brogue."

"Didn't know any of us settled down south."

"Plenty of us in Savannah. Hibernians all."

"Pleased to meet you, Patrick Houlihan."

"The pleasure is all mine. Now let's be getting me outta this swamp."

Patrick draped his arm around Terence and the two of them forced their way through the thick brush, creating a tremendous racket. After a few minutes, they froze in their tracks when they heard the unmistakable sound of muskets being cocked.

"Hold your fire," called Terence. "We're unarmed."

"Advance and be recognized," ordered a disembodied voice.

"I have a badly wounded man with me," said Terence. "We're coming forward."

"Slow and easy, son. Keep it slow and easy."

Stepping into the muddy lane, Terence looked around frantically for the man giving the orders.

"Ease the Reb down and put your hands high."

Terence laid Patrick in the road and raised his hands.

"I'm 1st New York Light Artillery, Captain Friedrich is my commander."

Another voice asked, "Ain't the first all Germans?"

"Not all. I'm Irish from Buffalo."

"Just as bad in my book," said the voice.

"Those boys fought hard," said the first voice. "Don't move. We're coming out."

Six men stepped out of the trees with their muskets trained on Terence and Patrick. The corporal walked up to Terence and eyed him closely.

"All right boy. Put down your hands. Who's this Reb."

"I found him bleeding a couple hundred yards back. He needs a doc."

One of the soldiers rested the point of his bayonet on Patrick's chest and muttered, "How many Union boys did you kill today, Johnny Reb? I think I'll save the doc the trouble so he can work on our own."

He probed Patrick's chest with the bayonet, but the corporal pulled him away.

"Leave off there. He might have some useful information. Take him to the doc. I'll let the Captain know he's there."

Two men hoisted Patrick to his feet and led him away.

"You look like you need some tending too," observed the corporal.

"I could use some water, a bite to eat and a warm spot to lie down," sighed Terence.

"Come along. We'll see what we can do."

After a day's rest, Terence was put back in the line with another unit and the fighting continued until the Union Army of the Potomac withdrew across the Rappahannock River two days later.

The First was sent to Brooke's Station to be refitted and pick up replacements for the lost men. After the horrors he'd been through in battle, it took Terence a while to be able to sleep through the night. Every sound brought him instantly awake, ready to fight for his life. The light duty and regular meals helped the young boy process the carnage he had witnessed, and he found more acceptance from the rest of the unit now that he had proved himself in battle. A grizzled veteran at fifteen, he fell into the routine of camp life relishing the boredom and dreading the thought of coming battle. His dreams of the glory of battle had been swept away by the savagery and horror of modern warfare. There was no glory in death, only bloody, mutilated bodies.

At first his mates in camp withdrew into themselves, trying to come to terms with the reality of war. Sunken-eyed, barefoot and dressed in rags some refused to leave their bunks or begged to be sent home. The rear echelon officers in charge of the rest and outfitting camp went easy on the men when they first arrived, but for the army to be rebuilt, discipline had to be restored, recruits had to be trained and recuperating men from the ravaged units had to be reassigned. The officers sent sergeants to roust the malingerers. Men were dragged from their bunks and forced to stand at attention for hours on end. If that didn't bring them around, they were given penalty tours carrying heavy logs or backpacks filled with stones around camp. Men who resisted the minor punishments would be bucked and gagged. This involved forcing a stick in their mouths like a horses bit. Their hands would then be bound and a stick was shoved over an elbow, under the knees and over the other elbow forcing them to sit hunched forward in the sun. The excruciating pain soon brought most men around. When a soldier rebelled and struck back at a sergeant or officer, more strident punishments such as flogging were meted out. This was rarely done though, since the goal was to get the men back on the line ready and able to fight.

Terence was always a dutiful lad, and he made sure to follow orders to avoid these unpleasantries of camp. Some men broke under the pressures of battle and army life and deserted in spite of the firing squad that awaited those caught deserting in a war zone. On his third day in camp, the entire camp was ordered to assemble on the parade grounds for an execution.

The troops were drawn up in two double ranks, forming three sides of a square. The inner ranks were ordered to take two steps forward and do an about face so they faced the outer ranks. The provost-marshal rode his prancing horse between the ranks around the square followed by the regimental band which stuck up Pleyel's Hymn, an oddly lively tune for such a solemn event. Next came twelve armed soldiers who deployed enclosing the open end of the square to cut off any chance of escape. Four men followed carrying the prisoner's coffin and after came the prisoner, accompanied by the chaplain and a single guard on either side. Finally came the twelve man firing squad. Each man carried a musket that had been loaded by an officer, one of which contained a blank charge allowing each man to hope his was the blank shot.

The coffin was place in the center of the open end of the square and the prisoner was seated on the bottom edge. The chaplain bent low and whispered something to the man before saying a final prayer. The provost-marshal tied a blindfold around the man's eyes and read the general order for execution.

"By order of the court-martial, Private Stephen Poliachik is hereby ordered to be executed by firing squad for the heinous crimes of desertion and treason, this tenth day of May, in the year of Our Lord, eighteen hundred and sixty-three. May God have mercy on your soul."

The provost-marshal raised his sword and called, "Ready arms."

"Aim - true, boys," stammered Polchek.

The firing squad aimed their muskets and fired when the provost-marshal slashed down with his sword. Private Stephen Polchek threw his arms convulsively into the air and fell backward into the coffin. The regimental surgeon examined the body and declared him dead. The troops were marched past the open coffin and on to breakfast. Terence looked at the corpse and thought that, "Another man dead, where is the shame or glory in that?"

Due to the number of German speaking troops in his unit, an assistant commissary was assigned while his artillery unit was being reinforced and outfitted after the debacle at Chancellorsville. Terence thought he had seen him before but couldn't quite place the man. The portly officer was red-faced and mostly bald with scraggly mutton chops joined by a full mustache. He glowered at all who came to the commissary, especially the few Irish lads in the unit. The stub of his arm was usually tucked inside his coat in a poorly executed imitation of Napoleon Bonaparte. Once he had appeared on the scene, their rations never seemed to go as far. Terence was convinced the man was using hollow weights to measure out their allotments. The officers ignored the men's complaints since their allotments, particularly the whiskey, seemed to last much longer than before. The shouts and laughter of drunken officers became a nightly occurrence around camp.

When Terence first went to pick up his rations and told the German his name, the man looked up from his list and stared into his eyes.

"Terence Curly is it?"

"Yes, Sir."

"From Buffalo?"

"Yes, sir."

Terence saw the German squint at the list and put a star next to his name.

"Would you be any kin to Micah Curly?"

Terence hesitated. He didn't want anyone telling his father his exact whereabouts.

"And you are?"

"You have the same eyes and nose, I'm thinking," the German commented thoughtfully. "Jeremiah Dietz at your service."

"You know my Da?" replied Terence uneasily.

"An honest man," said the German. "No finer constable in the city."

"He always tried to do his best to bring down the wicked."

He handed Terence his rations and frowning disagreeably he replied, "That he did. That he did."

Terence picked up his rations and left feeling uneasy after the encounter. He was sure he had seen the man before, probably on the streets of Buffalo, but he could not remember the circumstances. He looked back and saw the German pointing him out to one of the commissary aides.

Two days later, just before reveille, the Captain of the guard marched into his tent and turned the squad out to stand in the early morning chill. The captain emerged from the tent a few minutes later holding Terence's pack.

"Who belongs to this?" demanded the captain.

" 'Tis mine, sir," answered Terence.

The captain reached in the pack and pulled out a meerschaum pipe.

"Can you explain how the Colonel's pipe got in her?"

Terence gasped, "I never seen that afore now, sir."

"It was right where I expected to find it," said the captain. "You were seen taking it."

"I never."

"Are you calling me a liar, private?"

"No, sir, but whoever said he saw me take it surely is one."

"Take him to the guardhouse," ordered the captain.

As he was being led away by the guard, Sergeant O'Neil appeared on the scene.

"What's the problem, sir?" he asked. "Can I be of any assistance?"

"It is all taken care of, sergeant. Private Curly was just caught red-handed with the colonel's prize pipe."

"It canna be, sir. Private Curly is me best man."

"Oh it was him all right. He was seen by the colonel's tent after stable call, and we found the pipe in his kit."

"After stable call you say?

"Yes sergeant."

"Yesterday?

"Must I repeat everything I say?"

"No, sir. It's just that yesterday, Private Curly was out of camp foraging with me squad until just before taps."

The captain glared at the sergeant.

"Can you verify that?"

"All these boys was there. You can ask them yourself, sir."

The men nodded simultaneously. The captain bit his lip and hurried after the guard.

When Terence returned the sergeant was waiting for him.

"Seems you have an enemy in camp," mused the sergeant. "Any ideas?"

"None that I can think of, sergeant. I mind my own business."

"Just the same, somebody is out to cause you ill. Best keep your eyes open."

"I surely will."

Emil Engel, aka Captain Heinkle, aka Jeremiah Dietz, aka the German, fumed that his plan of vengeance had been so easily thwarted. His henchman, Barton, had to disappear after the botched attempt. The idiot could have checked his story before he went to the captain. He should have known that Terence was out of camp the day of the theft. Now Engel was left to come up with something on his own. Micah had driven him from a lucrative enterprise and he was going to get even by doing his boy harm. He had used the bonus monies he accumulated signing men up to desert and sign up again and again to set himself up as the commissary and sutler for the camp. Now, he would have to curry the favor of senior officers to accomplish his vengeance. Whiskey would be the means to the end. He visited the officers every evening bringing plenty of the devil's brew to go around.

After a month of R&R, the 1st Light Artillery received great news. In mid-June they were sent north to a sleepy little town in Maryland on the Pennsylvania border. Terence was glad to know they would be withdrawn from the battlefields of the south to be held in reserve in the backwater between Emmitsburg, Maryland and Gettysburg, Pennsylvania. He had had enough of Virginia and Robert E. Lee.

27

THE MOTHER HOUSE

The sultry summer air lost some of its oppressiveness as it wafted through the dark corridors of the Gothic Hall. Emmitsburg could try the soul of even the most ardent follower of Christ when weighed down by the heavy habits of the Sisters of Charity. Sister Mary Brigid wearily removed the stultifying wrap hanging the sweat dampened robe on the hook at the foot of her cot. With perspiration glistening on her forehead, she knelt in her slip to say her evening prayers. The week's exertions had sapped the last of her energy and she hurried her prayers, mechanically reciting the time worn words. The horror of Antietam still hung on her a like foul odor and she began to weep. She wept for the lost souls, the shattered bodies, the senselessness of war and for herself. A wave of self-pity swept over her and she collapsed on the floor overcome by the pitiless world. Her wracking sobs subsided and she lost herself intoning the words over and over as she lay on the floor.

"Hail Mary, full of Grace
Blessed are thou amongst women…"

Eventually she pulled herself up and crawled onto the cot where she lay staring into the darkness. Father Smith had instructed them to Baptize as many of the dying men as they could so he could hear their confessions and ease their passage into Paradise. She and Sister Elizabeth had moved among the shattered men bringing them cool water to ease their tortured bodies and bringing the waters of salvation for their lost souls. The frightened men had looked to them for comfort and she had done what she could. Her works of Mercy had taken a heavy toll physically and mentally. It had taken her years to forgive God for what he had taken from her, and now seeing the savagery of war that plagued the nation, she felt she was losing her Faith yet again. How could a merciful God let such things happen to good men? At least the armies had moved on and she could rest and pray for understanding.

Father Smith had said it was not for mortal man to question the ways of God, "Our duty is to accept His will and follow the teachings of Christ. All will be made clear when we join Him in Heaven."

The Irish in her found it hard to blindly accept what she couldn't understand, even though she knew she must. Why couldn't God be like her Da? He had always explained things to her and never expected her to just accept things because he told her so. She missed her family so, but she had chosen this life, and her love of God was all that she had, and now her doubts were jeopardizing even that.

Strange sounds came out of the darkness. Nights were usually quiet, punctuated by the cries of night birds or howling coyotes, but little else. Sometimes coon hunters could be heard in the hills following the baying of their hounds with the occasional report of a musket punctuating the successful conclusion of the hunt. This was different. At first it was a low rhythmic pounding that was not so much heard as felt. As it drew closer, it grew in volume to be joined by creaking axles, sudden bangs and jingling harnesses. Others in the Gothic Hall must have noticed the alien noises, because she heard sisters stirring in the corridors. The neighing of horses confirmed her fears. She pulled on her habit and joined the other women on the porch. Lanterns could be seen in the distance and the curses of mule skinners drifted across the fields to settle ominously on the Mother House. An army was setting up camp on the grounds of the convent.

"What does this mean?" asked Sister Clotilde.

"Are they Union or Southern?" asked another.

"It must mean a battle near us," said Sister Brigid.

"Maybe they are just passing through," suggested Sister Clotilde.

"From your lips to the Lord's ears," said Sister Brigid blessing herself.

The nervous women shivered in the cool night air trying to peer through the darkness as the army encamped. Many of the sisters prayed, silently wondering what the light would bring until the Laud's bell called them for the communal morning prayer.

When they emerged from the chapel, the sun had risen and they could make out the results of the night's disturbance. The field by the Vincentian Father's house which had been covered with clover at sunset was now a barren muddy quagmire. Not one shred of vegetation remained. Countless horses and mules were tethered to multiple ropes near hundreds of wagons and caissons in the muddy, rutted field. Tents could be seen farther on and what looked like thousands of soldiers swarmed like ants along the road and in the hills around them.

Soon squadron after squadron descended on the sisters house to requisition food and medical supplies. The sisters distributed bread and coffee to the hungry men until they were called to Sunday morning Mass. While the sisters were engaged in the Mass the soldiers helped themselves to the goods, pushing aside the boy left to watch the convent's bakery. The sisters returned and shooed the marauding men from the building and sent for a superior officer. Finally a guard around the Mother House was set up by General Trobriand. The men were dutiful and only accepted food when the captain of the guard gave permission. The guards gave the sisters a breather since they only had the sentries to feed while they proceeded to bake as much bread as they could. About four o'clock more troops arrived taking up positions covering all of the sister's grounds. Officers were billeted in the white house, the priest's residence and in other houses nearby. Unsure of what was expected, the sisters took on the task of feeding them and the other men crowding their farm.

Father Burlando and Father Gandolfo accompanied by a contingent of Union officers arrived after vespers.

"The general has declared Military Law," Father Burlando informed Mother Ann. "You are restricted to the immediate grounds during the day and to the convent at night. No one may leave without a pass. The guards are here to prevent any from entering or leaving as long as the army is encamped."

"Are we prisoners then?" asked Mother Ann.

"We are servants of God, who will use this opportunity to bring comfort to the men facing death."

"Yes Father."

Mother Ann bowed her head and turned away as the officers placed the guards and issued the orders, "Let no man pass here this night."

Mother Ann took precautions of her own, assigning Sisters Clotilde and Brigid an interior watch, lest one of the guards should steal into the convent. The two women spent the night wandering the corridors of the Gothic Hall in total darkness, starting at every sound, while an army of tens of thousands slept in the surrounding hills.

The next day scores of ragged, half-starved soldiers, many no more than boys, appeared at the bakery. The grime of forced marching covered their tattered uniforms and many stood barefoot in the mud. The sisters cheerfully fed the men and many of the lonely soldiers then sought out the priests to make their confessions. Word spread and more and more hungry soldiers crowded the grounds, the fear of death in their eyes. The sisters fed and comforted the homesick and the priests absolved the men, easing their fear of divine retribution. Death walked with the men, and as the days slipped by the sisters and priests did their best to prepare them to meet him. Then one morning a sudden order was issued to strike tents and march to Gettysburg. Within fifteen minutes the men were marching north and quiet returned to the Mother House.

Father Gandolfo, unaware of the army's departure, was halted by Confederate pickets as he rode to the convent to say Mass. Not realizing he had been stopped by Southern troops he responded petulantly to their challenge.

"I'm on my way to St. Joseph's to say Mass. Don't you realize we have General Meade staying at our house?"

"Now, I'm not sure about this," drawled the Confederate soldier, "but I don't think General Lee would take too kindly to you offering hospitality to that damned Yankee rapscallion. What do you think Sergeant Davis?"

Father Gandolfo turned white as a sheet.

"General Lee is a gentman, suh," replied the sergeant. "He respects the clergy, even when they lie down wid dawgs."

"I expect you're right, sergeant. You can go now, Father. Tell Jennie Butts that her Uncle John sends his regards."

"Our student, Jennie Butts?" asked the bewildered priest.

"The same."

The men rode off leaving a shaken Father Gandolfo to stare after them. A number of southern girls were enrolled at the school, and some, Jennie included, had to be kept inside to prevent them from provoking the Union soldiers. Over the next few days, Confederate troops passed through and the southern girls came out to cheer them on.

The sisters kept the bakery going and fed the hungry men the same as they had the Union boys. Sensing the coming conflagration, they readied the Mother House and stockpiled supplies to care for the inevitable casualties. Muttered prayers for the strength to cope with the impending disaster and for the souls of the men, filled the halls as the sisters went about the gruesome business of bracing to deal with the aftermath of battle.

28

MAN PROPOSES AND GOD DISPOSES

Passing through the Maryland countryside on the way north had restored Terence's spirits. The lush farmland, unscarred by the war was a balm to the battered psyches of the men. They yearned to return to their homes far from the ravages of modern warfare. Yet nagging at the fringe of their minds was the need to redeem their pride and prove that they could stand in the face of adversity. They had been driven from the field of battle and all their dreams of glory had been shattered. As much as they wanted to leave war behind, most longed for the chance to show the world that they were made of sterner stuff. Rumors of Rebel movements disturbed the march and encampment, but Terence dismissed them as no more than the fantasies of idle minds. They had left Robert E. Lee far behind and were now safely over the Mason Dixon Line.

As regimental surgeon, Captain Danny Reddy was assigned a comfortable seat in the first car of the train bound for Harrisburg. Upon reaching the Pennsylvania border he got out to stretch his legs and find his old friend Nelson Baker. Danny wove through the scores of soldiers from the 74th milling about as the train took on water and wood. Blasphemous curses directed at the open cars they were obliged to ride, along with boasts of fighting skill and tobacco smoke floated on the warm night air. He found Nelson stretching his cramped muscles by the water tower.

"How are you, Nelson?" he asked.

"Well if it isn't the good doctor come to inquire after my health. I'd be a mite better if I got to ride in a proper carriage instead of on a blasted flatbed."

"Privileges of rank, Nelson. Some of us are looked on more kindly by God and the army. Someday you might be so blessed."

"You're an evil, thoughtless man, Danny Reddy."

"Well, 'tis not so nice as you imagine. We're running low on whiskey, you know."

"Lord save us. To think that such fine men as you officers would have to endure these hardships."

The men laughed and Danny patted Nelson on the back.

"What do you think lies ahead for us?" he asked.

"It is war we are going to. I expect it will be bad."

"Aye. All the newspaper reports are so hard to believe. Tens of thousands lost in a single day. How could that be?"

"Hard to believe, but true."

"Are you afraid?"

"Yes. I put my faith in God, but I am still afraid. Are you?"

"Aye. Though I will be behind the lines tending to the wounded, I am still afraid of cannonading or capture. And I'm afraid for my brother and my nephew. There is no end to the fear I harbor."

The train whistle blew and the soldiers started boarding. Danny stared at his friend that he and Michael had once saved from a pack of wild dogs and wondered if he would be called upon to save him again or worse, be forced to watch him die on the operating table.

"Guess 'tis time to go," said Danny. "Stay safe. God go with you."

Nelson nodded gravely and added, "God's Will be done."

They arrived at Harrisburg and were immediately dispatched for Mt. Union eighty miles to the west. Reports of Confederate troops in Pennsylvania were rampant, but battle lines had not been established and Union and Rebel patrols bumped into each other and many short, sharp engagements ensued. No one knew where the Rebels would strike next. Nelson's company was ordered to guard a railroad bridge that had suddenly become strategically relevant to the coming battle.

Underneath the light of a full moon, Nelson stood watch in the ancient forest surrounding the rails. He had been lulled by the soothing night sounds of the dark woods. An owl hooted sporadically in the distance, closer by frogs croaked in a tireless rhythm, and closer still, June Bugs crashed into trees and mosquitoes buzzed in his ears.

In the peace of the brooding trees Nelson lost himself in thought. Fear of the dark and the danger that could lurk within was always with him, but at the same time he pondered the World and his place in it. What did the future hold for him? Did he have a future at all, or would his life end suddenly and violently at the hands of the rebels? He tried prayer, and it helped somewhat, but the fear of what lay ahead lay heavy on his heart.

A sharp crack of a breaking twig caused his heart to skip a beat and he hunched down peering into the darkness. Rustling drew his attention to the dark woods across the way, impenetrable in contrast to the moonlit clearing.

"Probably a deer or a skunk," he thought as he crept closer to the clearing and lay down next to a bordering tree.

His breathing increased and he was afraid a man with a sharp ear could hear him in the still of the night. The noise increased and the hairs on his neck stood up as he waited. He cocked his musket and the sounds ceased. Nelson waited, every nerve on edge, his finger twitching on the trigger. A Rebel soldier stepped into the moonlight.

"Halt or I'll shoot!" ordered Nelson.

The man stopped and raised his right arm. His other arm hung lifelessly at his side.

"Help me."

"Are there others,?" demanded Nelson.

"I am alone. Please, I can go on no farther."

"Keep your hands where I can see them."

Sticking to the woods, he made his way closer to the man. Seeing him sag to his knee and collapse on his face, Nelson stepped into the moonlight and ran over to the man. The man's carbine lay a few feet away in the brush and his scabbard was empty. Nelson noted the cavalry insignia on the soldier's collar and quickly checked him for weapons.

"What happened?"

"Pickets shot at us on patrol. We rode off, but one of the minnie balls found me. I fell off in the dark as the rest of the boys hightailed it out of there."

"I didn't hear any shots."

"Been walking for hours, trying to come across some of our boys, but I was getting so weak, I can go no farther."

"Well, you're lucky. We got the best surgeon in the whole Union army."

Nelson helped the man to his feet and across the moonlit meadow. He led him down the tracks to the bridge and called across.

"Corporal of the guard!"

A voice answered, "Step forward and identify yourself."

"Private Nelson Baker. I have a wounded prisoner."

Three men emerged from the woods and trotted across the trestle. They took charge of the prisoner and led him off. Nelson returned to his post and waited to be relieved at sunrise.

In the early afternoon Nelson stopped by the infirmary to check on the prisoner. He found Danny packing his bags.

"What's this?" asked Nelson.

"I've been ordered to Gettysburg. There's a major battle developing and they will soon need all the surgeons they can muster."

"Are the rest of us bound for Gettysburg?"

"Not that I know of. This crossing cuts off one of the Rebs' paths of retreat."

"What happened to the prisoner?"

"I heard you captured him."

"More like he surrendered. He just needed a doctor. Even a damned Yankee suited him just fine."

Danny laughed.

"He lost a lot of blood. Never would have made it through the night. I patched him up and they are interrogating him now. They'll ship him out sooner or later. The war's over for him."

"When do you ship out?"

Danny looked at his pocket watch and snapped it shut. He picked up his bag and stepped into the sunlight.

"Train due in five. Take care, Nelson."

The half day ride to Gettysburg from Mount Union wound through the mountains, following the meandering paths carved by the West Branch. At first, the ride was pleasant enough. Riding on the rocking flatbed, Danny fell to sleep, lulled by the gentle rocking and the warm wind. He was awakened by a man's shouted curse and the other riders scrambling to find some cover on the open car. The cracking of muskets was followed by splintering wood and the soldier next to him falling from the car with blood spurting from his neck. Danny flattened himself against the floor and wormed his way behind a stack of hardtack boxes just as another round of fire thudded into the car. The train chugged on, rounding a curve and leaving the sniper fire behind.

Seeing that the danger had passed, Danny grabbed his bag and hurried to help any of the wounded. He found three men who had been hit. None of the wounds were life threatening and he quickly patched the men up and returned to his place behind the hard tack. While he had been busy tending to the wounded the rest of the men had restacked the cargo to provide protection from other snipers who might be waiting in ambush.

Danny tried to relax as the train forged ahead for the next hour. He had never been under fire before and his heart had just stopped racing when the train slowed rounding a curve and then suddenly screeched to a halt sending a few of the men tumbling.

"To arms!" screamed Captain Reilly running along side of the train.

The men grabbed their muskets and leapt down to follow him. Danny followed behind the running men. Up ahead he spotted a squad of Rebel soldiers sprinting across a trestle. They looked almost comical as they pranced gingerly across from railroad tie to tie with a couple men trying to run the rail.

The Union soldiers reached the span and fired. One of the men on the rail fell screaming to his death on the rocks below and two more men stumbled and struggled across to the other side. When the union men tried to follow, they were driven back by gunfire from the other side.

The Confederates had pried up rails and were starting a fire to twist them out of shape when the train caught them in the act. Captain Reilly deployed some of the men to provide covering fire, and dispatched the rest to recover the rails and repair the track. The men worked swiftly and the Rebel raiders emerged from the woods onto the tracks beyond gunfire range and taunted the Union soldiers.

An officer unsheathed his sword and waved it defiantly, "Hurry along, boys. General Bobby Lee and Stonewall Jackson is waiting to take your measure!"

He reared his horse, pivoted and called out as the Rebel cavalry trotted away, "Death waits for you, for Lincoln and for all tyrants!"

"Feck you and the horse you rode in on!" shouted a Union corporal to the cheers of his fellows.

Danny arrived in the sleepy town of Gettysburg later that night on the 29th of June.

After all of his preparations, Micah found himself lost in a tangle of Army red tape. Days, then weeks, then months went by in a series of orders and counter orders. His request for a commission was first approved and then withdrawn by the mayor. Rumors of Confederate saboteurs in the border area and racial tensions arising from the draft were on the rise and the mayor was reluctant to let Micah go. The 74th had left in early June for Pennsylvania and the supply of reliable men was dwindling.

After the endless delays, he was afraid he would never be able to catch up with Terence. The urgency of finding the boy eased after another letter had arrived from Terence. He had seen some action, but they knew he was safe in southern Pennsylvania for the time being. It appeared the boy was capable of taking care of himself. But Micah still felt the need to go and keep an eye on the boy.

As time sped along, Micah decided to bring his appeal directly to Governor Seymour and traveled to Albany only to find the governor was in New York City conferring with Mayor Opdyke and Superintendent of Police, Kennedy. Apparently, anti-draft and racial tensions were a growing concern in New York as well as Buffalo. With no other options available, Micah continued on to New York to try and persuade the governor to intervene on his behalf.

When he disembarked in New York, newsboys were shouting out the headlines of troops massing for a major battle in Pennsylvania at a town called Gettysburg. His fears for Terence leaped to the fore once again and he hurried to City Hall to find the governor. When he arrived, he was told the governor was in meetings and was not available to the public. He wrote a quick note requesting a meeting as soon as possible, handed it to the mayor's aide and took a seat on a horsehair bench. About an hour later the door to the mayor's office opened and Superintendent Kennedy stepped out. He told the aide to send for lunch and another bottle. The aide gave him Micah's note and nodded toward Micah seated on the bench. Kennedy glanced at Micah and the note and went back into the office closing the door behind him.

A moment later he reappeared and announced, "The governor will see you now."

Micah followed the Police Superintendent into the mayor's ornate office. Mayor Opdyke and Governor Seymour were standing over a long mahogany table covered with maps of the city. They looked up as he and Kennedy entered the office.

"Micah Curly?" asked the governor.

"Yes sir."

"I'm pleased to meet you. I received your letter and one from your mayor, Will Fargo. I'm afraid I'm going to have to disappoint you both."

"Sir?"

"I am going to assign you to Superintendent Kennedy at least until the heat of summer is past. We need men with your knowledge and background as a peace officer here to avert a disaster."

"But how do you know I am what you are looking for?"."

"Mayor Fargo outlined all you have done in that hell hole along the Buffalo waterfront. He spoke so highly of you that I couldn't let this opportunity pass."

"But my son…"

"Your son is doing his duty the same as thousands of other brave lads."

"He is just a boy."

"As are many others. For now there is nothing you can do about it. His unit is in the line at Gettysburg, and you couldn't get there before the battle is history, even if I gave you orders to go there. Every train in the northeast has been commandeered to transport troops and supplies. You will stay here and lend your expertise to Superintendent Kennedy."

"Yes, sir."

The mayor's aide scurried in and handed the governor a telegram. The governor frowned and looked at Micah.

"The battle is underway. God save our boys."

Word came down just after the evening meal. The sergeant told Terence and his crew that the 1st was moving out at dawn. Fortunately, there were almost three hours of daylight remaining and the boys scrambled to put everything in order for the march. Caissons were stocked, axles greased, gear stowed and harnesses checked before the last light faded. Next their attention turned to the tents and their personal kits. How much to bring was always the quandary. Not knowing where they were marching made the choices even harder. The weather had been hot, and it promised to stay that way, so Terence laid out his kit, packing his poncho and setting his blanket to the side. He decided to bring as much as he could carry to make the next stop as comfortable as possible. He could always toss it to the side of the road it if the march was too long or grueling. Others in his tent were struggling with the same issue and spent a lot of time going over their choices with each other.

Before first light the sergeant had the men taking down the tents and breaking camp. The men talked quietly in the darkness. After the rout at Chancellorsville, the men were determined to make a good showing in the coming battle. They had been the brunt of derisive taunts after the defeat, unfairly scapegoated for the Union defeat, even though they had made the desperate stand that covered the Union retreat. Tagged the "Flying Dutchmen," after the defeat their proud rallying cry of "I fight mit Sigel!" acquired the mocking addition, "and I run mit Schurz!"

Boots and Saddles sounded and fifteen minutes later Terence was perched on a caisson with the XI corps advancing along the Baltimore Pike toward the town of Gettysburg. As the sun climbed higher and the men slipped into the rhythm of the march, conversation petered out to be replaced by the creaking of wagons and the tramping of thousands of boots. Nearing the town, the Corps fell out and the men took shelter in the shade of an orchard while the officers reported to receive final instructions. The light breeze shifted and the faint report of massed musketry drifted to the men resting under the trees.

"Ol' Robert E. Lee musta got up early today," observed Lutz looking to the north.

"Sounds like a powerful lot of firing," said Terence uneasily.

"I expect we'll be in the thick of it soon enough."

"We'll be ready this time," affirmed Terence.

"Ach, we were ready last time," said Lutz.

"Well, I sure wasn't. I was just digging into that roast pig when the Rebs come out of the woods. I think we learned our lesson. I know I did."

"Fall in!" shouted the sergeant.

The weary infantry groaned, hoisted on their packs and fell into line for the march. Terence and his crew checked the horses and equipment and fell into line behind. A grim silence hung over the men as they advanced toward the gunfire. Then Captain Weidrich rode slowly past, his hat held high in salute.

"For the Union, men!" he called and the men of Battery I burst out in cheers.

The corps commander, General Howard, was informed that Confederates were approaching from the north. He kept a third of his troops, artillery and supply wagons in reserve atop Cemetery Hill. Finding that General Reynolds had been killed and that he was temporarily in overall command of the Union forces, he left General Schurz, the unfortunate subject of other Union commanders' scorn, in command of the XI Corps.

Schurz advanced the depleted corps through Gettysburg to defend the Union Army's right flank and discovered 20,000 Rebel soldiers about to strike. With the memory of General Howard's failure to properly deploy at Chancellorsville, he made special provisions for General Barlow to angle his line toward the southwest to deny the Confederates a flanking move.

Reaching his assigned position, Barlow spied a slight rise in front of him. Instead of obeying General Schurz's order, and unaware of the fifteen hundred Confederates hidden on his right, he moved his two thousand men to the top of the rise. In an incredible repeat of the missteps at the battle of Chancellorsville, half the men assigned to the flank were now disconnected from the rest of the corps, breaking the defensive perimeter around the town and exposing them to enfilading fire on two fronts.

Seeing the blunder, the General Jubal Early, the Confederate commander, attacked. In short order, Barlow was wounded and despite fierce resistance by the proud German defenders, the unit was swept from the field. They fought obstinately and withdrew in fine order sustaining covering volleys as they retreated through town. The rest of the Union line soon followed suit and by 5 PM Terence watched as the battered remnants of XI Corps were climbing to the relative safety of the Union position on Cemetery Hill.

All the next day, XI Corps worked to strengthen their position atop Cemetery Hill while the battle raged below them. I Corps had taken up the position next to them and Terence felt that the men in his unit under Captain Weidrich, were ready for anything. Throughout the day, they were harassed by sniper fire from the town. They had strict orders not to fire upon the town and the men labored on stoically as the bullets riddled their position. The fire was mostly ineffective, but it added to the already unbearable tension. Terence's nerves were reaching the breaking point. They spotted a sniper who had climbed to a church steeple, and the fire became more accurate. A number of horses were hit multiple times, and bullets started pinging into the gunpowder stores.

Finally, when Lutz went down with a bullet lodged in his leg, Terence cried, "Enough is enough!'

He swung the Napoleon around and the crew leapt to action. The gun was sighted, the charged rammed home and cannonball was on its way two minutes later. The shot went wide and slammed into the side of a brick building beyond the steeple.

Terence adjusted the elevation while the crew reloaded the cannon, took a second sighting and yelled, "Fire!"

This time the aim was true and the sniper and the steeple were obliterated.

Temporarily secure in their position, the men were able to watch the battle unfold below them to the south and the west until the thick smoke hid the action from view. Terence trembled as the roar of hundreds of cannons and tens of thousands of muskets echoed through the hills accompanied by the fearsome screams of men charging, firing and dying unseen beneath the drifting clouds of smoke.

The last of the troops had moved on and peace returned to the Mother House. Oppressive heat had settled in and there was not a cool place to be found on the grounds. Sister Brigid and the others were thankful for the time to rest and reflect, but sleep was hard to come by even in the darkest hours. On the first of July the thunder of distant cannons could be heard to the north and the sisters prayed for the souls of the men they knew were bleeding and dying there. Father had instructed them to be ready to travel as soon as the battle ended. Countless soldiers would need their care.

She wondered if any of her kin were there. It seemed likely. Two great armies were fighting for their lives and the future of the nation only a few miles away. Lee was taking a great gamble committing the full strength of the Confederacy in a desperate gamble and the Union had to respond in kind. She offered her prayers for all the men, Union and Confederate. How could men do this to each other? How could God let them?

29

AT SUCH A COST

The sun beat down mercilessly on the wounded and dying. As the day wore on, the sickening stench of death mingled with the acrid gun smoke making breathing painful and stomach wrenching. During lulls in the battle the pitiful cries and moans of the thousands of wounded took their toll on the men on Cemetery Hill waiting for their impending trial by fire.

Captain Weidrich paced back and forth nervously, trying to discern something of the battle below. It was impossible to determine the tide of battle. Would it swing their way next?

Once more Terence checked the gun and ammunition. Double canister rounds were stacked at the ready. The foot long canisters were crammed with egg-sized lead balls, screws, iron scraps, anything that could shred a man, all packed tightly with sawdust into the casing. The blast was devastating. It could take down a swath of charging men, disintegrating any at close range.

About 4:00 pm Confederate artillery commenced bombarding nearby Culp's Hill. Captain Weidrich ordered the battery to fire on the Rebel batteries, and along with the other units deployed on the east side of the hill, they soon silenced the Confederate guns.

The battery turned their fire on the infantry advancing up Culp's Hill and soon the combined musketry and canister fire inflicted heavy casualties and drove the attackers back. The men cheered when they saw the Rebels retreating and turned to ready for another assault. They didn't have to wait long.

The Louisiana Tigers, the Confederate unit that had routed them at Chancellorsville, struck as dusk settled on the battlefield. The same unnerving Rebel's yell shattered the stillness that had finally settled on the battlefield and the Tigers charged up the hill. The steep slope of the hill impeded the Union artillery, because the cannon barrels could not be directed low enough to strike the attackers.

The Tigers charged, relying more on bayonets than musketry. Rank after rank was cut down by the Union fire, but the Rebels kept coming and soon swept over the Union forces arrayed along a stone wall at the base of the hill. The infantry broke and the Tigers pressed on sweeping into Weidrich's battery. A volley from the charging Rebels felled two of Terence's gun crew and the rebels were upon them.

Terence grabbed the sponge staff and beat back the first man upon him. He turned to parry a bayonet thrust from another advancing on his left. The bayonet slipped down the shaft and raked his ribs from his armpit to his stomach. He reeled to face the man when a shot from Captain Weidrich dropped the Rebel at his feet. Everything descended into chaos and with blood gushing from his slashed chest, Terence fought on. The defenders were driven relentlessly back and one of the Rebels managed to plant his unit's flag before being shot down by the retreating Union soldiers.

Terence and the others fought tenaciously as they fell back, fearful that the abandoned guns of the battery would soon be turned on them.

Captain Weidrich cried, "Rally on me, boys!" just as reinforcements from the west side of the hill ran double-quick out of the darkness. Together with the reinforcements they charged and pushed the Rebels from the battery. The infantry continued on, sweeping the exhausted Rebels from the hill and back across the stone wall. The Union men dove to the ground behind the wall, allowing Terence and his crew to fire canister rounds into the fleeing Confederates.

The instinctive firing procedures took over and the gun crew unleashed charge after charge of devastating canister shot into the retreating soldiers.

"Advance the charge!" ordered the corporal.

Terence rammed the charge.

"Fire!"

The gun recoiled and was pulled back into position as Terence cleared the barrel.

"Prepare the charge!"

Terence stepped back.

"Advance the charge!"

Terence rammed the charge.

"Fire!"

After six successive firings, the Rebels were beyond the range of canister shot, and a bone weary Terence slumped against the red hot barrel singeing his hand.

"Shite!" he exclaimed through gritted teeth as he stomped away to plunge his hand into the water bucket.

The infantry below started cheering, and the artillerymen on the hill joined in. Ignoring his wounds Terence took up the captured flag and waved it defiantly at the fleeing Confederates. He heard the distinctive click of a pistol being cocked behind him and turned to see a blood soaked Confederate officer lying half covered by a dead Union man rise up unsteadily with a pistol in his hand.

"Damned Yankee," he growled firing point blank at Terence.

Terence spun around, dropping and collapsing on top of the captured flag as he sank into darkness.

The stench of rotting flesh had long since stopped plaguing Danny. He had grown accustomed to the smell covering his blood soaked clothes. The boy he was hunched over prying a mini ball from, moaned and expended his last breath on the table. Danny stood up straight and wearily stretched his aching back. He signaled the orderlies to carry the lifeless boy away. Before they bore the body off, Danny closed the boy's eyes and said a prayer for the boy and his mother who would never see her cherished son again. He turned to get take a drink from the water dipper and stumbled over the gory pile of severed arms and legs at his feet.

"And get these damned clippings out of my way!"

A blood soaked negro rolled a wheel barrow to the table and tossed the shattered limbs in. Danny watched the man casually exit the tent to dump the severed limbs into the pile outside. The wheel barrow hit a bump and a discarded forearm tumbled out. Without pausing, the man stooped to pick up the limb and continued on his way.

Danny stepped out behind to get a breath of fresh air and grimaced when the man added his sickening cargo to the growing pile of gore. The sun was rising and the steady sound of thousands of marching feet portended more evil work to come. He sighed, brushed the hair out of his eyes and went back into the dimly lit tent. A terrified boy lay on the table. A tourniquet had been tied around his thigh slowing the flow of blood from his shattered knee.

"Help me, doctor. I hurt so bad. I'm all me mother has in the whole world."

Danny smiled at him and tied a rolled leather gag in his mouth.

"Close your eyes boy, and bite down on the leather. This will hurt, but If you ever want to see your mother again, you have to be brave."

The boy closed his eyes and whispered, "I'll be brave for me mother, sure as I am lying here."

Danny picked up his saw and rinsed it off in the bucket. He wiped it clean with a bloody cloth and motioned two burly orderlies over to the table.

"Hold him tight, lads," he ordered.

Steadying his left hand on the boy's hip, he began sawing through the boy's thigh impervious to the ear-splitting shrieks coming out of the boy. Thankfully the boy passed out as Danny methodically sawed through the thick bone. He pushed the shattered limb to the floor and tied off the arteries before stitching the wound closed, bandaging the stump and loosening the tourniquet.

"Find him a shady spot, lads and bring on the next," he murmured. "It's up to God now."

Sunday morning, the 5th of July, Sister Brigid again heard men talking outside the mother house. The distant sounds of battle of the last few days were missing, and the quiet conversation in the predawn darkness could be heard distinctly.

"We was lucky to get by those damned Yankee pickets."

"We was lucky to be get by anywhere. God only knows how many thousands of our boys are lying dead and dying back there?"

"I pray the sisters wake soon and have bread enough for us. If we don't move on soon, the Yankees will be sending us to die as prisoners in one of their hell holes."

Sister Brigid opened the door and called to the men.

"Take some rest and get water over yonder. We will prepare food and coffee shortly. Are any of you injured?"

"Thank you kindly, m'am. We are tired but none has any serious wounds."

"Sister."

"Apologies, Sister, m'am."

"What of the battle?"

"We fought with Pickett and give a good showing, but we was licked good. Fighting ended last night. Most of our brigade was mowed down, and we skedaddled when we got the chance. Not much point in getting killed or captured. We'll get those Yankees yet."

"Thank God it is over."

"Yes, Sister. Thousands of boys was killed, Southern and Yankee."

The vanquished men were soon fed and then, fearing imminent capture, left for parts unknown.

Father Burlando and Mother Ann summoned her and Sister Clotilde after the men departed.

"We are getting a mission of Mercy together," said Sister Ann. "Father will take you in the carriage and fourteen others in the omnibus to the battlefield to care for the wounded. The reports from the battle say thousands lay dead and tens of thousands lay wounded."

"Dear Lord," whispered Sister Clotilde.

"We must bring the Lord's mercy to the men," said Father Burlando. We leave as soon as the supplies are loaded. You two will ride with me so we can plan how best to be of assistance."

"Yes, Father," they answered together.

They passed a few Confederate stragglers making their way south, but otherwise the ride was quiet and peaceful. Not knowing what lay ahead, Sister Brigid prayed fervently for the strength to persevere in the trial facing them. Remembering Antietam, she had a good idea of what awaited them. She prayed that her challenged Faith and courage would be enough to see her through another visit to Hell.

About two miles shy of Gettysburg, they were halted by a blockade of trees spanning the road. As Father Burlando reined in the horses a squad of pickets rushed out to surround them with muskets leveled. When they spotted the distinctive coronets of the sisters they lowered their muskets and stood at ease. Father tied a white flag to his cane and approached the pickets. The barricade was soon removed and the soldiers signaled the driver to proceed. As the sisters passed the soldiers, the men removed their hats and bowed.

"God bless you sisters," said the corporal. "The boys will be glad to be seeing you sure."

A few hundred yards beyond the pickets, the horror of what had taken place manifested itself. Hundreds of bloated bodies intermingled with fallen horses and mules, lay on either side of the road with many lying in the road itself. The odor rising from the corpses was overpowering, and as the driver maneuvered around the fallen littering the road, the sisters clutched handkerchiefs to their nostrils in a futile attempt to cover the stench of death.

Men were busy digging burial pits for the fallen, one for the Confederates on the left and another for the Union on the right. Another crew was already tossing bodies of Rebel soldiers into a previously dug pit. There seemed to be fifty or more already lying there. The astounded sisters tried not to look, instead raising their eyes to the heavens and praying for strength. Some cried openly and others wept silently at the folly and wretchedness of men. Where was the glory to be found in a bloated fly infested corpse?

The bodies strewn along the road slowed their progress and the passage into town was cruelly slow. The town was in an uproar. The acrid smell of gunfire and burning woods still hung in the air as the full impact of the furious battle became apparent. Officers ran hither and yon issuing orders, couriers galloped through the streets dodging the ambulances bearing the wounded and a few bewildered local inhabitants wandered aimlessly amidst the chaos. No women or children were to be seen. They appeared sporadically over the next few days venturing up from the cellars where they had lay hidden during the battle. Frightened and shell shocked, they stared open mouthed at the devastation wrought by the opposing armies.

An officer directed the omnibus to McClellan's Hotel, which was turned over to the sisters for their use. Taking only a moment to unload their personal belongings, the sisters asked to be taken immediately to the wounded. Accompanied by some officers, Father Burlando drove the sisters to the aide stations that had been set up throughout the town, leaving one or two at each site. The wounded lay in the court house, in every church, every school house and many private homes. The sisters immediately brought food and water to the wounded, changed bandages and prayed with the dying. Misery lay over the town like a smothering blanket on a warm night, and the sisters returned to the hotel late that night for a short rest before going back to the endless task before them.

The following morning, sisters from Baltimore arrived to help. With the makeshift hospitals overflowing and the wounded still lying on the battlefield, Sister Brigid and others obtained the loan of an ambulance and started searching for the men still waiting for help in the fields. Tents and farmhouses were used as aide stations by the sisters and many more men would have perished from neglect and thirst if the sisters had not taken it upon themselves to find and care for the injured.

Straw was spread for the men to lie upon, giving them protection from the ground. The sisters bandaged the men, gave them water and noted the location to send ambulances to pick them up. In the late afternoon Sister Clotilde noticed a red flag with a sign declaring 1700 wounded this way. The driver took them down the hill to a wooded area where they found the wounded scattered about in terrible conditions. The men had been awaiting removal for more than a day. Lying in the sweltering heat the battered men cried out to the sisters for water, for relief from the insects swarming over them, for a bit of bread. The men were covered with swarms of lice and the bites of hundreds of mosquitoes. Some had maggots crawling in their bloody wounds and the suffering was sapping their life force.

A doctor and three orderlies were making their way through the men, assessing their wounds to decide who were worth the effort and who would be left to die. The ones who could be helped were tagged for pickup and the doctor returned to the aid tent to work on the men selected.

The sisters fanned out amongst the wounded, providing water and comfort to the men. They plucked the maggots from the festering wounds, combed lice from the men's hair and prayed with the dying. They stayed throughout the night, circulating with lanterns to bring comfort to the suffering and dying.

Sister Brigid moved deliberately from one man to the next in the darkness. The men lay about everywhere, and she had to step carefully to keep from stepping on a shattered limb or stumbling over a half seen body. The men were dying at an alarming rate during that dark night and realizing she could reach only so many, she became despondent but forced herself to continue on in spite of it.

A man snared the hem of her habit and pleaded with her to stay by him.

"Sister, don't take the light and leave me in the darkness."

"But there are so many that I must help," she replied.

"Stay and pray with me. I shan't be here long."

"You will be fine," she lied.

"No I won't. Please stay and pray with me. I am afraid for my immortal soul. I have not been a wicked man, but I haven't been a particularly good man either, and tonight I shall meet my maker."

She knelt by his side and took his hand.

"If you ask God, He will forgive you."

"Are you sure?"

"I am," she lied again.

He gripped her hand tightly and together they prayed the Lord's Prayer.

"Bless you, sister," he sighed. "Again."

They started the prayer and he gasped, clutched her hand tightly and breathed his last. She laid his hand on his chest and rose to her feet.

"Erin?" questioned a voice in the darkness.

"Yes," she answered furtively

"Erin, is that you for God's sake? It's me Terence!"

She raised the lantern and saw him propping himself up on one elbow.

"Terence!" she exclaimed.

She rushed over and hugged the boy, releasing him awkwardly when he grunted in pain.

"Easy," he said. "I'm hurt bad."

She laid him back down, waved the lantern high above her and called to the ambulance driver, "Here! I need you. I found my sister's boy!"

They loaded him into the ambulance and drove to the aid station where the doctor was still busy at work.

When they arrived, the orderlies were carrying a soldier out of the tent and she heard the doctor call, "Next!"

"This boy," she told the orderly and he and the driver carried Terence into the tent.

"What have we here?" asked the doctor.

"Bullets in the shoulder and elbow with a deep saber wound down the side," replied Erin.

Noticing Erin standing by the table he said, "Glad to have you sisters about. Got so much more than we can handle. Take off his blouse. Get those maggots out of his side and wash the wound while I pick the ball out of his shoulder."

"Yes, sir. He's my sister's boy," explained Erin.

Terence gasped in pain as Erin and the orderly wriggled the blouse off. She looked hopefully to the doctor and picked out the maggots crushing them between her forefinger and thumb. She took a wet cloth and wiped the dried blood away, revealing the extent of the slash.

"The wound is clear, doctor."

The doctor squinted at the wound in the dim light and said, "Should live, if the wound doesn't fester. Now let's see about that mini ball still in the shoulder."

"Oh Gawd!" cried Terence as the doctor probed for the bullet.

"It will be all right, Terence," soothed Erin.

The doctor raised up, moved the lantern closer and looked at the boy and then at Erin.

"Erin?" he asked.

"Danny!"

30
OF THE DARKNESS AND THE LIGHT

"I am not too sure what the Mayor and the Governor expect," admitted Micah. "But more important, I need to know what you expect."

"I am not certain what they expect either," replied Superintendent Kennedy. "I have good lads working for me, Todd on the waterfront, Copeland on Mulberry, Steers on Delancey to name just a few. Don't need another precinct captain. I think it would be best if you just worked with me as an advisor of sorts."

"But I don't know your city."

"No, but from what I hear, you know men. In the heat of battle, that can be all the difference."

"You think it will come to that?"

"Sure as I am standing here. The city is divided twixt the rich and the poor, twixt the Irish and the Germans, twixt the Whites and the Blacks. No good can come of it. Copperheads are out there stirring up the hate in every saloon in the city. Why back in '61 Mayor Wood tried to get the Aldermen to declare New York an independent city, because the cotton merchants were losing money. Almost got them to do it."

"Big money has a big voice," agreed Micah.

"The free Negroes fight for the same jobs as the Irish, keeping wages low and animosity high. And now the draft. I am afraid the city will explode."

"That I know something of. The lads in Buffalo went after the Negroes. Took the whole force, the militia and citizen volunteers to head them off. Still a lot of tension."

"The do-gooder's draft is going to be the match to set off the Irish powder keg. We are the only ones subject to the draft. Tammany Hall made sure the Irish was made citizens when they stepped off the boat to get their votes, and made sure that the other nationalities who might not vote the party ticket never become citizens. The draft is only for citizens. So the other immigrants and Negroes don't get drafted and the rich buy their way out for $300. Only Irish boys are getting called. There was a lot of angry talk at the first draw yesterday, but so far the peace has held."

"But no Irish lad wants to fight in the place of a Black man competing for his job and keeping his wages low or a dandy living high off his labor."

"You see what we are up against."

"Aye. If God hasn't been able to sort it out, how can we?"

"I do not know, Micah, but we must find the way. The next number draw is tomorrow. I want you to go down to the Provost Marshal's and keep an eye on things. The Captain has men there; no need for you to get directly involved. Just send me updates every half hour from the Marshal's telegraph office."

Micah arrived at the Provost Marshal's office a little after nine the next morning, July 13, 1863. The assistant marshals had just finished rolling the paper slips bearing the citizens' names and binding them with rubber bands. The drum was loaded and cranked to ensure they were thoroughly mixed and that the drawing would be fair. When a blindfolded clerk began to draw names from the drum, the crowd erupted into jeers and catcalls. The draft administers decided to continue the drawing while eying the mob anxiously.

The crowd outside began to swell, filling Third Avenue and spilling onto side streets. The crowd gathered to protest the Federal intrusion into their lives, but many were happy to have a chance to protest low wages and the poverty they suffered. As the crowd grew, it changed. A mob now confronted the Marshal's office. Men, women and children came armed with paving stones, clubs and pipes. Micah saw that it was not going to stay peaceful for long, and the thin line of policemen in front of the building fidgeted nervously in the face of the enormous mob.

Micah sent a quick telegram to Kennedy:

"Thousands of armed men in the streets STOP Riot imminent STOP Send help STOP"

The burly men of the Black Joke volunteer fire company forced their way to the front of the mob. Brandishing shillelaghs, they screamed taunts and threats at the few policemen barring their way. The Black Joke company's fire chief had been drawn on the first day of the draft, and they were hell bent on destroying the draft records and bashing as many skulls as they could.

A pistol shot rang out and the air was filled with stones, bricks and pipes. Two policemen went down, blood pouring from their heads and the Black Joke firemen surged forward overpowering the rest. Followed by the mob, they charged into the building, driving the marshals before them. The provost tossed the draft log into a safe and fled out the back door with the outnumbered police close on his heels.

The lottery drum was smashed. Desks, tables and chairs were piled together. Files were spilled on top and when the safe couldn't be opened, turpentine was poured on and the lot set on fire. People living above the offices barely escaped with their lives and black billowing smoke soon blanketed the skies.

Micah made his way around the crowd to a telegraph office only to find that the mob had cut the wires. There was more to this than just a riot. New York had a large contingent of Copperheads, southern sympathizers, and he was sure they had instigated the outbreak. He could do nothing but stand by as the rioters danced and cheered before the flaming building.

Then he spotted Kennedy making his way around the mob. Out of uniform and alone, he appeared to expect no trouble. After all, he was not a Federal and he had no interest in enforcing the draft. Micah started toward him.

A voice from the mob shouted, " 'Tis the bloody black and tan, Kennedy!"

He was immediately assailed with curses and threats. The mob surged around him. He raised his cane and tried to beat them back. A man grabbed his arm from behind, wresting the cane from his hand, and Kennedy was beaten to the ground by the crowd. He struggled to his feet and tried to flee, only to be knocked down again and cruelly beaten. Fighting for his life, he regained his feet again and again, only to be born down by the feral mob.

They roared for his blood and the energy of thousands was expended on the hapless man. The bloodthirsty mob caught him again and dragged him down.

He spotted a man he had once helped rushing toward him and pleaded, "John Egan, for the love of God, save me!"

By then Micah had reached the scene and he and Egan managed to convince the mob that the battered man bleeding from scores of knife and club wounds was dead. They covered him in gunny sacks and carried the bloody, seemingly lifeless man away from the mob. They carried him to a wagon which set off for police headquarters. Micah faded into the crowd to gather further intelligence as the wagon pulled away. The crowd was thinning somewhat. Many of the protesters wanted nothing to do with the senseless violence they had just witnessed. Micah was hopeful that the remaining rioters would drift off to one of the thousands of saloons to brag of their deeds as the rioters had in Buffalo.

Just then he caught sight of about fifty soldiers marching down the street to face off against the mob. There was something strange about the marching men. The customary precision was missing. Lieutenant Reade, the officer leading the march, limped on a heavily bandaged foot and many of the soldiers wore bandages on their heads, their legs, their arms or wrapped around their chests. It was the Invalid Corps comprised of men back from the war recuperating from their wounds. The only force available, they had been dispatched once word of the attack got out.

Reade arrayed his men facing the crowd and cried, "In the name of the U.S. Government, I order you to disperse!"

A hail of bricks and stones flew at the men and a few of them were knocked down. The soldiers aimed their muskets and fired blanks at the mob deterring them momentarily. When they realized the soldiers were firing blanks, the blood crazed swarm launched more missiles and surged toward the wounded men. The men reloaded and fired a volley of mini balls into the crowd, barely slowing the mob which surged over the fallen rioters and crashed into the line of soldiers. Slashing and clubbing the soldiers, they managed to wrest the muskets away from the injured men.

The soldiers ran from the vicious crowd. One, hobbling on a splinted leg that had been shattered by grapeshot at Fredericksburg, stumbled and fell. The mob swarmed around him like hounds rushing to slaughter a fox and stomped him to death. Another climbed a pile of rocks to make a stand against raging men and was soon overwhelmed. He was clubbed senseless, stripped of his uniform, slashed a dozen times and his naked body was gleefully tossed to the spectators below.

Helpless to intervene, fearful for his life, and sickened by the savagery, Micah stood transfixed by the horrifying tableau unfolding before his eyes. He saw that the riot was about much more than a draft. The violence implied a deeper despair, a darker hatred, a vengeful lust that had been simmering for a long time.

Like the squad of policemen before, the rest of the soldiers escaped leaving the mob to mill about aimlessly. Small groups pillaged local stores and saloons and set them ablaze, the newly liberated alcohol fueling the flames and their fury. Small groups set out looking for booty and any Blacks to be found,

"Dose two is ones what lies wid Niggers!" cried a women. "Annie has bore three pickaninnies for her Darkie."

Micah watched as about twenty men and women chased two screaming white women down an alley. A door opened and the women rushed inside bolting the door behind. The frustrated mob soon set fire to the building and were driven out of the alley by the smoke and flames.

Micah tried to make his way through the crowd to report to the mayor, but was thwarted at every turn. He passed the bloody corpse of a young Negro no more than nine or ten years old. Nearby hung the brutally mutilated body of an older Negro from a lamp post. He heard the drunken, men and women standing by the swaying body talk of burning the "pickaninnies" at the orphan asylum on Fifth Avenue. Aghast at the brutality, he decided to warn the unsuspecting men and women caring for th orphans of the mob's intentions.

He cut around the main cohort of five thousand rampaging men, women and children, and, stealing a horse from an abandoned stable, rode to warn the orphan asylum. He arrived at the imposing four story building just ahead of the mob and found the unsuspecting teachers going peacefully about the normal business of caring for the two hundred and thirty-three children. The children were busy in their classrooms, playing in the nursery, helping in the laundry or resting in the infirmary.

"The mob is coming!" he shouted running up the steps. "You have to get the children out!"

The Superintendent, William E. Davis, and the head matron, Jane McClellan, met him at the door, and seeing the mob coming on, let him in.

"They started at the draft drawing, and they drove off the police and the militia. They have gone mad and are killing any Negroes they come upon."

"Surely they wouldn't harm children," proclaimed Jane McClellan.

"I passed the body of a wee lad on the way to warn you. They were dancing like demons around the lad's bloody body. The Devil is loose on the streets today."

Superintendent Davis bolted the door and ordered, "Tell the teachers to get the children out the back door, orderly but hastily!"

A little girl who had been standing in the dining room doorway appeared carrying the asylum's Bible.

Smiling proudly she said, "See, Mr. Davis? I have the Bible. It'll be safe with me."

Davis patted her head lovingly, and said "Out the back with you."

The door reverberated to the pounding of the rioters outside and Jane rushed down the hall alerting the teachers, as Davis and Micah ran up the stairs to spread the word.

The children poured silently down the stairs with the anxious teachers hushing the frightened orphans. An axe splintered the front door, and the mob rushed through, intent on murder and mayhem. The staff quietly led the children out the back while the mob was occupied carrying off food, clothing, bedding, household utensils and furniture. They came across one young girl hiding under her bed and screaming obscenities dragged the her out from under the bed and beat the helpless child to death.

Others rampaged through the house, setting fires while the staff and children were making their escape. Chief Engineer Decker of Hook and Ladder Company No. 2 led the fire company into the burning building to fight the flames and the craven mob.

Seeing the chaos inside, Decker asked his men, "Will you stick by me?"

"To the gates of Hell!" answered the first behind him and the firefighters started extinguishing some ten or fifteen separate fires.

Hard as they struggled to douse the fires, it proved to be fruitless. The mob was hell bent on the asylum's destruction. A besotted, giant of a man waved an iron pipe menacingly in Decker's face and told him to let the fires burn or die.

Micah and his men stepped to the fore and declared, "In that you will have to pass over our dead bodies."

The man backed away, grabbed a kerosene lamp and smashed it on the floor in front of Decker sending a wall of flame reaching to the ceiling. The firefighters beat down the flames and the man was gone. Though the firefighters fought against the flames valiantly, the mob succeeded in destroying the building and driving the firefighters off.

When Micah went outside, he found the arsonists igniting fires down the entire block. Men and women were looking over their booty, while a group of men inexplicably gouged out the bark of large shade trees, ripped out decorative bushes, and tore down the iron fence by the street. The mob was out of control, venting their hatred and anger on anyone and anything. Sanity had been vanquished and fear reigned triumphant on the streets of New York.

Micah made his way to the Twentieth Precinct where the children were being sheltered. He reported to Captain Walling who told him what he knew of the riot.

"The hooligans don't seem to be interested in anything but burning and killing. They marauded up Lexington burning homes and leaving the valuables inside. They even set the mayor's home ablaze and burned two precincts for good measure. Mostly they are killing Negroes, shooting, carving, hanging 'em and such. Over the way they hanged three and the women sliced up the bodies and set them on fire. When the cowards went after the Times, Mr. Raymond brought out Gatling guns and his boys drove the mob off. It's bloody Hell out there. No telling when they'll get here."

"My God," said Micah. "How can we stop them?"

"They are an army now, and it will take an army to stop them."

Micah sent off a telegram to City Hall to the mayor describing the chaos he had witnessed and asking after Superintendent Kennedy. He was given a cup of tea and biscuits which he gobbled greedily before departing with a contingent sent from the precinct in plainclothes to help to ward off an attack on police headquarters by a mob of about 10,000 rioters. Wearing a uniform on the streets was begging for death.

Commissioner Acton led a force of about 125 officers against the mob at Broadway and Amity. When a uniformed officer from headquarters tore an American flag from a giant of a man at the forefront of the rioters, the mob exploded. A fearsome tempest of bricks and stones fell on the badly outnumbered police. Some in the mob opened up with firearms. Several policemen fell victim to the opening barrage. A man next to Micah groaned and clutching his head, collapsed to the pavement. Micah and the rest closed ranks and charged head long into the horde. Brutal hand-to-hand combat ensued, no quarter given by either side. Sweaty bodies slammed into each other howling with fury. The thud of nightsticks and the sickening crunch of shattered bones were followed by hideous shrieks of pain. A glancing blow knocked the club from Micah's hand and he bent low and charged forward slamming his head into his attacker's midsection. The man folded over and Micah wrenched the club out of his hand and rejoined the police salient crashing into the midst of the Irish horde.

After no more than two minutes, the men in the front fell back beaten or exhausted from the frenetic, adrenalin fueled battle. The next ranks stepped forward over the bodies of the fallen. Muscles ached and eyes burned as blood, sweat and tears splashed into the combatants' eyes and ran copiously along arms and legs stretched beyond endurance. The melee raged for a mere fifteen minutes, that seemed to Micah, a Hellish eternity.

Finally, the rioters broke and ran. Micah sat wearily amidst the dead, the dying and the disabled strewn about the street and stared morosely at their blood seeping between the cobblestones. One threat had been beaten back temporarily, but 70,000 rioters were left to wreak havoc on the sidewalks of New York with only 2,000 beleaguered policemen standing in their way.

30

LIFE, LIBERTY AND THE PURSUIT OF THE IRISH

Nelson felt as though he were crossing the river Styx. He stared uneasily at the fires dotting Manhattan as the train rumbled across the wooden trestle. The fires cast a red glow on the smoke rising from below and the scent of burning tar, garbage and flesh drifted out to assault his nostrils with the evening breeze. The sky was overcast as they pulled into the station, and the Hellish landscape didn't improve in the flickering light of the burning buildings. Overturned carts, dead horses, omnibuses, clothing, bottles and debris of every sort lay about lending the aura of Armageddon to the cityscape. He shivered in spite of the muggy, smoke filled air and was glad to climb down from the open car and stretch his cramped muscles while waiting for orders.

The 74th had received orders late in the day and had marched from camp to the train leaving much of their provisions behind. He was astounded when the sergeant told him that fighting had broken out in New York City, and that they were to put down the insurrection. The war was taking one unpredictable turn after another. They had been expecting to take on Rebs retreating from Gettysburg, and now they were landed in New York to fight Irish rioters.

The mayor dispatched Micah to lead the Buffalo unit to their station for the impending campaign to regain control of the city. He met with Colonel Waston Fox at the depot to bring him up to date as the men unloaded their scant supplies.

"Micah, it is grand to see you," said Col. Fox when he saw him approaching. "I didn't expect to find a familiar face in this den of iniquity."

"It is good to see you too, Watson. I may be the only friendly face you see for a while. Things have become desperate."

"Desperate? I was told a band of drunken hooligans needed tending to. We'll have them begging for mercy in no time."

"A band of hooligans 70,000 strong and armed to the teeth."

"70,000? Armed?"

"They have beaten back the police and the few soldiers left in the city able to fight. Death and mayhem has been the order of the day."

"Are we to stop 70,000 by ourselves?"

"Other units are arriving all the time and there should be 10,000 soldiers back from Gettysburg by morning."

"Who is in command?" he asked nervously. "Why are you here instead of an officer?"

"General Wool, the mayor and Governor Seymour are giving the orders. The mayor sent me because I've been here for the whole riot and I know the boys from Buffalo."

"Do you have orders for me?"

Micah handed him the orders.

"How'd the boys fair at Gettysburg?"

"We were on picket duty. Had a few skirmishes, but that was all. Minor casualties is all."

"What of Danny Reddy and Nelson Baker?"

"Danny Reddy was ordered to a field hospital at Gettysburg. Haven't heard anything since he left. Who was the other fellow?"

"Nelson Baker."

"I don't recall a Baker. What rank?"

"Private."

"Oh, I wouldn't remember every private. He must be about somewhere. Let's go over these battle orders for the morning."

The 74th marched to temporary headquarters for the night and incredible rumors that Nelson passed off as so much scuttlebutt, later proved to be true and spread through the ranks. The Irish commander of the 11th was torn to shreds and lynched by the mob after he fired a howitzer into a crowd killing a woman and her baby, who had the misfortune of living in the neighborhood. Blacks were being brutally murdered and lynched. The homes of the well-to-do had been set ablaze and any man of means became the target of the mob's fury. And the most alarming of all, only a few hours before the 74th arrived, a mob armed with muskets and cannon had routed Federal troops and beat to death the wounded soldiers left behind. Open rebellion had broken out and the city was on fire.

Nelson could understand the animosity of the mob, but not the violence. It could not be denied that the Irish Catholics were despised. Confined to the worst slums, they fell victim to disdain, discrimination, destitution, disease, drunkenness and depravity. The Nativist gangs, the so called "Know Nothings," proudly proclaimed the Constitution guaranteed the gangs the right to "Life, Liberty and the Pursuit of Irishmen" as they raided Irish neighborhoods preying on the vulnerable immigrants.

Now the objects of the Nativist's scorn were expected to step up and fight for their oppressors' way of life. To the indigent Irish, this was a rich man's war. The wealthy could pay $300 in lieu of being drafted or hire others to go in their place. Nelson had been disgusted back in Buffalo when he learned that the young Erie County District attorney, Grover Cleveland had paid a desperate Pole $150 to take his place. Men were willing to risk everything to provide a chance for their families and the rich capitalized on their destitution. Where was the sense of honor in that? God had commanded man to be his brother's keepers, not his brother's killers.

Nelson pondered the irony of it all as the 74th marched to relieve the exhausted police. The police department was defeated and sorely demoralized. They had fought valiantly but vainly against the tide of Irish fury. Hardly a man on the force had not been wounded in one way or another. After days of fighting against incredible odds the battered men could do little to protect themselves, let alone the city.

The 74th was one of the units assigned to clean out the Five Points, the epicenter of the insurrection. Tenements and sheds bordering the area on Mott, Mulberry, Cross, Orange, and Little Water streets were overflowing with the rioters and their loot. The finery from the mansions along Lexington and from stores like Brooks Brothers lay piled amidst the squalor of the dark, foul smelling hovels the downtrodden called home. The men of the 74th were told that order and property was to be restored at all costs.

Micah marched alongside Colonel Fox at the head of the column tromping through the desolation left behind by the rampaging mobs. Their passage was blocked by a company of bone-weary volunteer firemen manning the pumps on a fire wagon in the middle of Anthony Street while throngs of rioters taunted the firefighters and threw cobblestones at them. The column of marching men halted momentarily to watch the futile struggle against the inferno. The exhausted firemen pumped in slow motion, barely managing to keep the water flowing. The two men on the hose directed the feeble stream toward the second floor while the four floors above raged out of control. The chief ran back and forth exhorting the men to pump harder and the men on the hose to move in closer, but the hose men were driven back by the intense heat and the men on the pump had nothing left to give. A tremendous whoof sounded and the firemen ran for their lives leaving the chief screaming at them to do their duty. A huge rending crash echoed down the street and the façade of the cheap tenement came crashing down on the abandoned wagon and the hapless fire chief. His screams rang out, freezing the soldiers in place. A collective sigh escaped from the troops as they stared dumbfounded, listening to the buried man's screams fade into the roar of the flames. Seeing the brave man perish before their eyes horrified the soldiers who started to break ranks. Sensing their fear and loss of control prompted Micah to action.

"This way, Watson," he advised the Colonel and the unit executed an about face to cut around behind the fire and cheering rioters.

Back on Anthony Street, they began encountering people in the street glaring hostilely at the marching men. A boy scurried down the block shouting into the many saloons that lined the street. Surly men emerged and formed a mob blocking the unit's passage. Men broke off from the main mob facing the soldiers and disappeared to crowd into the tenements looming over the canyon-like thoroughfare.

"Halt!" ordered Colonel Fox.

The soldiers stood in ranks nervously awaiting orders.

"Make way for the New York State Militia!" shouted Colonel Fox.

"Feck off!" was the derisive reply from a beefy, red-faced man at the head of the crowd.

"Disperse or be fired upon," replied Fox.

"Have at 'em, lads!" cried the man in front.

The mob charged as bricks and cobblestones rained down from above on the soldiers still standing in rank below. The missiles found their marks and the soldiers staggered beneath the vicious bombardment.

"Fix bayonets!" commanded Fox. "First three companies form two ranks of skirmishers. Rear guard fan out and engage snipers."

Micah noted Nelson in the first line of skirmishers and spotted two of his Buffalo watchmen amidst the men kneeling and aiming at the ambushers on the roof tops. He ran to the men being pelted by the stones and split them into two groups sending one to each side of the street to cover the roofs on the opposite side.

"Flaherty, O'Brien, pick three men and follow me," ordered Micah.

The men rose and followed him through the door of a tenement.

"Reload and keep bayonets at the ready," he whispered in the gloomy hallway. "Lead the way, Flaherty. Use your bayonets on the way up the stairs. Keep still, but keep your eyes open. Don't fire until I give the order. We need to catch 'em off guard."

Climbing the rickety stairs brought back recollections of the Smith Block and he whispered, "Watch yourselves. Test each step before you trust your weight to it."

As they reached the top flight of stairs, they passed a filthy woman glaring at them from the dark interior of her room with a small, naked toddler clutching her skirts and sucking on his thumb.

"Fecking Black and Tan," she muttered as Micah noticed her.

"Just a Irish lad from Buffalo, dearie," he answered smiling broadly. "Now keep quiet and all will be well."

She snarled back, "Pig."

He started up behind the soldiers and she leaped on his back screaming, "They're coming for ye, lads!"

Micah screamed as she bit into the back of his neck and slashed his face with razor sharp brass fingernails. He tossed her to the floor and she charged back snarling like a mad dog, with his blood running from her mouth. She had filed her teeth into points to rip out the throats of the unsuspecting victims she waylaid on the streets of the Five Points. Micah back-handed her with his pistol, driving her to the floor again, and the bawling toddler ran over to the screeching harpy. She pushed aside the toddler and raked Micah's shin with her brass fingernails. He yowled and kicked her in the face. Blood splattered from her nose, her eyes rolled back, and she keeled over backwards. He rubbed his neck and stared at the insensible woman lying there.

"Jaysus," he muttered. "A succubus straight out of Hell."

The door to the roof burst open momentarily blinding the soldiers climbing the stairs.

A man in the door way called down, "Are ye all right, Maggie?"

Spotting the soldiers rushing up the stairs he slammed the door and screamed, "Soldiers!"

Micah dashed up behind the soldiers and yelled, "At 'em, boys!"

The door flew open again and a wooden barrel came tumbling down the stairs knocking the first man into the wall. The other soldiers pushed the barrel aside and rushed onto the roof bayoneting the man at the door. A shot rang out and O'Brien tumbled to the ground. The men fired into a group of eight or nine men facing them and charged with their bayonets. The ambushers broke and ran to jump onto the adjoining roof, with Micah and the squad in hot pursuit. A brief hand-to-hand skirmish broke out on the next roof when more rioters armed with clubs and three of them with muskets joined the first group. Micah emptied his revolver at the men with muskets dropping them on the spot, while the squad beat back the others, forcing the bushwhackers to the edge of the roof where they dropped their weapons and surrendered.

He stepped to the edge of the parapet and saw the battle raging below. The 74th was firing into the growing mob and retreating from the onslaught. Rioters on roofs across the way were still raining bricks and stones on the soldiers below and Micah ordered his men to fire on them. Across the way, a man maneuvering a cast iron stove onto the edge of the parapet clutched his chest and tumbled screaming to the wooden sidewalk below. Two more men fell as mini balls slammed into them and the bombardiers retreated from the rooftops.

Micah used his sleeve to wipe the sweat from his eyes and leaned over the edge to watch the action unfolding on the street. The mob had swelled and the 74th was badly outnumbered. He feared it would be another rout and that the rioters would win the day.

"Down!" ordered Fox and the skirmishers fell to their bellies.

The units' howitzer fired a round of canister shot over their heads. A dozen rioters fell and the mob staggered to a halt.

"Front rank fire!" screamed Fox.

The men rose to their knees and fired and stepped behind the second rank to reload.

"Front rank fire!"

The mob wavered before the concentrated fire.

"Down!"

This time the front rank of rioters dropped to the ground before the cannon roared and the canister shot flew over their prostrate bodies tearing into the men and women behind. The rioters who had taken cover rose and started forward again.

"Front rank, fire!" shouted Fox.

More rioters fell and the mob wavered.

A woman stepped to the fore, climbed atop an overturned wagon, and screamed, "Are ye cowards den? Dis is our home. Back at 'em, boys!"

The crowd surged forward again and a single shot rang out. The woman tumbled to the ground and the mob turned tail and disappeared into buildings, alleyways or fled headlong down the street. The 74th continued its march down the street, clearing each building of ambushers and arresting any who resisted along the way.

Micah followed along as the triumphant squad led the prisoners down the rickety stairs. Maggie, propped against the door frame rubbing her bruised face, glared hatefully at the passing men and bared her sharpened teeth when she spotted Micah.

" 'Tis enough for one day, Maggie," warned Micah leveling his pistol at her. "Any more from you and I'll put you down for good."

She spit blood on him and cursed, "The Lord'll take his revenge on you, sure. Any who would treat a lady like dat will burn in Hell, true."

He put his hand to the bloodied back of his neck and shook his head in disbelief.

"Lady? You're a mad dog, a wildcat that I should put down here and now, but I'll leave that to another depraved animal in this hell hole."

He cocked the revolver and sneered, "Get from my sight, before I change my mind, ye banshee."

She started to speak and he leveled the gun in her face. Staring into the gaping barrel, she thought better and disappeared into her room slamming the door and leaving her sobbing child behind.

Micah handed the boy a piece of jerky, patted him on the head and said, "Heaven help you, lad."

The boy sniffed and smiled in the darkness. He sucked on the strip of jerky nd waved bye-bye to Micah as he looked back from the landing below.

Washed with the blood of five hundred dead and countless wounded, the streets tired of the violence and an eerie calm settled on the city over the next few days. Smoldering fires, rotting food, and decomposing horse carcasses fouled the air, leaving the sun to shine blood red through the smoky haze onto the violated denizens of the great city. Martial law was declared and the unstoppable hum of commerce finally won back the sidewalks of New York.

Micah was thankful to leave the chaos behind and return to Buffalo with the 74th The governor relieved him of his enlistment in gratitude for his service during the riot, telling him there was no point now that Lee had been driven out of the North.

"We can lose the war at home if we are not careful," said Governor Seymour. "We need men like you to keep the rabble and the Copperheads in check."

With no word of Terence, his homecoming was somewhat muted. Mary started weeping when she saw him come through the door and just buried her face in his shoulder when he took her in his arms.

"Oh this wretched war," she moaned. "It tears at my heart, so."

"It canna be long now, Mary. Lee was sent running with his tail between his legs."

"But so many boys are lost. What shall become of us with Terence still in the fighting?"

"He's a good lad. He'll be fine."

She turned from him and took a seat by the window, staring down the busy street.

"The boys are off dying and here, here, everyone is busy making money off their sacrifice. It isn't right."

"No."

"At least you have come back. Danny, Michael, Da. They have yet to come home. I hope you are right and it all ends soon. The price is so high and the gain... Tell me Micah. What is the gain?"

He stepped to her side to put his hand on her shoulder and stare silently down the street. He had no answers, Lincoln had no answers and Micah had begun to wonder if God had any answers.

At the request of the mayor, he temporarily gave up his magistrate's position to return to the Watch. Tensions were rising across the city. To keep wages low, the owners were still playing the Negroes against the Irish dock workers. Most people had grown weary of the war and rival elements called for a negotiated settlement, or to let the Southern states secede, or for unconditional victory and the freeing of the slaves. Fear of spies and saboteurs was rampant, and the industrialists were growing fat from profiteering while merchants were suffering from the loss of southern trade.

The infected district was still the center of strife and nothing seemed capable of tamping down the passions of its wanton citizenry. Drunken brawls and full scale riots filled Micah's days and nights. The sailors and canallers murdered one another. Irish dockworkers beat and murdered Negroes. Muggers and whores murdered the immigrants. Soldiers were murdered and murdered the murderers as a part of the nefarious trade on Canal Street, and Micah found himself back in the thick of it.

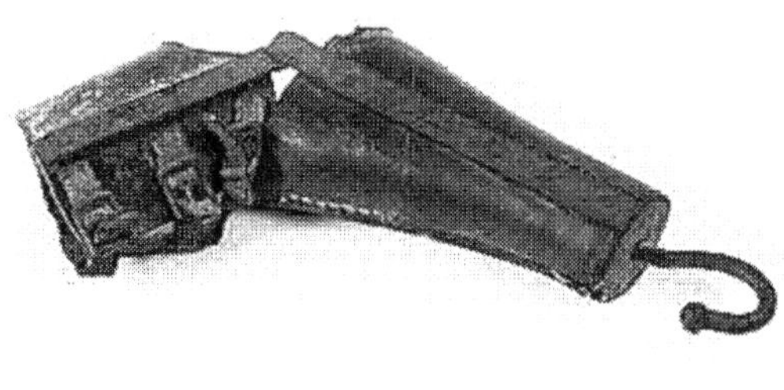

31

THE HOME FIRES ARE CALLING

Katie missed morning Mass again. It was getting hard to manage the mornings. Aching joints and hands that sometimes failed to grip were taking their due. This morning the huge coffee pot had slipped out of her hands and Jerry Molloy would have been scalded if he hadn't sprung to the side before the pot hit the table.

"Damnation, woman!" exclaimed Molloy. "What is wrong with ye?"

"It slipped. I'm sorry."

The boarders had to be content with water and biscuits this time. Katie knew it wasn't enough to carry them through the long day's labor ahead, but there was not enough time to boil another pot. A dock worker never had to worry about being late a second time. He would be free to sleep in every morning after the first time.

"I'll be expecting a few pennies back to buy something along the way."

Katie gave each of the men a nickel and sighed, " 'Tis only fair. It won't happen again."

Molloy took the proffered money and growled, "All right then. Have a good day Missus."

Katie stepped onto the back stoop to get the scrub bucket after the men left. A sliver of sunlight peeked through a gap in the surrounding buildings and fell warm upon her face. She bent down to pick up the bucket and groaned when she tried to straighten back up.

"Dear Lord," she sighed stretching her back and shoulders.

She shook her head, brushed hair out of her face and carried the sloshing bucket back in to clean the kitchen before leaving for Mass.

The faithful were pouring out when she made it to church. Father was standing by the door shaking Kira O'Toole's hand and listening patiently to the old gossip's litany of complaints.

"Dat Shannon lass will come ta no good, sure," whispered Kira. "Why I heard her coming in late again just last night. She needs a good talking ta, Faddah. She's a wild one, she is. And de lad she is stepping out wit. Dat's another t'ing all tageddah. Dere'll be a poor babe crying for de year is done."

"I'll talk to the lass, Kira. You go home and pray for her."

Kira spotted Katie trying to slip past into the church.

"Mass starts at seven, Katie Reddy," said Kira haughtily.

"Thank you, Kira. I am well aware of the time. Busy morning is all."

"Seems you've been having lots o' busy mornings lately."

"My mornings are between me and the Lord, ye old biddy."

"Hmmph. Just you remember, the day of reckoning is coming soon."

"Now, ladies," cut in Father.

"Forgive me, Father," sighed Katie glaring at Kira. "Will you hear my Confession before I have more to confess so I can pray in peace?"

Kira smiled triumphantly and declared, "Honestly Faddah, I don't know how ye bear de weight o' de sins o' dis wicked city."

Katie rolled her eyes and stomped into the church.

She heard Father tell Kira, "Go home and pray for God to open your eyes and keep your mouth closed."

After Confession, Katie knelt alone in the cool dark church. The war was a strange mix of good and evil. Fighting had not reached Buffalo, but fear of saboteurs and invasion from Canada infringed on the peace of the city. Buffalo had become an important war materials manufacturing center. The turrets for the ironclads had been cast just down the street and talk of Confederate spies was everywhere. Amidst all the fear and uncertainty, there was the boon of work for almost everyone. Money flowed through the Great Lakes and the canal making the elite of Buffalo prosper on the sacrifice of the nation's youth. The dockworkers grumbled. Whispers of strikes and sharing the wealth had become louder and ever more ominous. Things would never be the same again was the only thing Katie knew for sure.

Michael, Daniel, Terence and Micah were now on that sacrificial altar, fighting to survive the brutal conflict. Was the Union so important? Why was it the responsibility of her family to free the slaves? What would be left of her family and the Union when the fighting was done? And now Sean was gone. Called to Washington by the War department, he would be gone for the next two months. Worry and failing health had taken over her life.

With so many of the men gone, women were forced to assume the role of provider. War fueled inflation and shortages stretched the little money coming home from the poorly paid soldiers. The day to day struggle for survival on the home front manifested itself in the tired faces of the women. The men had gone off seeking glory, leaving the women and children to fend for themselves. Having no more time to reflect on her plight, she rose wearily from the pew. She had an appointment with Mr. Johnson to go over the bookkeeping notes Sean had prepared before leaving for Washington.

She walked down Main and over Church to the foot of Delaware where she boarded one of the elegant horse drawn cars that glided smoothly along the miles of double-track rails. Sean had regularly ridden out to see Mr. Johnson at his mansion, and even Mary sometimes rode it when she had been working at the house, but Katie had never experienced the luxury. Leaving behind the clutter and hubbub of the poorer side of the city, she found the ride was almost as smooth as a cruise along the canal and the scenery was breathtaking. Katie marveled at the wealth displayed. Magnificent homes with liveried servants lined the thoroughfare. Elegant women passed in rich carriages while others strolled the wide boulevard on their top-hatted husbands arms, smiling graciously at their equally elegant neighbors. It was a world of princes and princesses, a world beyond her imaginings.

She stepped off the omnibus and stood to the side as it continued up the street. She took a deep breath of the heavenly air filled with the scent of a thousand flowers and a fresh breeze from the lake. She started to cross the street and jumped back when a carriage rumbled around the corner and across her path. Katie peered cautiously both ways and started across when she hard a voice from the carriage.

"Katie?"

She stopped and looked to the carriage, wondering who she knew who could ride in such a stylish rig. A woman peered back from the side window.

"Katie? Oh it is you!" exclaimed the voice.

Katie stared back dumbly.

"Back up Joshua!" commanded the voice

The carriage backed awkwardly toward Katie and halted alongside. The horse snorted impatiently and a beautiful woman stared appraisingly at Katie. A feathered broad brimmed hat sat jauntily atop the woman's pale visage. She wore a cranberry intricately stitched silken dress with a high collar open at the neck revealing an exquisite white lace blouse beneath.

"You are Katie Dailey, are you not?" inquired the woman excitedly.

"I was," she replied hesitantly.

"I knew it! You've aged, but those eyes are the same."

"I'm sorry but…"

"It's me. Elizabeth!"

"Elizabeth?"

"Elizabeth Schmidt!" she exclaimed climbing down from the carriage.

"Oh, Saints preserve us. Elizabeth, child. I've often wondered."

"I've missed you so. You were the only happiness in my childhood. I was sure you had died when Papa abandoned you for my step mother."

"That was a hard time, true but you mustn't blame your papa. He gave me a home when I was lost and hopeless."

"He brought you in to get us off his hands. Mama killed herself because of him. There was no joy in our home until you came, and then he cast you out for that greedy woman who sent me off to school."

"You were just a child."

"I was lonely and lost. I missed you so. I prayed that you would come and steal me away."

"Me? I barely survived as it was."

"Oh, I know it was a foolish dream, but now here you are. We shall become such friends again."

"Your father became a grandee and I heard he died a few years back, but you were never around. What happened to you after school, Elizabeth?"

"I married well and lived in New York City. My husband provided me everything but love. After I bore him a son, he moved in with his mistress and only visited us on Sundays. God has cursed me for what I know not. Herman was murdered on the streets last month in the riot, and I have come to Buffalo to reopen my father's home."

"You will settle here?"

"There is nothing for me in New York. There never was."

"Oh, Elizabeth."

"But now I have found you," she said brightly. "It will be such a joy to have you over for tea. We have so much to catch up on. Do you still miss living with the Indians? Did you marry?"

"I am Katie Reddy, now, and I am on my husbands business. I'm afraid I must hurry or I will be late. I am so happy to see you, Elizabeth, but we still live in different worlds. You need to establish yourself with the right kind of people and not be seen to favor the Irish."

"I do favor you. I don't give a fig about what others think, and you shall come to my home Saturday for tea. I will not take no for an answer. I will send Joshua for you."

"Elizabeth.."

"I will not discuss it further. Don't you understand? You are the only person who has ever cared for me, the only one who I have ever cared for. Joshua will come for you at four."

Elizabeth wrapped her arms around Katie and hugged her tight.

"Katie Dailey, you were the only mother I had, my own true angel. Hurry about your business and don't be late for tea."

She climbed back into the carriage and waved out the window as the carriage pulled away.

"Saturday at four!"

The errant winds of the war years buffeted Katie to and fro. One minute she was thrilled to be doing God's work, the next she was worrying about her children, a moment later, and she was overjoyed to find Elizabeth. Then upon returning home, Cara handed her a letter with unfamiliar handwriting.

"I went looking for a letter from Seamus and found this waiting for you," said Cara.

"I wonder who it is from," mused Katie carefully opening the envelope.

It is post marked Washington," said Cara.

"Hmm, I see."

She stepped over to read it in the light from the window.

"Oh Lord," said Katie drawing in her breath and placing her hand on her heart.

"What is it?" asked Cara.

Katie waved her off and kept reading panting heavily. She let the letter fall to the floor and collapsed beside it.

"Katie?" asked Cara.

She knelt beside the sobbing woman and picked up the letter and read:

Mrs. Reddy,

As I pen this missive, your husband, Sean, is too weak to write and asked me to take this down for him. I will send it off in the morning with any updates on his condition.

Sister Marie Francis

Katie Dear,

I have been stricken with the cholera and fear that I shall not survive. I cannot leave you without trying to say what it is that you have meant to me.

When first I met you, my heart was too small for any but myself and then there was you. You wrangled your way in, stretching it and filling the small vessel to the brim. Again, there was room for no one else. I couldn't imagine any greater joy in this cold world than to love you and have you love me. Then along came our son, James, a tiny red-faced lump feeding at your soft, white breast.

I was afraid.

You were obsessed with him and jealousy darkened my heart. He was my son, and I knew I would do my duty. I would raise him to be a man, but I did not love him. Soon though, as both you and he became stronger, my fears faded, and I found

I had room for James in my heart as well. That tiny, helpless child managed to storm his way into my stony fortress heart and soften it to warm and grow around him.

When it was time for Mary, I knew my heart would make room for her. Next came Bernadette, Erin and the twins. Then Margaret and Micah joined the family and the grandchildren followed soon after. I came to know that the heart grows to meet the demands put upon it, enriching and expanding our lives even as it strains to meet those demands. I love you now more than ever, and I love our family. They are different types of love but they are just as strong. I know now that the capacity of the heart is limitless and there will always be room for others.

I do not fear my death. My only dread is the loss of you. I pray that there is some truth to the teachings of the Church and that God is not a vengeful God, but a kind, loving and forgiving God who will keep us together in Eternity as we have been together in life.

May God keep you in the palm of His hands and forgive me my sins.

I shall always love you, Katie Dailey.

Sean

As I post this he is still with us, weak but hanging on. I pray that you shall be reunited.

Sister Mary Francis

Erin carried the shuttered lantern before her, treading softly through the dark, crowded ward. Careful not to disturb the convalescing men, she paused before each bed and lifted the shade illuminating the sleeping men to monitor their condition. The ward was less crowded now. Many of the men had recovered and been discharged and, sadly, many others had been claimed by their wounds. She had written many letters home for the dying, held their hand as they passed and prayed for their departed souls. She had entered the Sisters of Charity because of the great tragedy in her life, but after listening to the regrets and shattered hopes and dreams of so many dying men, she had grown indifferent to her loss. The lives of so many young boys had passed through her hands in the last few weeks that her personal pain paled in comparison. Regrettably her faith had faded as well. She did all she could to help the boys in her care, but now she did it for them, not for God.

"Sister Brigid," whispered a voice in the darkened room.

"Do you need something, Colonel Walsh?"

"Niall. The war is over for me. I'll not be needing military rank anymore. You look tired."

"I am."

"Then spare a few moments, sit and keep me company. I cannot sleep this night. I will be able to travel soon, and they will transport me out west to some prisoner of war camp as soon as I am fit. I've heard nothing good of the prisons, only tales of woe."

"It can't be for long. The war will soon be over."

"I don't think it will end any time soon."

"But after all the death at Gettysburg, how can you go on?"

"We Southern boys are a stubborn lot."

"Yankee or Confederate, it doesn't make any difference. You're all fools."

"Aye."

"You're Irish and fighting for the South and my nephew Terence is an Irish lad fighting for the North. 'Tis us fighting against ourselves, while others grow rich on our blood."

"We fight against Northern oppression, just like we did in Ireland."

"And Terence fights against Southerners who make slaves of other men. Ye can't both be right."

" 'Tis a puzzlement for sure. But I didn't ask you over to argue. You have been a blessing to all of us, Reb and Yankee alike. You are such a lovely lass, why did you leave the world to hide behind the habit as a sister?"

" 'Tis a long story."

"I have time."

"You are a gallant, silver tongued devil of a man, Niall. You could make me forget my vows, but I won't burden you with my woes."

"After all you have done for me and the other lads, the least I can do is share your sorrow.

Erin smiled at him.

"Thank you for that, but I think not. God put us here on Earth to do good unto others. We all suffer."

"Then what are the others here for?"

"That's blasphemous!"

"Those boys raining canister shot down on us weren't doing no good."

She looked at him sadly.

"And what were you up to? Picking flowers?"

"Aye, you have me there. I don't know why we were put here, but it sure don't seem like we were sent to do any good. If we were, we've been making a holy mess of it."

Erin blessed herself and said, "We must try everyday to remember God's purpose for us."

"How can you believe in a just and caring God after all of this? Is it faith, hope, desperation? What drives you?"

"That is my cross to bear, not yours."

He looked at his bandaged leg and back at her serene face.

"I am here with my brutally shattered leg and you stand there with talk of your merciful God. Only one letter difference between here and there, yet it seems nothing could bridge the gap."

"Faith, Hope and Love are the bridge. You must let God into your heart. He will show you the way."

Niall smiled wanly.

"Enough. I give up. I won't question your faith or your goodness. I am too grateful for it. Well Lass, if you won't share your tale, at least share your given name."

"I was christened Erin Reddy."

"Erin, A grand name for a beautiful land and a beautiful lass."

Erin blushed.

"You are filled with the Blarney, Colonel Walsh."

His eyes twinkled.

"Beauty brings it out."

"I have no time for your foolishness. Flattery, despair? What will you try next?"

Before he could answer a man cried out for water and Erin took over a dipper of water. The man drank greedily, thanked her and fell back to sleep. She started to return the dipper, stopped and frowned by Terence's cot. He was tossing back and forth moaning softly on his sweat soaked pillow. She leaned down and brought the lantern close to look at his injured arm. A foul odor assaulted her nose. Pus leaked from the bandage and the flesh around the wound was red and festering. The wound was burning hot to the touch and caressing his forehead she found his whole body raging with fever.

She undid his blouse, brought over a pan of water and mopped his chest and brow with water to bring the fever down. Terence sighed and settled down when she wiped the cooling water on his burning skin, but soon after he started shivering uncontrollably. Alarmed she went to wake Danny.

Danny rushed to the ward with her still buttoning his shirt. He placed his hand on the boy's neck to check his pulse and temperature. Frowning, he told Erin to cover the trembling boy and proceeded to unwrap the bandages.

"Shoulder and side are fine," he murmured. "Let's see that shattered elbow."

As he unwrapped the elbow his nose wrinkled at the foul stench.

"Oh Lord," gasped Erin.

"It's mortified," said Danny. "I have to take the arm."

"Not Terence."

"I take the arm, or the arm will take his life," he answered sadly. "Make ready, Erin."

Danny called for orderlies to move Terence to the operating table, slipped on his surgical coat and washed his hands while Erin wiped down the table and laid out the scalpel and bone saw. Danny poured chloroform on a linen cloth and held it over the boy's mouth and nose. With Terence insensible, Danny straightened the arm, handed the clothe to Erin and took up the scalpel.

Bearing down on the scalpel, he cut through the skin and muscle down to the bone, leaving a flap of skin below. With orderlies holding Terence's arm in place and Erin dripping chloroform on the cloth covering his face, Danny sawed through the bone with a few rapid strokes. He tossed the limb to the floor and tied off the arteries with silk threads. Next he scraped the edges of the bone smooth to prevent them from cutting through the skin and sewed the flap of skin over the stump leaving a small drainage hole to prevent swelling. Erin spread plaster on the stump and bandaged the arm securely.

Danny looked down on his young nephew and for the first time started to cry. How many boys had he butchered in the hopes they would survive? And what sort of life awaited the boys back home?

"Will he live?" asked Erin.

"It is a clean cut. He should be all right if the inflammation doesn't set in. It would be good if you were there when he wakes."

"I'll be by his side until he is back on his feet."

She walked along as the orderlies rolled him back to the ward and placed him in his bed.

"Will the lad be all right?" asked Niall.

"The elbow inflammation was amputated and as long as it doesn't return, he will live."

" 'Tis a damnable shame to have this happen to your sister's lad after all you have done for others."

"War is the Devil's work, not God's."

"That was not what I meant, Lass. I'm just saying 'tis not fair 'tis all."

Erin returned his earnest look with a wan smile of her own.

" 'Tisn't, but I'll see him through this."

"We'll see him through."

She looked at Niall, lying in bed and propped up on his elbow. She could see empathy in his hazel eyes. Empathy and understanding and something more.

"Thank you, Niall."

Three days later Danny found Erin, Niall and Terence sitting underneath one of the few trees remaining after the artillery duels of the recent battle. The shade and light breeze provided some relief from the oppressive, mid- summer heat. The wild flowers that might have lessened the faint stench of death that overhung the scarred Pennsylvania countryside had wilted under the sun's pitiless glare and bowed to the ravages of war and sun.

Still the scene evoked the idyllic. Erin held both men's hands, bridging the gulf between the warring sides of the brutal war. The three comrades, each wounded by events in their own way, talked animatedly of their hopes for a quick end to the war and the chance to move on to what lay ahead. Erin smiled when she caught sight of Danny.

"It is good to see the three of you up and about," said Danny. "How's the arm, Terence?"

"Dull ache is how. I don't notice, 'less I think about it. Side still devils me and I am still a mite weak."

"That's to be expected. It will get better day by day if you do what you are told. I have news. You are being discharged and sent home."

"When?" asked Erin.

"Tomorrow."

"But he's not well enough to travel all that way."

"That's why I want you to go with him."

"I can't just leave. I have work here."

"We are all leaving tomorrow. The able back to their units and the rest discharged or to the hospital in Baltimore."

"And the prisoners?" asked Niall.

"To the prison in Ohio."

"Oh, Niall," whispered Erin.

"We knew it would come to this," said Niall. "It can't be for long. The South cannot hold out forever."

"But will I ever see you again?"

"I'll come to Buffalo when this is over. There has been talk between Fenians both northern and southern of a war to win back Ireland. I have no doubts about fighting for the freedom of Ireland and the hand of a fine lass such as you."

He leaned close and kissed her.

Erin blushed unable to speak.

"It is destiny, Lass. I was named for King Niall of the Nine Hostages. He gained his throne through a test of the gods. When he and his brothers were searching the forest for food and shelter they grew thirsty and came upon a hideous hag guarding a well. 'Before ye taste the water ye must taste me lips,' she laughed. None of his brothers would deign to kiss so foul a mouth, but Niall. He agreed for the sake of the others and when he kissed her, she transformed into the most beautiful woman on earth and granted him sovereignty over all of Erin."

"That is a lovely tale, but it is only a tale signifying nothing."

Niall kissed her again.

"Niall! I have taken vows," she protested.

"You must put them aside and take another vow, a vow to be my wife."

Terence shouted, "Hurrah!"

"I can't," said Erin.

"You can," said Danny. "Take Terence home to his mother and wait for Niall. God will forgive."

This time, Terence got to ride in a passenger car. The north bound train had been set aside for the wounded. A doctor and two nurses checked on the men after they boarded and gave them the final o.k. for the trip. Terence was the only one lucky enough to have his own nurse along for the ride, but Erin spent most of her time seeing to the needs of other wounded men. It was a long hot ride through Pennsylvania and the two of them soon grew weary of the journey.

Watching the Susquehanna pass slowly by, Terence looked up to see the commissary Jeremiah Dietz (Engel) staring down at him. Blood dripped from under the bandage on the man's head.

"Private Curly, right? From Buffalo?"

"That's right."

"I was going to ask the good sister to look at my bandage and saw you sitting next to her."

"It is good to see you, sir. Allow me to introduce my aunt, Erin Reddy."

"Sean Reddy's daughter?"

"Why yes," answered Erin.

"What a small world this is. Micah's son and Sean's daughter on the same train as me. God must have ordained this."

"Let me look at your bandage," offered Erin. "Here, take my seat."

The stub of his arm slipped out as he took the seat next to Terence.

"Another badge of courage?" asked Terence pointing to the stub.

"No, no. An accident from long ago took the arm."

Terence raised the stub of his recently amputated arm.

"Then I will get by with this?"

"It can be done," Engel answered darkly.

"Ahh!" cried Engel when Erin pulled the last of the bandage clear of the wound. "Having a clipped wing takes getting used to, but you will."

"Nothing serious," said Erin as she cleaned the wound. "You waited too long to change the bandage is all. Make sure you have it looked at when you get home."

"Thank you, sister. I'll be getting back to my seat soon as I have a cigar. Care to join me on the platform, Terence?"

"A little fresh air would be good," said Erin.

The three walked to the back platform and Engel paused to light his cigar out of the wind as Erin and Terence stepped out. The train rocked gently back and forth generating a cooling breeze. Erin closed her eyes and arched her neck relishing the rush of fresh air. Terence stood silently by her side.

"Close your eyes and feel the wind, Terence. It's thrilling!"

Terence closed his eyes and the two of them held hands and swayed with the train laughing with delight when the car bumped unexpectantly over am uneven coupling.

"Isn't this delightful?" posed Erin.

They closed their eyes again and fell into the rhythm of the rails. A vengeful sneer transformed Engel's countenance and he hunched down and charged to slam his shoulder into Terence's side driving him and Erin off the train and over the embankment. Erin's scream was cut short when her head slammed into the trunk of a tree below. Terence tumbled down the steep hill trying to stop and get to Erin, but rolled all of the way to the bottom without stopping. The train rattled on with the sound of Engel's laughter rising above the rumble, leaving the two of them stranded along the Susquehanna.

Terrence made his way up to Erin, who was sitting against the tree trunk rubbing the back of her head.

"Are you o.k?" asked Terence.

"I don't know," she replied slowly. "I think so. I just hit my head. What happened?"

"Dietz pushed us over the side."

"Why?"

"I'm not sure, but I bet it had something to do with my Da."

"Micah?"

"Dietz was probably someone he locked up, I'm thinking."

"Someone my Da must of helped with."

"Probably. What now?"

"I guess we walk along the tracks to the next town to wait for another train."

After days of agony the telegram came. Katie couldn't bear to open it. she handed it to Mary and finding herself unsteady on her feet, sat on the bench.

"Here, you open it and tell me when he died."

Mary took the telegram tearfully and murmured, "Oh Ma."

Katie turned her face to the wall and said, "Read it."

Katie opened the envelope cutting herself on the paper. She stuck her finger in her mouth to suck at the blood and looked at the telegram. Katie turned to look and saw Mary's eyes go wide. She choked back a sob.

"Oh Ma! Oh, oh!" Exclaimed Mary.

"What?"

She read, "Katie dear STOP. I am on the mend STOP. Expect to be coming home soon STOP. Love, Sean"

The two women hugged each other and danced around the room.

"Buffalo Sean won't you come home tonight, come home tonight, come home tonight," sang Katie as she swung Mary in circles around the room until the two fell to the floor laughing like giddy little girls at play.

Feeling light as a feather Katie had waited anxiously for Elizabeth's carriage to call. Tea turned out to be beyond Katie's wildest imaginings. A liveried servant was waiting to help her down as the carriage pulled underneath the colonnaded portico. She took his proffered hand and stepped cautiously onto the gilded iron carriage step. She paused to take in the magnificent setting before her. The servant's ingratiating smile and the sweet scent of roses climbing the trellis lent an air of tranquility to the imposing stone edifice before her.

The huge oaken door with leaded glass sidelights crashed open and Elizabeth burst forth to rush down the stairs laughing like the child Katie remembered from long ago.

"Oh Katie!" exclaimed Elizabeth. "I though I'd just die waiting for you to get here."

She took Katie's arm and hurried her up the steps past the butler and the maid waiting to greet her.

"We shall start in the parlor," said Elizabeth. "You may serve the tea, Davis."

The butler opened the parlor door for the two women. Treasures from around the world cluttered the room. Jade figurines from China, a golden elephant from India, finely carved teak furniture from the Philippines, a bone china tea service on a silver platter atop a an exquisitely carved table, intricate landscape art on the walls and heavy brocaded curtains hanging from the windows were but a fraction of the dazzling items crowding the Victorian parlor.

Elizabeth virtually danced around Katie while the tea was poured.

"I can't believe it is true. I mean I hoped, dreamed wished this could be, but I never really believed I would find you. But there you are, right there. Did you miss me too?"

"When I was sent away, I was frightened for myself, but more so, for you. We were happy weren't we?"

"Oh yes."

"What happened after you left for Buffalo?"

"That woman sent me away. They wouldn't even have me home for holidays. She saw to it that they were in Europe or down South whenever I was free to come. She didn't want me interfering with my father. She had him under her spell. She arranged my marriage, and I was kept by my new master in a beautiful home to be paraded on special occasions and ignored the rest of the time. I bore his children who were put in the care of a nanny, so I didn't even have them to ease my loneliness."

"I'm sorry, Elizabeth."

"But all that is behind me now. I have you and we shall be such friends."

Katie briefly told Elizabeth about her children and grandchildren and what life had been like for them. She talked about growing with the city, and how in spite of all the setbacks, they managed to prosper together.

"Things are happening in Buffalo. We are one of the richest cities in the world and grow richer every day. Of course most of the money just passes by those doing the heavy lifting. Precious little finds it way into the hands of the Irish. We provide the means and others help themselves to the benefits."

Elizabeth shifted uneasily under Katie's stare.

"I suppose it has always been so," continued Katie. "That doesn't make it right, but things are what they are."

"When I think how Father treated you and all you had to go through, it makes me ill. How can people be so hard?"

"It is hard to look on others as we do ourselves. They are not the same, so they must be lesser beings. The Africans are slaves, the

Seneca are savages and the Irish are besotted brutes. I don't blame you for your father. I am sorry that he let that woman destroy your chance for a happy home. Let's talk of other things."

"Thank you, Katie. I suppose we could talk of the war news."

"Would you like to help at the Soldier's Rest?"

"What is the Soldier's Rest?"

"We give room and board to the boys traveling through. My boarders are eating and drinking out on Saturdays, so I volunteer for the Saturday four to midnight shift. Most volunteers want Saturday night to themselves, but Sean is away so I don't mind."

"I'm afraid I don't know anything of cooking and cleaning."

"There are a lot of ways to serve. The boys would jump at the chance to talk to one as pretty and refined as you. Other fine ladies visit. The Ladies General Aid Society runs the Rest and holds fairs and sewing bees to get the boys what the army doesn't supply. It might be just the thing to get you out and about."

"I don't know, Katie?, do you think I could?"

"Remember the wild child you were back on the Genesee. She wasn't afraid of anything."

"Oh the fun we had," laughed Elizabeth. "I can hardly believe that little savage swimming in the muddy river was me."

"She is still in there somewhere," said Katie with a knowing smile. "We'll bring her back."

James was back in port Saturday. He and Margaret stopped by the Soldier's Rest to help and visit with Katie after dinner. They found Katie, Mary, Cara and Elizabeth sitting in the parlor with two boys still recovering from wounds they received at Gettysburg on their way home to Michigan.

"My grandson was there, Private Engwall," said Katie. "Perhaps you know him."

"What unit?" asked Engwall.

"Oh what was the unit? The German lads from Lancaster and Alden," said Katie.

"Well I don't know," said Engwall.

"The New York First Light Artillery," said James. "Weidrich's Battery.

"Weren't they the boys on Cemetery Hill?" asked the other soldier.

"Oh yeah, they were in the thick of things," agreed Engwall. "Put up a brave fight."

"Oh dear me," said Mary.

"Sorry m'am. Gettysburg was a fearsome fight all round."

"We haven't heard anything," said Katie.

"Mail is pretty spotty sometimes. I'm sure he's o.k."

"Yes, yes," agreed Katie.

"I have to admit I am a little worn," said Engwall. "Guess I'll be off to my bed. Thank you for your company. Don't get to talk to fine ladies much lately."

"Goodnight Private. Have a good rest."

She turned to Mary, "I'm sure it means nothing, dear Mary. Terence will be fine. He's a bright lad."

Mary sniffed and dabbed at the tears flooding her eyes. She leaned into her brother James and let out a long sigh.

"I know, I know," she said. "It's just so hard not knowing. Every day I get over to the express office to read the latest casualty reports, terrified to find his name, but I have to look. I just can't bear it much longer."

James hugged her tighter and she wept against his shoulder

"Another train is due in an hour," offered Cara. "Perhaps there will be news."

"Did you hear of the Confederate spies?" asked James.

"I thought that was just a rumor," said Elizabeth.

"I'm sorry," said James. "We haven't had the pleasure."

"Oh, James!" effused Katie. "This is Elizabeth!"

He looked confused.

"From Geneseo, before I met your Da! You know. I've told you about her."

"But you said she was just a wee lass."

Katie rolled her eyes, "That was back a ways, ye eejit!"

"Of course I remember," laughed James. "It is a pleasure to meet you at last."

"And you, sir," responded Elizabeth. "You were saying about the spies."

"Oh they are real, sure enough. Been plotting attacks in Toronto for a while, and they were just caught trying to capture the Michigan and free the Confederate prisoners on Johnson's Island."

"The Michigan?" asked Katie. "Isn't she the only gunboat on Lake Erie?"

"The one and only. Me and Captain Carter, the Michigan's commander, was having drinks one night in Sandusky when this real friendly banker from Philadelphia name of Cole comes over and starts buying drinks for Carter and his fellow officers. Since I was sitting there, I was thrown in the mix and we had a helluva time. I barely made it back to my ship in time to sail. That was the last time I ran into Carter or Cole, but it seems they became good friends.

"Turns out Cole was really a Confederate cavalry officer who had escaped from a Union prison. He was working with other escaped prisoners and secret agents up in Toronto under the direction of a former Confederate privateer, name of John Beall. They planned to capture the Michigan which stood guard over the Confederate prisoners on Johnson's Island. Once they had the Michigan, they would free the prisoners and use the warship to shell Buffalo and other Lake Erie ports.

"Cole persuaded Captain Carter to let him host a banquet on board for Carter and the other officers. He planned to put a Mickey Finn in the champagne to leave them incapacitated and make it easy to take over the ship while the crew slept. Up in Canada the Rebs had commandeered a Canadian ship and sailed to Sandusky Bay about eleven o'clock to wait for Cole's signal to attack.

"When they sailed into the bay, the Michigan was laying at anchor, all appeared quiet. But Cole wasn't on board and scores of Union soldiers lay waiting just below decks for the Rebel raiders. Seems a Union man had recognized Cole and turned him in to Federal Agents who seized him as he made final preparations for the banquet and laid the trap for the others.

"Beall's raiders waited and watched the gently rocking boat across the bay. They became suspicious when the signal never came. Sensing something had gone awry, they quietly slipped out of the bay and back to the Canadian shore where they burned the captured ship and made their way back to Toronto."

"What if he hadn't been discovered?" wondered Elizabeth. "Buffalo would be under the Michigan's guns by now."

"And there isn't another warship on Lake Erie. They could have sunk every freighter on the lake. The Union would be cut off from the West."

"What of the Confederate spies now?" asked Katie.

"They are still up in Toronto plotting against us."

" "Tis a cruel and dangerous world we live in," said Cara. "No one is safe."

A whistle sounded in the distance and Elizabeth announced, "Here comes the next train from the east. Time to greet the boys."

The women picked up baskets of bread and biscuits and stepped onto the platform to pass them out to the soldiers traveling through the city on the train. Elizabeth primped her hair and straightened her dress while Katie fussed over the baskets as the train chugged slowly into the station covering them with soot from the engine.

"O.k. ladies, big smiles for the boys!" said Katie stepping up to the first car.

They passed along the train handing bread, water, biscuits and coffee to the grateful soldiers leaning from the windows. James, Cara, Margaret and Mary carried the extra baskets along behind while Katie and Elizabeth handed out the treats.

"Thanks m'am, Got any tobacco?"

"Here you go. Where you from?"

"Cleveland. Been gone a long time."

"Got a girl waiting?"

"Finest in the land. No offense m'am."

"I'm getting a little too old to be worrying about that."

Down the platform Katie spotted some wounded soldiers disembarking.

"Better get down there and see who has come home," she advised Mary.

Mary saw a nun step off the car to help a one-armed lad down. He stumbled and the nun caught his arm steadying him.

"Poor thing," said Elizabeth.

"Too many come home like that," said Katie, "Too many. Most just boys."

"Oh Lord!" cried Mary. "Terence!"

The one-armed man turned around, "Ma?"

Mary rushed down the platform and threw her arms around him.

"Oh! Careful," exclaimed Terence. "My side is still tender."

Mary backed off sputtering, "Oh my God, you're hurt."

"He'll be all right," said Erin. " 'Twas Danny himself that fixed him up."

"Erin," gasped Mary. "Ma! Come quick! 'Tis Terence and Erin home from the war."

32

COLD HARBOR

The soldier's life was not what Michael had expected. Mindless routine settled into stifling, boring days that stretched on endlessly. Anything that disrupted the monotony of camp life was a godsend. Foraging details, patrols, picket duty, even fatigue duty, provided a welcome relief. Minor skirmishes brought brief heart pounding moments of heightened awareness, but so far the 155th had missed the fierce engagements that dominated the newspapers. Michael was disgusted. He wanted to get into the action. When Lee dashed into Pennsylvania to invade the North, the 155th had been sent on picket duty in the defense of Washington while the rest of the Union forces beat Lee back at Gettysburg. He was tired of moping in the backwaters of the war.

The 155th seemed the orphan of the army. They were passed around from one unit to another like an impoverished relative. Along the way men had gone AWOL out of homesickness and boredom. Michael hoped they would finally see some real action. He was ready to test himself against Johnny Reb or go home himself. Men need a sense of purpose. Practical jokes and bouts of drunkenness are not enough to sustain an army.

As a boy Michael rolled his eyes every time his Da looked him in the eye and said, "Be careful what you pray for, Laddie; God might be granting it." Michael first learned the sorry truth of it that December of 1864.

After months of picket duty warding off raids by Mosby's Rangers , Company K was assigned to defend a strategic bridge over Pope Run at Sangster Station along the Orange Alexandria Railroad. Captain Mc Anally was a careful man who knew the significance of the bridge and immediately ordered elaborate defenses erected.

As usual, Johnny Burns griped the whole time, "Bloody Captain ain't got nuttin' better ta do than make work for de rest o' us."

"It's for our own good," said Michael.

"Ha! Dat'll be de day when a officer does sumptin fer de poor soldier's good."

"The Union Army needs the railroad for the attack on Richmond. General Lee ain't likely to welcome us at the station. Easiest way to slow us down is to destroy this very bridge."

"Ol' Genra Lee ain't got nuttin left a fight wid. We jus' wastin' our time."

"If the Rebs come charging down those tracks, you'll be singing a different tune. These logs will save the lot of us. Now pick up the other end and help me set it in place ye dead beat."

Burns grabbed the end of the log and groaned when he lifted it.

"Blasted Mc Anally, gonna be de death o' me."

Michael ignored his endless whining and hefted his end.

"Shut yer gob and come along."

The night of the 17th was beyond miserable. Fierce thunderstorms with high winds and blinding rain swept through one after another. Michael leaned against the log stockade, thankful he had not cast off his slicker and wool coat like so many others had during the march. He constantly brushed away the stinging rain lashing his face in a vicious sideways onslaught.

Riders had been seen during the day and Captain Mc Anally had seen to it that Company K was on alert for a raid. The men slept in their uniforms with boots on, ready to spring into action at a moment's notice. The men in camp were wandering back to their tents after mess while Michael strained to pierce the blackness, but the clouds and driving rain reduced visibility to a few feet. Lightning streaked across the sky revealing glistening rails receding into the distance. When the boom of thunder echoed down the valley, Michael thought that any who might have been planning to find sleep that night were sure to be kept awake by the storm rolling in. Flash after flash followed, tearing the sky asunder and shattering the stillness with the deafening crash of thunder. Michael involuntarily bent down behind the logs with each flash and shuddered when the peals of thunder followed close behind.

After a few minutes, the storm abated and stillness returned to the night. Michael shivered as he wiped the cold rain from his face and again peered into the gloom. No one stirred in the camp, though the light murmur of conversation from within the tents drifted to him. The hairs on the back of his neck stood up when he thought heard the creak of leather and the clop of a horse's hoof, but try as he might, he could see nothing in the murky darkness. A brilliant flash of lightning pierced the gloom, revealing a horseman raising his sword a hundred yards down the track.

"Alarm!" screamed Michael and the pickets by the watch fire rushed to the log barricade.

Another flash revealed hundreds of cavalrymen emerging from the woods to line up against the few men on duty.

"Oh, Jaysus," muttered Burns when he saw the men arrayed against them.

"Steady," ordered Michael. The rest will be with us before they charge."

Men were streaming to the strong fortifications defending the bridge. Captain Mc Anally arrived and asked Michael, "What did you see, Corporal?"

"Large force of cavalry. Must be hundreds just there."

The captain couldn't make out anything and asked, "You're sure."

"They're out there and ready to charge."

Mc Anally whispered, "If we can't see them, they can't see us. Fire on my command."

A horse whinnied in the dark and a thousand hooves moved toward them. Muttered prayers and the click of muskets being cocked signaled the Union men had heard.

"Steady, wait for my command," whispered Mc Anally.

From down the tracks came one shouted command, "Charge!"

Lightning illuminated hundreds of riders riding down on the seventy men of Company K.

"Fire!" shouted the captain.

The thunder of galloping horses competed with the thunder of the storm and the thunder of the Union muskets and cannon. Horses and men shrieked in agony as the concentrated Union fire tore into their marks. Darkness returned. The charge had been halted momentarily giving ample time for the defenders to reload.

"At 'em boys!" came out of the darkness to be followed by the high-pitched Rebel yell.

The pounding of horse's hooves filled the night and Captain Mc Anally screamed, "Fire at will!"

The cannon and muskets roared again with the same devastating effect sending the charging cavalry off into the woods on either side of the tracks. Sporadic, disorganized fire fell ineffectively on the defenders sheltering behind the barricade.

A bugle sounded and the rebels charged from all sides. Captain Mc Anally withdrew the company to keep them from being overrun by the vastly superior force. He knew reinforcements would be on the way and that they had delayed the Confederates long enough to thwart their primary goal of destroying the bridge and capturing the trains in the station.

A company of Confederates swept behind the men and into the union camp, sending the few sentries fleeing into the woods. The Rebels galloped through hastily setting fire to the tents, supplies and bridge before being driven off by reinforcements arriving at the double quick. The Union boys concentrated their fire on the horsemen and the Confederates withdrew into the night to escape the murderous fire, enabling a squad of Union soldiers to rush in and extinguish the bridge fire.

"Cease fire," commanded the captain.

The seventy men of Company K stared at the retreating Rebs, shocked that they had held off the charge of a over 1,000 Confederate cavalrymen and saved the key bridge from destruction.

Michael breathed a sigh of relief and slid down the barricade to sit in the muddy water pooling there. He looked over at Burns staring wide-eyed back at him.

"How – did – we – manage – that?" panted Burns.

"Did you see how many there were?" responded Michael.

"Oh, yeah."

"Jesus," said Michael.

"I like ta shite me self," said Burns. "Always planned ta die abed at a hundred, shot by de husband of some sweet lass. But dem Johnny Rebs had another idea altogether."

"So far, so good," said Michael with a broad grin. "We sent them off proper."

"Jaysus," sighed Burns when the skies opened up to pour icy rain down on them again. "Jaysus, Jaysus, Jaysus, what ye gonna t'row at us next?"

A bolt of lightning lit up the night revealing the bodies of the wounded and dead Confederates sprawled along the tracks before him. Blinded by the flash and sickened by the sight, Michael put his face in his hands and whispered a fervent prayer of thanks. He looked toward their burning camp and dreaded the prospect of trying to hold out against overwhelming odds until relieved, with no food or shelter to sustain them.

The winter passed slowly, the cold and monotony of picket duty broken by a few hot skirmishes with Mosby's Raiders. The war had changed. The original war fever had subsided to be replaced by a general malaise when the reality of ruthless combat had become clear. Tens of thousands had lost their lives and hundreds of thousands more had suffered debilitating wounds. Union or Confederate, the high cost of war was hitting home. Massive armies swept through the land like a plague of locusts devouring crops, confiscating animals and leaving a ravaged land behind with little left to feed the civilian population. Soldiers and civilians grew weary of the conflict and calls for a negotiated peace filled the land. War profiteers seemed the only ones in the land driving the conflict forward.

For the Union a sense of inevitable victory had taken root following Grant's victories in the west and Lee's defeat at Gettysburg. The

Confederate cause evolved into a desperate struggle to survive long enough to win a negotiated settlement.

The soldiers of both sides fought on in spite of the carnage, because that is what weary battle-hardened soldiers do. Officers talked of great victories and glory while the soldiers talked of home and carried on. The whole Irish Legion received another unexpected blow when General Corcoran suffered a stroke while riding with his staff. He was talking animatedly with his aides when he froze and fell from his horse. His aides swarmed around and carried him to the surgeon where he died shortly after. Colonel Murphy assumed command and the whole Brigade was cast into shock. A sense of doom hung over the men waiting out the dreary remainder of winter.

Michael's company broke camp and marched to Alexandria in May for the Rapidan Campaign. Marching through the streets of Alexandria, Michael spotted Newell carrying the Buffalo Regiment's green flag at the head of the 155$^{th.}$ There was a fierce wind blowing and the slightly built lad could barely keep the flag upright. He struggled gallantly against the wind and managed to carry the banner past the cheering crowd. The men boarded boats and were transported to disembark at Belle Plains Landing.

When they arrived, there were hundreds of Confederate prisoners waiting for transport north to Union prisons. The disheartened men were bloodied, ill-clothed, dirty and half starved. They stared at the steady stream of Union troops disembarking with hollow, unbelieving eyes. They knew the war was lost for them and would soon be lost to the Confederacy as a whole.

Marching from the landing, they passed scores of walking wounded Union soldiers and a steady stream of ambulances bearing the more seriously injured. Something big was happening and Michael braced himself for what lay ahead.

After a series of forced marches they joined up with 4th brigade of the 2nd Division, II Corps, just before dark on the 17th of May, 1864. The men were served a quick dinner and ordered to fall in for a silent march. There was just enough time to wrap tin cups and anything thing else that might rattle in cloth. Michael saw Corporal Casey writing his name on his blouse and underwear.

"Afraid some Reb is gonna steal your long johns?" teased Michael.

Casey looked up at him. Michael was surprised when he saw the fear and resignation in the man's eyes. Casey had been in the thick of everything so far, and never once had hesitated to do his duty.

"From de looks of dose Rebs back at de landing and dat lot of our wounded boys, 'tis going to be rough up ahead," whispered Casey. "I mean ta make it easy ta identify me body. Sometimes dere is only parts left. Me mother would want ta be sure she is burying de proper lad."

"Can I borrow your pen when you are finished?"

Casey handed him the pen and Michael hurriedly inscribed his name on his undergarments.

Captain Byrne came by and whispered, "Time to form up boys. No talking and be sure that nothing will rattle and give away our position. This is a big one. Chaplain asked me to tell you that any man shot in the back running away would not get past St. Peter this day. I assured him St. Peter won't have to be turning any of you lads away this day."

The men laughed nervously prodding one another and pointing the way to the front.

"Good lads," said Captain Byrne. "Sergeant, silent march forward."

The company marched into line shuffling silently in the darkness. They continued until just before midnight halting at the rear of a series of breastworks. The exhausted men were told to stay silent and lay down to rest but to keep their backpacks on and muskets handy.

Sergeant Coughlin passed through the ranks whispering, "Johnny Reb is just over there in the woods. The boys from the 164th. are just to our right. It's going to be a brisk fight in the morning. A lot of boys have laid down their lives for both sides over the last few days, but we'll show 'em tomorrow."

He moved on. Michael peered over the breastworks and could just make out the dark line of the woods a hundred yards across the meadow. As he drifted off to sleep, he wondered how many muskets were lurking in those trees, ready to spew death on any who dared venture forth.

The muted sounds of men stirring awakened Michael in the pre-dawn hours of the 18th just as the sky was beginning to brighten. Slightly disoriented, he lay on his side staring at the backpack of Patrick Cruise while trying to remember where he was. A loud fart followed by a sigh brought him fully awake and he rolled onto his hands and knees and stood up. He stretched and yawned taking in the hellish surroundings. As far as he could see in either direction, men lay asleep on the bank of an earthen breastwork. Here and there men had wandered off to relieve themselves in the shattered forest. The topless trees in the woods behind stood as stark sentinels to the violence of the past few days and the days yet to come.

A whispered command came down the line, "Prepare to fall in."

The men shook each other awake to take care of their morning rituals before the final order to fall in was given. Michael checked his musket, bayonet and cartridge belt and adjusted his backpack on his sore shoulders.

"Fall in," came a few minutes later and the men rapidly formed into lines.

Anxious glances and reassuring grins were exchanged between comrades and thousand of silent prayers were sent skyward as the men awaited the next command.

"Forward!"

The 155th crested the breastworks and were met by a volley of musketry. Men crumpled and fell all around him, but the line surged onward crossing the open ground to the woods. The Rebels retreated through the woods before the advance, with Company K close on their heels. Stepping into a clearing on the other side of the woods, they were hit by the waiting Confederate artillery.

A shell burst nearby Michael, knocking down him and six or seven other men. All but three stood up and continued forward through another line of woods and down a small hill where they came up against the Rebel's main line of defense.

Musketry and canister shot raked the advancing line, mowing men down all around him. The regiment marched on, calm and steady in the face of the withering fire. Michael watched as Major Byrne clutched his head and fell to the ground, but still the men advanced.

Blood oozed from Michael's right ear and his vision was blurred from the artillery blast that had knocked him off his feet. He staggered after his company, determined not to fall behind. Ignoring his injuries he trudged on until he stumbled over the blackened corpse of a man killed the week before. The dead man's stomach burst and a blast of fetid air from the putrefying flesh made him gag and empty the contents of his stomach next to the decomposing horror. He pulled himself back to his feet and pushed warily onward, careful to avoid the scores of rotting bodies littering the field.

The company reached the abatis in front of the breastworks, but caught up in the interlaced branches, they could go no further and were subjected to a merciless artillery barrage. Unknown to General Grant, Ewell's second Corps had reoccupied the former Confederate breastworks, taking the opportunity to greatly strengthen them before Grant ordered the Union troops forward.

Devastated by the concentrated Confederate fire, the Union attack was repulsed and Michael withdrew with the remainder of his company. A quarter of the company, over one hundred men, had been killed or wounded in the assault. Corporal Casey was one of them.

That night Lieutenant Mooney walked up to the campfire Michael was dozing alongside. He sat on the log and poked the fire back to life sending hundreds of sparks up into the dark night. He refilled his clay pipe and tapped the tobacco down against the log. Michael stirred and looked up at his friend from the saloon.

"Hard times," sighed Mooney.

"So many lost for nothing," agreed Michael.

"You hear tell of the two Army privates one a pessimist, the other an optimist?"

Michael chuckled sadly, " Can't say that I have."

"Well, after a particularly gruesome fight, the pessimist plopped down beside the campfire and whined, 'What a terrible day. I don't see how things could get any worse' and the optimist said, 'Sure they can!'"

"Aye, we have more of the same coming, maybe worse. But it's got to be done, Hugh."

"The truly sad thing is when this is all ended, we shall go back to being brothers."

"I don't see how."

"It is like two brothers fighting. They battle like hell between themselves, but let someone else have a go at one and the two lads will join together to defend each other to the death. The next day they'll be at each other just the same."

"You speak with the wisdom of the saloon keeper, Hugh."

" I have picked up my share along the way. Do you know how many Irish lads are fighting just over there?"

"You mean the 69th?"

"No, for the Rebs. Most of them Fenians just like us. Why I was writing regular to a lad from Atlanta about taking the fight to Britain before this broke out and now he's fighting against us. Makes no sense a-tall."

"That should put the talk of invading Canada on hold, I'm guessing."

"Can't say for sure. We are trained and blooded soldiers now. If we come together against the British, we could do it sure."

"After we've killed each other? It will be hard."

"True, but we are all sons of Erin. That is where our true loyalties lay. Men will do what they must for the cause."

"First we have to survive this. What's next?"

"Grant won't give up. He'll just keep throwing bodies at the Rebs until they have no men left to fight. We have more men to lose than they do. We'll just outlast them. Tell the lads to get plenty of rest. Won't be long before we're in the thick of it again."

"You sound like the optimist," deadpanned Michael.

Mooney laughed, "Got me there. What do you hear of Sean and Micah?"

"Both are headed for home."

"Well Godspeed to them and to all of us," he said rising from the fire and disappearing into the night.

A day later they were on the move again. Word was that they were going on a long flanking movement against the Rebels gathering to defend Richmond. Passing through the town of Bowling Green, Michael noted the stark contrast with Alexandria. The women who came out to see them pass had tears and hostility in their eyes. Almost no men were evident, so he assumed they were off fighting with Lee or were already lying dead on some battlefield. Alexandria rung with the cries of impending victory and Bowling Green wept from the sting of defeat. It was obvious that they were in the midst of a hostile land.

Uneasy with the knowledge gleaned from past mistakes, and using only boards from the hardtack boxes, the men dug elaborate breastworks when they camped along the Mattapony River. No one wanted to be caught in the open with marauding Rebels around. The next morning the regiment crossed the river and engaged the enemy in a short but costly skirmish. The regiment continued skirmishing intermittently until moving out for Totopotomy Run where they again constructed breastworks using a plow and hardtack boxes to dig trenches. The men no longer had to be ordered to build defenses. They had learned their lesson and readily took to the task knowing their lives depended on it.

With no Confederates in sight, Michael sat atop the breastworks with a few of the men watching the sun settle into the western horizon. Quiet conversation ensued as the men unwound in the stillness of the peaceful evening.

"Finally a chance to get a bit of rest," said Michael. "Things have been pretty rough."

"Ye t'ink dat is rough? Me Biddy is wanting another wee one," said Billy Duffy.

"Who'd she get the last one from?" asked Sergeant Garey.

" 'Twas no one but meself!" returned Duffy. "Dat lass is a Saint, she is. 'bout dis time o' night she is home cooking. I can smell her stew sure as I'm sitting here."

"Ever wonder who she be cooking fer tonight?"

Duffy tossed a clod of dirt at Garey and the two of them went at each other, tumbling into the trench just as a single shot rang out. A bright red dot appeared in the center of Dillon Riley's forehead and he slumped over. Michael dove into the trench followed by the rest of the men. He reached back up and pulled Dillon down, behind him. The man's dead eyes stared back at Michael seeming to ask what had just happened. Michael grunted in frustration, pushed Dillon's body up out of the trench and hunkered down waiting for darkness.

The next morning brought an extended artillery exchange with the men of the depleted 155th waiting for an attack that never came. Skirmishes took place along the line, but Michael's company was spared any further conflicts and received orders to march toward Cold Harbor the next morning.

The drained, foot-weary men arrived about 5:00 PM and were ordered to immediately form up for an attack on the enemies fortifications. The resigned men formed up but were told to stand down once their depleted condition was noted. The men in Michael's unit had adopted Corporal Casey's tactic of writing their names on their blouses or pinning pieces of paper to themselves to paint a sad, demoralized portrait of men facing their demise. Michael slept soundly, the dark nightmares of the past weeks mercifully giving him respite before the coming battle.

With the boys of Buffalo's 164th on their left, the 155th moved forward at 4:30 AM on the morning of June 3, 1864. By 5:00 AM more than half of them would be lost.

All along the line the Rebs had placed stakes to mark the range for the artillery and infantry fire and they put up a murderous fire as the Union armies advanced. Michael and the boys from Company I plunged ahead in the darkness and soon found themselves mired in a marsh. Michael immediately lost his left boot as he slogged through swamp, struggling to keep his musket clear of the water with bullets whizzing past and churning up the murky water. He heard men grunt and splash into the water, some gunned down, others just stumbling in the morass. It quickly became every man for himself. It was impossible to work as a unit in the waist deep mud and water. As the sky started to brighten Michael could see the 164th breech the Confederate lines to his left. They had firm ground before them and the lads quickly piled into the trenches, fighting hand-to-hand to drive the Rebels back. The fighting looked fierce, and he prayed that Seamus would come through o.k. He had promised Cara and Liam that he would look after the boy, but with Seamus transferred to the 164th there was little he could do. Even if the lad was standing next to him, there was nothing he could really do to protect him anyway. The lad had signed up and was on his own now. Michael knew you have to do your own growing, no matter how tall your father was.

"God be with you, Seamus," he murmured as he waded toward his own fate.

He came to a small hillock in the marsh, and grabbing onto the trunk of a tree, pulled himself up out of the water. He was immediately struck by three mini balls and fell forward. He came to a moment later and reached to pull himself up. A stabbing pain from his shoulder caused him to cry out and roll onto his back. Bullets whizzed by overhead and the cries of men collapsing and drowning in the shallow water filled his ears. He glanced over toward the 164th and saw them being decimated by artillery fire as they huddled in the trenches they had just taken. He could see that the attack was broken as all along the line men were struggling to get back to safety. He eased back into the swampy water and slowly made his way back to the Union breastworks hoping he'd find Seamus safe in camp.

In the hospital tent he heard that the 155th had lost one hundred and sixty-four men in that swamp in less than twenty-five minutes. He was out of the action for now, and within two weeks the 155th would be left with but seventy-five men of the original four hundred recruited in Buffalo. Their sister regiment, the 164th, suffered similar losses in the hand to hand combat and the merciless barrage they had endured in the Rebel trenches while the 155th was mired in the swamp. Many a home in Buffalo would have empty chairs that could never be filled with the laughter of loved ones.

33

WITH MALICE TOWARD NONE

After the loss of 620,000 in a brutal Civil War, it never crossed Katie or Sean's mind that one more death could shatter their world.

But shatter it did.

Commercial Advertiser

Saturday Evening, April 15, 1865.

LAST NIGHT'S DISPATCHES.

AWFUL TIDINGS!

THE PRESIDENT ASSASSINATED!

Attempt to Murder Secretary Seward.

THE PRESIDENT SHOT AT THE THEATRE.

Mr. Seward Stabbed in Bed.

THE ASSASSIN ESCAPED.

WASHINGTON, April 15—12:30 A. M.

The President was shot in a theatre to-night, and is perhaps mortally wounded.

SECOND DISPATCH.

The President is not expected to live through the night. He was shot at a theatre.

Secretary Seward was also assassinated. No arteries were cut. Particulars soon.

WASHINGTON, April 14.

Sean rushed home with the Advertiser and pulled Katie from her laundry to read the devastating report.

"What will become of us?" asked a bewildered Katie. "He brought us through this cursed war. Who will bring us through the bitter aftermath?"

"Oh my God, Katie!" exclaimed Sean. "It was Booth what done the deed!"

"Who?"

"John Wilkes Booth! That actor you were mad about. He played Macbeth at the Metropolitan a few years back. You and all the lasses were like to swoon if he looked your way."

"No."

"What madness. To endure so much to save the Union and free the slaves only to be shot down with the suffering ended. God can be a cruel master."

"We don't understand His ways is all."

"Well I know I don't."

Reports flowed in daily outlining the scale of the plot, the death of Booth and the capture of the conspirators to be met with disbelief by the loyal citizens of Buffalo and all of New York. With the war ended, hope for the future had flourished only to be crushed by the tragic murder of the great man. Now melancholy Buffalonians prepared to bid their final farewell when the funeral train passed through the Queen City of the Lakes.

"Hurry everyone!" shouted Sean in the predawn darkness. "Time to turn out or we shall never get close enough!"

The household stirred as the groggy residents hurried through their usual Sunday morning rituals sprucing up and donning their finest attire. Children were inspected and sent back to tame errant hair or wash both sides of their necks and then given milk and biscuits from the previous night's supper. Within thirty minutes of Sean's call, the extended family was tromping toward the depot, just as a faint gray light lit the eastern sky, chasing the stars before it.

"Will you look at all the people already ahead of us?" commented Erin.

"He was the most hated and loved man in Amerikay," said Cara.

"Aye, he made us look hard at ourselves," said Sean. "And when we didn't like what we saw, he showed us the way. Men may never agree whether he was a Saint or a monster, but they all have to admit he was a great man."

"Not all great men are good men," said Danny pointing to Terence. "I heard tell that 50,00 men lost their limbs besides all that lost their lives. I know I took my share of limbs."

"Aye, but this man was good as well as great," said Terence. "I may have lost my arm, but I found my soul in service to his noble cause."

"You still intend to join the priesthood?" asked Micah.

"I do."

"Strange how war changes a man," said Erin. I've watched some become bitter apostates and you aim to be a man of God."

"But all changed," added Danny. "You can't see war and stay the same."

The family waited somberly in the grey morning light for the funeral train to arrive. At six-fifty the pilot train, heralding the approaching funeral train, pulled into the station, sounding long whistle blasts and ringing it's bell. The crowd surged forward craning their necks to catch sight of the approaching funeral train.

Precisely at eight, a hush fell over the crowd as the exquisitely decorated engine, the Dean Richmond, slowly, silently came to a rest at the depot. A full length portrait of the President framed by the graceful folds of Old Glory, each trimmed with black and white crape draped over the sides of the engine, was set under the head light. The handrails were festooned with funereal rosettes and bright bouquets.

The burial party disembarked and were taken to the solemnly decorated Bloomer's Railroad Dining Saloon where they were served the finest the city had to offer while the thousands gathered hung their heads in respect. The crowd turned their attention back to the train, standing in awe of the ghostly image before them. The funeral car was draped in black with black curtains covering the windows. A silver soffit hung from the roof with loops of crepe with a silver star and tassel centered on each window. Katie blessed herself, bowed her head and wiped a tear from her eye.

At eight o'clock the crowd was herded back as Mr. Lincoln's casket was carried from the rail car and borne to the waiting hearse on the shoulders of the honor guard. Six magnificent white horses shrouded in black to their hooves whinnied nervously as the coffin was loaded. The burial party boarded the carriages provided and the cortege proceeded up Exchange Street to Main and on to the St. James Hall on the corner of Eagle Street, followed by the throng of mourners. In a sad reprise of the scene from a few years before, every window and housetop along the way was filled with a mass of onlookers.

As the Reddy family reached the vicinity of St. James Hall, they heard the angelic strains of the St. Cecelia Society singing the solemn dirge, "Rest, Spirit, Rest." Tears glittered in every eye as the somber melody swept over the crowd, driving home the terrible loss the Nation had suffered. The crowd waited patiently to view the great man as preparations were made within the hall.

A little after ten the doors were opened and the waiting mourners were allowed in to pay their respects. Sean was amazed at the decorum of the crowd. City dignitaries and grandees from mansions on Delaware Avenue were granted first access and then merchants, dock workers, prostitutes, hooligans and the destitute set aside their prejudices and mingled in the line patiently awaiting their turn.

When he finally passed into the hall, Sean scanned the interior as the line inched forward. The walls were bedecked with black and white crepe, lace and golden fringe. The center was set off by eight wreath draped columns with three arched entrances covered in elaborately folded cloth with ties of black and white. A glittering chandelier suspended directly over the dais completed the rich trappings prepared for the deceased President.

Katie gasped when she spied the open casket resting atop a double dais inclined to display the body. Rich drapes of black velvet fringed by silver rosettes surrounded the dais highlighting the President.

Dressed in plain black the "People's President" lay in repose before her. His slightly discolored face bore that same kind, sadly benign expression that characterized him when alive.

Katie choked back a sob when Sean whispered, "We can be grateful that he has been granted the rest for which he must have so often sighed during these troubled times."

The walk home that day was long, sad and silent.

34

1866
BROTHERS IN ARMS

Life at the Reddy household had returned, if not to normal, to a new normal. Sean was back to work with a higher salary and with more responsibilities and healthy as he ever was. Danny, Michael and Erin were under the roof once again healing from wounds physical and pyschological. James was happily wintering at home with Margaret, and Terence was back with his parents, so only Bernadette was missing from the family circle. From the latest letter from California Katie learned that Bernadette was again with child and that her husband Tommy was well. Seamus had come unscathed through the conflagration, and the boarders were hungrier than ever at the table. All was well, and the future once again looked bright.

Her men, however, they were another story. Lately they had been gathering at Mooney' Saloon to meet with the Fenians. Michael had already joined the group and Sean and Micah were strong backers. The ongoing British occupation of Ireland was always the topic since before the Civil War, and many had fought just to learn the art of warfare.

Lately the Fenian Brotherhood had broken into two camps, those who wanted to smuggle weapons to Ireland to arm the populace to retake their homeland from the British, and those who wanted to invade Canada and trade it for Irish independence.

The brotherhood numbered in the tens of thousands. Men who had fought for the South and men who had fought for the North were now joined together in the Irish cause. The Fenians met openly and the U.S. government seemed to give tacit approval to their activities. War surplus weapons were made readily available to the Fenians, and most Americans held a dim view of Britain's recent recognition of the Confederacy's belligerent rights. Finally Manifest Destiny still rang true to most Americans and they believed that America should be a continental nation. Doubts about the Fenian agenda were raised only in border cities like Buffalo.

Sean came home a little later than usual and announced, "Well it has been decided. It will be Canada."

"But Sean, that makes no sense," said Katie.

"The people of Canada tire of British oppression just as we do. They will not fight to stay under the Crown's thumb. Once we defeat the few British troops, the King will be forced to trade Ireland for Canada."

"A fool's errand if ever there was one."

"This is man's business."

"How will you stand against professional soldiers?"

"Most of us have been well trained during the war, and the British exile their poorest soldiers to the wilds of Canada."

"I hope you don't think I'm letting you go fight."

"No, I am too old, but Michael may choose to go."

"Hasn't he seen enough blood?"

"It is for Ireland, woman."

"Don't use that tone with me. We are Americans now. Ireland is behind us."

"Tomorrow night Micah, Terence, Michael and I are to meet a war surplus dealer to pick up muskets and powder. We will bring the supplies to Mooney's and a few other storage sites."

"Terence? The lad who is going to be a priest?"

"He's Irish first."

"God comes first."

"The British drove me out of Ireland and Killed your Ma and Da, Katie. This is God's work."

"Making war is the Divil's work, Sean Reddy, and you know it."

"Hard times call for hard choices."

"Men! You're like two rams butting heads at every turn when you could just as easily walk around."

Katie's eyes flared then softened.

"Won't the army or the Watch try to stop you?"

"Half of the lads are Fenians. If they don't out and out join us, they will look the other way. Any way we will be moving the arms in the wee hours with no one to see."

"Where will you meet the gun runner?"

" 'Tis best if you don't know anything about it, just in case."

Katie's eyes flared once again and she stormed from the room.

The next night at Mooney's Saloon the four men nursed a growler of beer between them while others around them lost themselves in blackjack, straight rum or whiskey. Sean never developed a taste for blackjack. It was the cheapest and surest way to get drunk, but molasses and rum and whatever else might be mixed in made for a strange flavor that didn't satisfy the thirst. Loud raucous voices filled the saloon allowing the conspirators to discuss their plans with, Hugh Mooney, Michael's lieutenant from the 155th.

"Good to see you lads looking so rough and ready," said Mooney pulling a chair over to their table.

"Ready for duty, lieutenant," replied Michael.

"That was good for Cold Harbor, Michael. 'Tis Hugh now."

"Aye, aye, lieutenant."

"Hugh."

"Hugh."

"Now that we've settled that piece of business, I've a few concerns about tonight's business," said Sean.

"The wagons are hitched and waiting back of the Batt's Brewery. No one will think twice about brewery wagons on a grain run."

"Good. Who do we contact?"

"A German calls himself Weisbeck. You say, "Pleasant night," and he will answer, "Not to my liking."

"A German? Can we trust a German? I put my faith in sons of Ireland, but I don't know about a German. What's to stop him from laying a trap?"

"Money. I don't know about most Germans, but this one loves nothing else."

"O.K."

Then you answer him with, "Good for getting some work done. Got it?"

"Aye."

"Take one load to St. Brigid's and bring one back here. Nothing to it."

Sean nodded thoughtfully and shrugged his shoulders.

"Time we cast the dice. Ready Micah?"

"We will have to unload quickly so no one will take notice," remarked Micah.

"I will have men waiting here and at St. Brigid's. Anything else?"

"Erin Go Bragh!"

Hugh laughed and replied, "Slán abhaile, (safe home.)"

The men left with the last of the drinkers and strolled casually up to High Street to Batt's. Two wagons were hitched and waiting by the stables behind the brewery. Michael and Sean climbed onto the first and Sean took up the reins and guided the team out to the street. Terence and Micah took the second and followed along. The clop of the horses hooves echoed from the buildings in the still night air. Sean was sure it was loud enough to wake the dead, but in a bustling metropolis like Buffalo, people were used to the steady stream of commerce that passed by at all hours.

Twenty minutes later they pulled alongside a canal boat moored at the foot of Mechanic. A lantern resting on the cabin roof cast a feeble circle of light revealing the shadowy figure of a man leaning against the tiller with a straw hat pulled low over his face and a scarf covering his mouth and nose. His arms lay tucked inside his coat pockets.

"Pleasant night," greeted Sean.

"Not to my liking," came the muffled reply.

"Good for getting some work done."

"Come aboard."

"Mr. Weisbeck?"

"Will do for tonight, the swag is laid out below. You have the money?"

Sean nodded to Micah, who took the lantern and peered into the cabin.

"Looks about right," said Micah emerging a few moments later.

Sean began counting out the money as the others loaded the muskets and ammunition into the wagons. A musket slipped from Terence's arms and thumped onto the deck.

"Careful, boy, you'll attract attention," said Weisbeck looking up. "Don't want some nosy Watchman coming along. Move along quickly."

Sean saw Weisbeck's eyes widen when the man caught sight of Micah's face in the pale light of the lantern.

"Everything all right?" asked Sean.

"Thought I heard something down the street is all."

Sean quickly scanned the street.

"Must be nerves is all," said Weisbeck.

He swept up the money using only one hand, put it into a pouch and tucked it into under his tightly buttoned his coat. Sean figured the man had a concealed pistol in the other hand, and keeping one eye on Weisbeck, joined the others. The wagons were loaded ten minutes later. The men climbed back onto the wagons and were about to pull away when Weisbeck called, "Micah, did you get the box of grenades in the aft cabin?"

"Didn't check there," said Micah climbing down.

He hopped onto the roof of the boat and met Weisbeck waiting by the cabin door.

"Just down to the left," said Weisbeck pointing the way.

Micah ducked down followed closely by Weisbeck.

Terence started and exclaimed, "How did he know my Da's name?"

Sean grabbed his shillelagh and jumped from the wagon onto the roof of the gently rocking boat.

"Watch your back!" screamed Terence as Sean ran across the roof.

A shot rang out below decks and Sean rushed in shillelagh held high. Micah, with blood oozing from his side. was struggling with Weisbeck.

"You fucking Irish," growled Weisbeck trying to gouge Micah's eyes with his hook hand. "You've taken everything from me. I done for your boy on the train and now I'll due for you. The Divil with the consequences!"

Micah was weakening from the gunshot wound, but Sean laid Weisbeck low with one thump from the shillelagh. Micah sat on a bale of cloth and felt his side. Sean lifted his shirt and looked at the wound.

"Doesn't look too bad. We'll have Danny look at it."

"I turned just in time to deflect his aim," panted Micah. "He'd a killed me if Terence hadn't yelled."

"What the hell got into him? Didn't he figure we'd get to him even if he got you? Do you know him?"

Terence and Michael rushed into the cabin and Terence pulled Weisbeck's scarf from his face.

"It's Dietz!"

"No, that's Engel, the German."

"No, he's the commissary, the man who threw Erin and I over."

Micah looked again.

"Evil has a way of turning up everywhere. That's Engel all right. Is he dead?"

Terence leaned close and Engel buried his hook in the back of the boy's shoulder.

Terence screamed and pulled back from the maniacally laughing man. Sean beat Engel's head into a bloody pulp and Michael freed the hook from Terence's back.

Taking back the money and leaving the German where he lay, they hurried from the boat and drove their teams rapidly through the deserted streets to Mooney's.

"We had trouble," said Sean reining in the team outside the saloon.

"Is everyone all right?" asked Mooney.

"Micah and Terence are hurt. Have some of your men take care of the wagons while Michael goes for Danny. We'll wait inside for him."

"Help yourself to the jug."

"For God's sake, Michael, don't wake your mother," warned Sean.

"I'm not fool enough for that, Da."

Word reached them in May of the aborted Fenian raid on Campo Bello Island in New Brunswick. The Fenians had planned to take the island to gain control of shipping into Canada, but they had been turned back by British and American gunboats leaving the men stranded in Maine.

Contradictory rumors and orders sent Fenians back and forth across the Northeast with men traveling both east and west on the railroads. A plan had been proposed to capture land across the St. Lawrence as a base for privateers that would stop all British shipping to the interior. While these Fenian movements were taking place, Fenian soldiers from all of the states were quietly moving toward Buffalo.

Released from the prison on Johnson's Island a month earlier, Colonel Niall Walsh joined his Southern Fenian brothers on the Buffalo bound train. Gaunt and unsteady on his feet, he bore the evidence of years of captivity in a Union prisoner of war camp. Haggard as he was, he was welcomed by Colonel O'Neil and the 150 ex-Confederates who had left Nashville the 27th of May to be joined along the way by lads from Louisville and the Northern lads from Cleveland. Niall wasn't sure whether he was more excited to join the planned invasion or to finally see Erin again.

Just as the train was pulling out of the station at 10 PM in a light rain, the telegraph operator ran up to the window and handed Colonel O'Neil a telegram.

"Hmpf," he muttered. "Seems the Buffalo Guard is waiting to take us into custody."

"What are we to do?" asked Niall.

"A Michael Reddy is to meet us before we reach the station on Exchange. We are to slow the train to let the men jump off and the Buffalo lads will take us to hiding spots to await final orders."

"I know his sister."

"Is that the reason you're here?"

"One of them, but I am loyal to the cause."

The train reached the outskirts of Buffalo in the gray light of dawn with a light rain falling and Niall spotted Michael holding a green flag by a curve in the tracks. About ten others stood by. The train slowed and men leapt down to rally around the Buffalo Fenians. Niall stumbled when he hit the ground and fell unceremoniously to the ground. As he brushed himself off, Michael offered him a hand up.

"Thank you, Michael," said Niall.

"How do you know my name?" he asked.

"The telegram and you are the spitting image of Erin."

"How do you know Erin? Wait, you must be Niall."

"Pleased to meet you Michael Reddy, Colonel Niall Walsh at your service."

"Well I'll be damned."

"Not if Erin has anything to say about it," joshed Niall.

Over three hundred men were spirited away by the Buffalo contingent to be hidden in warehouses, barns, and meeting halls. Michael kept Niall with him and the two of them watched as the gunboat USS Michigan steamed into the harbor with her decks lined with Marines.

"Seems the government has got a hold of the idea that the Brotherhood might be more than a view drunken Irishmen talking through their arses," said Michael. "We shall have to be careful."

They passed through the freight yards as more guns and ammunition were unloaded from a rail car. Strange men could be seen at every turn and the city buzzed with anticipation.

The underfed Niall was taken to the Reddy household to be fed and fussed over by the Reddy women. He was seated at the dining table mopping up beef gravy with chunks of fresh baked bread when Erin walked in. He had lost so much weight that she didn't recognize him at first, but when he turned with gravy dripping down his chin and smiled at her, she ran to him and stood over him squealing with delight.

"Niall! Oh thank the Lord. Niall! Praise God! Oh Niall, Niall, Niall you've come at last."

He hugged her and said, "Now Erin Reddy about that vow."

"I'd be proud to be your wife."

Seamus O'Connor burst into the room and blurted, "The orders have come! We cross at dawn!"

Michael, Seamus and Niall joined the mass of men making their way to Pratt's Blast Furnace at Black Rock where barges that had been supposedly rented to take employees across the channel for a picnic waited to ferry the men across the Niagara River. In the early morning hours a steam tug was returning from the Canadian shore after transporting arms and supplies to the other side when Sean, Micah and Terence arrived to wish the men well and witness the crossing. The Fenian raiders were already lined up to board the barges when Sean spotted Michael and the others waiting their turn.

"Your Grand Da died fighting here," said Sean placing his hand on Michael's arm. "You take care and don't do anything foolish. It is a grand cause, but I could not bear to lose you now that you came through the war against the Rebels."

"I know what I am about, Da."

"Just the same."

The order came to board and once the barge was filled, the tug towed them across the silent river. He saw Micah and Terence waving their hats and Sean standing at their side staring morosely at the tiny Irish armada out to conquer the British Empire.

Disembarking on the far shore, the men were issued the stockpiled weapons and ammunition. In short order Michael, Seamus and Niall were marching south toward Fort Erie with the excited Fenian column. Instead of grim-faced soldiers off to face death, the column seemed more like picnickers off on a grand outing. Meeting no resistance, the men boasted, teased and joshed on the march to Fort Erie. Scouts spread out from the column into the surrounding countryside, commandeering horses and bringing reports of approaching British troops. By 5:00 AM the Fenians had taken possession of the crumbling walls of the fort. Other units were off cutting telegraph lines and destroying tracks toward Port Colborne while the British were marshalling forces in Toronto, Hamilton and Port Colborne.

Breakfasting on commandeered biscuits and tea, Michael watched the activity on the river as the USS Michigan cruised into position. The Michigan sailors could be seen off loading howitzers onto steam tugs for picket duty along the river effectively cutting off the only means of escape. Michael turned when he heard three scouts leading a string of horses gallop up and rein in next to Colonel O'Neil.

"We've brought you a mount, Colonel," reported the scout.

"Any further sightings?" asked O'Neil.

"Canna be certain, but appears could be as many t'ree t'ousand coming down from de north."

"We'll be ready," said O'Neil confidently.

Hearing this Niall nudged Michael, nodded to the Michigan and drawled, "Wal, we better be. Ain't no going back now."

Michael replied grimly, "Expect we're in for it. "Hope you Southern boys are up for another tussle."

Niall peered at Michael over the top of his mug, "We're all sons O' Erin, now. Half the men here are from south of the Mason-Dixon."

"Sorry, just habit I guess. Spent a good part of the past few years cursing your black hearts and your damned rebel yell."

"Wal truth be told, we didn't have much good to say around the cook fires about you Yankee boys."

"Now we're brothers in arms."

The men spent the rest of the day erecting a defensive perimeter of bullet screens to the north. Rails were leaned against the top rail of fences and clods of dirt were piled onto the rails, providing an effective screen almost as good as trenches with a fraction of the effort. Michael was alarmed by the slow pace of the work though. Rumor had it that the British were moving down from Chippawa and the Fenians wouldn't be ready to meet them if they didn't hurry. He could see the Michigan maneuvering in the Niagara, preventing any further reinforcements from crossing. They were on their own facing growing numbers of British troops that were assembling to repulse the invasion, yet Colonel O'Neil seemed in no particular hurry to finish the defenses.

At officer's call, the Colonel looked annoyed at Michael when he pointed out the slow progress of the work.

"We are likely outnumbered twenty to one," muttered O'Neill in reply. "I find that encouraging, because a force that size will be unwieldy enough to make life easy for us."

Michael just stared back dumbly not believing what he had just heard.

"The British are here," he explained pointing to Chippawa on the map. "They will expect us to head along the river and so we shall. When they move to cut us off we swing inland and make for Port Colborne. They will not be able to react in time to stop us from destroying the canal and escaping across the lake."

He slammed his fist on the table and laughed, "They don't know who they are dealing with, lads. 'Tis the sons of Erin they are facing today!"

"And if we meet another army coming from the west?" asked another.

"Ask me when they see their canal in ruins. They won't know what hit them."

The gathered men exchanged worried glances.

"Don't you understand?" asked O'Neil in frustration. "They are falling into our hands!"

A short time later word came that troops were indeed massing at Port Colborne. Confronted with the coming pincer movement, with no contact from his superiors and with no reinforcements able to cross the Niagara, O'Neill retreated to his tent unsure of what to do. After a time mulling his predicament, he emerged with a vague plan to salvage the undermanned expedition.

The men assembled for the march to the north. On the way the bridge at Frenchman's Creek was set afire, three hundred extra muskets were tossed into the blaze and the badly outnumbered column marched to face the enemy.

Enemy scouts saw the blaze lighting the sky and hurried to report the Fenians on the move. The British commander calmly reacted to the intelligence by telegraphing the information to Port Colborne and by sending reinforcements to Black Creek to counter the Fenian advance. Heartened by the news, the British generals laid plans to trap the invaders between their two armies. Luckily for O'Neil, the British and Canadian forces did not coordinate their plans. Moves were made without waiting for confirmation from each other, paving the way for the sorely outnumbered Fenians to set their plan in motion.

Under cover of darkness, as the British reinforced the defensive position at Black Creek and moved troops by rail from Hamilton to Port Colborne, O'Neill turned his column inland to the west. After a short pause to rest and regroup, he led the men up to the top of Lime Ridge, the only high ground for miles around, about a mile north of the tiny hamlet of Ridgeway.

While this was transpiring, Colonel Dennis of the Queens Own Rifles took a force of eighty men to Fort Erie to cut off any Fenian retreat and left the bulk of his men waiting in Port Colborne, effectively quashing the planned pincer envelopment.

The other British forces proceeded as originally planned moving to envelop the Fenians near Stevensville. Colonel Booker, the militia commander from Hamilton, started on time but the force at Black Creek was delayed waiting for a possible Fenian advance to the north.

Booker's inexperienced men had spent most of their sparse training learning to march smartly. Few had even fired a weapon. To make matters worse they were issued new breech loading rifles that none had ever fired and issued limited ammunition, and the supply trains were sent away. One of the ill-prepared companies marched into battle somehow forgetting to bring along any ammunition at all. They soon found themselves face to face with veterans hardened from four years of the most brutal war ever seen, grimly waiting behind professionally constructed bullet screens.

"Going to be a hot one," said Seamus as he dumped a few more clods of dirt onto the bullet screen. "Should have piled the biscuits here instead of in me stomach."

"You call this hot?" asked Niall. "Might get to eighty or so. That's top coat weather in Savannah. Biscuits wouldn't do no good. Too many ricochets flying around."

"You Reb boys will be suited just fine for where you're going."

"Not sure about that. Might have to ask Ol' Scratch himself to throw a few more coals on the fire after our time up north fighting alongside ye damned Yankees."

The men laughed and stretched out on the grass.

"Now you Yankee boys," began Niall.

"Wait. Hear that?" asked Michael.

The men stopped and strained to listen to a faint, distant rhythm growing louder with each passing moment. The sound faded and then the report of sporadic fire from Fenian skirmishers brought home the fact that battle had been engaged. A furious fusillade followed and Michael could see the skirmishers beating it back to the main defensive line ahead of the advancing militia that was spreading out behind them in the orchard.

Some of the advancing British were armed with Spencer repeating rifles and they put up a steady hail of lead that the Fenians could not match. Bullets thudded into the bullet screen, and the three comrades fired a volley and dove for cover to reload. They were able to return one shot for every seven or eight unleashed at them and O'Neil ordered a withdrawal from the orchard to reform the line. The British were so swift in the pursuit that gaps appeared in their line. Sensing a chance against the larger force of inexperienced fighters, O'Neil dispatched mounted officers to lead a counter charge.

A cry of "Cavalry" ran through the British ranks and they broke off the charge to form the traditional "defensive square" that had been used so successfully during the Napoleonic War .

"They are done for now!" Niall shouted triumphantly. "Have at 'em."

The Fenians unleashed a brutal volley into the tightly packed British square standing exposed in the middle of the road. Over thirty went down dead or wounded and the Fenians, with bayonets fixed surged forward driving the British before them. They pushed them three miles back through the village of Ridgeway before cutting off the charge.

Michael and Seamus stood bent over trying to catch their breath as Niall continued on another hundred yards before he realized he was alone and turned back to the scattered line of Fenians.

"We showed them," panted Seamus. "They won't be back any time soon. Ireland will soon be free of the Crown!"

"It was a good showing, for true," agreed Michael. " 'Tis not over yet." There are many more where they came from and with all the desertions since we landed, we are in for a tough go of it."

"Turn about, lads!" called Lieutenant O'Reilly. "We are on the march to the east."

"What's happening?" asked Michael.

"More bloody British than ye kin shake a stick at on the way. We're making for the fort."

Marching into the village of Fort Erie with the vanguard, they came under intense fire from British soldiers. The Fenians returned fire and were driven to cover where they waited for the main body to arrive. When the British saw the main column pouring into the village they broke and ran. Some of the militia rushed to the waterfront and tried to board a tug tied to the wharf. The captain of the tug saw them coming and cut the mooring lines with an axe, leaving the terrified men with no choice but to jump into the river and hide under the wharf. The rest scattered into the village, hiding in a number of houses, to fire on the advancing Fenian column.

The men ran out of the line of fire and Michael called for skirmishers to provide cover while Niall, Seamus and he crept behind the first house. A constant fire kept the British holed up in the house pinned down as they made their way around to a wood pile in the back.

A lone British sentry stood partially exposed in the rear doorway. He was hunched over peering anxiously toward the front of the house trying to follow the action and periodically turning to scan the rear for a sneak attack.

"Make ready," said Michael.

He crawled to the side of the wood pile and sighted his rifle on the man in the doorway. When the sentry leaned out to look around, Michael fired and the soldier collapsed into the yard. Niall and Seamus rushed forward with Michael right behind. The soldiers taken by surprise immediately dropped their weapons and threw up their hands before the three muskets aiming point blank at them. The officer put up the only resistance turning to fire his revolver and hitting Seamus in his bicep. Seamus fired back striking the officer in the leg. Breaking out the front door and underneath a swarm of bullets the officer ran toward the river emptying his revolver as he fled. Limping badly with the Fenians hot on his heels, he cast his revolver aside and rolled into the river attempting to escape down stream. Michael ran along the riverbank, leapt in and hauled him out of the water taking the bedraggled man prisoner.

Michael heard that in the ensuing chaos the British Colonel Dennis hid himself in the Reeve's (sheriff's) house, shaved his beard and put on a maid's dress to escape capture. Forty British soldiers, left to fend for themselves, had taken refuge in a larger house a little further down the road and loosed a volley on the Fenians. Shrieks of terrified women and children trapped inside with the soldiers followed the thunderous report of the volley. The Fenians rushed the house and Michael saw Colonel Bailey tumble from his horse run through by a forgotten ramrod left in the barrel by a frightened sixteen year old Canadian. The Fenians returned fire and a furious exchange ensued. Thousands of onlookers gathered across the river on the American shore cheered with each volley. Finally after twenty minutes of battle, a young woman appeared in the second floor window waving a white sheet and the Fenians ceased fire. After inflicting twenty-one casualties, the British laid down their weapons and surrendered to O'Neil.

With two victories to his credit, O'Neil found his situation growing ever more desperate. His force, now less than four hundred men, was left to face five times their number. The U.S.S Michigan controlled the river and he could expect no reinforcements. He abandoned the town and moved to a better defensive position at the old fort with his men and prisoners. When Michael brought the wounded British officer to him at the fort for questioning, O'Neill ordered Michael to take him across to Buffalo for treatment.

"Wait for the gunboat to swing to the north and then make for the American shore," ordered O'Neill. "Row hard and you can make it before they can react."

"Yes sir," replied Michael.

"Tell them that I can't hold out long without reinforcements, but if a movement is going on elsewhere along the border, I can turn the fort into a slaughter pen."

Michael had two men carry the officer to a skiff on the river's edge and bearing O'Neil's grim missive, he and Seamus ferried the wounded man across the river to the waiting Fenian General Lynch.

"Tell Colonel O'Neil that we cannot get past the Michigan," said the officer. "The planned attack across the St. Lawrence River was interdicted and he is on his own."

"We have fought bravely, but the cause is lost if you don't send reinforcements," explained Michael.

General Lynch pointed at the iron hulled Michigan waiting in the mouth of the Niagara River and answered, "There is nothing we can do. To go under her guns is suicide. 'Tis better to live to fight another day."

Michael returned in a drenching rain with the bad news and O'Neil just gazed through the haze toward Buffalo.

"What was it all for?" he asked dismally.

"You did all that any man could expect," returned Michael.

"Go back and have them send transportation. We shall withdraw."

"And the Michigan?"

"Better an American jail than a British noose."

After crossing once more with Colonel O'Neill's request, Michael was joined on the American shore by Sean, Micah and Terence. Along with hundreds of others they watched as the scow A.P. Waite was towed across to pick up the surrounded Fenians. Fearful of being left behind, the invaders crowded aboard the scow leaving no room to sit and sorely trying its capacity. When the captain of the Michigan saw the tug pull the overloaded barge into the river, he moved to intercept the craft. A shot was put across the bow of the tug and the tug heaved to for a boarding party. O'Neil waited for the Michigan's launch, climbed aboard with his fellow officers and immediately surrendered his exhausted army to the captain.

35

FORWARD AGAIN

" 'Twas a noble endeavor," sighed Michael.

"Could we have been so foolish as to think it could succeed?" asked Sean.

"We've waited so long to have it end this way," said Micah.

"We were the only ones to carry out the plan," explained Michael. "If the others had done their part, who knows how it would have ended? All those fine lads bound for prison."

"And Niall among them," added Sean. "Can't the lass have even a bit o' luck?"

"We seemed a cursed race," added Terence. "I should have gone with ya."

"I thought you were for the priesthood," said Michael.

Terence spit in disgust and growled, "The divil take the lot o' them."

"They won't have him," explained Micah.

"Won't have him?"

"The Bishop told us that a priest must have both hands to perform the Sacraments. Anything less would be an affront to God."

"The same God who put this evil war upon the land and took me arm away," said Terence bitterly.

"You can't blame God for our folly," said Micah. "We did this to ourselves."

"I watched thousands on both sides lay down their lives in the name of God and country, and now he won't let me atone for the killing I've done. What sense is there to this? I wish I'd died in the mud with the rest."

He stormed off, leaving the men staring after, not knowing how to answer the lad.

"I better go to him," said Micah. "No telling what he'll do now that his faith, as well as his arm, has been taken from him."

Michael shook his head and said, "The good fathers send us off to war with prayers for victory and proclaiming God is on our side. What foolishness that they would turn away a lad with such a burning desire to serve that same God. An affront to God, my arse! Is a man who lost his arm doing The Almighty's work not good enough to serve God in peace because of the sacrifice he made for God and country?"

"Don't let Ma hear you go on like that," said Sean. "She'll skin you alive. I know it doesn't make sense, but Terence will get through this. We all need to get away from the war and forget. We have become daft enough to think six hundred men could conquer a country of millions. Let's go home. There is nothing we can do here, and the women will be worrying. I'll see about getting Niall and the others off that barge. They can't do any more damage now."

"Aye. Beth will be worrying. She told me she'd never speak to me again if I went with the brotherhood, but I know she didn't mean it. I hope."

The men walked home in a cold drenching rain suited to their dark mood.

Sean and Micah shuttled between the mayor, Fort Porter and the U.S. Attorney's office trying to intervene on behalf of the ill-fated Fenians aboard the barge in the harbor. With no shelter or sanitary facilities, little food and only water from the lake, the men suffered extreme deprivation during four days of rain before arrangements could be made to move them to Fort Porter.

O'Neil and the other officers were arraigned and released after giving their word to appear before the Federal Circuit Court in

Canandaigua. The rest of the soldiers were paroled and given free rail transportation back home, while a few, suffering from exposure, Niall among them, were taken to the hospital for treatment along with the wounded.

Weak from his time as a Union prisoner of war, Niall came down with pneumonia and had to be carried off the barge. When Erin saw his ghostly pale complexion as he was carried into the ward, she almost collapsed. Memories of the hopeless hours spent at Johnny's bedside watching helplessly as he faded away overwhelmed her with foreboding. Could God be so cruel as to take away Niall just when she had decided to share her life with him?

"Ah lass, I feared I might not rest my eyes on your lovely face again," said Niall with a tired grin when she leaned over his cot. "You're called to be my angel of mercy once more."

"I will not leave your side."

A spasmodic coughing fit consumed him and Erin placed her hand protectively upon his breast until it subsided.

"You need to rest," she told him when he tried to sit up.

"No, I need you to tell me you'll walk by my side and bear our children."

Erin closed her eyes and whispered a quiet "Ave." Taking in a deep breath she purposefully removed her Cornette, set it on an empty bed and shook her hair loose. She shed the bib and carefully laid her precious, dark walnut Rosary on top of the pile, made the Sign of the Cross and took Niall's hand in hers.

"I shall always be at your side."

Niall smiled and closed his eyes to do as he was told. A while later Sister Clarice entered the ward and saw Erin sitting by Niall's bed with her head exposed.

"Why, what is this Sister Brigid?"

" 'Tis Erin from this moment forward. I cannot serve two masters."

"But your vows."

"I can no longer keep them. I will make a new vow."

Sister Clarice blessed herself and hurried from the room.

A short time later Katie appeared and placed hers hand on Erin's shoulders.

"I hear you have made up your mind to leave the sisterhood and go with Niall."

"I have."

"It is a hard path you have chosen. Are you sure?"

"I am. I have served God, now I will serve the blessed man he has sent me."

"Serve?"

Erin chuckled.

"As well as any Irish lass can serve a man who needs a considerable bit o' fixing."

Katie laughed along with her and said, "With a little hard work on your part, he'll do just fine."

Erin did not wait his time. No superstition could stand in her way. On Saturday June 16, 1866 the Reddy clan gathered to witness the marriage of the two star-crossed lovers at St. Brigid's. Sean gave away the bride, Terence served as best man and all sensed the easing of hardship and the mending of the great rifts brought on by years of war. Hard work, family and faith would see them through.

A few weeks after the Fenian fiasco, the reunited family gathered for the Fourth of July celebration anticipating good times to come. Katie, Sean, their children and grandchildren filled the room with laughter and conversation. A great midday meal was shared in the dining room while the borders were off to livelier pursuits on Canal Street.

Danny raised a glass at the end of the feast declaring, "Raise a glass for Ma and Da. May they live a hundred years with another year to repent, for as we all know, the older the fiddle the sweeter the tune, Slainte!"

"Hear, Hear!" resounded off the walls and a good deal of fine whiskey rushed down the throats of the family.

Mary leaped to her feet and grabbing Katie's arm commanded, "Come along you two. We have a grand surprise waiting by the river.

Katie grabbed her Da's shillelagh and used it to steady herself as the family excitedly dragged their parents down the street laughing all the way. At the foot of Main Street Katie pulled up and asked, "Now what is this?"

A huge hydrogen filled balloon hung before them tethered to the ground by a single cable. A faded Eagle graced the fabric and a large straw basket dangled beneath.

"We bought you a ride!" exclaimed Mary. "They say you can see all the way to the falls!"

"You'll not be seeing me up there," declared Katie. "God will be calling me up soon enough to suit me."

" Tis safe as can be. It is Union surplus. They used them all over the country during the war and with no one to shoot at you, you'll be safe as if you were home in bed."

"I don't know," said Katie as they led her to the stairs by the basket.

She and Sean climbed aboard and Michael nodded to the operator who started turning the crank, letting the craft rise. Katie made to climb out but Sean pulled her back.

"Sit tight, Katie dear," he said. "we are already too high to get down."

The balloon had already risen above the richly decorated buildings. Red, white and blue bunting was everywhere. The streets had been "greened" for the Fourth of July celebrations. Small trees were attached to lamp posts and branches hung from every available spot on the homes and businesses below. Katie stared nervously down at the raucous crowd hanging from balconies and lining the streets to drink freely from every imaginable type of container. As they rose higher, Katie could see the parade the people were waiting for assembling at the fort. Martial music drifted upward and occasional pistol shots were fired into the air.

"I thought Michael said we didn't have to worry about people shooting at us," Katie observed dryly.

"Only some lads letting off a little steam," answered Sean.

At that moment ships moored in the harbor sounded their whistles and the parade began marching down Canal Street to the cheers of all gathered.

"Isn't it wonderful?" asked Katie.

"And you didn't want to get in."

"I mean Buffalo."

The balloon rose higher still, and the city spread out in panorama below. Main Street stretched on before them, lined by one impressive brick edifice after another as far as the eye could see. A canal stretched off to the east toward their home and the Buffalo River snaked back and forth behind filled with all sorts of water craft. The Michigan still lay at anchor at the mouth of the Niagara and a mass of redcoats could be seen drilling in Fort Erie.

Sean pointed to the north and said, "Look there, Katie. You can see the mist rising from the falls."

Katie squinted down the Niagara River and exclaimed, "Oh I see it! I do!"

They spent a few more minutes looking down from the heavens at the magnificent Queen City of the Lakes below. Katie took Sean's hand and pulled him close pointing to the happy faces smiling up at them.

"Look there," said Katie. "Our children and grandchildren. What a world we are leaving them."

"It has been a long hard journey. We've had to fight the whole way, but the future looks bright for them."

"I remember when the world was a small cabin at the edge of a tiny village. Now Buffalo is a great city, a city of wonders and promise."

Sean hugged her close and picked up the shillelagh.

"Aye," he agreed. "Your Ma and Da fought and slaved over this land, and we have done the same. Now 'Tis their time."

He waved the shillelagh toward the sprawling city and said, " 'Tis your Da's Legacy, the shillelagh and the city."

The End

Made in the USA
Charleston, SC
29 July 2014